gilt
hollow

**Other books by Lorie Langdon
(with Carey Corp)**

Doon
Destined for Doon
Shades of Doon
Forever Doon

gilt hollow

LORIE
LANGDON

BLINK

BLINK

Gilt Hollow
Copyright © 2016 by Lorie Moeggenberg

This title is also available as a Blink ebook. Visit www.zondervan.com/ebooks.

Requests for information should be addressed to:
Blink, 3900 *Sparks Drive, Grand Rapids, Michigan 49546*

ISBN 978-0-310-75185-4

Any Internet addresses (websites, blogs, etc.) and telephone numbers in this book are offered as a resource. They are not intended in any way to be or imply an endorsement by the publisher, nor does the publisher vouch for the content of these sites and numbers for the life of this book.

Cover design: *Brand Navigation*
Cover photo:
Interior Design: *Denise Froehlich*

Printed in the United States of America

16 17 18 19 20 21 22 23 24 25 /DCI/ 20 19 18 17 16 15 14 13 12 11 10 9 8 7 6 5 4 3 2 1

For my sons Ben and Alex—
You both inspired parts of Ashton
with your strength and sensitivity.
Being a hero doesn't mean
you'll never have challenges; it's how you face those
challenges that inspires others.
Love you to the moon and back!

CHAPTER One

Brilliant sunlight stabbed Ashton's eyes as he stepped into the exercise yard for the first time in a week. He raised his hand to his forehead and paused just outside the door, fighting a wave of dizziness. After five days in solitary, the last thing he wanted to do was appear weak, as if it had beaten him. So he squinted, lowered his hand, and strode forward with confidence.

His first time in "the void," as everyone called it, had been torture. Locked inside the eight-by-eight windowless cell with nothing but his own thoughts, an aching jaw, and a broken rib had forced him to face his demons. And it hadn't been pretty. But as much as being cut off from everything and everyone sucked, when Ashton's gaze landed on Stanley Swindoll standing in the corner, his dark, toothpick arms pumping the basketball as if it were his only friend, he knew he'd do it all again.

Right about then Stanley spotted him. His eyes widening, he raced across the concrete, driving the basketball like an extension of his hand. "Ash! You're back. I'm so sorry, man. I had no idea—"

Ashton clasped the boy's bony shoulder. "Don't, okay? They had it coming."

"But when those guys jumped you—"

"Seriously, kid. I don't need a play-by-play." The heat of a heavy stare pulled Ashton's attention to the bleachers. DW— aka Dip Wad—glared in his direction. Ashton flashed him a grin, thrilled to see that the bruise around the bully's left eye had turned into a molten mess of yellowish brown.

"Did Dip Wad or the others give you any trouble?" Ashton asked, keeping his easy grin in place as DW bared his teeth in a grimace, his mammoth frame stiffening. Ashton seriously had no idea how the guy maintained his girth on the slop they were fed in this place.

"Nope." The rhythmic slap of the basketball began again. "Not since they transferred Jay."

Ashton's gaze jerked down to Stan's dark eyes. "Wait. What did you say?" As hierarchies went, Jay was the king of JJC. If you wanted something smuggled in—cigarettes, candy bars, drugs—you went through Jay. His uncle was the assistant warden, so he got away with everything short of murder. And the jerkhole couldn't handle that a thirteen-year-old black kid could wipe the court with him every single time.

"Jay's gone." A smile the size of Texas spread across Stan's face. "The ward called me in day before yesterday, and I told him everything. How Jay had been threatenin' me since that day I trounced him one-on-one. How he put that junk in my food that made me sick. How you jumped in when they pulled the knife on me. Guess the ward had been doing an investigation of Jay because some district head guy's comin' in next week for an inspection."

Stan paused in his dribbling and palmed the basketball with both hands. "That's the rumor anyway." He shrugged and set the ball in motion again.

Struck speechless, Ashton followed the five-foot-nothing kid over to the court. No wonder Dip Wad had stayed glued to the bleachers—without Jay, he was a powerless meatbag.

For the first time in three years, eleven months, and twenty-nine days, Ashton felt a spark of warmth in his chest.

He figured after the beat-down he'd given Jay and his buddies, it would only be a matter of time until it was his turn. In solitary, he'd gone through countless strategies on how to avoid the inevitable retaliation—only to find out now, it would never happen. He'd cut the head off the beast.

Ashton slapped the ball out of Stan's hands, faked right, and then used his height advantage to lay the ball in the hoop.

"Smooth!" Stan praised. "I might make a player out of you yet."

Ashton grinned, even as he bent over and clutched his aching side.

"Keller!" A guard approached the court, one who had repeatedly turned deaf ears to Ashton's complaints about Jay's reign of terror. "The warden wants to see you."

Ashton passed the ball to Stan and cleared his face of all expression. Even if he'd just broken out in a cold sweat, he wasn't about to show fear.

Stanley smiled and nodded his encouragement, as if the ward intended to give Ashton a medal or something. But he'd been around long enough to know that wouldn't happen. Even if he had saved the kid's life, the fact remained that he'd beaten up several inmates in the process, breaking the zero-tolerance policy for fighting.

The guard turned and walked away, expecting Ashton to follow. His feet like bricks, Ashton trudged after him.

"Hey, see you at dinner," Stan called.

Ashton lifted a hand without looking back. The guard pulled his club as they passed the bleachers and pointed it straight at DW. "Daniel Winston, you're next."

Any hope of an accommodation dissolved in that moment. If Dip Wad was on deck, this couldn't be good. Ashton stared DW down as he passed.

But apparently the jerk was even less intelligent than he appeared, because he shouted, "I ain't followin' no murderer." Then he hawked a loogie that arched straight onto Ashton's boots.

Red washed over his vision, and Ashton rushed toward the bleachers. With Jay as a shield, this coward had tormented him for years. *No more.* Ashton threw back his fist, and DW flinched hard.

But the blow never landed. The guard caught Ashton's arm from behind and hissed, "Throw that punch, Keller, and you're back in the void."

Blood roared in Ashton's ears. No longer a scrawny kid, he outweighed the guard by at least thirty pounds. He could easily pull away and get in a good slam to DW's blubbery face before the other guards could reach him. He'd already screwed up—why not go big?

He wrenched his arm out of the guard's grip but then lowered his fist. This pissant wasn't worth another week of confinement. Instead, he leaned in and growled, "Touch Stanley or any other kid here again and I'll put you in the ground."

Another guard approached and yanked him back, but not before Ashton saw a satisfying quiver of fear pass over DW's face. He stared him down until the guards forced him away. He'd had enough of others controlling his life. Those days were over.

Ashton let the guards escort him into the building without a fight. Their boots echoed down the long hallway like jackhammers pounding in his temples. He clung to the familiar heat of anger, but it wasn't enough to hold back the questions. Did the ward want to hear his take on the Jay situation? No, that didn't seem necessary now that Jay was gone. Or could this be a status change? If they took away his work assignment on the farm, he would freakin' lose it. The afternoons bailing hay, tending crops, and looking after the animals were what kept him sane. But the ward wouldn't mess with calling a face-to-face meeting for something so mundane. He'd just send new work orders through the chain of command.

Then as they climbed the stairs to the administrative wing, it hit him—this was the meeting to inform him he'd blown his chance at early release. All the blood drained from his head and sloshed into his stomach. He'd expected it was coming, but the thought of another year of nights lying in his bunk staring at the ceiling, of holidays when no one came to visit him, and endless hours gazing at the world through a barbed wire fence almost brought him to his knees.

They stopped at the last door at the end of the hall, and the first guard shoved his baton into Ashton's chest. "Don't move a muscle, kid."

He disappeared behind a door marked Conference Room.

That's when Ashton realized the warden's office was at the opposite end of the building. He searched his brain for a reason why anyone would call him here, but before he could grasp onto a theory, the guard returned, seized his arm, and ushered him through the door.

Three men sat at a long table. The guard led him to the single chair on the opposite side and ordered him to sit.

Memories of his police interrogation flashed; the rapid-fire questions, men screaming in his face, the mind-numbing fear that had kept him silent—and taken away almost four years of his life. Stiff as a board, he lowered into the chair.

"That will be all, York." Warden St. James nodded, and the guard left, shutting the door behind him with an ominous thud. The ward had always reminded Ashton of Samuel L. Jackson. Not just his wiry muscles or his clean-shaven head, but his no-nonsense, I-could-put-you-down-in-a-heartbeat attitude.

Silence filled the room, and Ashton took stock of his situation. On St. James's right sat his counselor, Mr. Larkin—or Bob, as he encouraged Ashton to call him in their weekly sessions. And to the warden's left was a middle-aged man Ashton didn't recognize, his thinning hair pulled into a low ponytail.

Warden St. James cleared his throat. "Relax, Mr. Keller."

Realizing his shoulders were hunched, Ashton ratcheted them down a notch but remained alert.

"This is Mr. Reed." The ward gestured to ponytail man, who stood and reached across the table, his hand extended.

A handshake was a show of respect that hadn't been offered to him by an adult since his incarceration. Following a moment's hesitation, Ashton rose to his feet and shook the man's waiting hand. "Good to meet you, Ashton. Call me Zane."

"Okay . . . Zane." With no idea who the guy was, the greeting came out more like a question.

The ward continued, "And I think you know Mr. Larkin."

Bob gave him a brief wave. The man resembled a teddy bear, but Ashton knew his beady stare could turn hard as coal when he didn't obtain the answers he wanted.

Ashton nodded in Bob's direction and took his seat again.

"Mr. Keller, you've just finished a stint in solitary, correct?" St. James asked.

"Yes, sir."

The warden shuffled the papers in front of him before raising reluctant eyes back to Ashton. "I must apologize for that. But it was for your own safety."

Ashton blinked, unsure he'd heard correctly. "Sir?"

St. James ignored the question in Ashton's tone and continued. "When I became aware of Jay Hanover's unwarranted power within this facility, I took swift action. He has been transferred to Warren County and his uncle discharged."

Ashton cocked an ear to make sure he'd heard right. A dozen other kids had reported Jay before, but the warden had never cared. "What changed your mind?"

The warden leveled a sharp stare in his direction. "Excuse me?"

Ashton clenched his jaw, thinking about all the kids who'd been tormented by Jay since he'd been there and the fear they'd all lived with waiting to see who would be Jay's next victim. He folded his hands on top of the table, mirroring St. James's posture. "Why believe us now? We've been telling you, Bob, the guards, anyone who would listen, about Jay for over a year. Why now?"

St. James pressed his already thin lips together as his gaze burned into Ashton. But Ashton didn't look away. He'd take whatever punishment they were about to give him, but he wouldn't waste this chance to make them see the truth.

"Mr. Keller, this is unnecessary and disrespectful," Bob said in his odd, singsong voice.

Ashton felt the comforting heat of anger descend on his shoulders like a buffer against the world. He leaned forward but kept his voice even. "You say you took swift action, but I have a broken rib and a friend who was almost stabbed to death that say otherwise."

The warden steepled his fingers in front of him. "Mr. Keller, I've already stated that I took care of the issue *as soon as* I became aware of it. And it is not your place to question the management of this facility. Nevertheless, this . . . *incident* has raised my awareness to the vulnerabilities of our inmates, and I assure you, their safety is my number one priority." St. James paused and regarded Ashton over his glasses. "However, it is no longer yours."

Every function in Ashton's body seemed to freeze as he waited for the other hammer to drop.

St. James continued. "Your willingness to stand up for a fellow inmate, even at risk to your own safety, demonstrates strength of character and confirms the positive progress you've made in Mr. Larkin's recent reports." He gestured to Bob, who nodded.

Sickening anticipation began to rise in Ashton's gut, like the feeling he got inside an airplane as it hurtled toward its point of takeoff.

"But"—St. James leveled his fierce stare at Ashton, sending his hope straight off the runway—"that does not mean I condone your methods. Fighting is still a first-grade offense in this facility."

Realizing his fate hung in the balance, Ashton bit off the smart reply on the tip of his tongue and nodded. "Yes, sir."

"Given your demonstration of leadership, your high GPA, and your strong service reports from the agricultural center . . ." St. James cleared his throat and glanced down at his paperwork. "Your early release has been approved."

Ashton sucked in a sharp breath and placed his hands flat on the table in front of him. Was St. James joking? He wouldn't be so cruel. Would he?

The ward continued, "Mr. Reed—"

"Zane," ponytail man interrupted.

St. James's eyes gave an impatient flicker, and he pronounced the name by holding out the vowel. "Zaaane here is your parole officer. After today you'll be required to report in to him every month . . ."

But Ashton didn't hear the rest over the roar of the jet engine as it rocketed into the atmosphere, taking his stomach with it. He felt weightless. Light-headed. He was out of here? Today? He glanced out the second-story window at the tree line on the other side of the fence and felt the insane urge to crash through the glass, jump to the ground, and sprint as far and as fast as his legs would carry him. But then a single word sucked him back into reality.

". . . mother signed the release."

Ashton turned to St. James. "Wait. What did you say about my mother?"

"Your mother signed the papers for your discharge last week. But since you turned eighteen yesterday, it became unnecessary. You can be released into your own custody now." St. James's lips pressed together.

"My mom . . . was here?"

"Yes, Ashton."

Of course she hadn't wanted to see him.

He hadn't seen or heard from his parents since his conviction. All his so-called friends had abandoned him. Even the girl he thought would stick by his side through anything had disappeared from his life. Apparently loyalty through a manslaughter conviction had been too much for her. But he didn't need them to start over. He didn't need anyone. Not anymore. Ashton swallowed the rejection that never seemed to fade, set his jaw, and lifted his chin. During the past week in solitary with nothing but his deepest fears and past regrets to keep him company, it had become clear what he needed to do. And who he needed to make pay.

Zane went over his release paperwork, the schedule for check-ins, and all the terms and conditions. If Ashton so much as stepped a toe on the wrong side of the law, he would violate the terms of his parole and risk ending up back in jail. Not here, but an adult joint. The real deal. No way would he risk it.

Ashton signed the papers and then shook hands with Bob and St. James—who actually flashed a genuine smile—and then turned to his parole officer.

"A taxi's waiting for you out front. Here's fifty bucks. You'll need to contact me with your new address within twenty-four hours, and we'll set up a home visit within the week." Zane handed him the cash, and they shook hands for the second time. "Where're you headed?"

Before Ashton could answer, the image that haunted him flashed across his mind—Daniel's broken body, his blood mixing in the water that lapped against Ashton's skin as he searched for a pulse, the horrible grief and fear when he didn't find one. Ashton would uncover his friend's true killer and make them pay for every hour that he'd lost in this place.

He leveled his gaze on the probation officer. "I'm going back. Back to Gilt Hollow."

CHAPTER Two

The familiar squeeze enveloped Willow's chest as she ducked behind the cappuccino machine. Sweat coated the back of her neck and a chill raced across her shoulders. She peeked out, searching the faces in the one-room café until she found the petite blonde perusing the shelf of organic pastas and sauces. Why did she have to come in *here*?

Mrs. Turano hated Willow with a passion that bordered on psychotic. Avoiding the woman did Willow little good. In such a small town, their paths continued to cross.

The room began to shrink.

No, no, no! Not now! She lifted her eyes to the paneled ceiling as she attempted to shake the tingling from her fingers. Her second day on the job; she *so* did not need this right now.

"Willow!" her manager barked. "I asked for a slice of carrot cake to go."

Wishing she could disappear, Willow ruffled her bangs so they fell over her eyes, rushed to the display case, and squatted behind it. Her arm shook as she slid the spatula under an icing-coated wedge, and she barely managed to wrangle the cake into a plastic container before she heard the voice like nails on a chalkboard.

"Margaret," Mrs. Turano snapped. "I thought you had better judgment."

Reluctantly, Willow stood and met pale blue eyes—the same shade as the woman's late son Daniel's—lined with a road map of red. Mrs. Turano had been drinking again.

"I refuse to be served by the girlfriend of a murderer!"

A hard silence descended on the room, every set of eyes darting between Willow and the poor woman who'd lost her son. Which, by default, made Willow the villain.

She longed to defend herself, to yell that she'd had nothing to do with Daniel's death. That she'd never been Ashton's girlfriend. But she knew from experience that denial wouldn't help. The woman would only insist that Willow admit Ashton's guilt. Demand that Willow denounce the only true friend she'd ever had. And Willow would walk away without saying a word. As always.

"Claire, I—" Willow's manager sputtered, her face flushing a deep red.

"There's no excuse, Margaret! If *she* works here"—Claire Turano pointed a trembling finger at Willow's head—"then you've lost my business. Which includes catering the annual art fund-raiser *and* the Sleepy Hollow Ball!"

The panic attack in full force, Willow's airway constricted as if she were breathing through a straw. Wheezing, she backed away from the counter.

Margaret glanced over her shoulder. "Willow, take a break, *now.*"

Gladly.

Willow spun on her heel and ran through the kitchen and out the side door to the shaded patio. She could feel people staring holes in her back, but she didn't care. She fell into a chair and searched for her focus color. Directly across from her, above a sign advertising the CC Café, she found a sky-blue flag with a peace symbol in the center. It would have to do.

Gasping for breath, she concentrated on the blue fabric and blocked everything out. The loud chewing of the woman beside her. The scrape of iron chairs against cobblestone. The mumble of voices . . .

Inhale through your nose.

1, 2, 3 . . .

Fall into the blue.

Exhale through your lips.

After three repetitions, the fog in her brain began to clear, but the pain in her chest persisted. Her shrink had given her a "panic script"—phrases to talk herself down. Unfortunately, it only worked when she said it aloud.

"Here goes nothing." Still focused on the flag, Willow recited, "This is an opportunity for me to learn to cope with this problem."

Cue the furtive glances and scurrying away.

Deep inhale.

"I have survived this before, and I can survive this time too."

Slow exhale.

The slam of her heart gentled to its normal beat. She could feel eyes on her, hear them gathering their things and whispering to one another, but she didn't dare look. She knew what she would see—condemnation and fear with a sprinkle of pity that equaled nothing but ignorant judgment.

Willow stared up at the fluttering green and yellow leaves and then drew a strong, clean breath before chancing a glance at the woman beside her—the only one who didn't leave. But the old lady's unwavering gaze made her swallow and look away.

"It's all right, dear. I talk to myself all the time."

Willow didn't respond, hoping the lady would get the hint and go away like everyone else.

The woman lifted half of her sandwich in arthritic fingers. "Want some? It's ham and cheese." The woman grinned, her cheeks plumping and eyes glittering in sweet enticement.

Willow blinked. Everyone knew you didn't accept food from strangers, especially not old women with stained dentures, but she'd made the sandwich herself not ten minutes ago and she hadn't eaten since breakfast. Her stomach growled like an angry beast, making up her mind for her. "Sure."

Accepting the offering, she peeled back the paper and sank her teeth in for a bite. The salty ham and creamy cheese melted in her mouth, dissolving the last of her anxiety. Willow slumped against the back of her chair.

"So, why are you so upset?"

Willow chewed, her eyes darting in search of an excuse not to talk to a complete stranger about her screwed-up life. But they were the only two left on the patio. When she glanced back at the woman's expectant face, she shrugged and answered, "Old decisions coming back to haunt me, I guess."

"I see." The woman's eyes narrowed. "Well, do you have a friend you can talk to?"

A lump of bread and lunchmeat lodged in Willow's throat. How much of the truth did the lady really want to know? That after Ashton had been convicted of killing Daniel Turano and was sent to juvie, he hadn't responded to any of her letters? That her one true friend had abandoned her and left her here to defend his innocence? That everyone at school either treated her like she was invisible or a freak of nature? Would she want to hear all that?

Willow rolled the sudden tightness out of her shoulders and attempted a light tone. "Not really."

"I see. Well, you can talk to me if you like."

Willow concentrated hard on her sandwich. When she finished, she folded the empty wrapper into a perfect square. She didn't want to confess the evil weed that had sprouted in her heart as Mrs. Turano yelled in her face—that her life would've been much easier if Ashton had been the one to die that day at the falls. Then *she* would be the martyr of the story.

But even so, she couldn't wish it were true, and she certainly couldn't tell a complete stranger. "Thank you, but—"

"Oh, there you are." Margaret stopped in front of her.

Saved by her not-for-long boss.

"We need to chat." She patted down her dyed blonde hair and retied her apron strings before meeting Willow's gaze.

Of course we do.

Reluctantly, Willow rose and followed her manager's retreating form but then turned back. "Thanks for the sandwich." Willow extended her hand. "I'm Willow Lamott."

"I'm Mrs. McMenamin, but everyone calls me Mrs. M." They shook hands, a red plaid sleeve falling across the woman's papery skin.

Willow glanced down and saw scuffed cowboy boots peeking out from the ruffled hem of the woman's flannel nightgown. She remembered then that Mrs. M had taught English at the high school but retired years ago. Everyone said she was a few clowns short of a circus. Though after her meltdown moments before, Willow didn't feel qualified to judge.

Mrs. M. held her gaze and leaned in close. "All heartbreak fades with time. Don't be afraid to move on."

The woman shuffled away, calling over her shoulder, "And don't be a victim!"

■ ■ ■

Willow lugged her overloaded backpack up the winding, cobblestone walkway to her new home. Three stories of Gothic Victorian loomed above her, blocking out the setting sun.

Sagging wrap-around porch, chipped gingerbread trim, wood siding stained a dirty gray, and, like the topper on a Tim Burton wedding cake, a rusted-out weathervane leaning precariously from the third-floor turret room. She shifted her backpack to the opposite shoulder and walked into the shadow of the dilapidated mansion.

Everyone in town believed Keller House was haunted, and for Willow it was true. But the specters that disturbed her were not of the ethereal variety.

Willow, bet you can't do this!" the boy with the shaggy dark hair and smiling eyes chants as he leaps over the porch railing and jumps to the ground.

"Seriously, Ashton," Willow muttered, "if you can't get out of my head, I'm not living in your stupid old house. Even if this is my mom's dream job." When her mom had landed the job of caretaker to Ashton's rundown family estate, you would've thought they'd won the lottery. But for Willow, living in her ex–best friend's house was a form of slow torture.

She jerked as the double-arched doors swung open with a baleful creak. But her fright was short-lived. Her mom posed in the doorway like a character in an old movie, hands on gypsy-skirted hips, heavy salt-and-pepper dreads looped in a lopsided bun. She spread her arms wide. "Velcome home, Villow! Hov vas your day?"

Willow bit her lip to trap a laugh. "Awesome, Count Chocula. How was yours?"

Her mom's face fell into a pout as she dropped her arms. "I was trying to be Elvira."

"Who?"

"You know, Mistress of the Dark?"

"That old chick with the black wig and the low neck-lines?" Willow asked.

Her mom nodded and stuck out her chest, making Willow giggle as she slipped into the foyer. "You've made some progress in here." The dust cloths had been removed from the entry table and parlor furniture. The cherry wood floors gleamed, and the bright scent of lemon filled the air.

"Only one problem," Mom huffed, pointing up.

Willow tilted her head back and stared at the centerpiece of the two-story foyer, a massive chandelier dripping crystals and cobwebs.

"Can't find a tall enough ladder," her mom grumbled.

"I don't know, I kinda like it." She met her mom's dark-chocolate eyes, the exact shade of her own. "Could go a long way for the Elvira image."

"I want to keep it for Halloween!" A four-foot ball of energy in the form of her little brother sped past, his bony elbow knocking the backpack off her shoulder.

"Hey!" Willow called to the boy who'd sped around the corner. "How was school?"

Rainn poked his head out and threw a sock at her head. "Good!"

Willow flicked the tiny stink bomb from her shoulder. For such a little kid, his feet sure packed a punch. Rainn's satisfied snigger echoed back to her as he disappeared into the house.

"Oh, I almost forgot." Her mom walked to the entry table and returned with a wooden picture frame. "I found this while cleaning out Ashton's old closet."

Willow gaped at the intricate pencil drawing of the tree house at the back of the Keller property. She and Ashton had spent so many hours there in the summer months, their parents had jokingly referred to it as their vacation home. It brought back happy, uncomplicated memories of before—before her best friend went to jail for manslaughter.

She took the picture and opened her mouth to make a witty remark about the property value skyrocketing after the scandal, but only managed to mumble, "Thanks."

Her mom bent to pick up the discarded sock. "I'm working at the soup kitchen tonight. Want to come?"

"Not tonight." Willow hefted her bag back onto her shoulder.

"What happened? Something's bothering you."

"I'm fine." Unwilling to admit she'd lost another job, she turned and began climbing the wide wooden staircase. "Tons of homework—trig, lit, chemistry . . ."

"No one told you to take all those honors classes!" her mom called after her.

If Mom had her way, Willow would stay home and attend Annherst next year. With no traditional grading system and classes like Experimental Body Art and Media Conspiracy Theory, the liberal arts college attracted freethinking societal anarchists from all over the country. And while the school infused the town with an eclectic mix of people and produced an inordinate number of famous musicians and actors, it didn't offer undergraduate degrees in biochemistry.

Willow opened the first door at the top of the stairs and inhaled a cloud of dust and powdery Shalimar. A sneeze rocked her chest, and she slumped against the mahogany wood frame, pushing her glasses up on her nose. This had been Kristen's room . . .

    Ashton turns, shoots Willow a wink, and sets the baby-blue glass bottle on the vanity table. She reaches out and adjusts it to the proper angle, even as butterflies war in her stomach. "What if she gets it in her eyes?"

With a drawn-out sigh, he says, "Why would she spray perfume in her eyes? Besides, it's only vinegar. The perfect complement to my sister's sweet personality."

The click of high heels echoes in the hall, and he grabs her arm, tugging her deeper into the room.

"We have to go!" she hisses.

"No time." He ducks and slides under the dust ruffle of the bed, and she scrambles after him just as the door opens.

Lying flat on her stomach, she watches Kristen apply fresh lipstick, run a brush through her long blonde hair, and lean into the mirror. "Flawless," she says to her own reflection before reaching for the blue bottle.

Three squirts, and a screech rents the air.

Willow jerks and shrinks farther under the bed, but Ashton's face is right there. Flashing a broad crescent of straight, white teeth, he squeezes her hand, and something like an inflating balloon fills her chest.

"Ugh." Willow's ribcage expanded as if her fingers were still entwined with his. She took several slow breaths and blew the dark veil of bangs out of her eyes. By sheer force of personality, Ashton had imprinted on this house—and on her.

She forced her feet to move. In theory, her own massive bedroom should make her ecstatic with joy. But in her heart, she wished her mom hadn't accepted the caretaker job. Willow preferred their cozy two-bedroom cottage to this abomination of hardwood, stained glass, and endless memories.

But even if she could convince her mom, it was too late to go back. A couple of newlyweds had rented their old house and turned it into a tattoo parlor/holistic healing center—as if Gilt Hollow needed another one.

Willow flopped down on the king-sized bed and tucked a pillow under her head. Most of her homework wasn't due until the end of the week. She could afford to close her eyes for a moment . . . A chill of awareness tiptoed up her spine, like when a teacher caught you texting in class. She twisted around, ready to yell at Rainn for sneaking up on her. But there was no one else in the room.

■ ■ ■

Willow couldn't sleep.

There's no such thing as ghosts, said the scientific part of her brain. But the little girl, the one who'd listened to all of Ashton's spooky stories, the one who used to have nightmares about the ghoul who lived in the attic, shivered under the covers. Ashton had sworn for years that he'd seen things in this house. Lights flickering. Chairs rocking in empty rooms. Doors swinging open by themselves. And as she lay straining to hear every sound, a part of her believed him.

She rolled onto her side and clutched a pillow to her stomach. The harsh digital display seemed to throw the time in her face—3:04 a.m. Propping up on an elbow, she spied the drawing of the tree house leaning against her lamp. In the moonlight, she could just make out the shape of the tiny dwelling that she and Ashton had helped her dad build the summer before he passed away. They'd scouted for weeks for the perfect spot. When they'd found the sprawling oak on the back of the Keller property, her dad went to Mr. Keller for permission, hoping he'd join them in the project. When he'd granted them the land but declined to help, her dad had made a big deal about Ashton being the architect.

Willow flopped onto her back. The dark paneled walls and twelve-foot ceilings loomed, stretching and contracting in the shadows as if they had a life of their own. She should go downstairs and make some warm milk or peppermint tea, but the thought of walking through the spook factory of a house in the dead of night kept her glued to her mattress.

A low groan sounded from somewhere close, followed by a clacking like metal against wood. A shiver skittered across Willow's shoulders, and she tugged the comforter up to her chin.

Ugh! She needed to relax. The noises were just the house settling.

Working to calm her thoughts, she pulled a long breath in through her nose and blew it out through her mouth. Her eyes drifted shut and she pictured a white-sand beach, turquoise water, the gentle rush and ebb of the tide, the warm sun on her skin . . .

Bam!

Willow sat straight up and held still, waiting for the sound to come again. Had it been a door slamming or something heavy crashing to the floor? Visions of Rainn falling out of Ashton's old four-poster had her springing out of bed. Without turning on a light, she ran around the corner and down the hall, the slap of her bare feet the only sounds. She rushed into Rainn's room and found her brother sleeping peacefully, his stuffed ninja turtle clutched to his chest.

Breathing a sigh of relief, she tiptoed to her mother's room and heard her snores before she even reached the door. So what had made that loud slamming noise?

She wrapped an arm around her waist as she crept back into the hall and toward an arched picture window. There were hundreds—maybe thousands—of trees on the five-acre property. The noise could've been one of them falling against the house.

When she reached the window that faced the overgrown back garden, a cloud obscured the moon, turning the yard into a tangle of dark shapes and twisted silhouettes. Leaning close to the glass, she didn't see any broken limbs or branches close enough to scrape against the siding. She recalled the sound and realized it had seemed to come from below her on the first floor.

And then something moved.

She jumped back from the window, her heart pounding into her ears. The quick, furtive movement had been a living being. Something large. Gathering her courage, she stepped closer to the glass. It was probably a deer. She'd seen plenty of them leaping through the woods between their old cottage and the Keller property.

Capturing her nightshirt sleeve in her fingers, she wiped a circle of dust from the window pane and peered into the yard. Directly below, a circular stone walkway bisected the unkempt lawn overrun by tangles of weeds and wildflowers. Beyond, the trees stood sentinel in a thick line, their leaves rustling in the wind.

Willow scanned the edge of the woods, skimming broad trunks and sweeping pines. Her eyes darted back to a group of narrow birch trees. The gloom between their silver trunks moved, and she pressed her nose to the cool glass. Had it been a trick of the light? Or . . .

Then the clouds shifted and revealed a figure. A midnight shade between ghostly white trees—tall and solid, its features in shadow—it turned and disappeared into the forest.

Willow stumbled back. Had he seen her watching? Her

pulse ratcheted into overdrive. Had that person tried to break into the house?

She ran. Not caring if she woke her family, she ran down the creaky staircase and through the drafty, cobweb-infested hallway, flipping on every light switch she came to. When the first floor blazed like daytime, she ensured all the doors were locked. But there were too many windows to check. Should she wake her mom? Call the police?

And tell them what? She heard a noise and thought she saw a shadow in the yard? The cops would laugh all the way back to the precinct, joking about the girl who lived in the haunted house of her ex–best friend, the murderer.

Willow stood in the middle of the kitchen shaking, the room spinning around her. Maybe she was losing it. Her chest tightened as the panic attack tried to steal her breath. *Not again!* Determination pushing back her fear, she poured a glass of milk and gulped down her anxiety with the cold, soothing liquid.

Her equilibrium restored, she wandered from room to room, switching off all the lights, and then climbed the stairs. After checking on her mom and brother once more, she went back to Kristen's room—*her* room—and locked the door.

CHAPTER Three

The words blurred in front of Willow's eyes and her cheek slipped from her fist, but she caught herself before her face smacked into her chemistry text. Finding a table outside at lunch had seemed like a good idea, but her lack of sleep the night before caused the late-summer sunshine to feel like a cozy blanket.

"Hey, there you are." Lisa rushed over, her navy star-covered skirt forming a pouf behind her. She plopped down on the bench across from Willow and handed her a Coke. "Looks like you need this more than I do."

Willow sighed as she cracked open the soda, knowing it would make her stomach bloat like a balloon, but too desperate for the caffeine to care. She took in a long sip of the cool bubbles and thanked the girl who seemed determined to be her friend. Lisa Gifford had moved to Gilt Hollow over the summer. She and Willow had bonded over their love of fried Oreos at the Gilt Hollow Street Fair, and then Lisa had shown up on Willow's doorstep the next day with two lemon shake-ups and invited her to watch a local band. Lisa had been the first person who didn't treat Willow like the weirdo who used to be friends with a convict. In fact, when Willow confessed the whole sordid tale, the ex–New Yorker shrugged and said, "That was a long time ago."

Willow grinned at the crystal headband holding back Lisa's blonde curls and her swoosh of heavy eyeliner topped by silver shadow. In Gilt Hollow her ultrachic look stood out like a Coach bag at a mud volleyball tournament. But she didn't give a fig what anyone thought. Just one of the many things Willow liked about her.

"It's the second day of school. How could you possibly have"—Lisa lifted the front of her textbook so she could see the cover—"chemistry homework?"

Willow took another swig before answering. "We have a quiz this afternoon."

"Okaaayy . . . you know those are just to gauge the students' memories from the previous year. It's not for a grade."

"I like to throw the curve. Gives me an advantage on the first few tests."

"Remind me to never take any classes with you, brainiac." Lisa took a bite of an apple, and her eyes narrowed on Willow's face. "If you let me put some mascara on you, you'd at least look more awake."

Willow set down her half-eaten strawberry and almond butter sandwich and shrugged. "I don't like to wear makeup."

Lisa opened her mouth, but her words were drowned out by a large group of guys bursting out of the cafeteria doors with a football. They jogged past the table on their way to the green space, and Willow buried her nose in her book. When the back of her neck tingled, she glanced up and met the pale blue gaze of Colin Martin. He jogged by as he tied his dark blond hair into a knot at the back of his head. In his Nike shorts, topped with a ripped, tie-died T, he was part jock, part tortured poet. And every girl within a twenty-mile radius lusted after him.

Seeing that he'd caught her attention, his lips tilted in a cocky smirk. "Hey, Weepy."

Willow jerked her eyes back to her textbook.

Lisa leaned forward and whispered, "A good friend would probably be asking why he called you that, but I can't get past his blinding hotness. You *know* him?"

"Sorta." Willow began packing her books away. "We used to hang out when we were kids." And he'd been one of the boys who'd testified against Ashton.

"I'm gonna need an intro." Her friend's eyes followed Colin's agile form as he snatched the football out of the air and took off toward the Solo-cup-marked end zone.

"Okay, sure." Willow stuffed the remainder of her lunch into her insulated sack. "Then we can eat a tub of Chunky Monkey and watch chick flicks after he uses you and dumps you on your star-spangled butt."

"Star-spangled butt?" Lisa rose to her feet and rotated her American-flag-print skirt so the stars were in the front and the stripes were in the back. "There. Now can I meet him?"

Willow burst into riotous giggles and, for once, didn't care who was watching.

■ ■ ■

Willow's chemistry quiz had been a total bust. She couldn't stop thinking about the shadow in the trees or the sounds she'd heard the night before. Had someone tried to break into the house? Would they come back and try again?

As soon as she got home, she changed into shorts and a T-shirt and headed out back.

When there were no signs of the trespasser in the over-grown yard or near the stand of birch trees where she'd seen him, Willow entered the forest. The cool, moist air was a respite from the mid-September heat, and she drew in a deep breath as she kicked a carpet of pine needles, releasing their brisk, earthy scent. She wandered deeper, the noise of cars and neighbors fading, branches linking overhead to blot out the sun.

She pushed a sapling limb off the path, and a bird rushed out, giving her a jolt. The forest felt hushed, as if waiting.

Variegated light cast shadows all around her, and goose bumps rose on her arms. This might be the part of the movie where people yelled for the character to turn back to the safety of the house.

Willow quickened her stride. Those were the same people who came up with sayings like "Curiosity killed the cat." The status quo-ers who were afraid to rock the boat. Not people who discovered cures for killer diseases. Her future career as a research scientist depended on delving into the unknown and daring to theorize based on the tiniest shreds of evidence.

Determined to find clues to her current mystery, she forged ahead until the path became more distinct and then ended in a steep gorge. The old swinging bridge appeared intact, but a layer of khaki moss coated the boards, hiding possible rot and decay. Willow took a tentative step onto the creaking wood, and when she didn't fall into the creek below held on to the rope and bounced up and down. Satisfied it would hold her weight, she crossed the bridge in resolute strides.

The wood parted on a sun-dappled clearing, the familiar sprawling oak pushing back the rest of the forest. She hadn't been here in years, despite Rainn's attempts to convince her otherwise, but cradled in the tree's powerful eight-hundred-year-old branches, the tiny house appeared unchanged.

At some point, it had occurred to her that the figure she'd seen the night before could be a druggie or a vagrant using this place as a crash pad. Moving quietly across the clearing, she reached for the ladder nailed to the trunk and secured her toes on the first rung. She couldn't allow her little brother to stumble on some scary bum's hideout. So she climbed, her heart thumping a steady rhythm in her ears. Unsure what she'd do if she discovered a grown man curled up inside, she hoisted herself onto the tiny porch as silently as possible. A board creaked beneath her feet, and she almost jumped back to the ground.

Willow froze for several seconds, and when she didn't hear any signs of movement inside, she grasped the railing and poked her head into the interior. The single room was empty. She let out a slow breath.

A crack rang out behind her, and she whirled, hitting her head on the low doorway. "Ow," she mouthed as she rubbed her aching skull and peered over the balcony.

Chin down, hands shoved into his pockets, a guy strode into the clearing. As if sensing her stare, he stopped and glanced up. Tall and skinny with a long nose and Ron Weasley-red hair . . . Brayden Martin—Colin's first cousin.

"Oh, hey, Willow." Color dotted his pale cheekbones. "I didn't know you still came out here."

Memories of Brayden and Colin chasing her around with sticks when they were kids made Willow swallow before she answered. "I . . . don't. I mean . . . I haven't been here in a while."

"Well, if you want . . ." He ran a hand through the shaggy layers of his hair. "I can go."

All little boys did stupid things. Rainn was evidence enough of that. She'd had several classes with Brayden last year. He loved to joke around, but when he did participate, she could tell he was way smarter than he let on. "As long as you don't bring any sticks. Come on up."

A grin flashed across his face, and he climbed the ladder in three quick steps. Willow sat and let her legs dangle over the edge of the porch. Brayden lowered beside her.

"Do you come here often?" Willow asked.

Brayden snickered, and she realized she sounded like a cliché.

Willow laughed, her cheeks heating.

"Actually I do," Brayden replied after a moment. "It's kinda peaceful out here."

"Yeah." The leaves swayed and a soft breeze pushed Willow's bangs off her forehead.

"Except when we played war." Brayden chuckled.

War, or capture the flag, had been their favorite game as kids. Brayden, Colin, and his little brother Cory had made a formidable team. Visions of the Martin cousins sneaking through the forest in camouflage while she and Ashton defended the tree house with Nerf guns stilled the swinging of her legs.

Suddenly she could see him perched on the railing. Tousled black hair, olive skin, nose sprinkled with freckles, and those dark blue eyes, like a starless night. Ashton wore his trademark expression—closed lips quirked in a one-sided grin that hid a thousand mischievous plans. Her heart did a funny little blip, and then she squeezed her eyes tight, pushing away the image.

Oblivious to her distraction, Brayden kept talking. "Remember that time I set a trap for you guys on the rope bridge and it caused you to fall and twist your ankle? Ashton tied me to a tree and left me there for hours. He wouldn't let me loose until I promised on my dog's life to never do it again." He shook his head. "Keller was pretty extreme, even then."

When she didn't respond, he glanced over, his brown eyes thoughtful. And she noticed that despite his red hair and pale complexion, he didn't have one freckle. "It's still hard for you, isn't it? What he did?"

"What do *you* think?" Willow snapped, digging her nails into the wood planks of the deck. Asking him up here had been a mistake. When would she learn all people wanted from her was a reaction? Some outburst or juicy detail they could take back to their friends to feed the rumors.

Willow lifted her heel and started to stand up, but Brayden touched her leg. "Wait. I'm sorry, okay? I didn't mean it like that. I just . . . Ashton was my friend too, you know."

A muscle jumped in the back of his jaw as he searched her face. He and Colin had both been at Heartford Falls the day Daniel Turano died. They'd both seen it happen.

"I think about that day . . . and . . . and how things used to be before." He snatched his hand from her leg and glanced away.

"Oh." Willow settled back to a seated position. "Sorry."

"You don't have to be sorry. I guess you're used to expecting the worst, huh?" He offered her a small smile.

Willow tilted her lips to one side, thinking about the job she'd lost because of Mrs. Turano. "You could say that."

"People are stupid." Brayden gripped the handrail and rested his forehead against the wood. "It's not like you had any control over what happened."

Willow nibbled her thumbnail as she let his comment sink in. After a moment, she lowered her hand and asked him something she'd wondered for a long time. "Do people grill you about it? Like random people asking personal questions out of morbid curiosity?"

"Not much anymore. My dad told me to tell people I couldn't answer any questions without my attorney. That clams people up real fast. Occasionally one of our friends will get curious, but Colin shuts that down with a raised fist."

Willow's chuckle didn't hold much humor. "Yeah, I don't have either one of those weapons at my disposal."

Brayden glanced over his shoulder. "I think people are curious because you always stuck by him. Even with all the evidence, you refused to stop defending his innocence." He pulled up one leg and bent it in front of him, facing her. "I always admired you for that."

"Seriously?" Why would he say that when he witnessed the whole thing? Testified *against* Ashton. "Why?"

"You're one stubborn chick, that's why." Brayden grinned, and in that dimpled expression she could see why the girls in her class swooned over him. "I've always liked you, even when everyone said you were a snob. I never believed it."

"A what? Why would anyone think *I'm* a snob?"

"Well, let's see . . ." The grin was back, and he counted off with his fingers. "*One*, you walk around school with your nose in a book and don't talk to anyone—besides that new girl, Lisa."

Willow threw up her hands. "But I—"

"Nope, let me finish. *Two*, you dress like some preppy boarding school elitist." His grin widened. "If you ask me, those little skirts and knee socks are kinda hot."

Wait. Is Brayden Martin flirting with me?

He wiggled his auburn brows. "But you don't even attempt to fit in with the rest of us mortal folk."

"I . . . I . . ." she sputtered. This was so crazy, it was bordering on ridiculous. Was that how people really saw her?

"And *three*—" His voice softened and he scooted closer. "You're beautiful, which intimidates the heck out of us."

Willow blinked repeatedly. Was this guy for real? She wouldn't use the word *ugly* to describe herself, but *beautiful*?

Brayden leaned over and grabbed her hand, linking his

fingers with hers. Willow's heart accelerated, but not from excitement. Alone in the middle of the forest, in a tree house with his big body blocking the exit. Nope, she didn't like this one bit. She disentangled her fingers from his and scooted over half an inch. His mouth tipped into a frown, a strained silence filling the air.

Then her snarkiness came to the rescue. "So *that's* why I'm so unpopular—I'm smart and beautiful and better than everyone else? Thanks for explaining that." She stretched her lips into a grin.

Brayden's gaze shifted to his battered blue-and-white Chucks. "I'd like to take you out sometime." He shrugged one shoulder. "Coffee or something. No big."

Willow surprised herself by saying, "Sure." She'd never been on a date, and despite her earlier freak-out, she liked him.

His cinnamon-brown eyes sparkled. "Cool! Gino's? Friday, after the football game?"

"Okay." She'd forgotten he played on the team. She never went to football games or any other social events. Maybe he was right. All these years, she'd thought people avoided her. But maybe she'd been the one to pull away.

"I guess you heard the rumor?"

Suddenly wanting to talk about anything but herself, Willow pulled her legs up and crossed them in front of her. "Not unless you're referring to the buzz about the next install-ment of the Marvel franchise. 'Cause I'm totally on board with Loki getting his own movie."

Brayden barked a short laugh, but it melted quickly into a frown. "I'm not sure I should be the one to tell you this, but . . ." He became intent on poking the tip of his shoe-lace into each one of the metal holes in his Converse. "It's why I came out here, actually. I needed some time to process the news."

Something sparked in Willow's gut, a completely illogical warning that dried out her mouth and made her palms sweat. "What news?"

He glanced up under the fall of his bangs. "I heard Ashton got released early."

"What? How?" she managed to choke out.

"Isaiah Kagawa told me. You know him, right?"

"Yes." She didn't really *know* Isaiah, but he'd been one of the boys at the falls the day Daniel died. His dad was also the chief of police.

"You're trembling." Brayden rubbed her shoulder.

Willow felt the rough boards of the tree house press into her back. She pulled away from his touch and shot to her feet. "I . . . I have to go. My mom will be looking for me."

"Willow, I—"

"It's fine." Willow shook her head. "I'm fine." She needed to be alone so she could think.

Brayden watched her, his brow furrowed. "I didn't mean to upset you. I just thought you should know."

Willow kept talking as she climbed down the ladder. "Thanks for . . . telling me. See you at school tomorrow."

She jumped down the last few rungs and landed with a jolt. But before she could escape, something skittered across the ground and came to rest on the white strap of her flip-flop. She bent and picked up the piece of trash and sucked in a sharp breath. Trader Joe's Swiss dark chocolate with hazelnuts.

Ashton's favorite.

CHAPTER Four

Ashton turned onto Main Street, and a cluster of people his age rushed toward him. Not ready to make a comeback while wearing his dad's old clothes, he tugged his cap lower over his eyes and focused on the scuffed toes of his boots. The group funneled around him without a backward glance and filed into Gino's Cappuccinos. Ashton blew out a breath and raised his head, pushing down his nerves. Not that they would've recognized him anyway. He'd grown almost a foot since he'd gone away.

He shoved his hands in his pockets and strolled down the familiar tree-lined street. The town felt different but looked the same. This place that had once been his wonderland had become a means to an end.

He walked around a group of musicians squatted cross-legged in the middle of the sidewalk having an impromptu jam session. Then he peered into the bookstore with the same old dust-coated volumes piled to the ceiling and the same tired Christmas track blaring from the open door. He paused, shocked to see the fat orange-and-white tabby in the window. Memories of a girl with wide dark eyes and a long ponytail petting the enormous cat caused an uncomfortable expansion in his chest. That girl no longer existed to him.

Forcing his fists to unclench, he turned away and almost smacked into a guy wearing a pink tutu and black high-top Converse. "Excuse me, sugar." The guy's black-lined eyes gave Ashton the once-over as he passed.

Patting the string bag on his back to make sure it was still secure, he continued on.

His father used to say that if the people of Gilt Hollow got any more open-minded, their brains would fall out. Ashton didn't know if he agreed—he just hoped their open-mindedness extended to him. Otherwise his plan would end with him driven out of town by an angry pitchfork-wielding mob, or, worst case, back in lockup.

When he'd returned, he hadn't expected to find the house inhabited. So he'd snuck in through the kitchen window, grabbed some supplies, and headed to sleep in the tree house. Considering he had zero experience with breaking and entering, it was no surprise that he'd totally botched it. And when he turned back to see if he'd woken anyone, the outline of a girl stood in the upstairs window. He was lucky whoever it was hadn't called the cops.

But in desperate need of cash, he'd snuck back into the house earlier that day, grabbed some clothes, and searched the attic for something he could sell. When he'd found Gram's old record collection, it felt like an answer from heaven. He had been his grandparents' favorite, and they'd left him all of their belongings, including his grandfather's motorcycle collection—which he planned to dig out of the garage as soon as he figured out how to convince the current tenants that he wasn't some random kid off the street.

But first he needed to see if Twisted Beauty was still in business. The store was so "exclusive" it didn't have a sign. Ashton turned into the tiny clothing boutique and climbed the narrow stairs to the second floor, where the pounding guitar riff to "Back in Black" greeted him. Ashton smirked at the irony.

Rock posters lined the walls of the small landing. Ashton

poked his head around the corner. Wooden bins of LPs filled the room, and the familiar smell of molded plastic laced with dust and a bit of herbal remedy drew him in. Ashton had spent many hours in this stuffy, second-floor shop, running his fingers over the accordion of colorful covers, helping sort stock, and learning to appreciate real music. Behind the counter, the owner, Jeff White, screeched into an invisible microphone.

"Still rockin' the classics, old man?"

Jeff glanced up mid-headbang, flicked shaggy bangs out of his eyes, and then lowered his fist by slow degrees. "Ashton? Is that you?"

So much for not being easily recognized.

Ashton tugged off his hat and ran his fingers through his hair. "Yeah."

Jeff leaned over and turned the music down. "How you doin', kid?"

Ashton met Jeff's unwavering gaze. When he saw no fear or condemnation in the man's clear gray eyes, the tightness in his chest released. "I can't complain." He shrugged and thumbed through the movie soundtrack section.

"Are you in town to stay?" Jeff leaned on the counter, the sun streaming through the windows behind him highlighting the silver streaks in his brown hair.

"For now." Ashton picked up a double album of an old musical he'd liked as a kid. He and Willow had watched the DVD until it warped. He dropped it back into its slot like it burned his fingers.

"If you need anything, kid, anything at all, just say the word. My couch is open if you need a place to crash. It ain't much, but it's cushioned more important butts than yours." He chuckled at his own joke.

Ashton slanted a glance at the shop owner. "You still giving cash for vinyl?"

"You know it! Whatcha' got for me?"

"How about the Beatles's *Can't Buy Me Love?*"

Several beats of silence passed. Ashton glanced up to find Jeff's jaw unhinged. "You better not be yankin' my chain, kid."

A grin tilted up one side of Ashton's mouth as he lifted the record from his bag and placed it on the counter. "Nope. It's the original 45."

"Hot dang! This thing's worth a small fortune." He ran his fingers over the mint-condition cover reverently. "Where'd you get it?"

Ashton's jaw locked up. He couldn't tell if the guy thought he'd stolen it or if he was just curious. But he sure as heck hadn't come here to defend himself. He narrowed his gaze and growled, "Do you want to buy it or not?"

Jeff's eyes widened and he took a step back. "Sure . . . sure . . . of course." Then he blinked, as if remembering he'd known Ashton most of his life, and a goofy grin spread across his face. "Does Steven Tyler wear leather pants?"

The tension left Ashton's shoulders. "How much will you give me for it?"

Jeff moved over to his computer and typed in silence for several moments. Practically vibrating with excitement, he turned back to Ashton. "How does five hundred sound?"

Ashton knew his records, and this thing may not be the holy grail—that would be John Lennon and Yoko Ono's *Double Fantasy*—but he wasn't about to get screwed on the deal either. "You know it's worth four times that, Jeff."

"True . . . but I have to put up the cash not knowing what I'll make in return." He perched on a stool and began typing again. Ashton thumbed through the selection of singles, a dull pain radiating through his lower back. He lifted his arms and stretched, popping several vertebrae. He'd slept like a baby the first night. The fresh breeze flowing through the tree house tasted like freedom. The second night had been a different story. Crashing on a stoner's sofa wasn't the answer though. Jeff may be cool, but Ashton needed to stay as far away from illegal activity as possible. Maybe he could convince the tenants living in his house to break their lease early. He had a home visit from his parole officer coming up in less than a week.

"Eight hundred is my final offer."

Ashton strolled back to the counter. "I've got more where this came from . . ." He let his words trail off as Jeff's gaze sharpened like a laser. The others weren't worth as much as this one, but together it would be enough for food, school fees and supplies, and some clothes that didn't stink like mothballs. "Make it a grand, and it's a deal."

"Okay, kid, but just because I know you."

Ashton nodded, already imagining the reaction of his "friends" when he walked through the doors of Gilt Hollow High. It was time for some payback.

CHAPTER Five

D o you think he'll come back here?" Lisa asked as she laid a slinky black skirt on top of the growing pile of clothes in Willow's arms.

The logical part of Willow's brain told her Ashton would never return—to the scene of the crime, where Daniel's parents still grieved, where he would forever be seen as a criminal. But the part of her that knew Ashton Keller better than anyone else on the planet knew he'd never run from a challenge in his life.

The question that wouldn't stop playing through her mind since she'd heard he was released, since she'd seen that freaking candy wrapper, was whether or not she *wanted* him to return. She'd tried to reach him for almost a year after his conviction, but with every day she didn't hear from him, her heart had broken a little more. And even though she'd never admit it to anyone, she began to wonder if the darkness she'd seen growing in him after her father passed had eclipsed the Ashton she used to know—the boy in her daydreams.

"Willow?"

Recalling the shadowed figure she'd seen watching the house, Willow suppressed a shiver and forced her attention back to her friend.

"Or will he go to . . . Where did you say his parents moved—Columbus?"

"Cincinnati," Willow corrected. "Not sure." Willow mouthed a relieved "thank you" as she unloaded her burdens into the arms of a clerk.

"What's your favorite color?" Lisa called from behind a multihued display. "Or more importantly, what's Brayden's favorite color?"

"I have *no* idea." A scarlet halter dress appeared in her arms as if by magic.

"All boys like red," Lisa pronounced as she flounced over to the jewelry counter.

They were shopping for her date—even if she didn't know if that's what it was—at the only upscale boutique in town. Lisa had turned her nose up at every other clothing store they entered, declaring them "too hippie," "too vintage," "too . . . disgusting!"

Unemployed—again. The money Willow had managed to scrounge together wouldn't go far. She turned toward the fitting rooms. "I'm going to start trying stuff on."

Lisa was close behind. "I found the perfect necklace for that dress!"

Willow stared at the rainbow of clothing hanging in her fitting room. The majority of it was way out of her comfort zone. She gravitated toward muted colors and comfortable fabrics. But she had to admit, the jewel tones Lisa had picked out for her were gorgeous. She selected a sapphire-blue sweater and held it up under her chin.

Lisa yanked open the door and appeared in the mirror behind her. "That blue really makes your eyes pop. Try it on," she ordered as she slammed the door.

Willow drew her loose gray shirt over her head.

"And take those glasses off!"

"Oh. My. Gosh. Bossy much?" Willow laughed as she removed her cat-eye frames and placed them in her purse. Ever since Lisa learned the glasses were only for seeing at a distance, she'd been bugging her to ditch them. Willow slipped on a pair of soft charcoal leggings and turned to admire how long they made her legs look. And they were comfortable.

She opened the door and met Lisa at the three-way mirror. Her friend wore a sleeveless jumpsuit that managed to look relaxed and chic at the same time.

"That really is your color. Wait—" Lisa jogged into her dressing room and came back out with a wide belt that she looped around Willow's waist. "Voila! Instant figure."

A blast of bass shook the mirrors in front of them.

"What's up there? A rave? It's five o'clock on a Wednesday. Geez, this town is weird." Lisa turned and looked over her shoulder to check out the back view of her outfit.

"It's a record store." Willow adjusted the belt on her hips. "I love that jumper, by the way. I could never pull it off, but it looks great on you."

Lisa's blue eyes met hers in the mirror. "A record of what?"

"You know, albums. Are you sure you're from a big city?"

"Yes, genius, but record stores are only for stoners and old guys reliving their glory days." Lisa smirked. "Now go try on that sexy red dress."

Willow did as ordered, and after ten more outfit changes they were at the checkout. The prices more reasonable than anticipated, she decided on the leggings and blue tunic, as well as the scarlet halter dress. She had no clue when she would wear it, but it actually made her look curvy instead of like a stick figure.

"Want to grab dinner?" Lisa asked as she paid for her jumper and three other outfits with matching accessories.

"Can't. I've got homework." Anxiety churned in Willow's gut. For the second night in a row, she'd barely slept, and now she had at least three hours of studying ahead of her. A huge yawn escaped and she covered her mouth. If she didn't fall asleep first. This was exactly why she never procrastinated.

Ready to be home, Willow gathered her bags and they made their way toward the door.

"Do you want to go to the game with me Friday night?" Lisa asked, stopping to admire a black tulle skirt. "Oh, I love this!"

"I think you've bought enough, and that's way too Madonna," Willow teased as she tugged Lisa away. "And yes, going to the game sounds fun." After talking to Brayden yesterday, she'd realized she'd spent too much time worrying about what other people thought of her. She had a new friend and a date with one of the most popular boys in school. It was time to let go of the past and live her life. Enjoy her senior year.

"You should come to my house first. I'll do your makeup for your date with Braaayden."

"If you say his name like that again, deal's off," Willow threatened.

Just as they reached the cramped entryway, a guy came out of the stairwell from the record shop. Tall with the lean muscles of an athlete, his T-shirt stretched tight across his chest and shoulders, a black baseball cap pulled low over his eyes. Something about the way his dark hair curled against the olive skin of his neck, the way he moved . . . she *knew* him. As he reached out to push open the door, he turned, and Willow's heart dropped into her feet.

Ashton.

Time seemed to stop as they stared at one another.

He was still Ashton, but transformed, as if a sculptor had chiseled away the softness of his face to reveal the sharp angles beneath. Broad cheekbones, strong chin, square jaw clenched tight. But his eyes were the same deep blue of a lake at midnight. He was Ashton all right, but all grown up.

Then something clicked behind his gaze and turned hot like a gas flame igniting. Willow sucked in a sharp breath as the planes of his face hardened into a mask of rage.

And for the first time in four years, Willow believed Ashton Keller was capable of murder.

CHAPTER Six

W illow froze, unable to move or speak. Ashton's expression slammed shut and he pushed through the door, the shop bell clanging like a wakeup call in Willow's ears.

Really? After being the only one to defend his innocence, *this* is what she got? A lethal glare and silence? If anyone should be glaring, it should be her!

Heat flooded her cheeks, and something snapped. Ex-convict or not, it would take more than a dark stare to erase their years of friendship. Nearly vibrating, she stalked to the door.

"Wait—" Lisa reached out to stop her, but Willow shrugged off her hand.

Out on the street, she spotted Ashton almost at the corner of the block. For a wild moment, she considered rushing after him and tackling him to the ground, but instead she stalked forward and yelled at the top of her lungs, "Why did you come back here?"

He stopped, his shoulders tensing as his head tilted, and she caught a glimpse of his hard profile. Willow waited, glaring at his back, bracing for a fight. But Ashton didn't take the bait. He just turned and walked away, dismissing her like they hadn't been friends since they were five, like she hadn't written to him every day for months.

Willow puffed out a breath and spun on her heel, heading in the opposite direction. She walked fast—down the sidewalk, around a couple holding hands, past Bill's grocery, her heart racing as if she'd done a 100-yard dash. The lights of the outdoor patio of Postman's Tavern streaked her vision, laughter and the clink of glassware swirling in her ears like a funhouse recording.

Willow slowed her pace at the corner, waiting for a car to pass, her breath coming in short gaps. *Oh no.* Fighting against the rising panic, she didn't hear Lisa approach.

"Hey, you dropped this back there."

Willow took the bag of clothes in numb fingers and crossed the street.

Oblivious to Willow's escalating distress, Lisa quipped, "Who was *that* mouth-watering specimen?"

"Ashton." Willow scraped a breath through her pinched throat.

"*That* was Ashton?"

Willow couldn't find enough air. But she pushed her legs faster.

"If all felons look like him," Lisa continued, "I'm signing up for prison guard duty today!"

"Lisa! Not helping." Willow clutched a fist to her heaving chest.

"Hey." Lisa gripped Willow's arm, pulling her to a stop. "Are you all right?"

"I just . . . I just . . ." Willow couldn't focus, her eyes darting, her fingers tingling.

Lisa gasped. "You're *not* okay." She grabbed Willow's hand and led her off the main road and into a tree-shaded park.

Trembling, Willow stumbled to the closest bench and sank down. The world spun as she leaned her head back. She hated this. Hated that her body betrayed her at the first sign of stress. Hated that her new friend would see her weakness. Glimpsing a patch of vivid blue between the pink and purple streaks of the setting sun, she focused on it and began to mumble her panic script.

When the steel bands loosened from her chest, she sat up and turned to meet Lisa's wide eyes. "Sorry about that. I . . . er . . . sometimes—"

"Freak out when you run into your ex–best friend four years after he was convicted of murder and he looks at you like you're his next victim?"

Willow huffed, blowing the bangs off her forehead. "Um, yeah."

"It's cool." Lisa shrugged. "My granny used to have panic attacks. But hers weren't triggered by stress . . . more like lack of attention."

"What did you do when she had one?"

"Pretty much ignored her until she shut up."

Forgetting her own troubles, Willow's eyes widened. "You didn't!"

"We learned early on that woman could suck the joy out of any occasion if we let her." Lisa's grin faded. "But you aren't anything like her."

"Thanks . . . I think." Willow grimaced, making Lisa laugh.

"Anytime, Lamott. What are friends for, if not to make you feel less weird?"

A streetlamp sputtered to life next to them, and Willow gathered her bags. "I better go. Calculus quiz tomorrow." But as she stood, something Lisa had said made her pause and sit back down. "So do you think he hates me now?"

Lisa chewed on her bottom lip before answering. "I think he seemed angry. Whether or not that anger is directed at you is hard to say."

"Oh, I think the direction of his anger was pretty clear. But I don't understand." Suddenly too warm, Willow yanked down the zipper of her jacket. "I supported him when everyone else had turned away, and got *nothing* in return. Shouldn't I be the one who's angry?"

A couple strolled by and stared at Willow. She knew her voice had risen to a shrill screech, but she couldn't care.

"I have a feeling he sensed your ire." Lisa grinned. "That was pretty ballsy, yelling after him like that. If he stared me down, all dark and brooding, I probably would've run away with my tail between my legs." She wiggled tawny brows. "Or thrown myself into his arms. Hard to say."

Too wound up to go there, Willow glanced down at her clenched fists and forced her fingers to uncurl. "That's just it . . . anger wasn't my initial reaction. When I saw him and realized who I was looking at, it was like a huge weight lifted. Like I could finally let out a breath I'd been holding for the last four years."

All traces of humor gone, Lisa placed a calming hand on Willow's arm. "Maybe he just needs some time. He's been through a lot."

Willow slumped back against the bench, blowing out a breath. She couldn't begin to imagine what Ashton had been through, or how all of it had changed him. Or the reasons why he'd shut her out.

"There's something I don't get though." Lisa rubbed Willow's arm in comforting circles. "Why would he come back here if his family is gone and everyone in town believes he's guilty?"

"I don't know." Willow shook her head. "Obviously, it wasn't to rekindle old friendships." Willow tugged the cuffs of her sweater down to cover her suddenly cold hands, and then got to her feet. "I need to go."

"Do you want company? I can walk you home."

"Thanks, but I need some time to think."

Willow wandered through the park, taking random turns along the path. Could she have misjudged Ashton? Had she wanted to believe so badly in his innocence that she'd ignored the facts?

Questions crowding in, she ambled through short pools of streetlamps and long stretches of darkness, until she realized the shadows had taken over the light. Willow came up short. Rolling hills dotted with ancient trees, the scent of fresh-turned earth. She'd wandered into the Sanctuary.

She hadn't been here since . . .

Trees, angels, and headstones spin around her as she hightails it from her father's gravesite. Away from the crying. And the stares. The expectations.

Footsteps pound.

"Wil, stop!" A hand grasps her upper arm.

She staggers to a halt, grips her knees, heart pounding inside her throat.

"Are you okay?"

Stupid question, but she pants, "Yeah."

"Really? 'Cause you don't look so good to me." Ashton bends over and meets her gaze. "Kinda pukey, actually."

She shoots him a steel-melting glare.

He offers a grin, but it collapses like a house of cards, and he tugs her into his arms. "Come here."

She rests her head on his polyester suit–clad shoulder, the chemical smell of fresh dry-cleaning melding with his warm, citrus scent. Breathing deeply, she feels her world slowing into its regular rotation.

That was the Ashton she remembered—the side of him no one else knew.

Instead of turning back the way she'd come, Willow headed deeper into the cemetery. The air had cooled with the setting of the sun, and she tugged her jacket tighter around her. Odd that she remembered the way after so many years. But when she reached the correct section, she couldn't recall which row it was in. The darkened stones blended together—memorials of various shapes and sizes, some topped with flower arrangements or surrounded by flags, others dark and lonely. The day they'd put her father into the ground, it had felt like his grave was the only one there.

A tinkling sound like fairy bells drew her eye to a spiral wind chime twirling on a shepherd's hook, and she knew she'd found it. Only her mother would create such a monument.

Picking her way toward the grave, careful not to step on any freshly tilled ground, she wished she'd chosen to come here during the day. It wasn't that she felt some melodramatic aversion to cemeteries or that she couldn't stand the thought of visiting her father's final resting place, she just couldn't imagine paying homage to a slab of granite and a cadaver. She knew her father wasn't here buried under the dirt, tucked into a box. That was just his body—a body that had failed him. His soul resided elsewhere.

She had to believe it.

After a short but fierce battle with colon cancer, her dad had passed away when she was thirteen. She stopped in front of the three-by-six plot and smiled. Her father had been a silver-lining kind of person. When they had no money for a vacation one summer, he'd created a "tropical beach" out of a kiddie pool, a strip of plastic and a hose, water balloons, and seashells made out of cardboard. Willow had reclined on her Hello Kitty towel with her face to the sun while he described the ocean in such detail that she could smell the salt and hear the surf.

He'd brought light into every situation, which made the winding path of painted rocks that led to his marker, and the multicolored beads and crystals ringing music on the wind, a perfect tribute. A tiny handcrafted sign rose out of the ground at the end of the rock path. Willow tiptoed forward, careful not to displace the stones, and strained to read the words in the dark.

I LOVE YOU TO THE MOON AND BACK, DADDY.

A sob caught in her throat. It was written in Rainn's messy handwriting. This phrase had been whispered, yelled, sung, and even signed in their house more times than she could count. Willow dropped to her knees and brushed imaginary dirt from the top of the granite. "Hi, Dad, er . . . it's me . . . Willow. I'm not sure if you can hear me . . ." She sank back on her haunches with a sigh and ran a finger over the indention of his name. People always talked to dead loved ones in movies and it seemed perfectly normal, but this felt awkward. She traced the engraved dates. He'd only been thirty-three years old.

Maybe it didn't matter if he could hear her or not. Maybe it was more about the process of letting go. So in a soft whisper, she told him about school and Lisa and all the ways Rainn was like him.

"Oh yeah, and Ashton's back. You'd probably be disappointed in me. I wrote him tons of times, but when I didn't hear back after a while, I stopped. I tried to convince Mom to take me to see him, but she was always busy, and I just gave up. Now I'm pretty sure he hates me . . . or blames me or something. Which is totally unfair. But you know how he can be."

Her dad used to joke that Ashton swept in like a turbulent wind, smiling and content one day, changeable and fierce the next. The Lamotts's cottage had been his safe place to land between adventures or after a storm.

Willow began to pull a few taller pieces of grass that had grown up around the stone. "All I've done since he went away was defend him, even though the entire town believes he did it. I didn't think it was possible . . . until tonight. He changed after you left, Dad, and not for the better."

Shortly after her dad's death, Ashton began to pull away from her family. He'd started hanging with a different crowd and getting into fights. He was even arrested for vandalism and petty theft when he and some other boys "borrowed" all the garden gnomes in town and filled the school lawn with them. It would have been a hilarious joke if not for the lone pointy-hatted statue that had smashed through the science lab window and landed on Mr. Edward's desk.

Right after that, Ashton started showing up at their cottage, jittery and restless, and would take off without warning. Almost as if searching for something. Maybe the security he'd never known with his own family. Or the closeness he'd had with her father that he couldn't recreate—even with her.

She made a pile of the grass clippings and smoothed a hand over the bumpy surface of the pebbles. "But I'm trying to put all of that behind me now and enjoy my senior year. Brayden Martin asked me out. Can you believe—"

A crunch and the snap of a twig made her whirl around. The moon provided enough light to see the closest plots, leaving the rest of the cemetery in silhouette. Maybe it had been the wind in the trees. Slowly, she rose to her feet. It was late anyway.

She ran her fingers over the beads in the wind chime, sending them spinning. "Bye, Dad." He may not be able to hear her, but she knew if he could, it would please him that she had made the effort. Willow kissed her hand and then rested it on the top of the headstone. "Love you to the moon and back."

CHAPTER Seven

Ashton plunked down a good chunk of his cash at the town hardware/sporting goods/drugstore, and headed outside wearing new black combat boots, cargo pants, a T-shirt, and a buttery-soft leather jacket. Feeling much more like himself, he dropped the sack containing his dad's old clothes into a trash can and turned toward home.

Home? The thought of storing his new wardrobe in paper bags, using the creek as an outhouse, and spending another sleepless night on the hard floorboards of the tree house slowed his steps. He'd served his time, paid for whatever role he played in Daniel Turano's death a thousand times over. Yet he was living like an escaped convict.

No more.

With decisive steps, he headed back to the trash can, where he yanked the black baseball cap off his head and tossed it in. Raking a hand through his hair, he turned and strode down the lamplit street. A middle-aged woman stared him down, and he lifted a corner of his mouth in a slow smirk. She blinked rapidly and jerked her eyes away. He didn't recognize her, but after his conviction, he was sure his face had been plastered all over the news. He could just imagine the headlines: *"Trust-Fund Teen Kills Classmate."* Or *"Illustrious Keller Family Tainted By Scandal."*

Ashton turned down Oak Avenue and passed the Dairy Shed. Yellow fluorescent bulbs washed everything within a twenty-yard radius in a familiar jaundice glow. *Vanilla on a sugar cone with extra sprinkles.* Willow's high-pitched voice echoed in his head. The girl would order the same blasted thing every time, without fail. No matter what special flavors were offered or how much Ashton goaded her about it.

Ashton walked faster, away from the sallow-cast patrons and their animated chatter. And the memories. Seeing Willow had hit him harder than he'd expected. For some reason, he'd never pictured her as anything other than the awkward fourteen-year-old girl in braces, her hair shorter than his. Definitely not the girl he'd seen today—luminous eyes, high cheekbones, and soft lips.

"Why did you come back here?"

The twine handle of the shopping bag dug into his palm, and he loosened his death grip, but he couldn't undo the sting of her words. He wasn't sure why they even bothered him. He'd written off Willow Lamott long ago. Just as she'd done with him. But when he'd decided to come back to Gilt Hollow, his need for retribution had blinded him to how hard it would be to just walk down the street. He hadn't been prepared for the memories punching him in the gut at every turn.

A For Rent sign in the window of a brownstone slowed his steps. His parents' old office building. He'd come there after school for years, hoping to get a moment of their precious time. He'd sit in the back office listening to his parents on the phone with clients, negotiating contracts or making plans for future deals, until they'd force him to head home, where he'd take his dinner into the den and watch reruns of *Full House* until he fell asleep. Nanny or the cook would usually wake him and send him to bed. He'd lived for the moments when one of his parents would come home, help him up the stairs, and tuck him in, even if his mom was chastising him all the while.

Ashton could almost see her sleek blonde head through the window . . .

Catherine Arnett-Keller straightens the jacket of her Akris suit—worth more than most people earn in a month—and sits in the folding chair across from her son. She holds her purse in her lap, as if afraid to let the police station germs touch her belongings.

Ashton meets her dark blue eyes, the same shade as his own. "But I'm telling you, I didn't do this. Mom, please believe me," *he pleads, tears clogging his throat.*

She puffs out a long sigh. "Then why did you tell the police that you did? Why have Colin, Brayden, and Isaiah—the chief of police's son—come forward to say they saw you do it?"

Ashton digs his fingers into his hair. He had confessed, but only because his fear and confusion had jumbled with the responsibility he felt for Daniel's fall as the cops were screaming in his face.

"You get suspended for fighting at school, stay out all hours of the night, and then lie about where you've been . . . How do you expect me to believe you now?"

It's true. Since Adam Lamott's death, he'd gone off the rails, running from grief that always caught him in the end.

"Have you even thought about how your actions are affecting your family? Your father and I have a business to run that depends on our respectable image."

Ashton draws in a deep breath. "Where's Dad?"

"He can't see you right now. He's too disappointed."

Ashton's heart twists painfully in his chest. He and his dad didn't have a perfect relationship, but at least his father wasn't a heartless robot.

"The prosecuting attorney is pushing to try you as an adult for aggravated manslaughter. I've spoken with our lawyer, and he's negotiated a plea bargain for the lesser charge of involuntary manslaughter."

"I—"

She silences him with a look. "The other boys testified that you and Daniel have been fighting for weeks. That they've all been worried you would blow and do something to really hurt him."

"It's not like that! Daniel has been . . ." Ashton has to swallow as the image of Daniel's broken head reminds him that his friend is dead.

Mom continues as if she hasn't heard him. "Considering that you were arguing with Daniel just before the fall, we're going to take the deal. We'll settle out of court to avoid a drawn-out trial and further negative publicity." She sighs. "As it is, your father and I will have to relocate if we have any hope of salvaging the business this family has spent decades building." She patted her hair and rolled her eyes to the ceiling. "Thank goodness your sister is going to UCLA in a month."

Ashton stays silent, afraid the hurt and fury mixing in his heart will spew out of his mouth like poison.

His mother stands. "Ashton, I'm doing this for your own good. If my parents had been stronger with my brother . . . let him deal with the consequences of his choices . . ." Pain flickers across her face. Her younger brother had been a druggy whom their parents treated like a disabled child instead of an adult with an addiction. They'd bailed him out of jail, paid for dentures when his teeth fell out, bought him a new car every time he wrecked the last one, paid his rent, you name it . . . until he'd overdosed. Mom never spoke to her parents after that, blaming them for her brother's death. "Well, you know the story."

She turns her back and steps toward the door. Without looking back, she whispers, "I love you, Ashton, but I won't be your enabler. You need to learn to stand on your own."

That was the last time Ashton saw her.

He'd spent years burying the rejection of his family and friends, but now he embraced it—let it fuel him. She'd wanted him to stand on his own, and he'd *more* than learned that lesson. It was time to begin reclaiming the life he'd lost, starting with a more comfortable place to rest his head. Setting his jaw, he turned onto Walnut Street.

A block and a half later, Ashton pushed against the front gate, which opened with a screech, and stared up at the familiar—or not so familiar—face of his ancestral home. The once beautiful Victorian looked like a faded old woman, barely holding herself together. The facade, once a blend of soft green, deep blue, and eggshell had faded and chipped, exposing the gray boards beneath. Shutters hung off their hinges, boards covered a window on the third floor, and the broken porch stairs made the entire house appear crooked. What had happened here? He knew his parents had moved out of town, but it appeared as if they'd abandoned the house along with him. Grandpa Keller would bust out of his grave if he knew his pride and joy had fallen into such disrepair.

Keller House had been built in the 1800s by his great-great grandfather, one of the original founders of Gilt Hollow. Ashton's dad used to tell the story at dinner parties, school events, the grocery line—any chance he got to brag that their family had been part of the abolitionist movement, and had migrated from the East Coast with the aim of creating a utopian society. But the idealistic community plan dissolved, due in no small part to Ashton's ancestor marrying a Filipino woman. Apparently incorporating other races into their Shangri-La didn't include procreating with them. Run out of town, Grandpa Keller bided his time and returned a decade later, instituting the Little Miami Railroad, becoming mayor, and building Keller House.

As a kid, Ashton had been proud that his home was one of the oldest in Gilt Hollow. He loved that everyone knew he lived in the big Victorian on Walnut.

Not anymore.

Suppressing a shudder, he walked up the weed-infested path. The closer he got, the worse the place looked. He bent down to inspect a hole in the lattice beneath the porch where an animal had gnawed through the wood, and no doubt still resided. At the juvie agricultural center, he'd learned everything from barn repair to tractor maintenance. Ashton straightened and gazed up at the old mansion again. Maybe he could use what he'd learned to fix up the place.

Clearly his parents had given up on it, but they couldn't legally sell it. As part of the trust from his grandfather, this house, along with a sizable fortune, would rightfully be Ashton's when he turned twenty-one. So whoever lived inside had to be renting. He would just explain to the current tenants that there'd been a mistake and give them two weeks to vacate. The house had eight bedrooms, not including the old servants' quarters in the attic, so staying on the premises until they'd found another rental shouldn't be a problem.

Anticipating a soft place to sleep and a hot shower, he loped up the crooked stairs and lifted a finger to the doorbell. A screech and pounding footsteps from inside made him step back. Squeals of laughter sounded, and Ashton leaned in to peer through a panel of wavering glass next to the door. A little boy with a mop of blond hair raced by, holding something small and black above his head.

Dark hair flying behind her, a girl raced after him. "Rainn! I swear, if you don't give that back . . ."

Ashton's breath caught as a woman with salt-and-pepper dreads and a weary frown marched into the entryway. "Rainn, that's enough. Give Willow her phone."

Oh no.

He stumbled back from the door.

Turning on his heel, he leaped off the porch and ran into the tree line. Really? Of all the people in Gilt Hollow, why did it have to be *them*? He'd once considered the Lamotts more family than his own. Until they'd ditched him too.

Blood boiling, he crashed through the trees, branches scraping, damp leaves smacking his skin. Soon the lights of a neighboring house cut through the gloom of the forest. He pulled back into a circle of spruce and squatted, lowering his head into his hands. No way was he spending another night hiding in that godforsaken tree house.

He could find shelter at the lone seedy motel in town or one of the multiple bed-and-breakfasts, if they'd take cash—doubtful. But that wasn't the point.

He clenched his fists against his thighs. If it had been anyone else, he would have rung that doorbell and asked them to start packing. But the Lamotts had been the one solid he thought he could count on. He'd waited for months, hoping every visiting day, every holiday, every mail run would prove they still cared. Until one particular day, six months after his incarceration . . .

Dude, you're like a caged animal today. What's your deal?" Toryn demands.

Ashton turns from the cell door and flops down on his cot, staring at the random bumps in the popcorn ceiling. "What time does the mail run again?"

"Same time as every other day, man." From the opposite bunk, his cell mate releases a long sigh. "Four o'clock."

Ashton sits up and swings over the edge of the bed, legs jumping, feet tapping a silent melody.

"Seriously, what are you expecting? An Xbox? A flat-screen TV? A bikini-clad girl jumping out of a giant cake? 'Cause if you are, I'll blow off arts and crafts time to see that."

"No, I . . ."Ashton trails off as the mail cart enters their hallway.

"Mallory!" Rumble. Rumble. Squeak. "Hudson!" Rumble. Rumble. Squeak. "Rozelle!"

Toryn rolls off his cot, takes the letter, and tosses it onto the desk. He turns to face Ashton. "See, no big. Just my mom ranting about my grades and what I'm planning to do with my life after this. Blah, blah, blah . . . You should be glad you don't get that bull from your parents."

I don't get anything from my parents, bull or otherwise, Ashton thought. "I just hoped"—Ashton shrugs, swallows the baseball in his throat, and lies back on the *cot, hands behind his head*—"*that somebody remembered my birthday.*"

In that moment, it hadn't been his real family he'd wanted to hear from. They'd made their disassociation clear. But a tiny part of him had hoped for something from the Lamotts. Some acknowledgment that he was alive. That he mattered. But mostly, that his best friend hadn't forgotten him.

And now she lived in his house with no thought as to where he might be staying. Well, he didn't owe her a damn thing. She could sleep on the street for all he cared. Shooting to his feet, he took several strides toward the house and stopped. He couldn't do it. With a growl, he slapped a pine bough, needles and cones falling at his feet. Their rich, clean scent calmed him as he drew in a ragged breath.

If nothing else, he owed Adam Lamott that much. The man had been more of a father to him than his own. Ashton knew in his gut that if Adam were still alive, he never would have abandoned him. For his sake alone, Ashton wouldn't try to force his family out on the street.

But he wouldn't spend another night out in the cold either. Shuffling through the crisp carpet of fallen leaves, he found a relatively comfortable trunk to lean against, pulled a sandwich out of his bag, and settled in to wait. If he knew the Lamotts, they'd be snug in their beds by ten o'clock, and then he'd make his move.

CHAPTER Eight

W illow closed her locker and leaned against it with a sigh. For the third day in a row, she felt like the walking dead. The night before, Keller House had hit a new level of creeptastic. Sometime after midnight, she'd been startled awake by a noise that faded before she'd fully awoken. Her heart beating in her throat, she'd lain stiff as a board under the coverlet. Just as she'd begun to relax, a creak echoed through the hall, followed by a soft thud, and another, and another—footsteps. She'd pulled the covers over her head like a frightened child and slept fitfully the rest of the night.

In the light of day, she began to suspect the noises had less to do with ghosts and goblins and more to do with a certain individual whose house she now occupied. At one point during the night, she'd heard running water, followed by the metallic bang of pipes. Unless her mom had started sleep-showering, they had an uninvited houseguest.

"Nice outfit, Lamott." Lisa approached, eyeballing Willow from her red Converse to her oversized sweater and ripped jeans, to her sloppy ponytail and glasses. Then Lisa hooked her arm through Willow's and tugged her into the flow of traffic. "I'd hoped my fashion tips might've begun to rub off on you, but this is even a step back from your usual preppy Gap-girl look."

"I'm not even sure my socks match." They turned into the arts hallway and then into the choir room, their only class together besides Study Hall.

"Another sleepless night in the haunted mansion?"

Willow dropped her books on the floor and rotated her stiff neck as she climbed the risers, Lisa on her heels. "Or were you having evocative dreams about Mr. Dark and Brooding?"

Willow frowned and narrowed her eyes at her new friend before plopping down on the top bleacher.

Lisa sat beside her and raised her hands in a pleading gesture. "Whoa, sorry, didn't mean to offend."

Students streamed into the room, bringing with them an almost deafening chatter.

"No, I'm sorry." Willow sighed and met Lisa's concerned gaze. "*He*'s just a sensitive topic right now. And a big part of the reason why I'm so exhausted today."

"Wait." Lisa gripped her upper arm, blue eyes flaring wide. "What?"

As Willow opened her mouth to share her theory, Yolanda and Ona climbed the alto risers, bringing with them a choking wave of incense and musk. Yolanda tossed the blue-black sheet of her asymmetrical bob out of her face, dropped her binder with a loud smack, and then crossed her arms, pulling her crochet knit top tight across her braless chest. "Only the strongest voices get top row."

Ona flipped her wheat-colored cornrows over her shoulder and gripped her bohemian-print-clad hips, giving a tight nod. "Yeah." She'd gone to Jamaica with her family in July, where she claimed to have met her spirit mate, who told her never to unbraid her hair. She hadn't washed it since. It was September.

Secretly, Willow had always thought of the hippie-emo twins as Yoko and Ono, but since they pretty much ruled the school, she'd kept it to herself. Besides, knowing them, they'd take it as a compliment. It wasn't. The two of them had been relentless in their quest to break Willow down in the weeks after Ashton's arrest. And when they finally taunted her until she ran to the bathroom in tears, they'd christened her Weeping Willow—which was shorted to Weepy and adopted by their entire crowd.

In no mood for their usual sass, Willow shot to her feet.

Before she could open her mouth, Lisa rose beside her and jabbed a french-manicured nail toward the bottom row. "Well, good thing there's still room for you two down in front." She might look like a delicate fashion plate, but she was also a New Yorker.

Mrs. Adders, the instructor, clapped her hands three times. "Students! Find your seats. We have a lot to cover before our concert next month."

Yolanda narrowed her black-lined eyes. "I'd rather be in the front row than near you two tone-deaf crows. Come on, O." Grabbing their things, she shoved her way into the front row, Ona on her tail.

"At least I don't smell like I use skunk oil for deodorant!" Lisa tossed after them. "Take a bath once in a while!"

Willow lifted her sheet music folder to hide her idiotic grin.

"What *is* that stench, anyway?" Lisa hissed out of the side of her mouth as they began to sing scales.

"You know, Patchouli—*mi mi mi mi mi*—everyone wears it."

"*Do . . . re . . . mi . . . fa . . . so . . . la . . . ti—*"

"*Oh*, is that the reek I smell every time I walk into this building? I thought it was just clove cigarettes," Lisa muttered.

"Open your folders to page sixteen of your song books," Mrs. Adders directed.

"That too," Willow replied.

"I'm just glad you don't wear it. Might've been a deal breaker." Lisa read the title of their new piece and smirked, one perfectly made-up eye flashing in a wink before she waved her copy of *Send in the Clowns* above her head. "Oh look, Yo, it's a song just for you!"

Willow doubled over laughing.

■ ■ ■

After giggling their way through several more songs and earning a stern talking to by Mrs. Adders, Willow and Lisa headed to their lockers. Imitating the look on Yolanda's face when Lisa shouted they were singing her song and the entire room burst into laughter, Willow didn't at first notice the hush in the air. Groups of students clustered together, whispering behind their hands, others ducking into their lockers like turtles.

As Willow reached into her own locker, she felt a shift in the atmosphere and the hairs rise on the back of her neck. She turned in slow motion, and all the air whooshed out of her lungs. Waves of dark-tousled hair falling over midnight-blue eyes, broad shoulders thrown back, cargo-pants carelessly tucked into combat boots, Ashton Keller sauntered down the senior hallway confident yet alert, as if an attack could come from any side—and he was ready for it.

A gasp sounded from nearby. "Is that who I think it is?"

His name ricocheted like an out-of-control Ping-Pong ball, as more and more students flocked to the scene.

Coolly indifferent, Ashton didn't seem aware of the disturbance around him. His eyes shifted in Willow's direction, pinning her to the spot, then without a change of expression slid away to a cute redhead walking toward him. His lips tilted in a slow grin. After a startled blink, she returned his smile with a tentative one of her own.

"Holy hotness, what is *he* doing here?" Lisa hissed in her ear.

Willow had forgotten her friend still stood beside her. Pain pierced her consciousness, and she peeled herself away from the metal shelves digging into her back. She was practically inside her stupid locker. With growing disgust, she spun around and threw her songbook onto the shelf and then grabbed the text and notebook for her next class. She slammed the metal door with so much force it bounced back and smacked her knee.

"Ugh!" She kicked it, this time making sure it closed.

"Lamott, talk to me." Lisa adjusted the string bag on her shoulder and followed Willow to the stairs, whispering, "Can't have you going into overload mode."

"Too late," Willow spat. "What the heck is he doing? Does he think people will welcome him with open arms? That they've forgotten? Did you see the way he looked at me? Like I don't even exist?"

"Yes, I get it. He's an idiot." Lisa tugged on Willow's sweater. "Slow down, Speed Racer."

Realizing her legs had sped up with every word out of her mouth, and that she'd practically run to Advanced Lit class, she paused and faced her friend. "I think he snuck into the house last night."

"*What?*" Lisa squawked, her mouth dropping open in a cartoonish mask of shock.

"Technically, it's his house, right? But—" The warning bell rang. Willow sighed. "You better go." Lisa had gym second period, which was on the other side of the building.

"Right." She glanced at the clock and began to jog, throwing over her shoulder, "See you at lunch!"

The morning passed as if in reverse. Every class Willow

waited, tense and watchful, for Ashton to walk through the door. In second period Bio, Brayden had tried teasing her, but when all his jokes fell flat, he turned silent. She could see in the tense set of his mouth that Ashton's return took its toll on him as well.

In Historical Music Appreciation, the classroom door clicked shut, and Willow sank back into her seat. Maybe they wouldn't share any classes. He might even have to take some lower-level courses to catch up. Despite Gilt Hollow's graduating class having fewer than two hundred students, their academic standards were above average. And, Willow imagined, well above that of a state-run juvenile detention facility.

Mr. Rush tapped his baton on his desk, calling the class to order before he began to conduct—with wide sweeping gestures—a lecture on the influence of Greek theory on medieval music. But at the moment, Willow couldn't care less what the class was about, as long as Ashton wasn't in it.

Just as Willow settled in to listen to a reproduction of "A Troubadour Love Song"—which sounded more like a dying cow accompanied by a toddler playing the lute than the "prodigious classic" Mr. Rush touted it to be—the door swung open. Willow jerked upright. Mr. Rush stopped the song and glared. "*Yes?*"

Ashton strode into the room and handed the teacher a slip of paper. Her pulse creeping into her throat, Willow watched Mr. Rush scan the note and gesture with his baton to the only empty desk. Right next to hers. "Take a seat, Mr. Keller."

At the sound of the name, whispers and giggles broke the unnatural silence in the classroom. Gripping her pencil, Willow focused on breathing normally as Ashton sat, leaned back, and extended his long legs into the aisle, his booted feet resting inches from hers.

"Now, let's get back to it, shall we?" Mr. Rush started the torturous song from the beginning and closed his eyes, waving his arms in ecstasy.

Willow ran through her schedule, trying to figure out the earliest opportunity to meet the guidance counselor. She was *so* dropping this class.

"So . . ."

The deep voice, so close to her ear, made Willow jump. Livid that she'd shown a reaction, she turned, shooting daggers.

Ashton stared straight at her, his strong features mere inches away.

She swallowed. Hard.

"Sleep well last night?"

They were the first words she'd heard from him in four years. His voice, smooth and low, was almost unrecognizable. But the cadence, the slight mocking, hadn't changed.

Careful to keep her tone flat, she answered, "What do you think?"

One side of his mouth quirked and something undefinable sparked in his eyes before he leaned back. His posture languid, he shrugged. "How would I know?"

Jerk.

Willow fixed her gaze on the squiggly lines moving to the music on the Smartboard, but her thoughts were far from the screeching love song. Ashton knew exactly why she looked like a zombie with sleep apnea, and his goading confirmed it. He'd broken into her house last night, taken a shower, slept in one of the beds, and probably ate their porridge. Except she was no bear and he definitely was not a cute little blonde girl.

She glanced at him from the corner of her eye—over six feet tall, his T-shirt sleeves stretched over biceps that could have fit on a professional fighter. Nope, not Goldilocks, more like the Big Bad Wolf. Willow forced her gaze back to Mr. Rush, who'd begun to pontificate on the wonders of ancient melodies, and zoned out.

Even if the house belonged to Ashton's family, her mother had signed a contract allowing her to live there as caretaker. He had no right to bust in like he owned the place. She had to confront him, convince him to leave before her mom freaked out.

When the bell rang, Ashton stood, grabbed his things, and left without a glance in her direction. Willow blew out a gut-level breath. People filed out, whispering and casting surreptitious glances in her direction. Should she shoot a cocky smile? Ignore them? Make a joke about an ex-convict, a nerd, and a monk?

With a disgusted sigh, she dropped her aching head into her hands. She'd *finally* begun to break out of the stigma surrounding her. She had a new best friend and a real date. Was it too much to ask that she could have a normal senior year?

The second bell sounded and she lifted her head. If she didn't get to lunch, Lisa would likely make a missing-person's announcement over the PA system. But as she gathered her things, she saw that she wasn't alone. Isaiah Kagawa flicked his tied-back dreads over his shoulder and met her gaze.

His dark, almond eyes drilled into her, assessing, before he turned and walked toward the door.

And so it begins. Willow shoved her notebook into her string bag. As one of the boys who'd testified against Ashton, Isaiah had kept his distance for years. But recently that had seemed to change. Last year he'd asked her to join his group for a history project, and after that he'd gone out of his way to say hello. It would seem Ashton's return had screwed that up too.

"What does he want?"

The quiet words gave Willow a start. Isaiah hovered inside the doorway, shifting on his feet as if he couldn't decide if he wanted to stay or go.

Willow looped her bag over her shoulder and stood, deciding a bit of honesty couldn't hurt. "If you mean Ashton . . . I have no clue."

Isaiah's brow lifted in surprise. Why everyone assumed she had the inside track on Ashton's thoughts, Willow couldn't say. Just because she'd defended an old friend didn't mean she could read his mind. Especially not now.

"He shouldn't be here."

Willow cocked her head. His decisive tone almost seemed like a warning. "Why?"

Isaiah stared down at the yellowed linoleum, shuffled his feet, then glanced back up, not meeting her eyes. "A lot of people don't want him here, that's all."

Willow moved forward slowly. "That's kind of obvious, but you mean someone specific, don't you?"

Yells and the sound of running jerked their attention to the hallway. Willow passed Isaiah and found a circle of students, their excited whispers indicating a fight. Dread twisting in her gut, she pushed to the front of the crowd. Ashton and Colin Martin faced off like two bucks about to lock horns.

"Don't touch me again, Keller." Colin shoved a finger into Ashton's shoulder. For all his blond prettiness, the varsity quarterback gave Ashton a run for his money in the muscle department.

"You were in my way," Ashton growled, just before his gaze shifted from Colin and found Willow. As if a switch flipped, the tension leeched out of his shoulders and he stepped back. But before Willow could register relief, Ashton's eyes shuttered and his mouth slid into a dangerous smirk. He may have changed over the years, but that expression still spelled a million kinds of trouble.

Fear burned in Willow's chest, and she took a step forward. Someone had to stop him. He didn't come back here to be expelled the first day. A hand gripped her arm and pulled her back. She glared over her shoulder and found Brayden shaking his head. "Stay out of this," he hissed.

"What's the problem, Colin?" Ashton had crossed his arms over his chest and widened his stance. "Are you *afraid*?"

"What the frick is that supposed to mean?" Colin lurched forward, strands of hair falling out of the knot at the back of his head. "This is *my* school. If anyone should be afraid, it's you."

As if confirming Colin's words, a few of the other football players raised their fists and began to chant, "Martin! Martin!"

Ashton lifted his chin. "Go ahead, pretty boy. I'll give you a free shot."

Colin's muscles coiled, but he hesitated. Ashton cocked a brow in challenge.

"Break it up, gentlemen." Mr. Rush pushed his way in and stood between the two boys.

Colin relaxed, his face taking on a plaintive moue. "I didn't do anything, Mr. Rush. He rammed his shoulder into me." He rubbed his bicep and grimaced like his arm might be broken.

The boy should skip sports and follow his true calling in the drama club.

"Mr. Keller." The squatty teacher spun on Ashton. "Violence is not how we conduct ourselves at GHH. This is not juvenile detention!"

Ashton's expression didn't change, but the color drained out of his skin. Recovering quickly, he snapped to attention and raised a hand to his forehead in salute. "Yes, sir!"

Only someone who knew him well would detect the mocking in his voice and the anger darkening his eyes. Mr. Rush wasn't one of those people. He straightened his own rounded posture and gave Ashton a quick nod. "Very good. You may go."

Obviously, Colin Martin wasn't the only hidden thespian in their midst. The group began to break up, and Willow pulled away from Brayden, striding after Ashton's retreating form. She had to jog to keep up with his long strides. When he turned into a short hallway that led to the quad, Willow called his name.

He stopped, turned to face her, and crossed his arms over his chest. Jaw set in a hard line and brows lowered, he looked so menacing Willow had to fight the urge to turn tail and run. But she'd been running from life long enough. She lifted her chin and met his eyes, the familiar deep blue flecked with gold giving her courage.

"We need to talk."

CHAPTER Nine

The bones of Ashton's face appeared to harden beneath his skin. "I have nothing to say."

To you. At the unspoken words, a spark flared inside Willow's chest. Being around him was like a knife striking flint, her emotions going from a single flame to a burning inferno in a matter of seconds. She mirrored his stance, crossing her arms and arching a brow. "Does that mean I don't have the right to speak?"

His cheek rippled, and she could hear his teeth grinding as he searched her face. Willow bit the inside of her lip in an effort not to squirm. After several seconds, he clipped, "Then speak."

She cleared her throat and decided on a direct approach. "You can't stay in the house."

He took two steps forward, standing so close she could feel his warmth and smell his spiced citrus scent. *How does he still smell the same after all these years?* An involuntary shiver raced down her spine as she tilted her head back to meet his shaded gaze.

"It's *my* house and I'll stay there if I like." His words were low and controlled, but the underlying threat hovered just beneath the surface. "The question is, what are *you* doing in it?"

Was it possible that he could kick them out? Override the contract they'd signed? Where would they go? Keller House was not only their shelter, but her mother's sole source of income. A change of tactic was in order. Willow took a step back and broke eye contact. Able to breathe much better with some space between them, she pushed the bangs off her forehead and forced her tone into more polite territory. "My mom signed a contract to take the caretaker job. We moved in last week. She's been working hard to clean up the place, but the last guy let it go for years."

When Ashton didn't respond, she jerked her gaze back to his face, then wished she hadn't. His mouth had parted as he searched the wall behind her head, his face unguarded for the first time. He dropped his eyes to the floor and scrubbed a hand down the back of his neck. "Just give me some time."

Without waiting for her reply, he pivoted and pushed out the door.

Willow slumped against the wall as a realization slammed into her—he had nowhere else to go.

■ ■ ■

The rest of the day passed in a blur. Willow didn't see Ashton again and heard rumors he was doing admittance testing. In his absence, he was still all anyone could talk about, with reactions ranging from fear that a "killer" walked among them to twitters from girls about how he wasn't like the other boys—his bad-boy persona only fueling their fascination. Willow found herself thrust into the center of it all and faced their voracious curiosity with as much nonchalance as she could manage.

All the while, her own thoughts swirled in her head. Ashton appeared so strong and independent that she hadn't given a thought to his plans—or lack of options. And why would she? Between his ominous glares and irritating taunts, there hadn't exactly been room for a heartfelt reunion. But she was beginning to see through his facade.

By the time she jogged up the front steps of Keller House after school, she'd decided to talk to her mom about him staying there—temporarily.

The acoustic stylings of James Taylor's "Fire and Rain" greeted her as she entered the house, along with her mom's sweet soprano singing, "But I always thought I'd see you again . . ." Willow dropped her backpack on a chair in the entryway and followed the music to the formal parlor, where her mother had thrown open the damask cream drapes and stood on a ladder cleaning one of the floor-to-ceiling windows.

The rounded room with its silk upholstered sofa and matching loveseat wasn't exactly cozy, but she'd been enchanted by it as a kid. She turned in a circle, and as her eyes landed on the curio cabinet packed with colorful hand-painted teacups, saucers, and pots, the urge to have an *Alice in Wonderland*–style tea party came rushing back.

"Oh, hey, Willow." Mom backed down the ladder and turned the radio off. "How was your day?"

"Fine," Willow muttered as she perched on the Queen Anne sofa. "Can I talk to you?"

Her mom pulled one of the dust covers back over the edge of the love seat before sitting in her dirt-stained clothes. Willow's belly lurched. The enormity of the favor she was about to ask made her wish she hadn't eaten the cafeteria meat loaf.

"I actually need to talk to you about something as well." Mom's dark eyes leveled on her face, her full lips pressed tight.

That look—the parental "we need to talk" expression—made Willow sit straighter. Such a rarity in their relationship, it caused her to blurt the first thing that came to her attention. "Hey, that's my T-shirt."

Mom tugged the shirt away from her slim chest and

glanced at it, the Goonies Never Say Die letters cracked over the faded skull and crossbones logo. Willow had worn it out the summer she turned fourteen—which brought her thoughts back to Ashton.

"Mom, I—"

"Willow—"

They spoke over each other and then both laughed. But it was less like their usual camaraderie and more like a nervous giggle. Curious, Willow conceded. "You go first."

"I ran into Chief Kagawa at the market today." She flicked the tail of her dreads behind her shoulder and tilted her head. "Did you know Ashton was back?"

Willow nodded. Isaiah's dad must have told her, and her mom was hurt that she hadn't shared the news. "That's actually what I—"

"Have you seen him? Talked to him?" Her mom's brows lowered, her back stiff as a board.

"Yes . . ." Confused, Willow stumbled over her words. "He . . . er . . . he came to school today."

"I don't want you associating with him, Willow. I know you were friends once, but he's not the same boy you remember."

Willow searched her mother's face for signs of fever or possession. This could not be her open-minded, peace-loving parent talking. "How would you know? You haven't seen him in years."

Mom continued as if she hadn't heard the question. "Chief Kagawa is going to be keeping a sharp eye on him, and I don't want you anywhere nearby if he gets arrested."

"Arrested?" Willow leaned forward. "Why would he? Do you think he's in town to case the local bank? He just got out of jail!"

Mom slumped back in her seat and pinched the bridge

of her nose. "Willow, I know you cared for him once, but drowning people will only drag you down with them. You may not realize it until you're ten feet under and suffocating, and then it's too late."

A breeze fluttered through the open window, brushing Willow's exposed skin with an early taste of autumn. She shivered and rubbed her arms against the chill. Ashton had been her *best friend*. She'd spent almost every day with him between the ages of five and fourteen. If Mom thought he was such a monster, why had she allowed the friendship?

Then she recalled overhearing a rare argument between her parents one morning before a trip to the zoo. Although she hadn't been able to make out all the words, Ashton's name had come up repeatedly, and she'd had to tell him he couldn't come with them as they'd planned. It all began to make sense now . . . her mom setting up playdates with prissy little girls Willow had nothing in common with, the sudden enforcement of a nine o'clock curfew—even in the summer—and her best words of comfort after Ashton's conviction: *"Maybe you're better off without him."* Willow had assumed those words had been her mom's way of trying to comfort her because she didn't know what else to say. But she'd really meant them.

"Why, Mom? What happened to make you feel this way about him?"

"Sweetie, that's not important now." Mom rose and then sat beside her on the sofa.

"But he has no one," Willow muttered, staring blindly into space.

Mom took Willow's numb fingers, connected to an arm that felt like boneless rubber. "I never thought we'd have to deal with this . . . never thought he'd come back here since his parents left so long ago. But I don't want you spending time with him." She squeezed until Willow met her intense gaze. "Do you understand?"

Where had this woman come from? When did she become judge, jury, and executioner? Fury uncoiled in Willow's chest, heat flooding her neck and cheeks as she stared at her mother.

"All these years, I defended him and you didn't say a word. You watched me suffer under the weight of this town's judgment. Lose my friends, and every job I've ever had, and you said nothing!" Willow yanked her hand back and shot to her feet.

"We raised you to have your own opinions. I just never shared mine."

Willow whirled. "That you thought he was guilty. That he *killed* Daniel Turano!" It wasn't a question.

Mom crossed her arms under her chest, her chin jutting out. "Regardless. I don't want you seeing him."

Willow coiled her fingers into fists at her sides to hide their trembling. She'd heard people complain about their unyielding, autocratic parents—something she never thought she'd have to deal with. Angry tears burned her eyes as she spat, "You're nothing like I thought you were. Dad would be ashamed."

Before she could digest the hurt crumpling her mother's face, she stomped out of the room.

* * *

Ashton leaned his head back against the wall, Linkin Park's "Numb" thumping in time with his riotous thoughts. Some things never changed. He'd been blowing off class and hanging out at Twisted Beauty since he hit middle school. The place was usually dead during the week, just a few Annherst students trickling in between classes. Jeff probably had the internet gods to thank for his ability to stay in business.

Half a day at that cesspit of a school had Ashton beginning to regret the strings his financial attorney had pulled to get him into Gilt Hollow High. The whispers behind his back. The terrified stares, like he might whip out an Uzi and go Call of Duty on their zombie butts. And worst of all, the morbid fascination, being poked at like some kind of circus freak. A kid had actually snapped a picture of him on his cell in the flipping restroom.

In computer science, Yolanda Shepard had plopped down at his lab table, propped her chin on her fist, and ogled him like they hadn't known each other since kindergarten. Ashton had never had a confidence problem. His sister used to tease that he'd been born with a superpower that attracted the opposite sex. But outside of the toothless cafeteria lady at JJC—who used to slip him extra rations—it had been a long time since he'd been around any females. And they were *way* more forward than he remembered.

Yolanda had run her hand down his bicep, her black-lined eyes heating with appreciation. Then she'd invited him to "hang out" at the snack shack by the football field at lunch. He'd let his gaze sweep over her and replied, "If you're looking for a relationship, I'm not interested."

Her hand found his thigh beneath the table. "We don't need commitment for what I have in mind."

He should've jumped all over it. She was hot, and part of Colin and Brayden's crowd, but something held him back. Maybe the way she kept glancing over her shoulder to see who was watching. Like being with the ex-convict would solidify her reputation as a rebel. He'd told her no and moved his leg from under her hand. Before flouncing away, she'd made a comment about it being his loss and spent the rest of the class texting. Probably relaying their conversation to half the school. He'd just have to find another way to infiltrate the Martin cousins' inner circle—one that didn't require him hooking up with a soulless clone.

On second thought, the absolute worst part of his day had been seeing the boys who used to be his friends—Isaiah, Brayden, and Colin Martin. He hadn't been able to look at any of them without the memory of their soulless eyes as they stared down at him from the top of the falls the day of the accident. Bumping into Colin had been an accident, but when Colin had lifted his chin and shot him that smug I-got-you-sucker look, Ashton's instincts had kicked in.

"Hey kid, you want a drag?"

Ashton turned to find Jeff holding out a hand-rolled cigarette, a tendril of pungent smoke curling to the ceiling. He shook his head and offered a grin. "In case you haven't noticed, I'm like half a foot taller than you. I'm not exactly a kid anymore."

Jeff took a long drag, walked to the open window, and shrugged. "You are to me. You've got your whole life ahead of you." He swept his arm wide.

Great. Ashton had forgotten how Jeff loved to wax philo-sophical. He used to find it funny, but right then he couldn't think past the next day, let alone his undefinable future. Mr. Zane Ponytail Reed would be coming to Keller House tomor-row for his first parole visit, and Ashton had no freaking clue what to do about it.

The Lamotts weren't there under a normal lease. And Willow had made it clear he wasn't welcome. He gripped the edges of the wooden stool beneath him. She brought out something primal in him, all the hurt and disappointment boiling to the surface every time he looked at her insolent little face—the tilt of her chin denying their history, her eyes flashing rejection.

Which was fine by him—he had no need for her approval. Ashton leaned his stool back on two legs and pushed his shoulders into the wall as he admitted he wasn't being entirely truthful. He did need something from Willow. He just had no idea how to go about getting it.

In accordance with his herbal-enhanced mood, Jeff changed the LP to a mellow, and only slightly less angsty, band from the eighties singing about finding a destination under the Milky Way. Ashton closed his eyes and let the song flow through him. He'd missed this. The way music could either transport you or gut you like a pumpkin, leaving your innards exposed and vulnerable.

His eyes popped open and he reached over to open a nearby window. Evidently, one didn't have to hold the cigarette to experience its calming effects. *Not* what he needed at the moment.

He leaned close to the screen and sucked in a cleansing breath before bringing up his dilemma with the only person he had to talk to. "So, I've got this parole officer visit tomorrow, and I kind of gave him the Keller House as my place of residence."

Unfortunately, his sounding board was as high as a cherry bomb on the Fourth of July. Jeff swayed a bit and squinted at him through a haze of smoke. "So what's the prob? It's your house, right?"

"Not legally until I turn twenty-one. Plus someone's

already living in it. Dee Lamott signed a contract as the live-in caretaker."

Following a long drag, Jeff flicked the stub into an ashtray under the counter and asked, "Aren't you tight with the Lamotts?"

"Used to be."

Jeff's gaze sharpened. "They put you out with the trash after your conviction?"

Ashton gave a tight nod.

"Why not ask them if you can crash for a few days? That place is like a McMansion, dude. They could totally spare a room."

Ashton smiled at Jeff's Shaggy-meets-surfer speak. But despite his old friend's herbally-induced rose-colored glasses, Ashton knew the truth when he heard it—asking Mrs. Lamott if he could stay in the house until he found a place of his own was the best option. If Adam were alive, it wouldn't even be a question.

Jeff began typing on his computer. "Or, like I said before, you can always crash—"

"Ashton Keller?"

The authoritative bark of his name whipped Ashton's head around. Chief Kagawa, stiff-necked and broad as a bulldozer, stood in the doorway, arms crossed, legs spread wide.

Jeff caught Ashton's eye—neither one of them had heard him come up the old, rickety staircase.

Slowly, making sure his hands were visible, Ashton stood. "Yes, that's me."

Jeff lifted the needle from the record with a screech, dead silence settling on the room as the chief gripped the top of his nightstick and strode forward. "I'm going to have to ask you to come down to the station, Mr. Keller."

Ashton tried to stay calm. This was probably regarding a routine procedure. Like a registration following his release or something. But the hard set of the chief's features said otherwise. "Can I ask why?"

"Harassment, theft, destruction of property . . . any of this ringing a bell?"

Ashton's muscles locked, his pulse ratcheting into overdrive. "What?"

The cop stopped a few feet in front of him, pulled out his cell phone, and held the screen up to Ashton's face. "This look familiar?"

The picture showed a football jersey with the number twelve embossed on it, pinned crucifixion style on a door. There were gaping slashes all over it, like someone had taken a blade to it. Ashton leaned in close to read the name on the back. *C. Martin.*

"Colin's jersey was stolen from his locker during practice, urinated on, shredded, and nailed onto the gym door."

"When was this?" Ashton demanded.

"He's been here all afternoon, chief." Jeff spoke up for the first time.

Kagawa ignored Jeff, his dark eyes never leaving Ashton's face. "Sometime between three thirty and five. According to the school office, you signed out at one thirty today to take care of personal business."

Ashton didn't appreciate the inferred air quotes around "personal business," but he kept his voice calm and stuffed his emotions deep as he perched on the edge of the stool, his feet still on the ground. "I've been here since three."

"That's right," Jeff chimed in. "I remember the time he came in because he helped the UPS guy carry a shipment up the stairs. They're always here around three o'clock."

Chief Kagawa lowered his phone and slipped it into his pocket, his gaze laser-focused on Ashton's face. "Everyone saw your altercation with Colin today. That gives you motive and opportunity."

"I wouldn't call it an altercation, exactly." Ashton cocked a brow. "More like a misunderstanding."

"Where were you between one thirty and three this afternoon?"

So he *had* heard Jeff say he'd been here all afternoon. Ashton almost smiled. The chief's evidence was unraveling. Colin had worn his jersey during school, and practice started at three thirty. Ashton was already at Twisted Beauty by that time and hadn't left. The school was on the other end of town, making it nearly impossible for him to slip out, do the deed, and be back to the shop before Jeff noticed. But Ashton knew how to play this game. Keeping his voice neutral, he replied, "When I left school, I went directly to Harrison's Electronics and purchased a cell phone. Then I stopped at CC's for a sandwich and walked here after I finished eating. I think I've got the receipt in my pocket." With deliberation, so as not to make any sudden moves, Ashton dipped his hand into the pocket of his cargo pants and pulled out the cell and his lunch receipt.

The chief snatched the piece of paper out of his hand, scanning the tiny print.

Ashton continued, "The people at Harrison's and CC's could tell you I stopped in. I'm fairly certain, by the way the manager at CC's glared holes in my back, that she knows exactly who I am."

Taking out a small black notebook, Kagawa scribbled down a note and then handed the receipt back to Ashton. "What's your cell phone number?"

After rattling off his new number, Ashton held up the small device. "It's just a basic call and text phone. No data plan." A smirk tilted his lips. "In case you wanted to follow me on Instagram. I won't be there."

Chief Kagawa lurched forward, his face so close Ashton could smell the tacos he'd eaten for lunch. "This isn't over, Keller. I don't need Instagram to see your every move. If you so much as drop a tissue on the sidewalk, I'll hear about it. Understand?"

Ashton squinted into Kagawa's dark, hooded eyes and answered through clenched teeth. "Yes. Sir." He'd had just about enough of authority figures treating him like dirt, but he didn't dare make a move. Not yet anyway.

The chief gave a tight nod and stepped back. He turned to where Jeff hovered by his computer. "Is that pot I smell?"

"No, sir. Just cloves and incense."

"That better be all it is, or I'll be back with a warrant," the chief snapped before stalking out.

After they heard the bell clang and the door slam downstairs, Jeff let out a ragged sigh. "Dude, you should get out of here. I need something stronger than tobacco. I'm closing up shop for the day."

"Sure, man, I have something I need to do anyway." Asking for help didn't come easy for Ashton, but having a place of residence with a respectable family would go a long way toward helping him earn credibility with Mr. Ponytail Reed and the local authorities. It was time to bury his true feelings about the Lamotts and charm his way back into their lives.

CHAPTER Ten

Willow made her way down the front stairs while uncomfortable tingles raced across her shoulders. She paused and scanned the deep shadows gathering beyond the arched doorways branching off the dark foyer. She couldn't say why the house had this effect on her even after she'd discovered the identity of their "ghost." But it almost felt alive, as if the home had a spirit of its own, and it didn't approve of its new residents.

Gripping the handrail, she took another step down. The tick-tock of the grandfather clock in the entryway echoed in her ears, her pulse throbbing in time. Was Ashton already in the house? He'd asked for more time, and she would give it to him, but how much time? She couldn't hide his presence indefinitely.

Another step.

She wouldn't be downstairs alone at all except she'd skipped dinner, and her rumbling stomach had forced her out of hiding. Rainn's high-pitched whine echoed down the hall from his room, indicating that Mom had her hands full as they worked on her brother's homework. Good. Willow had no desire to rehash their argument.

Another step.

Wind pushed against the house, shaking the windows in their frames like a death rattle in an old man's throat. Willow gripped the railing tighter. The eves above answered with a long moan. Visions of the resident ghosts at Hogwarts made her glance up at the ceiling, but in the gloom the crossbeams held tight to their secrets. Maybe she wasn't hungry after all.

A resounding gong boomed through the house. Willow swallowed a shriek and race back up three stairs before she recognized it was the doorbell. She stopped to catch her breath and then jogged down into the foyer, yelling that she'd get it.

The side windows, with their original now-warped glass, were useless, so after a second's hesitation, she cracked one of the double doors. Her hand on the lock, she peeked out, ready to slam it shut again if . . . if what? A robber stood at the door? Unlikely.

Straightening her spine, she swung the door wide. Ashton stood to the right of the entryway, a steady breeze lifting the hair off his forehead.

"What are you doing?" Willow gasped.

Ashton raised a darkly amused brow. "I thought I was ringing the doorbell."

"Who is it, Willow?" Mom called.

Willow's gaze swung back to Ashton, who offered a smile. "I came to talk to her . . . your mom."

Footsteps sounded from the second floor.

"It's just a kid selling tangelos for band, Mom! No need to come down."

"Okay, tell them I already bought some from the neighbor."

"All right!"

Grabbing Ashton's hand, Willow tugged him through the door, shut it behind her, and led him to the farthest corner of the dim living room. A rush of electricity traveled up her arm and flared in her belly as she registered that his strong, warm fingers had closed over hers. She stopped in front of the empty hearth and yanked her hand away, spinning to face him.

Ashton's closed lips quirked up on one side, but the

expression didn't reach his eyes. "I had no idea you'd be so happy to see me."

"Lower your voice," Willow hissed as she glanced at the ceiling and then back to him. But she had to readjust the angle of her gaze to account for his height. How had he gotten so . . . large? She'd grown maybe an inch or two, but it was like he'd doubled in size in four years.

"Like I said," he continued in his deep rumble, "I came to talk to your mom."

"Well, she doesn't want to talk to you." Ashton's jaw flexed and Willow bit her lip, wishing she could take back the tone of her words. What was it about him that brought out this thoughtless aggression? "I mean . . . um . . ."

Ashton pushed out a sigh, strode past her to the mini bar, and drew a glass of water from the faucet. Willow watched him, how comfortable he seemed, like he belonged in this rambling old mansion. Because he did. He'd been born into a life of wealth and privilege that she could only imagine. The Kellers had been like Gilt Hollow royalty—until that fateful night when one boy's actions toppled them from their pedestal with a resounding crash.

After downing a second glass, he turned and leaned against the granite counter, crossing his arms and ankles in front of him. "I have a parole officer visit tomorrow, and it would be best if I'm not homeless. I'm trying to do the right thing by asking for your mom's permission to stay here . . . just for a few days."

"That's going to be difficult since she kind of forbade me to see you." Willow slumped into one of the leather chairs by the hearth.

"Why?" His brows shot up, and then he pinched the bridge of his nose and shook his head. "Never mind."

"Did you already give him this address? Your parole officer, I mean."

"I kind of thought this was my house." Ashton dropped his hand, crossing his arms again. "So, yeah."

His words dripped sarcasm, but Willow pushed down her defensiveness. She couldn't imagine what it must be like to come back after four years and have your old life completely changed. Your family gone. Turning to face him, she whispered, "What about your parents?"

Shadows obscured one side of Ashton's face, giving him a haunted look. When he spoke, his voice was void of emotion. "I haven't seen them since my sentencing."

Willow clutched the arms of the chair as something cracked in her chest, a heartrending pain for the boy she'd once adored. She'd known that his parents had their faults, but how could they abandon him when he needed them most?

Outside the window, fireflies sparked and plunged through the purple dusk, and Willow's stomach swooped along with them. She'd been a rule follower her entire life. Structure and order were her greatest comfort. After the fight with her mom, she'd spent the whole evening organizing her clothes by season, frequency of wear, and color. It calmed her, gave her a sense of control. But in this one rare moment, none of that mattered. She knew what she had to do. "What time is the appointment?"

"Seven o'clock."

"Tomorrow's Thursday . . ." Willow nibbled on her thumbnail, thinking through ways she could get her mother out of the house. Then she remembered St. Vincent's soup kitchen, where they volunteered twice a month. Surely her mom wouldn't object to the suggestion that they were short on help. She lowered her hand and stood to face him. "I can give you an hour and a half . . . maybe a little more."

The monotonous tick of the antique clock on the mantel filled the silence as Ashton stared at her, unmoving. Time seemed to reverse and they were once again connected, their friendship the biggest thing in their world.

Ashton unfolded his arms and pushed off the counter. He walked toward her, his heavy-lidded eyes searching her face. "Willow, I—"

Sharp footsteps echoed above their heads, cutting off his words as they both stared at the ceiling. "That's my mom," Willow hissed. "Take the back stairs."

He took a step closer and touched her shoulder, the pressure of his hand warming her all the way to her fingertips. "Thank you."

A creak sounded on the stairs, and Willow pushed him away. "Go!"

He shot her a grin—a real one that lit his eyes like a sky full of stars, then turned on his heel and slipped into the dark.

Willow forced out a shaky breath, a rush of light-headedness causing her to grip the chair. Her mom rounded the corner and appeared in the arched doorway. "Did I hear voices?"

"Just me talking to Lisa." She whipped her cell out of her pocket and held it up. "I had her on speaker phone."

Mom stepped into the room, moonlight catching on the glittered thread woven into her skirt. "Willow, about earlier—"

"It's okay," Willow rushed to interrupt the looming lecture. "I understand where you're coming from." Which she did. She just didn't agree with it. "Hey, can I go to Lisa's after school Friday? We want to get ready at her house before the football game."

Mom's eyes lit up. She'd been bugging Willow to "have fun with kids her own age" for years. "Absolutely."

Willow walked forward, keeping her mom's attention away from the back hallway. "We'll probably go out after too." She hadn't told Mom about her sort-of-date with Brayden Martin, and didn't plan to. "If that's okay?"

"Sure." Her mom hugged Willow's shoulders as they walked side by side. "There's leftover paella in the fridge. Let me heat it up for you."

A few minutes later, as Willow savored the perfectly seasoned shrimp, vegetable, and rice mixture, and her mom finished the dishes, she brought up St. Vincent's being short of help.

Her mom stripped off her rubber gloves and turned. "They serve at seven. We should be there by six thirty to help set up."

"Perfect," Willow said before taking a long swig of lemonade to hide her smile. Wow, that was easy.

A ping sounded from her pocket, and she took out her cell to find a SnapMail notification. She hadn't used that app since last year, when one of the girls doing a group history project had to communicate with her iPod because she didn't have a cellphone. Curious, Willow clicked open the message to find a picture. It looked like a GH football jersey tacked to a wall. She used her fingers to enlarge the image and noticed the shirt was stained and in tatters. She zoomed in on the letters at the top. *C. Martin.*

Weird. Why would someone do that to Colin's football jersey? And send her a picture of it? She checked the return address to find a series of random letters and numbers.

The picture disappeared, reminding her that this app allowed the sender to set a period of time that their message could be viewed. Her phone pinged again, a text popping up from the same unidentified sender:

> Rein in your boyfriend before
> somebody gets hurt.

Willow read the words four times before it clicked in her brain. A chill spread down her spine one vertebra at a time. If the destroyed jersey belonged to Colin Martin and her "boyfriend" was Ashton . . . Had Ashton done this in retaliation after their fight at school? Whoever sent this message certainly thought so.

"I'm going up to bed, hon. Need to start on the front landscaping tomorrow before the weather turns." Mom leaned over and kissed the side of Willow's head. "Hey, you all right?"

Willow clicked off her screen, but the message had already vanished. "Yeah, I'll be up in a few. Need to make some chamomile."

"Okay, good night."

But Willow didn't make tea. She sat staring at the blank screen in her hand, the mutilated jersey burned into her eyes. Colin had been at the falls and had testified that Ashton pushed Daniel to his death. The dark house seemed to shrink around her. Ashton's parents were long gone. He'd made it clear he wanted nothing to do with her, except when he needed her help. Why would he come back to Gilt Hollow at all? Unless . . . he'd returned seeking revenge.

Willow shot out of the chair and shoved it against the table. Not five minutes ago, she'd considered going up to the third floor to knock on his door, hoping they could sit and chat like old times. *What an idiot!*

Shutting off lights as she went, Willow raced up to her room and locked the door behind her.

How could she have forgotten, even for a moment, that she had no idea who Ashton was anymore?

■ ■ ■

Willow was on edge all morning. She'd half expected Ashton to show up on her walk to school. He hadn't. In the hallways, Colin's jersey was all anyone could talk about. She'd passed his locker, and a group of girls hovered and cooed over him like he was a wounded baby bird. Willow suppressed the urge to gag. God forbid anyone touch Colin Martin's sacred football jersey. Not that shredding and peeing on someone's clothes was okay. It wasn't. (And gross.) But the way people were reacting, you'd think his house had burned to the ground.

By second period she'd heard everything from "The police have cleared Ashton" to "Ashton ripped the jersey off Colin and shredded it in front of him." People were ridiculous, and it made her question her own assumptions. Which brought her thoughts back to who and why someone thought it their duty to send her the picture and warning the night before—as if she'd had anything to do with it.

Worst of all, Lisa had a dentist appointment and wouldn't be in until lunch, so Willow couldn't even discuss what happened with her friend. Not that she could share all of it. She'd texted Lisa the night before to tell her she'd been wrong about Ashton breaking in. A part of her felt bad about the lie, but *no one* could know that Ashton was staying in the house. Secrets that juicy had a way of leaking out.

In second period, Brayden slid onto the stool at their lab table, flicked his bright hair off his forehead, and then shot her a warm smile. "Hey."

"Hey." Willow sat a little straighter and put her glasses into her hair. She'd taken a little more time on her appearance that morning, returning to her usual plaid skirt, knee socks, and blouse-sweater combo. She'd even put on a little mascara and worn her hair down in loose waves around her shoulders.

Brayden scooted his stool over so they sat elbow to elbow. "So what's with the glasses? I've noticed you don't wear them all the time."

Willow took the dark, cat-eye frames out of her hair and put them back on. "Better to see you with, my dear," she cackled in her best wolf-in-granny's-clothing impression. Brayden hooted with laughter. She liked hanging with him. He reminded her there could be more to life than angst and drama. "I have a slight nearsighted astigmatism. It's not bad, but I need my glasses to read the small print on Smartboards."

"I see." Brayden's knee brushed her leg as he lifted his hands and slipped the glasses off her face. "Well, I like seeing your eyes."

Heat rushed into Willow's cheeks, and she resisted the urge to squirm as he stared at her. "Um . . . thanks."

He grinned and handed her glasses back as the teacher called for their attention. Once Mr. Edwards had turned his back to point to a diagrammed cell, Brayden leaned in, touched his shoulder to hers, and whispered, "I should be able to get to Gino's by nine thirty on Friday. Will you meet me there?"

Willow nodded.

"It'll be crowded, but there's a table in the back, set into a window alcove. Try to get that one, 'kay?"

"Yeah, I know the one." Willow's belly flipped. So it *was* an actual date.

By the time she reached Music Appreciation, she'd made a decision; she'd fulfill her promise to Ashton and then move on. No more helping him. No more drama. After the meeting with his parole officer, he'd have to find another place to stay.

When Ashton slumped into the seat next to her, she stared straight ahead and spoke under her breath. "We'll be at St. Vincent's from six thirty to eight thirty tonight. The house is all yours."

She could feel his gaze drilling into the side of her face, but she didn't turn. Several awkward seconds passed before she inclined her head so the sheet of her hair fell between them.

"Thanks," he finally said in a gruff whisper.

Willow felt the moment he turned his attention away from her, and let out a tiny breath.

After class she darted out the door and to her locker. Lisa, looking flawless as usual but holding an ice pack to her jaw, mumbled through half-numb lips, "Teeth extraction is so archaic."

Willow threw her books onto the shelf and grabbed her lunch bag. "Can we eat outside?" Catching a glimpse of Ashton's tall form out the corner of her eye, she didn't wait for Lisa's reply but began to steer her down the hall.

"Wha's the russ?"

"I'll explain when we get out of here." Her pulse accelerated with her feet as she skipped down the back stairs. Why she was running away, she couldn't say. She just needed a break from the stares and the speculation—and a certain pair of piercing blue eyes.

Once they were outside, she chose a shady table at the far edge of the commons area and plopped down with a sigh. "So I guess you heard about the jersey incident?"

Lisa propped her elbow on the tabletop and gingerly reapplied the ice pack to her jaw. "Who 'asn't?"

Willow began to unpack her food. "Yeah, well, somebody

thinks I had something to do with it." She pulled half of her turkey sandwich from the container. "Or maybe they think I could've stopped it . . . I don't know."

"It may be the Advil 500 I took, but I'm not following." She enunciated her words with deliberation before shifting the ice higher on her cheek.

Willow swallowed and whispered, "I got an anonymous message last night with a picture of the jersey and a threat to rein in *my boyfriend.*"

"Let me see the message." Ashton stood, arms crossed, beside their table.

Willow's heart smacked against her ribs. Clutching a fist to her chest, she spat, "You need to stop sneaking up on me like that!"

"I'm not sneaking. I followed you out here. You need to be more observant."

Willow shot Ashton a glare that he ignored, and he walked to the other end of the table.

Lisa's eyes flared wide as he sat on the bench beside her. She scooted half an inch in the opposite direction and then pulled a container of yogurt from her lunch bag. After watching her struggle with the lid for a few seconds, Ashton took it out of her hands, pulled back the top in one swift motion, and handed it back. Lisa blinked at her yogurt and then stared at him like he'd just saved her cat from drowning in a raging river. "Thanss." She shook her head and spoke her next words carefully. "I mean, *thanks.* I'm Lisa."

His mouth kicked up on one side. "Hi. I'm Ashton."

Lisa returned his smile in slow motion. *Good grief.* He was cute. So what? And he still had those adorable freckles across the bridge of his nose. Big deal. Lots of guys were attractive. The girl needed to get her priorities straight. With hard-won control, she gave Lisa a gentle kick under the table. "Don't mind my friend—she's doped up on pain meds."

Ashton faced Willow, his expression turning sharp. "So can I see the message or not?"

"Not." His brows crouched over his eyes. "They sent it on SnapMail."

"Okay . . ." He drummed the fingers of his right hand against the tabletop. "What did it say word for word?"

Willow repeated the message and then added, "Why someone would, first of all, think you're my boyfriend, and second of all, think I have some control over your actions is beyond me."

Ashton became very still. "You think I did this, don't you?"

Willow popped a grape in her mouth and didn't answer.

"You *think* I stole Colin's jersey right after half the senior class saw us face off in the hallway?" He lowered his chin, his brows hitching up.

Willow searched his face in silence. Yes, he'd changed physically and in other ways she could only imagine, but strategy had always been his thing. When they'd played war in the woods behind his house, he would develop contingency plans for every move the opposite team was likely to make. Chess matches with him were pointless. The only time she'd won a game, he'd had a fever of 101.

If anything, the whole jersey incident had worked in Colin's favor. Ashton was no saint, but he would never do something this stupid—even if he thought Colin deserved it.

With a curl of her lips, Willow handed him the other half of her turkey sandwich. He searched her eyes for several seconds before taking it, but when he did, Willow felt a knot unravel in her gut. It was almost as if they were friends again. *Almost.*

CHAPTER Eleven

Ashton accepted the sandwich with a solemn nod, seeing it for what it was—a peace offering. Willow had never liked sharing her food. She'd always hated when he'd steal a chip off her plate or taste what she'd ordered at a restaurant. It wasn't that she was selfish; she'd just always thought of sharing food as unsanitary.

After gulping down the turkey on wheat in three bites, he asked, "Who do you think sent the message? Maybe it's the same person who set me up to take the fall. Tell me the exact return address."

"I have no idea what the address was." Willow shrugged as a soft breeze blew waves of dark hair across her cheeks.

His mouth suddenly dry, Ashton snapped, "Then how do you know it was anonymous?"

She grasped the stray strands and tucked them behind her ear before rolling her eyes. "It was a series of letters and numbers."

"Why didn't you write it down?" he accused, his tone harsher than he'd intended.

Willow sat up straight, her shoulders rigid. "Oh, I don't know . . . I might have been a tad bit distracted by the threating nature of the picture and the actual message." Her cheeks flushed magenta and her dark eyes flashed. "It was on the screen for like twenty seconds tops."

Ashton gripped the edge of the wood slab in front of him. "Then how the h—"

Lisa slapped her palm on the table with a loud *whap.*

"Chill ou' you 'wo!" She shook her head and then spoke more slowly. "I *mean* if you two could stop bickering like old ladies, maybe we could figure this out." Her eyes flickered shut and she pressed the ice pack tighter to her face.

Willow's brow furrowed as she reached over and squeezed Lisa's free hand. "Hey, are you all right?"

"I'll be fine. Just *stop* already."

"Okay, okay." Willow took a deep breath and then turned to Ashton. "I don't remember the exact address, but it appeared random."

He nodded and asked, "Do you use that app a lot?"

"No, never." She pursed her lips. "Except . . ."

Ashton's gaze lingered on her pink mouth for several seconds before he forced his eyes away and shifted on the bench, his skin suddenly too warm. "Wait, what did you say?"

With an inpatient jerk, Willow flicked her bangs off her forehead. "I *said*, the only people who have my SnapMail address were in a small group with me last year."

"Who was in the group?"

The color drained from her face, and Ashton straightened his spine as she listed the names. "Chad Richards, Isaiah Kagawa, Brayden Martin, and Penelope Lunarian."

"Does Chad still live on his own planet?" The kid Ashton remembered had been an introvert to the extreme. It wasn't that no one liked him; he just didn't care what anyone thought. Unless you were willing to talk video games or old Godzilla movies, he wasn't interested.

Willow nodded. "Yep."

Ashton sucked in a deep breath. The other three were a different story. Isaiah and Brayden had both been at the falls the day Daniel died.

Before he could ask, Willow supplied, "Penelope and Colin have dated off and on for the last four years."

"Are they on or off right now?"

"Very publicly *off*." Willow glanced at the time on her phone and began to pack up what was left of her lunch. "First day of school, Penelope caught him in the janitor's closet with one of the girls from the soccer team. She flipped out and threatened to cut off his, um . . . you know . . . his *part*." She jerked her gaze away from his and focused on screwing the cap back on her water bottle.

Half a grin curved his lips before he could stop it. All this time and Willow still couldn't say it. "You mean his pe—"

Willow's eyes flew wide.

"Well!" Lisa spoke over him. "I think we have a candidate for who trashed Colin's jersey. Sweet little Penelope has a mean streak, and maybe with good reason."

Lisa was right. Ashton could not believe he'd let himself be distracted from the goal. Of course, it had to be Penelope. But would she send a threat to Willow? That part didn't add up. "Do you and Penelope get along okay?"

Willow shrugged. "I guess so. I don't think we've spoken since we worked on that project together last year."

The warning bell rang in the distance, and Willow shot to her feet like one of Pavlov's dogs conditioned to respond. Punctuality. Another one of her type-A quirks he'd forgotten. "Who does she hang out with?"

Willow braced her hands on the table and climbed over the bench. "She's the third spoke on the Yoko Ono wheel."

"Huh?" Ashton asked as he stood.

Lisa and Willow exchanged a look and a giggle, but Lisa's laugh turned into a groan as she readjusted her ice pack. Her dark eyes sparkling, Willow turned and met Ashton's gaze.

For several seconds neither of them looked away. His stomach did a funny swoosh, like when you jump your bike over a creek and land hard.

"It's what I call Yolanda and Ona. They've been kinda unbearable since you left." Willow began to walk toward the school. Ashton followed. "They even gave me a special nickname." She chuckled like it was a joke, but Ashton could tell that it wasn't.

His face must have shown his irritation, because Willow shoved her sack lunch into his chest. "Here. Looks like you need this more than I do."

Ashton paused and clutched the paper bag, watching Willow and Lisa join the flow of traffic into the building. He pulled out the half-full water bottle and chugged. It was one thing to set him up. Another thing entirely to involve Willow. He lowered the empty bottle and crushed it in his fist.

* * *

After gathering the books she needed for her homework, Willow took an extra lap through the senior corridor, hoping to have a chat with Isaiah or Penelope. Out of the list of individuals who'd been in her small group last year, she'd ruled out Chad—for obvious reasons. When she'd confronted Brayden about the message, he'd appeared genuinely shocked, and then he'd made a joke about her having a secret admirer. Willow felt sure that if he wanted to warn her, he would've done it to her face. So that left Isaiah and Penelope.

But besides a few stragglers and the old janitor, the hallways appeared deserted. Giving up on her quest for the time being, Willow headed out the front doors to join the masses soaking up the late-September sun. A subtle earthy dryness crackled in the air as she paused on the stoop and lifted her face to the warm rays. The tops of the sugar maples in the courtyard had turned fiery. As a kid, the changing colors of fall had signified the end of long summer days of play. She'd thought the variations of yellow, orange, and scarlet converging on the vibrant green meant the trees were losing their fight against winter.

Over the years, she'd learned to appreciate the cycle of the seasons and the coming crisp sweater weather, autumn festivals, and everything pumpkin spice. With a mind to swing by Gino's for her first hot cinnamon cider of the season, she skipped down the stairs but then froze. Straight across the parking lot, Ashton straddled a jet black motorcycle and then turned to put a helmet on a girl's blonde head. Hair flowing to her waist, antique lace skirt—Penelope.

Penelope Lunarian was one of those people who lived up to her name. Soft-spoken and uber-creative, she only dressed in clothes she made herself and never wore shoes unless forced. At first glance, she projected an ethereal, otherworldly quality, until one realized her quiet demeanor wasn't shyness but pretention.

Something in Willow's chest tightened as Ashton cracked a grin and snapped the helmet strap beneath Penelope's chin. Then he took her hand and placed it on his right shoulder. She hitched up her skirt with her other hand and climbed on the bike behind him. When she wrapped her arms around his waist and rested her head against his broad back, Willow turned away, unable to watch as they roared out of the lot.

No longer in the mood for a cider, she began to trudge toward home. Usually she and Lisa walked together until they reached the shaded intersection of Walnut and Second Street, where her friend turned to head home, but Lisa had texted to say she had to leave early and sleep off the pain meds.

So Willow set off with only her thoughts to keep her company. She kicked a pinecone off the sidewalk, little brown bits clinging to her shoe. Did Ashton really like Penelope? Or was he just using her to gain information? If he'd sought her out to get answers about the jersey, or even to make Colin jealous, he appeared to be enjoying his role a little too much.

But, whatever. Ashton could hang out with whomever he liked. Willow shifted her fifty-pound backpack onto her other shoulder with a huff. So why did she feel like someone had punched her in the throat?

■ ■ ■

Rainn grabbed a sloppy joe off the tray she carried and sped off with a giggle to join a group of his friends. Willow shook her head as she returned to the service window to replace the missing sandwich. St. Vincent's served all their meals restaurant style. Pastor Justin, who ran the soup kitchen out of the fellowship hall of their church, believed herding the needy through a cafeteria line was demeaning. He felt being served restored a bit of their dignity.

Willow had to agree as she delivered the hot plates of food to groups of chattering men and women. Squeaky clean faces and damp hair contrasted with their mismatched, worn clothing. The church allowed use of their shower facilities if people arrived early enough to sign up for one of the limited bathroom time slots.

"Sir, would you care for coffee or iced tea?" Willow smiled into the older man's ruddy face as she handed him a bundle of silverware. No paper dishes or plastic sporks were used, only real ceramic plates and metal utensils—even if they did disappear occasionally.

"Coffee with extra sugar, sweetheart."

"Coming right up." After taking drink orders for the rest of the table, Willow hustled off to the drink station. It used to break her heart looking into the faces of these people whose lives had somehow deteriorated beyond repair, but after getting to know some of the patrons, she learned that, as hard as it was to believe, many of them chose this lifestyle. They felt free of responsibilities, bills, and debt—even if it meant sleeping under a bridge.

She loaded her tray with steaming coffee and packets of sugar and cream. The plight of the mentally disabled and families with children still killed her, but it felt good to do her part to help them, no matter how small.

After delivering the drinks, Willow went back to her first table to clear dishes and fill empty cups. A woman lifted her mug with a trembling hand. "More sugar. I said I wanted extra sugar, and you only gave me one packet!" The drug addicts kind of scared her. She had no idea why, but they were obsessed with sugar.

Willow poured the woman's coffee and then reached into the pocket of her apron. "Two packets of sugar left." The woman knew the rules limited one sugar per cup. Willow set the tiny white envelopes on the table and slid them under a napkin, lowering her voice, "I won't tell anyone if you don't." She was rewarded with a moist-eyed grin.

Astonished and a little touched that something so small could mean so much, Willow pivoted and headed back to replace the coffeepot.

"Nicely done, Willow." Pastor Justin stood by the drink table, arms crossed over his barrel chest. A former college linebacker, six feet five and tattooed, he didn't fit the traditional clerical image. "That could've turned ugly fast."

Willow winked. "I've a few tricks up my sleeve."

He chuckled and helped her fill glasses of iced tea. "How's it going at the old Keller House?"

"Um . . . interesting."

"Don't tell me the place is haunted, like everyone says."

"In a sense . . ." Perhaps it was his superpower, like Wonder Woman's lasso of truth, but Willow found it impossible to lie to this man she'd known her entire life. "It's more the ghosts of the past turning up around every corner."

"Ah . . . you're referring to Mr. Keller." Pastor Justin's dark eyes narrowed thoughtfully. "Well, I have to commend you for forgiving the past and accepting him . . . even if it puts you in an awkward position."

Her mother must've shared with him that Willow wished to befriend Ashton again, but Willow wasn't sure she'd forgiven Ashton for anything. Right then, she couldn't think about him without her blood simmering. *Penelope. Really?* The girl had nothing in her head but rainbows and stardust.

Willow hated to disappoint, but she wasn't sure she could own up to accepting Ashton either. She lifted the tray of drinks and noticed that the pastor still watched her with something like concern on his face. "Wait. What aren't you telling me?"

Pastor Justin pulled a square of paper from his pocket and unfolded it. When he held it out for Willow to see, she dropped the tray back to the table with a clatter. Her heart in her throat, she took the flyer. Ashton's face glared back at her in black and white, his mouth set in a tight line, his brows lowered in anger. The picture wasn't very high quality, like someone had snapped it with their cellphone. Scrawled across the top in bold letters were the words Killer Keller, and on the bottom it said, "Stop harassing our students! Leave now!"

"Where did you find this?"

"I took this one from the bulletin board at Bob's Market."

"This *one*?" The paper trembled in her hand.

"I removed all the ones I came across in town, but they're everywhere . . . on telephone poles, mailboxes, store windows."

"Isn't that illegal? Like character defamation or something?"

"That's debatable." He shoved his hands into his pockets and shrugged. "Some may say they were only exercising their right to free speech. Not that I think it's right, mind you."

"Excuse me! Can I get some iced tea over here?"

Ignoring the request, Willow glanced back down at the flyer. Did Ashton know about this? Willow glanced up at the clock. It was almost seven thirty. What would Ashton's parole officer do if he went into town and saw these accusations plastered everywhere?

Willow untied her apron, lifted it over her head, and handed it to Pastor Justin. "I'm sorry. I have to go."

"Sure. I'll take care of . . ."

Willow didn't hear the rest because she was sprinting for the door.

CHAPTER Twelve

S o both of your parents are out of town?" Zane Ponytail Reed asked for the second time as he typed into his tablet.

"Yes." Ashton draped an arm across the back of the Victorian sofa. He'd led Mr. Reed into the formal parlor, hoping the less comfortable environment would make for a shorter visit. So far it didn't seem to be working. "They travel a lot."

"Before you turned eighteen, your mother signed the papers for your discharge but didn't visit while she was there." He glanced up, his expression carefully neutral. "I was under the impression that you hadn't seen your parents during your incarceration. Is that correct?"

Ashton forced his jaw to unclench. If *Zane* had access to Ashton's records, he knew the answer to that question. "That's right."

"But they were accepting of you staying here after your release?"

More like they didn't know or care. "It would seem so." Ashton answered, working hard to wash the sarcasm from his tone.

"What are you doing to stay busy? I haven't received any calls for employment references."

"I've enrolled full-time at Gilt Hollow High."

"They accepted you?"

"With a nudge from my family's attorney."

Zane sucked in his right cheek, causing his mouth to

contort as he paged through his tablet. The silence stretched on until Ashton leaned forward and rested his elbows on his knees. Mr. Reed cleared his throat and spoke without looking up. "Do the three individuals who witnessed your crime and testified against you attend Gilt Hollow High?"

"Yes."

Zane blew out a breath and took off his glasses. "This concerns me on many levels. Part of my job as a probation officer"—he sat straighter in his chair as if he were a supreme court judge, not a lowly government official—"is to ensure that after your release you are in no way jeopardizing the public welfare."

"Why would I—"

He raised the hand holding his glasses and cut Ashton off. "That remains to be seen, but I'm warning you now, I won't hesitate to pull you out of that school if there is a need. I spoke with Chief Kagawa on the phone, and he seemed *concerned* that your return to Gilt Hollow could cause . . . conflict."

Ashton's suspicions that Kagawa was out to get him confirmed, he pointed out, "Chief Kagawa's son, Isaiah, was one of the witnesses against me, so keep that in mind. Also remember that I pled *guilty* to my crime."

"Yes, *after* the other boys stepped forward as witnesses."

This man had no clue what Ashton had gone through as a minor shuffled though the justice system alone. All he wanted to know was that Ashton wasn't going to hurt anyone . . . else. Ashton met Zane's gaze and allowed his face to soften. "I just want my old life back. A second chance."

"I'm well aware that taking a plea bargain doesn't mean you've accepted your guilt. However, your counselor, Mr. Larkin, has assured me of your rehabilitation. So I'm giving you the benefit of the doubt." He replaced the glasses on his face and propped his tablet on his knee.

Silence loomed like a specter, stretching to fill the round two-story room and sucking the air from Ashton's lungs. This man, this *stranger*, held countless words in his hands that summed up the life of a juvenile delinquent. But those words didn't define him—his past or his future.

After what felt like hours, Zane removed his glasses again and raised his blank gaze. His next words sounded as if he recited them from some probation officer's guide on how to be a pretentious stooge. "The court has dictated that we meet every four weeks for the next six months, though it is up to my discretion to meet on a more frequent basis if I deem it necessary. I'd like to return in three weeks." He tapped the screen and then swiped his finger over the surface. "Perhaps if we meet on a Saturday afternoon your parents will be around?"

Knowing that wasn't going to happen, Ashton kept his reply noncommittal. "Yeah, maybe."

"Good." Zane tucked his glasses into his pocket and then grinned, his demeanor transforming as if someone had changed his internal TV channel. "The Ohio State game starts in twenty minutes. Want to head into town and watch it at the Postman's Tavern?"

Ashton would rather slit his wrists with a chain saw. But before he could come up with a good excuse, the door-bell gonged. Shooting to his feet, he asked Zane to wait and jogged into the foyer. He paused before opening the door. The only person who knew he was staying here was Willow. If he answered the door, he could blow that secret out of the water.

He glanced over his shoulder at Mr. Ponytail Reed, who

whistled an old Van Halen song while he packed up his things. Ashton couldn't afford the man's suspicion. Deciding he could talk his way out of anything, he opened the door.

* * *

Out of breath from sprinting the five blocks from the church, Willow clutched a fist to her diaphragm and sucked in air. What was taking him so long to answer? Was the meeting over already? She smoothed the hair back into her braid and lifted a hand to the gargoyle knocker. The hideous monster eyeballed her, but before she could pound its brass talons against the wood, the door swung open.

Ashton's face a mask of stone, he growled, "Yes?"

"I just needed . . ." Willow trailed off. She hadn't planned on how to tell him that someone had plastered his face all over town, accusations blaring from every page. The only thought in her head had been to warn him. "I . . . you . . ."

Ashton glanced over his shoulder and then stepped onto the porch, yanking the door shut behind him. "What the heck, Wil?"

Willow's heart gave a tight flutter and tears burned behind her eyes. No one called her Wil except Ashton and her dad. To hide her overreaction, she spun on her heel and stalked to the other end of the porch.

She felt Ashton come up behind her as the warped floorboards dipped. "Hey, what's going on?" A warm hand clasped her shoulder, flashing something like heat lightning down her spine.

Hyperaware and feeling raw, she jerked away from him and spun around. Concern etched his brow, and those dark blue eyes swept over her face, sending every rational thought tumbling out of her head. She crossed her arms under her chest and spat, "Do you have a motorcycle license?"

His mouth stretched into a flat line, and he blinked three times before answering. "Nooo . . . but I did get a driver's license as part of my prerelease program." He crossed his arms, mirroring her stance. "What is this all about? I'm kind of right in the middle of something." He jerked his head back toward the house.

"Well, you need a specific license to drive a motorcycle, and I saw you . . ." Willow cut herself off with a shake of her head before she sounded like a jealous sow. "Never mind, I came to show you this." She pulled the folded paper out of her jeans pocket. "Pastor Justin found it at Bob's and said they're all over town . . . on light poles, in shop windows. I can help you take them down. It's outrageous, really. I mean . . . it doesn't *mean* anything."

The hint of a smile curled up one side of Ashton's mouth. "Why don't you let me be the judge of that?" He held out his hand. "Can I see it?"

She set the paper in his palm as if it might explode, and honestly, she worried that *he* might. Whoever had done this wasn't messing around. Their intent had been to harm him—to rally the town against him. When she said it didn't mean anything, that wasn't the truth.

He unfolded the paper, and naked pain shot across his face.

Willow's heart gave a twist and she reached out but drew back before she touched him. "Ashton . . ."

The front door opened, and a middle-aged man with thinning hair poked his head out. "Ashton, the game starts in ten minutes. We'll be lucky to find a seat at the tavern."

Ashton folded the paper and stuck it in his pocket.

"Oh, hello." The man walked outside as he looped a messenger bag over his shoulder. "I didn't see you there."

The tension radiating from Ashton could've set a small town on fire, so Willow shook the man's hand and tried to hold his attention. "Hi, I'm Willow. Ashton and I are old friends."

His eyes widened before he could contain his surprise. Did he think Ashton lived in a bubble?

"I'm Zane Reed. Ashton and I were just headed into town to watch the game." He hitched a thumb over his shoulder. "Can't be much fun hanging out in this hulking place all alone." He laughed loud and long.

Willow offered a forced chuckle as her gaze strayed to Ashton. He leaned against the porch rail, booted ankles crossed, fists shoved into his pockets, a bored look on his face. Amazing. She doubted they offered acting class in juvie, but he was a master.

"You're welcome to join us," Mr. Reed said.

"Oh well, that's nice of you, but . . . I . . . er . . . just walked through town, and the streets are packed. Some kind of save our oceans rally or something . . . Besides, Ashton and I are supposed to study for a trig test tonight."

"Thanks for the invite, Zane," Ashton cut in, his tone perfectly cordial except for an odd emphasis on the letter Z. "But Willow's right. I have a lot of catching up to do. Maybe some other time?"

"Sure, that works." Zane shook Ashton's hand. "I'll see you, and hopefully your parents, in a few weeks."

Willow tensed at the mention of Ashton's absentee parents, but he responded with a nod. "Sounds good."

The parole officer made his way down the crooked front stairs. As soon as he'd backed out of the driveway, Ashton lifted an eyebrow at Willow. "Save the oceans rally? Not bad, Lamott. With a little training, you could join the accomplished fibbers club."

Not falling for the distraction, she cocked her head. "Your parents?"

"Sometimes you have to tell people what they want to hear."

"But what—"

"I'll make up another excuse." He shrugged a shoulder. "A lot can change in three weeks."

He said it like he could be in Jamaica next month, or maybe on Mars. Like he had no clue what tomorrow held. Didn't he have any plans for his future? For what came next? Willow'd had the next twenty years of her life planned out since she was twelve—graduate high school with honors, earn a scholarship to Miami University, finish her BS in biochem in two years, and then it was off to MIT for her graduate program. The thought of drifting with the wind made her skin crawl. Shaking off the sensation, she resumed their original conversation. "I saw you take off with Penelope after school." But the image the words conjured made her wish she could take them back. She ran a hand over her braid and cleared her throat. "Um, did you find out anything?"

"Other than that she hates Colin Martin almost as much as I do? No, but . . ." Ashton's gaze narrowed on her, searching. Willow stilled like a cornered animal, afraid to move. A whip-poor-will's haunting call echoed in the distance. He uncrossed his arms and pushed off the rail, closing the distance between them in two strides.

She took a step back and hit the house. Ashton didn't stop until inches separated them. When she looked up into his face, a smile played around his closed mouth and something like wonder flashed in his eyes. "You're blushing." Slowly he lifted his hand and, feather-light, brushed the crest of her cheek with his knuckles.

Willow's skin blazed in response to his touch, her pulse pounding so hard, she worried he might hear it. A breeze whispered through the leaves, whipping around the corner of the house and lifting the hair on Willow's neck. She shivered.

Ashton studied her face, his voice low and soft, "Are you *jealous?*"

When she didn't answer right away, Ashton's mouth kicked up on one side, breaking the spell.

"Cocky much?" Willow knocked his hand away and glared. "I happen to be seeing someone."

Ashton stepped back, his mouth spreading into a full-out grin. "You still didn't answer my question."

Willow rolled her eyes. "You're ridiculous. Downtown Gilt Hollow is wallpapered with your face, and all you can do is tease me?"

He looked up at the ceiling and shook his head. "What is it you think I should do, Miss Do-Right?" His mocking gaze lowered to her face. "Spend all night running around town, pulling down flyers? It's not like they're wanted posters. It's one ignorant person's opinion."

Willow unclenched her jaw. "Then I should've let your parole officer head into town?"

Ashton blew out a breath and shoved a hand into the back of his hair. "No. I appreciate the warning, okay? Is that what you want to hear?"

She'd seen the unguarded expression on his face when she'd shown him the flyer, but if he wanted to pretend it didn't bother him, fine. "Whatever, Ashton." She spun on her heel, her anger boiling hotter with every step. She risked a lot to help him, including her relationship with her mom. She'd have to invent another lie to cover why she'd left the church so suddenly. Flinging open the door, she paused on the threshold. "You should get out of sight. My mom will be home soon." And without waiting for his reply, she stalked into the house and shut the door behind her.

■ ■ ■

Willow read the paragraph for the fourth time before setting her book down and flopping back on the pillows. She stared up at the shadowed ceiling and willed a hole to open. Was Ashton up there? After their argument, she didn't know if he'd come into the house or not.

The old grandfather clock in the foyer struck the hour, and she counted eleven chimes. Did he have a decent bed up there? Blankets and pillows? She didn't even know. When they'd played in the attic as kids, she remembered a huge storage space, a few small bedrooms with sparse furnishings, and an old-fashioned bathroom. But that had been years ago.

She rolled over and stared out the window at the moonlit night. When she'd told her mom she'd had to leave St. Vincent's to email an assignment that was due by eight, Mom had totally bought the lie, but Willow felt horrible. And that wasn't even the worst of it. Her mom had no idea Ashton was sleeping in their attic—maybe this very moment.

Prickles raced across her skin. The way Ashton had looked at her today, like a mystery he wanted to solve. Or a mythical creature he'd longed to discover. No one had ever looked at her like that. Did he see Penelope the same way? Willow sat up and grabbed her history book, determined to kill her romanticized thoughts with a little Revolutionary War blood and guts. Ashton hadn't been around girls since he was fourteen years old; his hormones were likely ruling his brain.

Settling the book on her crossed legs, she reread the passage about Nathan Hale's last words before he was hanged by the British for spying: "I only regret that I have but one life to lose for my country." That was some serious loyalty. Willow got halfway through the next section before her phone pinged on the nightstand. She tensed. It wasn't the custom bird chirp she had programmed for Lisa or the melodic bells that indicated her mom. The last time she'd heard the generic sound, it had been an anonymous warning.

She stared at her pink OtterBox case for several seconds before grabbing it and swiping in her code. The screen showed she had a text, not a SnapMail message. Letting out a sharp breath, she tapped the icon. A number she didn't recognize popped up with the text:

R u asleep?

Willow stared at the number, racking her brain for who it could be. Brayden? No, she'd programmed his name in her contacts. Wondering if it was a wrong number, she typed:

Who is this?

SRY. It's Ash.

Ashton? How did he get her number? And he wasn't "Ash" any longer. That was the name of a boy she trusted. One that didn't confuse her with every word out of his mouth. The one she knew with all her heart was innocent.

Before she could ask, he typed:

Lisa gave me your #.

Willow would have to have a little chat with Ms. Lisa. Her phone pinged again.

So ur awake?

No, I'm sleep-texting.

> In that case . . . what r u
> wearing???

Willow laughed out loud despite herself. Glancing down at her yoga pants and ratty tank, she turned the tables on him:

> **Haha. What r U wearing?**

> Um . . . hold on a sec . . . let me
> take off my shirt.

Willow's face flamed as she speed typed.

> **WAIT!**

> Stop blushing. I was joking.

> **I wasn't blushing.**

Willow cupped her feverish cheeks with cool palms, but before she could regulate her temperature, another message popped up.

> If you want to see what I'm
> wearing . . . come up.

Temptation tugged at Willow's gut like a string pulling her forward. She took her history book off her lap and swung her legs over the side of the bed. Her toes touched the icy hardwood. She could sneak up the back stairs. Just see where he was sleeping, set her mind at ease.

Her phone pinged. She snatched it off the coverlet.

> On second thought, don't come
> up here.

Willow sat perched on the edge of the mattress, filing through all the reasons he didn't want her to come up to the attic, and landed on the most obvious: He didn't trust himself to be alone with her. Goose bumps rose on her skin, but his next message annihilated her fantasies with a kill shot of reality.

> Penelope admitted to trashing
> Colin's jersey out of anger. But
> don't think she threatened u.

Willow sighed at her own gullibility. He didn't want her up there because he just wanted to tell her about *Pennecelope*.

> **When did she tell u this?**

> **Just talked to her.**

Great. So he'd spent the evening talking with Penelope before deciding to text-flirt with her. A slightly gross and somewhat vindictive thought occurred to her, and she typed the question before she could think better of it.

> **She peed on it?**

> **Soaked it in the urinal.**

Was that better? Willow shuddered. She didn't think so. She typed:

> **Barf.**

> **I know, right?**

There was a pause, then he said:

> **U can't tell anyone. Her parents would freak.**

Really? He was worried about Penelope's parents? The lies Willow had told on his account were adding up by the minute. If Mom found out what she'd done, she'd ground her until she graduated. And Ashton would be out on the street.

> **Wil?**

Who did he think he was, throwing that name around like it meant nothing? Maybe to him, it didn't. She took off her glasses and rubbed her suddenly gritty eyes. Ready to end their emotionally draining conversation, she replied:

> **I won't tell. Good night.**

> **Wait. R u really seeing someone?**

> **Yes.**

And for the first time, Willow considered what Ashton's reaction might be to her dating Brayden—one of the boys who had helped put him in jail. Not good.

Who?

Brayden

She typed his name and then deleted it. They hadn't even gone on their first date yet. It could turn out to be nothing. Besides, she didn't own Ashton any explanations. So she repeated:

Good night.

Night. And thx.

Thanks for protecting Penelope? Thanks for saving his butt tonight? Thanks for keeping all of his secrets?

Willow silenced her phone and plugged it in to charge. Grabbing a blanket off the bed, she slung it around her shoulders and padded to the window. The wind bent the trees, thrashing the leaves into chaos. There wasn't a cloud in the sky, but the air felt heavy with tension. Poised. Waiting. A storm was rolling in. She could feel it.

CHAPTER Thirteen

The small coffee shop overflowed with students celebrating Gilt Hollow's victory. Removed from the excitement, Willow used her thumbnail to trace the cursive *G* on her paper cup, watching as the wax peeled off in a tight curl against her fingers. She'd come straight to Gino's from the football game and nabbed the back corner table, per Brayden's instructions. But he'd yet to show up. She checked her phone again. No messages, and it had been almost an hour.

Willow took a sip of her now *cold* hot cocoa and scanned the room, noticing a few of the guys on the team had trickled in. She decided to give Brayden twenty more minutes before she gave up and went home.

The day had passed in a blur. After school she'd gone straight to Lisa's, where her friend had given her a head-to-toe makeover. Willow had insisted on cute and comfortable. What she'd gotten had far exceeded her expectations. Lisa had insisted she bring the charcoal leggings and sapphire sweater she'd purchased, and then Lisa added a heather gray scarf, ankle boots, and a short leather jacket. Willow still felt like herself, but it was different enough that it gave her confidence. And what Lisa had done with her hair was magic—it hung down Willow's back in loose, shiny curls like something out of a shampoo ad. The makeup had been the most painful part. Mascara and lip gloss were about all she ever used. But by the time Lisa was done, Willow couldn't stop looking at herself in the mirror. She didn't recognize the girl with the glowing skin and mysterious eyes.

She'd felt stares on her throughout the game, and several boys she'd never talked to had smiled at her. Yoko Ono had even taken notice. As Yolanda walked past her on the bleachers, she'd snapped a snide, "Nice biker jacket, Weepy." Before Willow had been able to contrive a suitable comeback, Yolanda had hiked up to the back row. Willow had let it go, but the name calling had to stop.

"Hey."

Willow glanced up from her cup to find Isaiah Kagawa with his hands shoved in his back pockets, shoulder hitched up.

"I heard you were looking for me. Can I sit?" He indicated the chair opposite her.

She nodded, and he took a seat. He hadn't been in class that afternoon, but he appeared his usual healthy self.

"Were you sick today?" Willow asked, deciding it was a safe question to break the ice.

"No . . . I . . . um . . . had something in town I had . . . I mean something I had to do . . ." A screech followed by cheers pulled his attention to the other end of the room where a junior girl had jumped up on a table and began a rap/poem. Isaiah turned back around. "Did I miss anything in Music Appreciation?" He lifted his hands and made air quotes.

Willow sat back and chuckled. "Um . . . other than Mr. Rush making out with his baton? No." She wasn't even sure if that was true. The class had been torture. Something had changed between her and Ashton. They'd sat next to each other as usual, but a new awareness buzzed through her with every move he made—her pulse jumped as he tapped his pencil against his thigh, the hair on her arms rose when he leaned in to take the eraser off her desk. And when he'd braced a hand on the back of her chair as he returned it, his thumb brushed her spine and she thought she might fly out of her seat.

She hadn't seen him or Penelope at the game. Willow could only assume they were together, since they'd been joined at the hip all day at school. Willow felt a soft pop as her thumbnail sliced through the paper cup.

"So what did you want to talk to me about?" Isaiah pulled off his beanie, and she noticed his dreads were knotted up in an intricate design on the back of his head.

Pushing the mutilated cup away from her, she commented, "Your hair looks cool. But how do you do that? Can you reach it yourself?

He smiled and reached back to pat the loops of hair. "My sister did it."

Willow had forgotten he had a younger sister in middle school and that his mom wasn't around. No wonder he was so jumpy all the time. Living in a single-parent home with the staunch chief of police for a dad would make anyone a nervous wreck.

"You're looking nice. Are you waiting for someone in particular?"

Willow glanced at her phone. Still no messages. "I thought so, but maybe not." She shrugged, trying not to think about why Brayden would stand her up. "So I wanted to ask you something kind of weird."

"Um . . . okay." He took a swig of his coffee.

"Did you happen to share my SnapMail address with anyone after our group project last year?"

He lowered his cup slowly. "I don't think so." His lips compressed and his brows lowered as he thought, then he shook his head. "No, I'm sure I didn't. Why?"

"I got a strange message the other night but didn't recognize the address it was from."

"A threatening message?"

Why would he go there? Because his dad was a cop? Or because he knew something? Willow leaned forward and lowered her voice. "How did you know it was threatening?"

Isaiah blanched. "I didn't! I mean, it just . . ."

A rumble sounded outside, so low it vibrated the glass in the window next to them, drawing both their eyes to the source. A black motorcycle with the words *Indian Scout* scrawled on the side stopped at the curb. The rider hit the kickstand and drew off his helmet. Ashton ran a hand through his tousled hair before dismounting.

"Um . . . I gotta go." Isaiah's chair screeched against the floor as he pushed away from the table.

"Hey, pretty girl!" Brayden appeared at the table, freshly showered and grinning. "Sorry I'm late. Coach held a few of us back after the game. And my phone died." He lifted his black screen as proof.

Isaiah stood and met Brayden's gaze. For a fraction of a second, neither of them said anything. Then Isaiah clapped Brayden on the shoulder. "Nice moves out there tonight."

"Thanks, man." Brayden's words lacked his usual enthusiasm, but then he smiled and said, "And thanks for keeping my girl company."

"Not a chore, believe me." Isaiah turned to Willow. "Catch ya later."

As Brayden took Isaiah's vacated seat, Willow searched outside. Ashton was nowhere in sight. She scanned the other patrons, but the room was shaped like an L and she was sitting at the bottom of it, so she couldn't see everyone in the shop.

"Looking for someone?" Brayden shucked off his letter-man jacket and hooked it on the back of the chair.

Willow focused on Brayden, her lips curling up. "Just you."

"Ouch." He winced. "Sorry again, but Coach wanted to go over the game footage with us."

Deciding to let it go, she widened her smile. "Well, I'm glad you made it out alive."

He laughed and reached across the table, taking her fingers in his. "I'm glad you waited." His warm brown eyes crinkled at the corners and he asked, "Can I get you something to drink, eat? Run down to Gale's and bring you a lemon tart?"

Gale's was Gilt Hollow's only gourmet restaurant. People traveled from miles around to sample their creative, organic cuisine, but it was not cheap. Willow usually only went there once a year on her birthday. She squeezed Brayden's fingers. "How did you know Gale's was my favorite?"

He tapped his temple. "Because I can read your mind."

"Oh yeah, then what drink do I want?"

Brayden clenched his eyes shut, his nose and forehead crinkling like a pug puppy. "I'm sensing something . . . warm." He opened one eye. "Am I right so far?"

Willow nodded, biting her lip against a grin.

He laid his left arm on the table, palm up. "I'm going to need your other hand for this—it's a little hazy." Willow grasped his fingers, and he closed his eyes again. "It's coming to me now . . . chocolate . . . no . . ." He scrunched up his nose and a damp lock of red hair fell across his forehead. "I know! A chai tea latte!"

"Hot cinnamon cider." The deep voice cut through the air, making both of them start.

Ashton sat sideways at the table next to them, legs spread wide, elbows resting on his thighs as if he were engrossed in a good play. Willow's gaze traveled over his dark hair, disheveled and chaotic, his skin glowing from the sun and wind, and her heart did a funny blip. She tugged her hands out of Brayden's.

"What do you want, Keller?" Brayden clipped.

Ashton's gaze flicked from Willow to Brayden. "I need to talk to her."

"It's gonna have to wait. We're kinda busy." Brayden turned back to Willow, dismissing Ashton.

Out of the corner of her eye, Willow saw Ashton stand. "It can't wait."

Annoyance washed cold over Willow's shoulders. She just wanted *normal*. An ordinary first date without all the drama. Was that too much to ask?

With deliberation, Brayden rose from his seat. Ashton crossed his arms over his chest and planted his feet. They were nearly the same height, but Ashton appeared broader, more solid.

Brayden stared him down, his hands fisted at his sides. "Nobody wants you here, Keller."

Ashton's eyes narrowed as a corner of his mouth curled in a deceptively benign expression. But Willow saw it for what it was: danger.

Sensing the same thing, Brayden swallowed, and his Adam's apple bobbed. Ashton leaned in, his arms unfolding, fists clenching.

Willow catapulted out of her chair. This wasn't a game of capture the flag. And she *was not* the prize. "Stop it! Both of you!"

Neither of them looked at her. If Ashton got into a fight, it would only prove what people were saying about him. And if somebody called the cops . . .

Steeling herself, Willow shoved Ashton with both hands. He barely moved. "Ashton!" His gaze shifted to her, his eyes blue flame. She didn't give a fig. The jerk needed to listen for once. "If you want to talk to me, ask *me*!" she fumed, pointing to her chest.

He blinked, and life flooded back into his face as if he were waking up from some testosterone-fueled hypnosis. "Willow, I—"

"Willow, you don't—" Brayden talked over Ashton, and Willow cut him off with a glare. He didn't own her either.

She turned back to Ashton. "Brayden and I are here together. I'll call you later."

Ashton's jaw flexed. "It's kind of important."

Two intense stares drilled into her. Waiting. Willow glanced between them and wondered how she'd gone from invisible to two good-looking guys battling for her attention—virtually overnight. With a sigh, she turned to Ashton. "We'll talk later." She'd been looking forward to this date with Brayden. She wanted to try to make it work.

With a curt nod, Ashton pivoted on his heel and stalked off. But he wasn't really gone. As she and Brayden sat back down, her ex–best friend's presence lingered between them. In an attempt to break the tension, Willow smiled and said, "I'll take that drink now."

Brayden glanced over his shoulder, then back at her. "Keller is a freaking lunatic. You better steer clear of him before it's too late."

"Too late for what?" Willow's already frayed nerves felt ready to snap.

Brayden leaned forward. "If you don't stop hanging out with him, he's going to drag you down with him."

"Really?" His words were so like her mother's that she

immediately went on the defensive. "Are you saying that because you care about me or because you don't want to see me with him?"

"Both—" Brayden said, but Willow cut him off. "In the tree house that day, you said he'd been your friend too. But I don't think that was ever true. You're just like everyone else in this town who thinks they're the ultimate judge and jury." Willow grabbed her jacket off the chair and jammed her arms into the sleeves.

"Hey, wait." Brayden scooted his chair back. "Are you leaving?"

Willow stood and looped her purse over her shoulder. "Ashton and I have a long history. And if you and I are going to see each other, you're going to have to accept that."

Brayden stood up, his eyes pleading. "He's a criminal, Willow."

"And he's served his time, as I'm sure you're well aware." Willow breezed past him.

"Let me walk you home!" Brayden called.

"I'll be fine."

As she made her way through the crowded room, a sharp movement caught her eye. In the far corner, Ashton held a boy she didn't recognize against the wall. She moved closer, drawn like a pedestrian to a five-alarm fire. What was he doing *now*?

Ashton leaned into the kid's bug-eyed face and spoke words she couldn't hear. She skirted a table full of cheerleaders and moved around a guy carrying a cardboard tray of coffee cups. When Ashton came back into view, his face contorted with rage as he jerked the kid forward and then slammed him against the wall, snapping his head back. Willow's gut twisted and she rushed forward. She hadn't witnessed this side of Ashton since the first day she'd seen him in Gilt Hollow—when the intense fury radiating from his every molecule had caused her to believe he was capable of murder.

But before she could reach him, Colin Martin grabbed Ashton's arm and yanked him back. As the two argued, Willow approached the boy. He swiped at the tears in his eyes and shoved through the small crowd of people who'd gathered around the action. Willow followed him. "Hey, are you all right?"

Without answering, he pushed past her and out the door. Willow spun around to give Ashton a piece of her mind but collided with Colin instead. She attempted to edge around him, but he side-stepped and blocked her. Her frustration level already off the charts, she glared at him and barked, "Move!"

"Everything okay, Weepy?"

Willow lifted her chin and stared into Colin's cool-blue gaze. "Call me that again, and you'll be the one weeping."

"Oooh, put a little makeup on her and she gets mouthy."

Willow tried to step around him again, but he refused to move.

"You look good, Willow." Colin reached out and fingered the fringe of her scarf. "Maybe I'll call you sometime and we can hang out."

Really? Did he know she'd just walked out on a date with his cousin? Likely, the "king" of Gilt Hollow High didn't care. She arched a brow and jerked her scarf out of his hand. "Don't bother."

He threw his head back and laughed like it was all a big joke. Willow walked past him and searched the faces in the room, but none of them was Ashton's.

■ ■ ■

Willow plodded down Main, avoiding eye contact with everyone she passed. She'd never been good at hiding her feelings, and right then they were boiling over. What was wrong with Ashton that he thought violence was a valid way to communicate? And who was that kid? Ashton had said he needed to talk about something important. If she'd taken the few minutes to see what he wanted, maybe the whole incident could have been avoided.

No. He was *not* her responsibility.

Unclenching her fists, she took a right onto Elm and forced her legs to slow. No sense getting back earlier than necessary just to sit in her room fuming. Besides, the blisters forming on her heels made it painful to move too quickly. She and Lisa wore the same size in just about everything, even though Willow had a few inches on her in height, but the boots had formed to Lisa's slightly wider feet, causing them to slip and chafe with every step.

Turning onto Beckett Street, trees arched and knit into a canopy that blocked the moon, their branches creaking like dry bones. A chilled breeze chased down Willow's neck. She tightened her scarf and shoved her hands into her pockets, but the unlined jacket felt icy against her knuckles. Clearly the thin bit of leather had been designed for fashion, not warmth. The mournful whistle of a train wailed in the distance, and Willow suddenly noticed how far the houses sat off the sidewalk, their yards full of mature trees. And hiding places.

She pulled out her phone, deciding to text Lisa to see if she was still awake. But the screen cast an eerie glow, making her feel exposed. She tucked it away. It was only a few more blocks. She'd call her from the safety of her bedroom. A coyote howled in the distance, and chills rose on Willow's arms. But it wasn't the animal's cry that gave her the willies. A sudden awareness crept over her like eyes drilling into her back. She glanced over her shoulder. The sidewalk was clear. She picked up her pace, ignoring the pain in her feet.

Leaves skittered and danced across her path, the noises of the night closing in around her. Was that footsteps she heard or just branches tapping in time with the wind? A sharp crack, like a stick breaking, made her spin around. As she pushed the hair from her eyes, a lean shadow melded in with the trees across the street. Her heart hurtled into her throat. Someone was following her.

CHAPTER Fourteen

W illow spun around and tripped over the edge of the sidewalk. As she stumbled forward, her momentum propelled her into a jog. Should she knock on someone's door? Tell them she'd seen a shadow in the trees? Her steps slowed to a fast walk as she took her phone out and dialed 911. Her finger hovered over the dial icon as she squinted back to where she'd seen the shadow. Nothing.

Had her mind been playing tricks on her? Could it have been a low swaying branch or a deer? Her mouth dry, she scanned the street, searching dense clusters of shrubbery, parked cars, and shadowed porches. A person could follow her for blocks, rushing from one hiding place to the next. Her chest tightened, her breath coming faster as her feet sped down the sidewalk. But why? Why hide? If someone wanted to hurt her, they would have had plenty of opportunities since she left Main Street.

Then again, maybe they were waiting for the right moment to yank her into the mouth of a deserted alley or their dark van idling near the sidewalk. The words of the threatening message loomed large in her mind. *Rein in your boyfriend before somebody gets hurt.* Her heart hammered painfully against her ribs as she lengthened her strides. That *somebody* could be her. She turned around, walking backward as she scanned the trees, her hair flying into her eyes, a horrifying thought occurring to her—if anything happened to her, the police would blame Ashton. Then her stomach dropped. After witnessing the rage inside of him, maybe they'd be right.

She spun around, her throat tightening with panic. Had she made a mistake by allowing him back into her life? Had Brayden and her mom been right? Her finger hovered over the call button again as she strained to hear anything suspicious above the groan of the wind, and flinched when a low roar reverberated behind her, growing louder by the second.

She glanced back just as the jet black motorcycle pulled up beside her.

Ashton.

"Need a ride?"

"No!" She stared straight ahead and kept walking. Visions of Ashton's face contorting as he'd slammed that young kid against the wall caused her pace to quicken. Maybe she'd been wrong about Ashton all along and their friendship had blinded her from the truth of his guilt.

The bike's engine growled as he pulled up beside her. "I got my motorcycle license today, and insurance. So I'm totally legit."

"Go away."

"I'll drop you off down the street so your mom doesn't see." The amusement in his voice sparked a memory of a long-ago night when they'd snuck out to watch a local punk band perform at the street fair. Riding home on the handlebars of Ashton's bike, her ears burning from Origami's scalding lyrics and deafening bass, she'd kind of understood why her parents had told her she couldn't attend the concert. But the exhilaration of the night, of tasting the forbidden, had stayed with her long after Ashton had dropped her off at the corner of her block.

Proving they were on the same wavelength, Ashton's voice projected over the rumble of his bike as he sang the

138

chorus of Origami's only hit, "Night falls on your heart, and my world explodes with wonders untold—"

"Ashton, please, just go." Willow cut him off before he sang the racy part, but she realized her steps had slowed to the point that when she glanced at him, the engine idled and he walked the bike forward with his feet on either side.

"Sorry I screwed up your date." His tone said the opposite.

"No, you're not."

After a few seconds of silence, he admitted, "You're right. I'm not." The engine revved, and he sped off down the street.

Willow's breath caught. She hadn't expected him to leave her. But then he looped back, did a U-turn, and parked his bike half a block ahead. After putting down the kickstand, he turned off the engine, dismounted, and shoved the key into his pocket.

As Willow approached, he said, "I can't let you walk home alone this late. There's too much creepiness going on."

"I doubt there's anything scarier than you out here."

Without responding, he fell into step beside her. Had she hurt him? Part of her hoped so.

They walked in silence, and an odd tension stretched between them like two polarized magnets, attracting and repelling at the same time. After a few minutes, the strain became too much and Willow caved. "I noticed the posters were gone downtown."

Ashton made an inarticulate sound of agreement.

She looked over and noticed the tight set of his jaw. Fists shoved in his jacket pockets, his shoulders were fixed in a hard line. He was still angry, yet he'd come back to make sure she was safe. And she knew in that moment that her fears of him were unfounded. The edge of her own frustration softened, and she asked, "Did you take the flyers down?"

"No."

Deciding to throw caution to the wind, she asked, "Who was that boy at Gino's?"

"You saw that?" He scanned her face, his expression guarded.

"Yeah, I saw that. What the heck, Ashton? He looked like he was twelve."

"First of all, he's a sophomore." His eyes flashed as he pulled a hand out of his pocket and lifted two fingers. "Second, he took my picture in the bathroom my first day back at Gilt High."

That was odd, but if Ashton was going to smash the kid against a wall, why didn't he do it right after it happened?

Answering her unspoken question, he continued, "I glared at him as he snapped the photo, but didn't think much of it . . . until the flyers appeared."

The pieces clicked into place in Willow's brain. "That's what you wanted to tell me tonight, right?"

"Yeah, I'd found his name by looking at your old yearbook."

"But who is he? Why would he do something like that?"

"That's what I wanted to find out. When I saw him at Gino's right after . . ." He scraped a hand down the back of his hair. "Well, I kinda lost it."

It was no excuse, but she couldn't help asking, "What did he say?"

"He denied it at first. Said I was as crazy as everyone claimed." Ashton's eyes closed for a second and he shook his head. "Something just snapped inside me, Wil. I . . . I grabbed him out of his chair and told him if he didn't tell me why he put up the flyers, I would show him how crazy I could get."

Willow didn't speak, hoping her silence would coax him into continuing. But what he said next took her by surprise.

"It's different in juvie. If you don't go on the offense, you'll be the next victim."

Willow scanned the hard lines of his profile and remembered the boyish fourteen-year-old whose face had been plastered all over the news, all freckles and big blue eyes. Her throat closed. It was almost impossible to imagine that boy growing up in a prison.

Ashton stared down at her, his gaze wary. "Do you know why I got out early?"

"Why?" She could barely push the word past her lips.

"My friend Stanley." He released a dry chuckle. "The kid was skin and bones, but he was an amazing basketball player. Would whip guys twice his size on the court." He swallowed, his tone sobering. "Anyway, he was jumped by a group of guys who didn't like losing, and I stepped in. I don't remember half of it. Just that one of them had a blade and I was fighting for both our lives. When it was all over, Stanley and I were the only ones standing."

"That's why they let you out early?" Willow couldn't disguise her shock. "Because you got in a fight?"

"I spent a week in the void." He glanced over at her, hair falling into his eyes. "That's what we called solitary."

Willow nodded.

"And then they called me in and said I'd only been in there for my own protection, and what I'd done to protect Stanley had shown strength of character."

"Violence was rewarded," Willow mused.

"Not only that, but it was a way of life. Survival of the fittest and all that."

A gust of wind tunneled down the street, and Willow

felt herself drift closer to Ashton's warmth. "What about the guards?"

"They could always be convinced to look the other way. I think they were half afraid of us."

There was a brief pause before Willow asked, "So did that kid put up the flyers?"

"Naw. He said he received an anonymous text on SnapMail telling him that if he took my picture and texted it back, they'd pay him a hundred dollars." Ashton pushed out a sigh. "He started babbling about needing money for a marching band trip to Florida."

"So whoever put him up to it knew he was desperate for cash."

"Good point. I'll start digging into who he hangs with at school."

They reached the corner of Walnut and turned left, their steps in perfect sync. They'd walked this route together hundreds of times. But when his elbow brushed her upper arm, a charge shot across her skin, reversing their polarity. Ashton must have felt it too, because he pulled her to a stop in the middle of the sidewalk.

"Why Brayden?" His dark brows swooped down over his eyes.

Willow stared up into his face and suppressed her first reaction—to tell him it was none of his business. He'd lost the right to question her when he pushed her out of his life and refused to communicate with her the entire time he was away. But as his eyes searched her face, she caught a glimpse of something like pain. "I . . . I don't know . . . It just kind of happened."

"Do you have any idea what it felt like to see you with

him? Holding his hands, gazing into his eyes?" He scrubbed a hand over his hair. "Damn it, Willow. He. Put. Me. In. Jail."

Willow sucked in her bottom lip to hold back the tears. "I . . ." She looked down at their feet, his black boots dwarfing her size eights. When he'd left, their feet had been close to the same size. So much had changed, but he had no idea how much.

She raised her gaze. "I defended you the entire time you were gone, Ashton. I lost friends, jobs . . . I lost myself. When I didn't hear from you, I sat at home night after night, talking to the shadows. I threw myself into my schoolwork. Never went out. Never went to football games or parties or dances." She sucked in a breath, ignoring the muscle that ticked in his jaw. "When Brayden asked me out, he made me realize people hadn't shut me out as much as I'd shut *myself* out. And I was tired of it."

He glanced away and shook his head. "I never thought about . . ." His gaze darted back, his eyes fiery with emotion. "I never thought about what you went through." He grabbed her and pulled her against his chest, wrapping her in his arms.

Taken by surprise, Willow's hands dangled at her sides for a beat before she lifted them and pressed her palms against the strong planes of his back. As she drew in his warm citrus scent, she relaxed, resting her face against his chest, her head fitting just beneath his chin. The fierce beat of his heart made her smile. Ashton was real and safe, and he was here.

His arms still looped around her waist, he leaned back. "Was I right?"

Willow cocked her head. "About what?"

"Your drink order." His lips tilted in a mischievous grin, making her skin flush.

Clamping down her reaction, she retorted, "I like chai tea."

Ashton lifted a hand and hooked a strand of hair behind her ear. "But you *love* fresh, hot cider." His eyes were hooded, only a slit of blue visible beneath his dark lashes as he traced her jawline, his thumb brushing against the corner of her mouth. "The sweet and tart tingling on your tongue."

Willow's breath caught as he watched the path of his thumb sweep across her open mouth. Every one of her nerve endings caught fire and she rose on her toes, straining toward him. What would it feel like to have his lips replace his thumb?

Headlights swooped around the corner, bathing them with light. Willow pulled away as the car sped past. Reality splashed over her, dousing the heat in her veins. If someone saw them and told her mom, she didn't want to think about the consequences. She stepped back. "I . . . I need to get home. I can walk the rest of the way on my own."

Her face flaming, she took off down the sidewalk without looking back.

* * *

Ashton banged on the door for the second time. Knowing Jeff, he'd probably gotten tanked and passed out in his apartment. Resisting the urge to knock a third time, he slumped against the wall. He couldn't stay at Keller House tonight. After what he'd almost done, he didn't trust himself. And renting a room was out. Between new clothes, school supplies, and repairs and gas for the Indian, he was down to his last hundred bucks. Jeff was his only hope, which didn't give him much confidence.

Finally, the door rattled and unlatched, opened by a sleep-mussed Jeff wearing striped boxers and a faded Stevie Ray Vaughan T-shirt. "Dude, it's after one in the morning." He rubbed an eye with his fist like a sleepy kid.

"Can I crash here tonight? I promise I won't get in your way."

Jeff's eyes widened slightly and the slackness left his expression. "I have a friend staying with me in the apartment, but . . ." He glanced behind him and then back at Ashton. "I've got a small blow-up mattress we could drag into the shop."

"Perfect! I owe you one, man."

Jeff moved out of the doorway and gestured for Ashton to come in. "I'd say you owe me more than one at this point, kid." The three windows behind the counter allowed enough light for Ashton to see Jeff grimace. "That cop, Kagawa, won't leave me alone. He comes snoopin' around here at least once a day."

After inflating the air mattress, they carried it through the shop and laid it to the right of the counter, the only place with enough floor space. Jeff handed Ashton a flat pillow and a ratty-looking blanket. "You can use the public toilet, but there's no shower. How long do you need to crash?"

Ashton began to make his bed. He'd slept on worse. "Not sure, maybe a night or two." Or until he could trust himself to sleep under the same roof with Willow.

When Ashton straightened, Jeff put a hand on his shoulder. "Everything okay, kid? You're not in any trouble, are you?"

Ashton couldn't blame Jeff for not wanting to get involved, but this time he didn't need to worry. "Just girl trouble."

"*That* I can understand." He shook his head with a grin and walked back to his apartment. "Sleep good, kid."

Easier said than done. Ashton sat on the edge of the mattress and cradled his head in his hands. He was a complete and total idiot. After shedding his jacket and toeing off his boots, he flopped onto his back. But when his gaze fastened on the star-filled sky through the window, he saw Willow's eyes sparkling as they gazed up at him. He could still feel her soft lips against his thumb, smell her skin. Ashton rolled over on his stomach and punched the mattress.

He could've screwed up all the ground they'd gained with one stupid, thoughtless kiss. He'd promised Adam Lamott on his deathbed that he'd watch out for Willow. So far he'd failed miserably. But he'd been given a second chance, and he didn't think that included making out with her on the street.

Shifting onto his side, he tucked the pillow under his head and tried to shift his focus. Someone in Gilt Hollow wanted him gone. Badly. The flyers and the warning message to Willow indicated premeditation—especially now that he knew they had paid that kid to take his picture for the express purpose of plastering it all over town. Speaking of, he had no clue how the flyers had been removed so quickly. He'd driven through town that morning on his way to school and they'd been everywhere. Had the chief ordered them cleaned up, or did Ashton have a secret ally?

He tugged the blanket up over his shoulder, but his eyes refused to close. He had a feeling whoever was out to get him wasn't done yet.

CHAPTER Fifteen

W illow didn't see Ashton the rest of the weekend. At night she lay in bed straining to hear a footstep or telltale bang of pipes, but there were no signs of him. Except in her dreams, where he would show up uninvited, arms crossed, smirking as she danced in the garden in her bunny slippers, or arching an eyebrow as she fled from an enormous cartoon textbook.

Deciding it was best to put some distance between them after what had almost happened, Willow hadn't texted him or gone upstairs to check if he'd slept there—although fighting the urge took up more of her mental capacity than she cared to admit.

Brayden had called several times, leaving apologetic messages, but she was too confused to call him back, so she'd texted to tell him she needed some time. Time to figure out if she could date one boy and want another. Despite everything that had happened, everything Ashton had done, she'd wanted him to kiss her, wanted it from her tingling lips to the depths of her soul. What did that say about her feelings for Brayden?

To keep her mind busy, she'd reorganized the files on her computer, completed an extra-credit project for science, and helped her mom clean the library. Sorting the hundreds of books by author and genre had done wonders for her raging emotions.

■ ■ ■

On Monday morning Willow trudged down the stairs, wishing she could crawl back under the covers and hide. Maybe being invisible hadn't been so bad after all.

As she entered the kitchen, her mom, head stuck in the pantry, called, "Rainn, did you eat the entire box of granola bars yesterday?"

Willow slid onto a stool at the island. "Mom, you okay in there?" As if in answer, a bag of chips hit the floor, followed by more shuffling.

"And all twelve juice boxes?" Mom came out and eyed Rainn, who sat at the counter shoveling spoonfuls of oatmeal into his mouth, chunks of blond hair falling over his eyes. "Did you have a party I didn't know about, buddy? There are a whole bunch of bananas missing too. I was going to make muffins with those."

Narrow shoulders hunched, her brother didn't answer.

"Rainn Robert Lamott, what is going on?"

He scraped his bowl, ate the last bite, and then turned wide green eyes on their mother. "I gave them to the ghost."

Mom's brows winged up, her forehead crinkling. "Really?"

"Yup, he lives on the third floor."

The bottom dropped out of Willow's stomach.

Rainn slipped off his stool and walked over to the sink. "I hear him almost every night, but I figure if we give him something to eat, he won't hurt us. He'll know we're his friends."

Willow met her mom's amused gaze and then let out a low breath. If the woman didn't sleep like the dead, she would've heard Ashton by now too. But clearly a granola-eating ghost pushed the limits of Dee Lamott's open-mindedness.

Mom turned back to Rainn. "Baby, I don't think ghosts can eat."

Willow stifled a giggle as her brother spun around. "Oh

yeah? Then why is the food always missing when I go back the next day?"

"Well, I—" Mom arched a brow at Willow, accusing her of hiding the food.

Willow froze. Ashton was probably eating it because he thought she was leaving it for him. But before she could respond, Rainn explained, "He doesn't like everything." His little forehead scrunched up. "He didn't eat the rice cakes I left him Friday or Saturday, but when I checked this morning, the Pop-Tarts were gone."

He put his bowl and spoon in the dishwasher and then shrugged. "Maybe he only likes sweets."

Rainn grabbed his backpack and headed out the back door. Willow opened the refrigerator and stuck her head inside to hide her laughter. Ashton had a notorious sweet tooth. She grabbed the gallon of milk and, when she turned, almost tripped over her mother standing like a statue behind her.

"Stop encouraging him, Willow. His head is stuck in the clouds half the time, and he needs a bit of reality to keep him grounded."

Biting back her grin, Willow sidestepped her mom and grabbed a box of cereal off the counter. "Sorry, I didn't think it was hurting anything." Deciding to change the subject before her mom asked where she'd stashed the food, Willow poured her cereal and commented, "The flower shop is hiring. I thought I'd stop by after school and fill out an application."

Mom moved to the sink and picked up a small watering can, then turned to face her. "I've been thinking about that, and I'd really like to see you focus on your studies this year."

They'd struggled financially for as long as Willow could remember. When her dad was alive, it wasn't so noticeable.

Going on imaginary vacations and making homemade presents for each other had seemed normal, and Dad had made it fun. But after he passed, the life insurance went to medical bills and funeral costs. They'd had to sell their car, and Mom took a second job. "What about saving for college?"

Her back to Willow as she watered her window herb garden, she replied, "I have every confidence that you'll get a scholarship, and if it doesn't cover everything, you'll qualify for financial aid." She glanced over her shoulder. "I want you to have a normal senior year, honey. Go to dances and parties and act like a seventeen-year-old for once."

It was exactly what Willow wanted too, but for some reason, her mom's generosity made her belly twist. She put down her half-eaten bowl of cereal.

Mom faced her again. "Speaking of parties, I emailed the Keller House solicitor for permission to host a Sleepy Hollow Ball after-party here." The grin that spread across her face made her look like a little girl. "Wouldn't this place make an amazing haunted house? I found boxes full of Halloween decorations in the basement, and we could make creepy food, like blood-dipped candy apples and witch's brew punch with dry ice."

The knot in Willow's belly tugged tighter. This sweet, generous woman was trying to give her the senior year she'd always dreamed of, and yet Willow had done nothing but defy her wishes and lie to her face.

"Honey, what? We don't have to have witch's brew . . . is that too corny?"

Trying to wipe the worry off her face, Willow shook her head. "No, Mom, it's perfect. I just . . . I . . ."

Her mom rushed across the room and enfolded her in her arms. "I think I know what's wrong."

"You do?" Willow practically squeaked. Had someone told her mom she'd been in Ashton's arms at the end of their street? Or worse, had she figured out the identity of their ghost?

"You know how much Daddy would've enjoyed having a Halloween party here."

Willow slumped back against the counter. Picturing her dad's excited face made it hard to speak. "He would've . . . totally . . . loved it." She swallowed and then offered a small smile. "I bet he'd be sketching jack-o'-lantern designs . . ."

". . . And painting life-sized murals of the headless horseman," Mom finished for her.

"Exactly." Her dad would've loved the atmosphere of this place, seen it as a blank canvas. He also would've been the first one to offer Ashton a place to stay after his release. Willow's smile melted as she stared into her mom's glistening gaze. "Mom, I need to tell you some—"

The doorbell echoed through the house, making both of them jump. Saved by the . . . gong. "I'll get it," Willow said as she jogged out of the kitchen, down the hall, and into the foyer. When she cracked open the door, she was met by Lisa's wide blue eyes.

"Are you mad at me?"

"No!" She threw the door open. "Why?"

"You didn't return my calls all weekend!"

"I texted you," Willow responded lamely.

"With two-word answers!" Lisa pushed her way into the house. "I started to worry Brayden had roofied your hot cocoa and dragged you to his evil lair."

Willow winced. "Sorry. Introvert habits die hard. I just had a lot on my mind." She grabbed her backpack off the stairs. "Mom! I'm leaving!" Confession time would have to wait.

Out on the porch, Lisa glanced at Willow and then did a double take. "You're using the eye shadow I gave you."

Willow shrugged. "Yeah, it's fun to play around with the colors."

They reached the street, and she stared over her shoulder at the third floor. Had Ashton left for school yet? He must walk the motorcycle halfway down the block before starting it so Mom won't hear. What if he offered her a ride to school? Would she wrap her arms around his waist as she settled in behind him? Their bodies pressed together, his scent filling her with every breath . . . the rumble of the bike vibrating through her veins . . . wind flowing through her hair . . .

"Holy cow! What is that dreamy look on your face? Did you spend the whole weekend with Brayden? Is that why you didn't call?"

"No!" Willow walked faster. "We barely had a date."

"Oh, I see." Lisa caught up to her and hooked her arm through Willow's. "Tall, dark, and dangerous, right? Spill the deets."

So she did. All of it—from her interrupted date to Ashton threatening the kid in Gino's to their almost kiss in the street. The only parts she left out were the private things Ashton had shared with her about his time in juvie and that he was staying in the house.

For the first time since she'd known Lisa, she was silent. As they walked into the school lot, Willow unhooked their arms and turned to stare at her friend's stunned face. "So, what do I do?"

Lisa blinked at her. "About what?"

"About my mom, about Ashton, Brayden . . ."

"Well, if I were you . . . and I'm not gonna lie, I kinda wish I was . . ."

Her words were drowned out by a thunderous roar. Ashton passed within two feet of them and glanced over his shoulder, his eyes meeting Willow's for an intense, fleeting moment that had her toes curling in her Mary Janes. Then he was gone.

"That . . ." Lisa sighed. "I'd do *that*."

"Lisa!" Willow half cried, half laughed.

"You asked." Her brows arched, unapologetic.

Maybe Lisa was right. Fighting her growing feelings for Ashton was exhausting. Maybe she just needed to give in and see where it would take them. But could she trust him? There was so much she still didn't know about his past, about his real intentions for returning to Gilt Hollow.

"Looks like Bohemian Barbie might have the same idea."

Willow followed Lisa's line of sight to where Ashton walked across the parking lot with the golden-haired Penelope glued to his side. A bitter lump slid down Willow's throat and burned in her stomach. Was that where Ashton had been all weekend? Had he run to Penelope after they'd almost kissed? Stayed at her house? Pain squeezed Willow's chest. She lengthened her stride. You couldn't find anyone more opposite to Willow than Penelope *freaking* Lunarian. If that's what he wanted, more power to him. "Whatever," Willow spat as the couple disappeared into the building.

"Hey." Lisa bumped her shoulder. "Slow your roll, girly. They're just walking together."

"Mmm." Willow couldn't share that Ashton had been missing all weekend without telling Lisa that he was living on their third floor. But she decided to rein in her assumptions all the same. She'd never been driven by emotion, and she didn't plan to start now.

As they entered a side door, Willow pushed down the

lingering prickle of jealousy and forced herself to focus on Lisa as she chatted about a boy in her math class whom she'd texted all weekend.

"What about Colin?" Willow asked, referring to Lisa's crush and her fantasies of them double-dating the Martin cousins.

"After the way Colin talked to you this weekend, are you kidding me?" Lisa propped a hand on her hip. "Not even his Thor-like hair is worth that 'tude."

Willow laughed and glanced over to see the kid from Gino's lugging a tuba case half his size into the band room. The sight sobered her instantly. The sousaphone section of the marching band was a tight group. Crossing over age and social status, they spent tons of time together. And she was almost positive that Isaiah Kagawa played the sousaphone.

Before she could complete the thought, Ashton walked up beside her. "Spend all weekend organizing your underwear drawer, Lamott?"

Her cheeks flamed. Their history gave him unfair insight into her freakish tactile processing habits. The first time being after she'd flunked a fifth-grade science test and locked herself in their basement craft room. She'd ordered hundreds of old photos in sequence and glued them in scrapbooks, refusing to come out until her dad had sent Ashton to tap on the narrow window and make funny faces at her. His threat to moon her had finally pulled her out of her trance. Now she'd kind of pay to see that.

After her cheeks cooled, she dared a glance in his direction. "You make me insane, you know that?"

A smile hovered around his lips and his blue eyes sparkled like sunlight reflecting off the deepest sea. Her heart flipped in her chest as he leaned in close.

"What I'd really like to know . . . is if you cataloged them by style or color first . . ."

"Shut. Up!" She hauled back and punched him in the arm, only to yank back stinging knuckles. He hadn't even flinched. As he walked ahead through a narrow doorway, she let her gaze flow over him—half-laced boots, snug-fitting cargo pants, royal blue T-shirt pouring like water over his wide shoulders to the indentation of his bicep. With his lean-muscled build, he looked like an action figure, and after what he'd told her about the culture in juvie, she imagined that was deliberate.

They turned into the senior hall to find a crowd gathered around the first bank of lockers on the left. Approaching the edge of the group, Lisa asked, "What's going on?"

"Isaiah's locker . . ." a girl muttered, the first bell cutting off her voice.

Some of the kids cleared out, heading to class, and the view opened. The words YOU'RE NEXT! were spray-painted in red on a locker door, and Isaiah Kagawa knelt cleaning up crumpled pieces of paper that had spilled out onto the floor. Moving through the crowd, Willow picked one up and rejoined Lisa and Ashton. She knew what it was before she finished unfolding it.

She glanced back to where Ashton peered over her shoulder at the flyer with his face on it. A muscle jumped in his cheek, his eyes darkening before he moved around her and strode into the center of the gathering. There were several sharp intakes of breath, and half the group dispersed while the other more-curious half seemed to lean in.

A guy next to them whispered, "Isaiah was at the falls when Daniel died, right? Do you think someone thinks he had something to do with it?"

His friend responded, "That or Keller thinks Isaiah put up the posters and he's getting his revenge."

Immediately, Willow knew the guy was wrong. Even if Ashton thought Isaiah had something to do with plastering his face all over town, he'd just confront him about it. This was too . . . passive-aggressive.

Ashton squatted in front of Isaiah and began to help him gather balls of paper. "I'd be happy if I never saw this picture of my ugly mug again." He paused and then added, "I didn't do this, Isaiah."

The PA system crackled and Principal McNachtan's voice blared through the hallway, "Ashton Keller, please report to the office immediately."

Still staring at the floor, Isaiah replied, "Maybe not, but sounds like you're about to take the fall for it."

And whoever *did* do it had known exactly that. Willow glanced up and down the corridor, searching for a security camera. She knew the building had a few outside, but she'd never had reason to notice if they'd installed them inside as well. She scanned the walls above the lockers and found one mounted at the other end of the hallway.

"Ashton Keller," Mr. Rush barked as he entered the circle of students, scattering those who remained.

Lisa muttered, "I'll catch you in first period," and then took off like her feet had wheels. She'd seen her share of violent confrontations in her school in New York and had told Willow she had no stomach for them.

Ashton's shoulders stiffened before he looked up, his face void of expression. Mr. Rush stood with his legs spread, hands gripping his thick waist. Ashton rose slowly, towering half a foot over the music teacher.

"I believe the principal requested your presence." He grabbed Ashton's arm in a fierce grip. "That means *now*."

Ashton's fists clenched at his sides before he jerked his arm away from the teacher's hold and growled, "I can walk on my own."

Willow tried to catch his gaze, to communicate with her eyes that she supported him, but he stared straight ahead as they walked away.

"Man, he's totally screwed."

Willow turned to find Brayden watching Ashton and Mr. Rush head toward the stairs.

"Why?" Willow squeezed her book bag to her chest. "He didn't do it."

Brayden gave a noncommittal shrug. "I just came from the office. The police are here."

"For a locker prank?"

"No, something about a robbery at Twisted Beauty last night."

Willow's throat constricted as she watched the back of Ashton's dark head disappear down the staircase. If he was convicted of another crime this soon, they'd lock him up and throw away the key. And that fleeting glimpse might be the last she ever saw of him.

CHAPTER Sixteen

T he police station stank of burnt coffee and fear. Ashton shifted down on the metal folding chair, then stretched out his legs and crossed his ankles while trying to hold his arms still so the handcuffs wouldn't chafe.

He'd been waiting for over an hour for Chief Kagawa to come in and ream him. All the deputies would tell him was that Kagawa wanted to question him about a local robbery. Ashton fought against panic. *Questioning* meant he was a suspect, but he hadn't taken so much as a Tic Tac that didn't belong to him since he'd been in town. Surely they'd determine that quickly and he'd be on his way. But as another hour ticked by, he had to wonder if Kagawa had left him there to cool his jets as some sort of strategy.

Ashton gripped the unforgiving edge of the metal cuffs as he watched the deputies begin *another* game of paper-triangle football. If he had to sit in an office all day with these meatbags, his head would explode. The extent of their excitement in the last two hours had been booking a street performer for disturbing the peace and panhandling. No wonder Kagawa followed him around like a hound dog on a family of rabbits.

But as the phones quieted and the paper triangle rested on the corner of a desk, Ashton's thoughts journeyed down a twisted path to a memory he'd tried hard to avoid. The last time he'd been in this station had been the worst night of his life.

A boy is dead! Because of you . . ." Kagawa leans forward into his face. "We have three witnesses, Mr. Keller. Admit it and this will all be over soon."

The image of Daniel, head smashed on the rocks, blood everywhere, his neck at a grotesque angle, dominates Ashton's vision, blocking out the three sets of eyes drilling into him. Without hesitation, even though it was too late, Ashton had jumped over the falls after his friend. Screamed his name. Touched his fractured skull. Blood coating his fingers, he'd emptied his stomach in the water that rushed around him. Brayden, Colin, and Isaiah stared down from above. Silent.

Fire burns through Ashton's chest, scalding his throat and leaking out of his eyes. "Yes, it was my fault." A mumble, nothing more, but enough.

The door to the small windowless room bursts open. "Are you questioning my minor client? Nothing he's said is admissible, Kagawa, and you know it!"

Ashton snapped back to the present. The attorney had been wrong. Between the three witnesses who claimed Ashton had pushed Daniel, their argument moments before, and his whispered confession in front of the chief, Ashton's lawyer had convinced him to accept responsibility and take the plea bargain. But that guileless kid no longer existed. This time there would be no coerced admissions.

The double doors burst open, bringing a rush of cool, dry air and a flurry of dead leaves. The chief, flanked by an officer on each side, strode into the station. Ashton resisted the urge to straighten in his chair. "Mr. Keller, sorry to keep you waiting. We'll get all this business over as quickly as possible." He nodded to the deputies, who moved to stand on either side of Ashton. Before they could reach him, he bent his knees and shot to his feet.

Forcing a neutral tone, Ashton leveled his gaze on Kagawa. "What is it you're accusing me of, Chief?"

Kagawa's mouth flattened, but something in his eyes glittered. "Oh, not accusing, merely questioning. Didn't my men explain?" He shook his head as if shamed. "Twisted Beauty was robbed last night, and your bike was spotted parked outside."

Ashton felt his jaw unhinge but snapped it closed again. He'd spent the entire weekend camped in the store, which would look pretty damning. "I'd like to call my attorney."

The chief waved a dismissive hand. "No need, son. You aren't under arrest. As I said, we're just chatting."

Ashton's back locked, his eyes narrowing. He'd experienced the good chief's *chats*. "Then you have no right to hold me." He lifted his cuffed wrists.

"Oh, good gravy!" Kagawa let out a humorless chuckle and pointed at the nearest deputy. "Unlock those cuffs."

The cop complied, and Ashton rubbed the feeling back into his wrists.

"I must apologize. My men aren't accustomed to dealing with felons."

Ashton froze, already done with the games. "Since I'm sure you haven't found any evidence against me, I need to get back to class." He met Kagawa's beady stare. "I'm missing Music Appreciation." He strode forward, but as he passed, the chief snagged his arm.

"Not so fast." Nose to nose, Kagawa stared him down. "A few questions should clear this whole matter up quickly." Not releasing Ashton's arm, he steered him into a small, windowless room.

"I'm thinking my probation officer should be here for this," Ashton commented as the chief shut the door behind them. "Zane Reed? He told me he's been in contact with you." Although Ashton didn't relish his meetings with the over-zealous officer of the court, the man struck him as being 100 percent by the book. Unlike Kagawa, who liked to twist the law to his own purposes. "I think he'll be interested to hear how your deputies handcuffed me and hauled me in here when I'm not even under arrest."

"Have a seat, Mr. Keller." The chief pulled out a tarnished folding chair.

Ashton widened his stance and crossed his arms in front of his chest.

"Fine, you're welcome to stand, but I've had a rough day." Kagawa took off his hat, set it on the table, and perched on the edge, one foot anchored to the floor. "When, or should I say *if*, I contact your probation officer, you will become an official suspect. I don't think you want that."

Ashton lowered his chin and stared at the man who had taken four years of his life. Enunciating each word so that there was no mistake, Ashton said, "I didn't take anything from Jeff or Twisted Beauty."

"Oh, come on, Ashton. Jeff told us you admitted to him you were low on cash. Desperate times call for desperate measures. No one would blame you for trying to survive."

Thanks Jeff, Ashton thought, wondering if he'd also told Kagawa the rest of their conversation about Ashton deciding to sell some more of his grandma's records. He wasn't without resources. It just sucked to have to give up the things his grandparents had left to him—especially since they'd been the only true parental figures in his family.

"You're wasting my time, Chief, and I'd like to know why. I'm positive Jeff told you I didn't do this."

The cop's eyes turned to slits and he leaned forward. "I'm wasting *your* time? I've spent the last four hours investigating your screwups." Kagawa shot to his feet and crossed the room in two strides, stopping inches from Ashton's face. "Including my son's locker being vandalized!"

Seething, Ashton forced his arms to stay folded, pressed his fists into his sides, and leaned into the old man's beet-red face. "I. Didn't. Do. It. I didn't piss on Colin's jersey or steal from my only friend in town or trash Isaiah's locker . . . I didn't do any of it!"

A smirk twisted the chief's face, and he stepped back. Ashton's heart slammed against his ribs as he waited, racking his brain for what he'd said wrong. What he'd given away that Kagawa was about to use against him.

Resuming his perch on the corner of the table, Chief Kagawa tilted his head to the side, his next words draining the blood from Ashton's face. "Jeff White isn't your only friend in town, is he?"

* * *

"My mom said they never should've let Ashton Keller come back here. It's like letting a registered sex offender teach biology." Yolanda and Ona paused less than a foot away from where Willow stood at her locker.

Ona, ever the follower, chimed in. "I know, right? What if he loses it and kills one of us? They'll be sorry then."

Yolanda turned and bumped into Willow, knocking her sideways. "Oh, sorry, Weepy. Didn't see you there."

Willow's chest tightened and her heart shot out of the gate at a sprint. She sucked in air but didn't turn around as Ona added, "Yeah, looks like your *best friend* is headed back to the slammer." With cackles of hysterical laughter, the two girls moved on.

Panic creeping in, Willow gripped the rough metal edge of her locker door. Yoko Ono's taunts were no worse than what she'd been hearing all morning. In the eyes of Gilt High, Ashton had been convicted without a shred of evidence against him. After some deep breathing, her pulse slowed and she yanked her lunch bag off the shelf.

She slammed the door and turned to see Brayden approach, his expression set with determination. "Come on." He gestured for her to follow him.

"What?"

"You said it yourself in Bio earlier—they need to check the security cameras."

"Yeah, but . . ."

Brayden held her gaze. "I know it doesn't help him with the robbery charges, but at least we can do this."

She searched his cinnamon-brown eyes. Why would he want to help Ashton? Maybe it was his way to make amends and back up his apology with action. Willow nodded. "All right. Let's do it."

"Hey, can I tag?" Lisa joined them, her blonde curls frizzing out of her ponytail.

"Sure, we're going to the office."

"Whatever." She sighed. "I just can't handle being in the cafeteria with the Yoko Ono twins. For some reason, they're more obnoxious than usual today."

"Yeah, tell me about it," Willow muttered as they all headed toward the stairs.

Following a brief argument with the school secretary, during which Brayden pulled the "my mom's the president of the PTO" card, they were ushered into Principal McNachtan's office. Willow took a seat in front of the desk and sucked the humid air into her lungs. Something about the plants hanging from the ceiling, sprouting out of pots, and climbing the filing cabinets and credenza lowered her blood pressure.

"What can I do for you, kids?"

Willow sat straighter. "We . . . um . . ." She exchanged a quick glance with Brayden, who nodded his encouragement. "I would like to know if you've checked the security footage in the senior hallway to see who vandalized Isaiah Kagawa's locker."

The principal folded her hands on the top of the desk, her fingers encased in silver and emerald rings that wove around her fingers like vines. "And this is your concern, why?" Her dyed-crimson eyebrows arched into the fringe of her matching bangs.

"Because everyone in school thinks that Ashton Keller did it." Willow's voice rose an octave. "Don't you think he's been villainized enough?"

Mrs. McNachtan narrowed her gaze to the front of her desk, where Willow clutched the edge with white-knuckled intensity.

Forcing her hands to relax, Willow sat back. Disrespect would get her exactly nowhere. "I'm sorry, Principal McNachtan. I just—"

Brayden spoke over her. "Willow has a very strong sense of justice, ma'am. She only wants to see whoever did this receive the punishment they deserve."

The principal relaxed back into her chair and smiled at Brayden.

Who knew brownnosing could be a superpower? Willow glanced over at the boy beside her with new respect.

"As a matter of fact"—the principal addressed each of them as she spoke—"we've just reviewed the footage but were unable to make out any distinguishing details, so no one's been accused of anything. Mr. Keller . . . well, let's just say he's dealing with more serious issues right now."

Which Willow could do nothing about. But this, at least, she could help him with. "Ma'am, would it be possible for us to watch the footage?"

"Yes." Brayden gave a nod. "We might recognize details about the person that you wouldn't. Clues that could help you identify them."

Lisa, who'd remained silent up to that point, chimed in. "I'm great with details!"

The principal seemed to consider their request. After a moment, she conceded. "All right then, but there will be no conclusions drawn from this, and what you see stays in this room."

They each agreed as Mrs. McNachtan turned to her computer. "The time on the file shows that the vandalism happened late Friday evening." A few moments later, she swiveled her monitor so that they could all see the screen. Lisa moved behind Willow and Brayden, hovering over their shoulders. The recording was dark and grainy, but Willow recognized the senior hallway by the room numbers and the huge homecoming poster taped on the wall. After a moment, a tall figure, hefting a duffel bag, slunk into the frame.

Leaning in, Willow focused on the person's head, but all she could make out was a black mass. Then she realized he was wearing a ski mask. Searching for other specifics, she watched as he dumped the balled-up flyers into the locker ncern.” Willow met Mrs. McNachtan’s artificial green gaze, enhanced by contacts. How had she never noticed the woman

and slammed the door. “Wait? How did he open the lock? Can you go back?”

Mrs. McNachtan clicked on the back arrow and played from the part where the guy first arrived at the locker.

“There’s something in his hand,” Lisa pointed out.

“Yeah.” Brayden leaned close, his arm pressed against Willow’s shoulder. “Looks like he had the combination written down.”

They watched as he loaded the locker full of papers, slammed the door, and took a spray can from his bag, then turned and appeared to say something. Unfortunately, the video had no sound. “Pause it!” Willow rested her elbows on the desk and stared at the frozen image facing them. All dark clothing—boots, cargo pants, leather jacket.

“Does that look like anyone you know?” Mrs. McNachtan asked.

Willow slumped back. It couldn’t be. Someone had dressed like Ashton to purposefully let him take the fall. She shook her head. “No.”

The principal glanced between them. “Lisa? Brayden?”

Digging her fingers into the seat cushion, Willow waited for Brayden to throw Ashton under the bus. Both her friends had to have noticed Ashton’s usual uniform, but she had faith that Lisa would stay quiet.

“No, ma’am.” Brayden’s answer sent a shock wave over Willow’s skin, but she forced herself not to react. Why would he protect someone he clearly despised?

“Me either,” Lisa echoed. “Could be anybody.”

“Okay, then. Well, thank you for your . . . er . . . concern.” Willow met Mrs. McNachtan’s artificial green gaze, enhanced by contacts. How had she never noticed the woman

166

was such a character? "You should all get to lunch before the period ends."

Bumping into each other in their haste to exit the principal's office, they reached the hallway and collapsed against the cool tile wall.

"Why did you do that?" Willow turned to Brayden. "Why did you cover for him?"

He faced her, one shoulder propped against the wall, his eyes glinting with emotion. "Don't you know?"

"Well, that's my cue." Lisa started down the hall. "Call me later, Willow."

Brayden brushed Willow's upper arm with the back of his knuckles. "I like you, Willow. And I want to see where this thing can go between us. You told me I had to deal with Ashton being part of your life, and that's what I'm doing."

"Do you think that was him? In the video?"

His gaze flicked to something behind her head and then shifted back to her. "It looked like him. Don't you think?"

The height and broad shoulders could have been any number of boys at their school, and everyone knew Ashton wore a variation of the same outfit every day—easy to emulate. But she could also be avoiding the obvious. What was it her grandpa used to say? *If it walked like a duck and quacked like a duck . . .*

"Yes, but if it was him, I don't understand his motivation."

Brayden shrugged off the wall and held out his hand. She only hesitated a second before linking her fingers with his. As they walked, he theorized, "Maybe Isaiah put up the flyers and Ashton saw this as a way to get back at him."

Then something she'd seen that morning clicked into place—Isaiah and the kid who'd taken Ashton's picture both played the sousaphone in the marching band. Isaiah would know the boy needed money for their Disney World trip. He also had Willow's SnapMail address.

"But regardless," Brayden continued. "Keller has more to worry about than a stupid vandalized locker. I heard his motorcycle was spotted parked behind Twisted Beauty late last night, after the store was closed."

Doubts swirled in Willow's mind, mixing with what Ashton had told her about his time in juvie. It had changed him, made him into a person who took what he wanted, forced it if necessary. She'd seen that firsthand at Gino's. How well did she really know the person he had become?

"Do you think we can try again?"

Willow's attention snapped back to the boy holding her hand. "I'm sorry. What did you say?"

Brayden squeezed her fingers and pulled her to a stop. "I'd like to take you out." His eyes crinkled at the edges as he smiled. "On a real date this time."

Whatever was going on with Ashton was out of her control, but this boy liked her without any strings attached. He was normal. "Yes. That sounds nice."

Brayden's eyes danced. "Great! I'll pick you up tonight at seven."

■ ■ ■

Willow sat ensconced in the deep leather chair, her feet propped on the table, history text unread in her lap. A glittering beam of late-afternoon sunlight slanted through the window and across the face of the empty fireplace. Mom had taken Rainn to the library, and as the monotonous tick of the grandfather clock droned into the quiet, all the sleep Willow had missed in the last weeks weighed down her eyelids.

She almost ignored the soft ping when it sounded from

deep inside her bag, but when it happened again she recognized the generic signal. Pulling her legs off the table, she grabbed her phone and swiped in the code. Two pending messages on SnapMail.

With trembling hands, she clicked the icon. The text was from the same unidentified sender as before.

If you defend Keller to the police . . .

The next message was a picture of Rainn walking down the sidewalk alone. Willow's hands shook so hard, she dropped her phone.

As she reached down to pick it up, the text and picture disappeared, and a bang sounded on the front door. Taking a deep breath to steady her pulse, she stood on unsteady legs and walked into the foyer. Not sure if she should open the door, she called, "Who is it?"

"Gilt Hollow PD."

Her first thought was that something bad had happened to Mom and Rainn. She threw the dead bolt and flung open the door. "What is it? Is everything okay?"

Chief Kagawa and a deputy whose name badge read "Simms" waited straight-faced on the porch. Simms inclined his head. "Yes, Ms. Lamott, we just have a few questions for you regarding a pending case."

"Can we come in, Willow?" The chief slid the hat off of his buzzed head and held it in front of him with both hands.

"Of course." Her mind racing, Willow stepped aside as they entered the foyer. They had to be here to question her about Ashton. Had they figured out he'd been living here? Had he told them?

"Is your mother at home?" Kagawa asked.

Thank the Lord, no. "She took Rainn to the library for

a Lego building thing." Willow's heart clunked against her ribs as she led them into the front parlor, hoping the formal atmosphere would discourage them from lingering. She'd noticed that Ashton had done the same when his probation officer had visited.

The cops perched on the edge of the narrow Victorian loveseat, and Willow sat in the opposite chair, folding one leg beneath her. The turret room smelled of old wood and lemon polish. To calm her racing heart, Willow focused on the curio cabinet behind the officers and imagined herself as a well-born lady serving tea to the local constables. Picturing them in the old-fashioned domed hats they would have worn in the 1800s almost made her smile.

Chief Kagawa took out a tiny black notebook, then crossed his legs and pinned Willow with an unblinking stare. "Just a few quick questions, Willow. Nothing of an official capacity."

She folded her arms around her middle and then, deciding it made her appear defensive, unfolded them and laced her fingers in her lap. If this was so "unofficial," why did she feel like she was one wrong word away from her fingers being pressed in ink?

"You've been spotted around town with Ashton Keller. Is it safe to assume that you've resumed your friendship?" The smile that lifted the chief's lips didn't reach his eagle-sharp gaze.

"Sure." She shrugged a shoulder, figuring vague was best.

"It must be kind of . . . odd for him that you and your family are living in his ancestral home." He gestured to the two-story ceiling of the old Victorian.

Working to keep her voice casual, she replied, "Not really. He understands my mom took the caretaker job and is working to fix the place up."

"She's doing an excellent job," Officer Simms chimed in, earning a glare from his boss.

"Er . . . thanks." Willow addressed the younger cop. "She's hired a contractor to start repairs and painting on the outside."

The chief nodded absently while staring at his notebook. "Can you tell me where Ashton's been staying since his return to Gilt Hollow?"

Willow felt the color drain from her face. She covered with a smile. "No, well . . . he said he's been staying with various friends."

"Huh. He told me the same thing, but I wasn't aware he had any friends in town besides Jeff White." He raised his head. "And you."

Penelope Lunarian sprung to mind, but as much as Willow despised the girl, she wouldn't drag her into this. She remained silent.

"Has Ashton mentioned being short on money since he returned?"

"No."

"How is it that he has disposable cash, do you think?" He tapped his pen against the notebook.

If Ashton had spent all afternoon in jail, surely he'd already answered all of these questions. "I don't know."

"Apparently he sold a valuable album to Jeff, something from his grandmother's collection." He looked up again. "What I'm wondering is how he got ahold of it."

Because he broke in here and took it from the attic. Although it was rightfully his, she wouldn't do him any favors by being honest. "I let him in so he could collect whatever of his things he needed."

"Was your mother aware you let Ashton into the house?"

Dang. He was good.

"I don't think so . . . no."

"Where were you last night from midnight to seven o'clock this morning?"

She blinked. Twisted Beauty must have been robbed sometime between those hours. But the missing Pop-Tarts that morning told Willow that Ashton had been in the house, even if she couldn't be sure what time he'd arrived. Meeting Chief Kagawa's gaze, she replied, "I was here."

"Sleeping?"

She sat straight and put both her feet on the floor. "I don't see how that's any of your business." And that's when she realized she was going to lie. That she would perjure herself to keep Ashton safe.

Kagawa's brows raised a fraction. "Do you know where Ashton Keller was between the hours of midnight and seven?"

Willow opened her mouth and then snapped it shut, remembering the warning she'd received seconds before the police had arrived. Would they really harm Rainn if she defended Ashton? If the messages were from Isaiah Kagawa, as she suspected, she couldn't imagine him hurting an innocent person, especially considering his father was the chief. But if Ashton went back to jail, it wouldn't be juvie this time; it would be adult prison.

She could not lose him again.

Channeling the stress and fear she'd experienced in the last twenty-four hours, Willow stared into her lap. When she looked up, her eyes were shimmering with unshed tears. "Is what I tell you confidential?"

Chief Kagawa uncrossed his legs and leaned forward. "Of course."

"Ashton was here . . . with me . . . all night."

CHAPTER Seventeen

"Y ou questioned Willow, didn't you?" Ashton pushed off the table and sprung to his feet.

"I'd shut up and be happy I'm letting you go." Kagawa stood, arms crossed, by the open interrogation room door.

Ashton glared at the man and forced himself to relax his hands. "What did she say?"

"She gave you an alibi for the time of the robbery." The chief stepped to the side. "Now go, before I change my mind."

Ashton walked out of the tiny, windowless room and let out a heavy breath.

"By the way, I checked into who posted those flyers of you, but the security cameras in town didn't reveal any new information."

Ashton gave a tight nod. He doubted Kagawa had lost any sleep over it.

"Deputy Simms will give you a ride to pick up your motorcycle." The chief shut the door and then turned to him with a smile that might have been genuine. "It's a gorgeous bike. Where'd you get it?"

For once, the question didn't sound like an accusation. "My grandpa Willard left me his collection. The rest are stored in the garage at Keller House."

"Oh yeah?" Kagawa's brows arched up. "What else you got in there?"

"A couple Harleys, a BMW café racer, and a 1963 Triumph Bonneville."

"No! A Steve McQueen edition?"

Ashton almost smiled when the chief's eyes lit up like Christmas morning. "Yeah. They all need work." Ashton shrugged. "Maybe after I inherit the house, I'll start working on them."

His cop face sliding back into place, Kagawa's jaw set and his brows lowered. "When's that?"

Working hard not to get defensive, Ashton began to stroll toward the door where Deputy Simms waited in his cruiser just outside. "When I turn twenty-one, the house becomes mine along with a trust my grandparents left me."

"That's why you came back here." Kagawa walked beside him, and they both paused at the glass doors.

"Partly." Ashton met the chief's eyes, almost wanting him to dig deeper. When the time came, he would need this man to do his job. Maybe a part of the chief knew Ashton had returned to find the true killer, and that his son was on the list of possibilities. That's why he wanted Ashton gone. But that wasn't going to happen. "Well, this has been fun, and the saltines and water I had for lunch were fantastic, but a little more nourishment is in order."

Ashton pushed against the door, but Kagawa stopped him with a hand on his arm. "Be careful with Willow Lamott." He cleared his throat before continuing. "She's a good one."

And you're not. The unspoken words hung in the air between them. Ashton met the chief's stare and had to unclench his jaw before he could answer. "I'm well aware."

With a curt nod, the chief released him. Ashton pushed into the windy evening and took a deep draw of the crisp fall air before sliding into the backseat of the cruiser. As they took off, he watched the sun sink toward the horizon, the sky exploding with red, orange, and gold—flushing the treetops in glorious pink. The fiery colors reminded him of Willow's cheeks when he'd held her in his arms. He could paint her face from memory, the way she'd looked at him that night.

Whatever she'd told the cops had saved him. His lips lifted in an astonished smile that quickly dissolved into a grimace of determination. He'd risk anything for her, but he couldn't allow her to do the same. The closer he got to the truth, the more dangerous he became. His chest tightened like a vise around his heart. He knew what he had to do.

❋ ❋ ❋

A cool evening breeze pushed against Willow's skin, and she tugged a sweater over her shoulders as Brayden held open the door with a smile. He'd picked her up in his dad's BMW and taken her to Gale's. *Gale's*.

They'd just finished one of the best meals of her life— pan-seared, wild salmon with melt-in-your-mouth tomato risotto and fresh-baked bread. She could still taste the cream of the house-made herb butter on her tongue.

"You know what I'm craving?" Brayden asked as he draped his arm over her shoulders and steered her down the tree-lined street.

"Are you serious?" Willow chuckled. "What could you possibly want after that enormous helping of squash and pumpkin lasagna?" She'd thought what he'd ordered sounded gross, but when he'd given her a taste, her eyes had rolled back in her head, confirming that everything at Gale's was off-the-charts amazing.

"There's always room for ice cream."

"Okay, but I have to go home and change first. I'm about to pop a seam in this dress." Willow inhaled, the scents of roasted coffee and wood smoke mixing with the fresh night air. Orange globe lights hung from the trees like fat pumpkins, casting Main Street in a soft glow as people strolled arm in arm, ducking in and out of shops and restaurants, their laughter punctuating the night. In was surreal how much downtown Gilt Hollow resembled a small town television drama—or whodunit mystery, as the case may be.

Brayden's fingers squeezed her upper arm, and she glanced at him as they walked. "No changing. You look too gorgeous. Have I told you how good you look in red?"

Willow grinned. "Maybe once or twice." *Or ten times.* When she'd put on the red halter dress in her room, she'd taken one look in the mirror and changed into jeans and a sweater set. The dress was beautiful, and way out of her comfort zone. But she was sick to death of her comfort zone, and Brayden had advised her to dress nice. So she'd compromised by wearing it with a cardigan and boots instead of sandals. When she'd opened the front door, Brayden's face had lit up and she knew her risk had paid off.

Their dinner had been nice. She'd learned that his parents had been high school sweethearts who graduated from Gilt Hollow High, and that he had an adopted sister. His dad was a sales rep at a local environmental company, where his mom worked part-time in accounting. They had family game nights and went to the beach every summer, where Brayden had fallen in love with the ocean and decided to become a marine biologist. The conversation had flowed easily, but now an awkward silence descended.

"Have you heard from Ashton?"

The question caught Willow off guard, causing her to trip over the uneven sidewalk. Brayden looped an arm around her waist and pulled her close. "Whoa, no more root beer for you, young lady."

"Sorry, I didn't see . . ." Willow's words trailed off with her thoughts. She'd done her part to help Ashton, and she prayed her false alibi had been enough for Chief Kagawa to release him, but she wished Brayden would drop the subject.

"I heard he was at the station all afternoon. His bike was still parked at school when I left."

No such luck. Unsure of what to say, she nodded.

"Why do you think he came back here? To Gilt Hollow, I mean."

Willow's back stiffened, a buzz sounding in her brain that felt like a warning. "I don't know."

They stopped as a crowd spilled out of Neon Art Theater, and Brayden turned her to face him. "I didn't mean to upset you."

But Willow read something besides contrition in his searching gaze, something that made his throat contract and his neck turn red.

A boisterous group exited the theater dressed in Victorian costumes, the women wearing extravagant bustled gowns and elaborate feathered hats, the men in pinstripes and tall fedoras. They were singing "I Could Have Danced All Night."

Willow stretched up on her toes to watch the spectacle as they danced across the street. "I forgot they were showing *My Fair Lady*. It's one of my mom's favorites."

Brayden walked around to meet her gaze, blocking her view of the parading minstrels. "I'm sorry, okay? I was just curious."

Willow wasn't sure that he was being entirely honest. Ashton's return clearly made him uncomfortable. But if he expected her to feed him information on her ex–best friend, he would be greatly disappointed. What little she knew she would keep to herself. "Can we not talk about him tonight, please?"

His chestnut eyes searched hers. "Of course. But if you ever feel like talking, I'm—"

A familiar voice cut off Brayden's comment. "Willow?"

She turned to find her mother and, just beyond, Pastor Justin holding her little brother's hand. "Mom? What are you doing here?"

Her mom smiled sheepishly, her cheeks flushing pink. "Rainn and I ran into Jus—" She glanced up and exchanged a look with the man beside her. "We ran into *Pastor* Justin at the library and . . . um . . . he likes musicals too, so we decided to see the movie . . . er . . . together."

Willow lifted a hand in a lame wave. The man who'd baptized her, taught her the books of the Bible, and performed her dad's funeral nodded, not appearing in the least uncomfortable. "Hi, Willow."

Some part of her had suspected her mom's friendship with the never-married minister could turn into more, but the twist in her gut every time she thought about it made her push the idea away.

"Hi, Mrs. Lamott. I'm Brayden Martin." Her date reached out and shook her mom's hand.

"Hi, Brayden. I remember you."

After a round of reintroductions, Rainn tugged on Pastor Justin's hand. "Come on, guys. I'm starving!"

"Okay, buddy." Mom turned back to Willow, her eyes sparking with curiosity and perhaps a bit of something else. "We promised Rainn a burger if he sat quietly in the movie. So we better go. See you at home, by eleven?"

"Sure." Willow watched the threesome stroll away, her

mom walking close beside the tall pastor. It hadn't escaped Willow's notice that her mom had referred to them as "we."

Maybe she wasn't the only one keeping secrets.

• • •

Ashton pulled up to the curb just outside of the Dairy Shed's fluorescent glow and parked behind a VW Bug covered from fender to wheel in bumper stickers. Political and social statements screamed from the vehicle like a poster board for public activism. Save the Trees. Wake Up and Smell the Fascism! Support Organic Farmers. PEACE! Coexist. Hang Up and Drive!

It was so Gilt Hollow that Ashton grinned.

He shut off the engine and lowered the kickstand, reaching back to assist Penelope as she dismounted. After his near arrest, he'd resisted the urge to return to Keller House, and Willow. If he had any hope of separating her from this mess, he would need to put as much distance between them as possible.

Penelope unhooked her helmet, balanced it on the handlebar, and grabbed Ashton's hand. "I love this place! Don't you just love this place?"

Ashton offered her a smile as he climbed off the bike. "Sure."

Hanging with Penelope Lunarian wasn't exactly a chore, but tonight her joyous optimism grated on his nerves. His date skipped into the line, tugging her with him. "What's your favorite flavor? No, wait. Let me guess." Penelope tapped a finger against her pursed lips as she scanned the list of current offerings. The Dairy Shed always had a few exotic flavors mixed in with the usual chocolate, vanilla, and strawberry.

"I bet you like chocolate, but not plain chocolate . . ."

A dark-haired little girl in front of them ordered vanilla with extra sprinkles, and Ashton no longer stood with Penelope.

Willow takes a huge lick of ice cream, coating her tongue in rainbow colors, and then props a hand on her narrow hip with a glare. "Why would I try something else when I know what I like?"

"Because getting the same thing every time is boring!"

She smirks, vanilla dripping down her chin. "How're you liking that lavender lemonade sorbet, Mr. Adventurous?"

Ashton takes a huge bite and fights the sour puckering his lips, but his eye squints, betraying him.

Her uninhibited laughter tugs his mouth into a grin.

". . . Peanut butter and chocolate? Ashton, are you listening to me?"

A sharp yank on his arm brought him back to the present and the girl staring at him with narrowed eyes. "Um, yeah, that's good."

With ice cream in hand, they crossed the street to the town square, where couples lounged on blankets, a vendor sold kettle corn out of a converted wagon, and the town troubadour—as he liked to call himself—strummed a guitar and sang what sounded like a mash-up of Willie Nelson and Nirvana. They found a table inside a large gazebo covered in tiny lights and fall garland, and sat across from each other.

Penelope ate her kiddie cup of pistachio in uncharacteristic silence. That suited Ashton's mood perfectly. He barely tasted the salty-sweet Reese's sundae, which a few weeks ago had been the object of his dreams, as his mind ran over the events of the day. Whoever had vandalized Isaiah's locker went to a lot of trouble to make it look like Ashton had done it. The flyers stuck inside were the key, but he couldn't quite put it together. Was it the same person who'd posted them? What did the warning mean? And more importantly, had someone robbed Twisted Beauty, knowing he'd take the fall? Or had that crime been unrelated—an unfortunate coincidence?

"Why did you ask me out?"

Ashton snapped to attention at the wounded tone in Penelope's voice. "Huh?"

She pushed aside her half-eaten ice cream, hurt drawing down the corners of her mouth. "I thought you liked me, but I'm beginning to think you're just like Colin."

Not following, but sure he was nothing like Colin Martin, Ashton reached over and took her hand. "I do like you. But today was kinda crazy." That's when he realized that she hadn't asked him about his near arrest or the vandalism. Like maybe if she didn't bring it up, it hadn't actually happened.

"It's just that . . ." She looked over at a group of middle school kids laughing at the next table, her usual glow absent from her cheeks. "Colin wanted me on his arm like some kind of trophy. He didn't really care what I wanted or what was going on in my life." She turned back to him with pleading eyes. "I can't be in that kind of relationship again."

Shame washed over Ashton like a cold wind. Her parents were divorced and had both remarried, starting new families. She'd told him she often felt like an afterthought. He rubbed the back of her hand and leaned forward with a smile. "What's on your mind, Pen?"

She lit up in a way that only someone who was starved for respect and attention would understand. A need intimately familiar to Ashton.

"Well, I decided today to run for class president. My grades aren't the best, but student body government will look good on college applications, don't you think?"

Ashton agreed and let her talk for another thirty minutes, responding in all the right places. By the time they were ready to go, Penelope's excited chatter had soothed Ashton's stress and he found himself laughing as they made their way back to his bike.

But before he pulled away from the curb, a young couple strolling arm in arm caught his eye. The girl, in a killer red dress with shiny waves of dark hair down her back, had attracted more than just his attention. Every male in the vicinity watched as Brayden took Willow's hand and spun her out, then twirled her in a circle, her hair and dress rotating around her, the sweater falling off of her creamy shoulders.

Ashton's breath seized as Willow fell against Brayden in a fit of giggles. He needed to talk to her, but not here. Not like this. Not when his chest ached with the need to smash his fist into Brayden Martin's grinning face. Instead, he clamped on the accelerator and roared away, repeating over and over in his head that she deserved happiness, whatever the cost to him.

●　●　●

Willow swam through her dreams, kicking and pushing against resistance as she tried to break through the surface. A nebulous presence chased her, so close she could feel his hot breath on her neck. Icy fingers grasped her arm. She jerked away with a shriek. But she couldn't escape.

Something was there with her, just out of view. Emerging into consciousness, her eyes fluttered, working to focus in the dark. Prickles raced across her skin, her mouth going dry. She was definitely not alone.

As she blinked, a shadow separated from the wall. She started and shrank back, choking on a scream.

"Shh! Willow, it's me."

"Ashton?" She levered up on one arm as his form solidified.

"Yeah, I need to talk to you."

She sat up and smoothed her hair out of her face, then cleared her throat and rubbed her eyes before she asked, "Is everything okay?"

"Can I sit?"

"Sure." Willow scooted over to make room on the edge of the bed, her pulse accelerating as his large body sank the side of the mattress. He smelled like the night—open air and freedom. Her eyes adjusting, she watched him run a hand over his tousled hair, the leather of his jacket crinkling as he moved.

Willow had to swallow before she could ask, "Did you just leave the police station?"

"No, they let me go around six."

"They dropped the charges then?"

"There weren't any official charges." He raised one hand in an air quote. "They were just holding me for questioning. Not sure that's legal, but since Kagawa is king in this town, he can do what he wants."

"That man is a serious egotist."

"I was going to say something else, but that works too."

Ashton readjusted his perch on the edge of the bed and then slipped off his jacket, laying it across the coverlet. Willow suddenly found it hard to breathe. What was he doing in her room—on her bed—in the middle of the night?

"Ash—"

"Wil—"

He smiled, a flash of white teeth against dark skin, and Willow's belly effervesced, her head spinning like the time her mom let her drink champagne.

His voice a rough whisper, he asked, "Willow, what did you tell the chief?" He leaned in, a stripe of moonlight illuminating the turbulent sea blue of his eyes.

Their gazes locked and the intention she read on his face melted her bones like butter. They eased toward one another, the sound of her heartbeat pulsing in her ears. If she looked into his eyes another second, she would drown in them. Gladly.

"Wil, what did you tell him?"

Thankful to have something to focus on, other than the way Ashton had encased her hands in one of his, or his thumb as it moved in lazy circles across the backs of her fingers, she blurted, "I told him you were here with me all night."

His thumb stopped its rotation. "*With* you, with you?"

Willow shrugged. "I let him draw his own conclusions."

He withdrew his hand, his brows crouching over his eyes. "Don't ever do that again."

Stiffening her spine, Willow lifted her chin. "You mean claim we slept together, or save your behind from going to prison?"

"Both!" He pushed off the bed and began to pace. "I grew up in jail. On my own. With not one word of encouragement from anybody. I don't need anyone's protection." He stopped and stared down at her. "And most certainly not yours."

Willow scrabbled up on her knees to face him. "What do you mean, with not a word from anybody? I wrote to you *every day* for months! Did you throw my letters in the trash without reading them?"

He stilled. "I never got any letters."

She searched his face. Was he telling the truth? If she'd had the wrong address, the letters would've been returned. After several weeks of no response, her mother had called the facility and assured her they were going to the right place. *Her mom.* Willow sunk back on her heels. Mom had said it over and over: *"Maybe you're better off without him."* She'd never trusted Ashton—never believed in his innocence. Saw him as a bad influence on her only daughter.

"What?"

Willow stared at him, his reaction to her that first day finally making sense. The look of hatred on his face had been cultivated over years of assuming she'd abandoned him . . . along with everyone else. But she couldn't tell him about her mom's betrayal until she spoke to her and confirmed her horrid theory. Grasping for a change of subject, she confessed, "I received another anonymous SnapMail message."

Instantly alert, he stepped toward the bed. "What did it say?"

With a useless gesture, she pointed toward her phone resting on the nightstand. "It was a message that warned me not to defend you to the police, and then . . ." She glanced past him to the trees lashing outside the window. Why was she telling him this? He would feel responsible.

"And?"

Goose bumps rose on her skin, reminding her she wore

only a tank top and sleep shorts. Reaching behind her, she grabbed a blanket and wrapped it around her shoulders. "And . . . then they sent a picture of Rainn. He was alone, with his backpack over his shoulder, probably walking home from school."

Ashton shoved the hair off his forehead, clutching the strands as he spun away toward the windows. "Are you kidding me?" He dropped his hand and turned back, his face a mask of shock. "Then why would you do it?"

There was a tap on the door. Willow met Ashton's eyes, and he dropped to the floor like a cat, just as the door swung open. Rainn's blond head peeked in. "Sis, I heard something. Like voices."

"Sorry buddy, I couldn't sleep and I was listening to music." She smiled at his too-long hair sticking up on one side, his sleep-red cheeks, his wide green eyes, and a sudden terror gripped her. What if she'd really put her little brother in danger? He was defenseless, small for eight years old. His little arms stuck out of his TMNT pajama shirt like twigs. She crawled out of bed, rushed to the door, and squeezed him tight against her chest.

He returned her hug, and she leaned down to kiss his soft head. He smelled like watermelon—his "big kid" shampoo. "Want me to walk you back to your room and tuck you in?"

Pulling out of her arms, he propped a hand on his narrow waist. "I'm not a baby."

Willow smiled and ruffled his crazy hair. "I know. I'll keep my music down."

"'Kay."

She watched him pad down the hall and around the corner, then shut her door and turned the lock. Leaning back against the wall, she squeezed her eyes closed against tears. What had she done?

There was a shuffling noise and a muffled "Ow" before Ashton rose up from the other side of the bed, rubbing his head. "That was much easier when we were twelve."

Willow gave him a tight smile, but her vision swam with regret.

"Hey, don't cry." He came around the end of the bed and hesitated by the second post, indecision clear on his face. Then she watched his expression harden with resolve. "I won't let anything happen to him, Wil. To any of you."

She swiped at her leaky eyes. "I think I know who's sending the messages."

He crossed the space between them. "Tell me."

So she did. They moved to the plush chairs in the sitting area of her room, and she told him her theory about Isaiah Kagawa and his connection to the kid who'd taken his picture for the flyers.

Ashton leaned back and crossed one ankle over his knee. "But if Isaiah put up the flyers, who would stuff them in his locker?"

Willow arched a brow. "So, you didn't do that?"

His Adam's apple bobbed and his lips pressed together as both of his fists clenched, but he didn't speak.

"Okay, just checking." Willow put her hands up in a defensive gesture. "Whoever did do it looked a heck of a lot like you."

He uncrossed his legs and leaned his elbows on his knees. "How do you know that?"

She told him about the trip to the principal's office and what they'd seen on the security footage.

"And this was Brayden's idea?"

Willow nodded.

"Brayden Martin? The boy who almost punched me because I wanted to talk to you at Gino's?"

"Yes, he's trying hard to make that up to me."

Ashton muttered a curse under his breath that brought heat seeping into Willow's cheeks.

But then a detail from the security footage clicked into place. "Wait." She leaned forward. "At one point the guy filling Isaiah's locker faced the camera, and it looked as if he was speaking to someone."

"So he wasn't alone. I guess that makes sense. With everything happening it would take more than one person to pull off the posters and frame me for the robbery." Ashton shook his head. "But I still find it hard to believe Isaiah would threaten you or your family."

"Me too. That's why I decided to defend you anyway. Because if it is Isaiah trying to scare me, I don't believe he would hurt a fly."

"But what if it isn't Isaiah? Or what if Isaiah isn't who we think he is?"

Willow tugged the blanket tighter around her shoulders.

"What if I have a chat with Cory? He and Isaiah used to be tight."

"Cory Martin?" she asked. Cory was Colin Martin's little brother. A year younger but worlds apart. Cory had been studious, introverted, and played the saxophone like nobody's business. He was also dead. But Ashton wouldn't know that. "Um, Ash, Cory's gone. He was killed over two years ago."

His blue eyes flared wide. "What? How?"

She swallowed before launching into the story that, unfortunately, everyone in Gilt Hollow knew by heart. "It was a horrible accident. Colin, Cory, Brayden, Isaiah, Mr.

Martin, and Chief Kagawa were preparing for a hunting trip to West Virginia. The night before they were supposed to leave, the guys were sleeping over at the Martins', and Cory went out to the garage to clean his gun . . . and it went off." Willow's breath caught, and she took a deep breath before continuing. "He shot himself. Isaiah found him and called 911, but it was too late."

Ashton pressed a fist to his mouth and squeezed his eyes closed. Several moments passed, but she stayed quiet and let him mourn. They'd both known Cory almost their whole lives. But then she realized it was more than grief on his face. She could almost hear the wheels churning in his brain as he processed this news, fitting the piece into the puzzle of what they already knew. When he opened his eyes, the force of his gaze pinned her to the chair.

He stared at her for several long seconds before he sprang to his feet, grabbed his jacket off the bed, and stalked toward the door. He reached out for the handle and then paused. Without turning, he said, "What if it wasn't an accident?"

A tremor raced across Willow's shoulders and down her arms. The thought had never occurred to her, but now that he'd said it, she couldn't deny the possibility.

His back still turned, Ashton whispered, "I can't involve you in this any longer. Don't be upset if I don't talk to you at school."

Before she could figure out what to say, he slipped out the door and shut it behind him.

CHAPTER Eighteen

The morning following her midnight chat with Ashton, Willow suggested to her mom that Rainn *might* have issues with a bully, who could *possibly* take his show-and-tell items and/or push him around. As a result, it was determined that Willow would walk him to school and Mom would take the afternoon shift—even if Rainn wouldn't admit what was happening.

As she and her brother made their way down Walnut Street, the leaves fell like snow, laying a colorful carpet at their feet. Rainn crunched through the dead foliage, stomping his boots and making roaring noises like a baby T. rex. Willow fell back and let him clomp his way down the street, sucking in a deep breath of wood-smoke-scented air. She'd lain awake half the night thinking about Cory and Ashton and what he'd said before he left her room. Willow had never believed Ashton killed Daniel Turano, accidentally or otherwise. He was a protector. She'd known it from the day she met him when he'd stopped her from jumping her bike over a creek by convincing her that the angle of the ramp wasn't steep enough and she'd end up crashing into the opposite bank. Over the years, she'd watched him go out of his way to help old women carry groceries down the street, stop a kid from taking another kid's lunch money, rescue a pet hamster from a drain pipe—you name it. The kid had been born with a hero complex.

But there had been times she'd doubted what she knew about him. Brief flashes of uncertainty, like when he'd stared laser beams of hate at her when he'd first returned to town. Or when she read that he'd pled guilty to the charges, or when Isaiah, Brayden, and Colin spread their version of the story around school. But Ashton had been locked up when Cory died, and suddenly it seemed like too much of a coincidence that the same three boys were involved.

If Ashton was right and Cory's death hadn't been an accident, how did the police overlook it? Why? It all circled back to the Kagawas. Was mild-mannered Isaiah really a psychopathic rage monster?

As they reached the elementary school gates, her own little monster raced to join his friends without so much as a wave good-bye. After making sure he was safely inside the building, Willow crossed the parking lot and spied Ashton speeding away on his bike. She'd been so entrenched in her own thoughts, she hadn't noticed him following them. She smiled to herself as she headed downtown to meet Lisa at Gino's. It was definitely a pumpkin spice latte kind of day.

But later she wasn't smiling anymore. Ashton had ignored her, as promised. And even though she knew he was distancing himself because he believed it would keep her and her family safe, what she didn't understand was why he'd attached himself to Penelope like a tattoo. He even went so far as to eat lunch with her and the Yoko Ono twins. Forced to stay inside the cafeteria because of rain, Willow watched as Yolanda and Ona laughed at Ashton's jokes and smiled at him as if they hadn't been bashing him the day before. Then to put the cherry on top, in Music Appreciation Ashton asked to switch seats and moved to the opposite side of the room.

Past ready for the day to be over, Willow closed her binder after History and had begun to gather her things when the teacher called her name.

"Willow, please see me after class."

Clutching her book bag to her chest, Willow approached Mrs. Innes's desk. "Yes?"

Willow wasn't sure why she felt nervous; Mrs. Innes was one of her favorite teachers. Her enthusiasm for history made her class fun, and with her purple pixie hair and diamond-studded nose ring, she felt relatable.

Mrs. Innes finished typing before lifting concerned eyes. "Willow, I wanted to give you this test back personally because the grade is so uncharacteristic of you." She took out a stapled packet of papers and slid them facedown across her desk. Not a good sign. With a whoosh of light-headedness, Willow reached for the packet and flipped it over, revealing a fat, red D. Her eyes flicked back and forth between the grade and her name written at the top of the page. It was her paper all right. Slumping into a nearby chair, she admitted to herself that she hadn't studied. But only because she thought she knew the material.

"Is everything all right at home?"

"Um . . ." Willow didn't know what to say. She'd just discovered a fellow student may have been murdered; she was being blackmailed via text message; she was hiding her ex-convict/ex–best friend in her attic while trying to keep him out of jail and not fall head over heels in love with him in the process. Her world had turned upside down. So, no, everything was most certainly *not* all right at home. But none of that would change the D glaring back at her like a flashing emergency beacon, so she shook her head and muttered, "Sure, everything's fine. I just forgot to study."

"Well, if you need any help before the next test, let me know. I'd be happy to meet with you before or after school."

Willow thanked her, rose from her seat, and walked to her

locker without remembering how she got there. Exchanging her history stuff for Spanish—thankfully her last class of the day—she slammed the door and almost ran into Isaiah. Her heart jumped into her throat and she glanced around, realizing the hallway was nearly deserted. The second bell buzzed, sending the stragglers scurrying into their classrooms. Leaving them alone.

Willow stepped around Isaiah. "I'm late."

"Wait. I need to talk to you."

Really? He wanted to talk instead of sending anonymous texts? She stopped cold. "What do you want, Isaiah?"

His eyes darted up and down the empty corridor before he whispered, "Meet me in the school library after the pep rally. Alone."

Then he rushed off.

Willow did the same, slipping into class while Señora Jay's back was turned. But the Spanish words that normally came so easily to her bounced off her brain like gibberish. What did Isaiah need to say to her in private? The thought of meeting with him alone kind of terrified her, but this could be her chance to find out if he'd sent the threatening messages. And put a stop to it.

Sliding her phone from her pocket and into her lap, she texted Lisa and asked her to be her backup. Her friend agreed, and they planned for her to arrive before Isaiah to hide in the stacks.

By the time the bell rang for the pep rally, Willow was wound tighter than one of Lisa's infamous topknots. And as her fellow students rushed out of their eighth-period classes early, she was caught up in the stampede, unable to find Lisa or Brayden or anyone else she knew. So she let herself be pushed along with the flow until she reached the gym.

Hundreds of voices echoed off the walls, mixed with the squeak of tennis shoes on the waxed floor and the discordant shrills of the pep band warming up their instruments.

Willow despised crowds—the stink of too many bodies clustered in one place, people touching her she didn't know. Just as she thought it, someone pushed her and she rammed into the person in front of her, a large boy who turned and shoved her sideways into the bleachers. She muttered an insult and broke out of the herd, climbing until she found an open spot in the fifth row.

Who scheduled a pep rally in the middle of the week anyway? As the cheerleaders began their first routine, Willow glanced around trying to find Lisa's bright curls but instead saw Ashton two rows behind, his dark head melding with Penelope's platinum blonde as he whispered something in her ear. Willow whipped around, heat bursting into her cheeks, her rib cage squeezing her insides until she thought she might gag. It had to be at least a hundred degrees in there. Whatever Willow thought was between her and Ashton, the magnetic energy she felt when she was with him, must be one-sided. Obviously he preferred the beautiful, flighty type.

The band joined the cheerleaders in the school fight song, and people raised their fists to chant all around her. A buzz vibrated in Willow's pocket. Praying it was Lisa texting to rescue her, she whipped out her cell and swiped in the code. But it was another SnapMail notification. Unable to resist, she pressed the icon.

> If you don't stop helping Keller,
> what happens to you will be worse
> than this . . .

The next message was a picture of Cory Martin, lying flat, arms at his sides—dead in his casket.

The room spun in a hard circle, and Willow felt herself sway. Her heart pumped so fast it hurt. She gripped her chest, the room narrowing to a shadowy tunnel as the football players ran out onto the floor. It was too hot. Too close. Her lungs constricted until it felt like she was sucking every breath through a tube. She had to get out of there.

Turning, she pushed past the kids in her row, stepping on book bags and feet, stumbling into people as she swayed. But their protests were jumbled in her brain. If she didn't get air soon, she would suffocate.

Finally out of her row, she made it down two sets of stairs before a wave of dizziness turned the room on its side and she fell forward. Her arms flailed as she tried to catch herself. She smacked hard on her hands and knees, the angle of the stairs and the momentum of her bag knocking her flat on her face. Silence spread through the room like a wave.

Then someone yelled out, "Is she drunk?" Followed by laughter and "We've got a stoner here!"

"Wait! I think she's sick."

"Somebody call 911!"

The lucid part of Willow's brain knew she was hyperventilating and would pass out any moment. She rose up on trembling arms, her vision darkening. She had to get out of there.

The floor vibrated beneath her, and she fell to her elbows, a wave of nausea rolling into her throat. Then a warm hand pressed into her back, another one taking her arm in a strong grip. "Willow, you've got to breathe."

Ashton.

Gently, he turned her over and cradled her in his lap. She dug her fingers into his arm, her eyes darting as her chest heaved up and down in an effort to suck air into her shrunken lungs. But it didn't work. Like a fish flopping on dry land, she arched back.

"Look at me, Wil." Ashton cupped her face, leaned forward, and guided her head until all she could see was the midnight of his eyes. "Focus on my voice."

A tiny opening cleared in her airway. Greedily, she sucked in a ragged breath.

"That's right." Ashton's eyes smiled. "Just like that. You know how to do this. Inhale through your nose."

His words, soft and deep, blocked out everything else. She did what he said, taking a drag of sweet oxygen as she fell into his endless blue gaze.

"Exhale through your lips."

After three repetitions, the pain in her chest began to ease, but her throat still felt constricted and her vision hazy.

"What's the funny thing your shrink told you to say?"

Willow huffed out, "Panic . . . script."

"Yeah." His thumb brushed along her cheekbone, his hand supporting the back of her head. "Let's do that. How does it start?"

"I have . . . survived . . . this . . ." *Inhale.* ". . . before and . . . I can survive . . . this time too." *Exhale.*

Her airway opened and the darkness lifted. Limp with exhaustion, Willow let her eyelids flutter shut as she took several slow, reviving breaths.

"All right now?" Ashton's sweet sigh feathered across her face, and she opened her eyes with a smile and a nod.

"Good. Do you think you can stand?"

She pushed up against him, suddenly remembering they were in the middle of the bleachers at a pep rally. His arm tightened around her waist, and he helped her to her feet. A smattering of applause erupted into a few cheers.

Several teachers, including Mrs. Innes and Mr. Rush, waited at the bottom of the stairs. Mrs. Innes gave Willow a reassuring smile and Mr. Rush, his usual scowl in place, huffed up the stairs to Willow's side. "I'll take it from here, Mr. Keller."

Seeming satisfied that she could stand on her own, Ashton withdrew his arm from her waist.

"Ms. Lamott, please come with me to the infirmary." Mr. Rush reached out a hand. "I can carry your things."

Willow handed the teacher her bag and said, "One second." Then she turned to Ashton, and anchoring her hand on his arm, stood on her toes and planted a soft kiss on the scruff of his cheek. "Thank you, Ash."

Penetrating eyes locked on hers, ruddy color tinting his skin.

"Ashton Keller, are you blushing?" Willow said under her breath, teasing a hint of a smile from him.

"Willow! Are you okay?" Brayden raced past Mr. Rush, drawing Willow's gaze.

She glanced back at Ash, then to Brayden. "I'm fine now."

Brayden's gaze drilled into Ashton, his lips pressed tight before he turned back to her. "I'll take you to the nurse."

Between Mr. Rush and Brayden, Willow made her way on shaky legs down the bleachers. Her knees and hands ached from where she'd fallen, and the image of Cory's face was still burned into her mind, but deep inside a tiny flicker of warmth glowed. Ashton had tried to show the world that he didn't care about her, but he had failed miserably.

CHAPTER Nineteen

Mrs. Innes pulled her tiny yellow eco car into the driveway of Keller House and stopped behind a painter's van. Before Willow could even open the passenger door, her mom flew down the porch stairs with her zebra-striped dreads streaming behind her.

"Sweetie, are you all right? The nurse called. I was so worried!"

"She's fine, Mrs. Lamott," Mrs. Innes reassured as Willow climbed out.

"What happened? The message only said she collapsed at a pep rally."

Willow walked around the front of the car, working to disguise the way her bruised knees caused her to limp. "I'm fine now. It was a panic attack." She leaned into her mom and wrapped an arm around her shoulders, inhaling her familiar scent of lilac and herbs.

Mrs. Innes propped her bent elbow on the open window and winked. "I think it helped that a cute boy came to the rescue."

"Really?" Mom gave Willow's arm a squeeze and asked, "Who's that?"

"Um . . ." Willow needed to change the subject . . . or did she? Maybe if her mom heard something good about Ashton, it would improve her opinion of him. "It was Ashton, Mom."

Willow felt her mom stiffen, but before she could respond, Mrs. Innes gushed, "You should've seen him! He held her in his arms and talked her through it. It was like they were the only two people in the world."

She let out a dreamy sigh, and that's when Willow remembered Mrs. Innes and her husband were new to Gilt Hollow. As part of the staff, she had to have heard the rumors about Ashton, but she hadn't let them cloud her opinion of him, making her Willow's favorite teacher of all time.

Willow faced her mom. "He remembered the breathing techniques and the panic script the doctor gave me right after Dad passed away. I was on the verge of passing out, but he pulled me back from the edge."

Her mom's lips tilted in a mechanical smile. "I'm just glad you're all right." She turned to Mrs. Innes. "Thanks so much for bringing her home."

Willow and her mom waved as Mrs. Innes drove away, then looped their arms around each other's waists and walked back to the house in silence. Wood-and-metal scaffolding was set up on two sides of the house. Men in white uniforms worked like busy little ants, painting and repairing siding. One even dangled from a harness from the third-floor turret, welding the iron railing of the widow's walk. The dizzying height sent tingles down Willow's spine, and she looked away. She'd always been terrified of heights.

They mounted the porch stairs, skipping the broken step in tandem. Inside, Willow put down her book bag in the foyer and looked up at the grimy, cobweb-covered chandelier, unable to meet her mother's eyes. "If we get permission to have the Halloween party here, let's not dust that."

When her mom didn't respond, Willow lowered her gaze. Arms crossed over her narrow chest, jaw set, brows slightly arched, Dee Lamott gave Willow the *mom look*. Willow swallowed. Her mom had asked her to stay away from Ashton, and Willow had done the exact opposite. Maybe it was time to come clean.

Mom held out her hand. "Let's make some tea and have a chat."

Perched on a stool at the kitchen bar, her hands wrapped around a steaming mug of chamomile, Willow struggled with how to begin. After Mom agreed to let her talk without interruptions, Willow decided on a selective truth. Some things, like Ashton breaking into the house, would only freak her mom out. So she started with how Ashton had been sleeping in the tree house because he had nowhere else to stay, and how he'd given his parole officer this address as his place of residence. When she got to the part where she'd told him he could sleep in a third-floor bedroom, Mom sucked in a breath and gripped her mug until her knuckles turned white, but she remained silent.

"He wanted to ask for your permission to stay here, but I kind of talked him out of it." Willow took a slow sip of tea and watched her mom bite her lip, her cheeks flaming. She rushed ahead to explain. "I knew what you would say, and I couldn't kick him out of his own house. I couldn't let you do it either."

Mom opened her mouth, shut it, and then opened it again.

Willow hated arguing with her, but this confrontation had been coming for weeks. Mentally bracing herself, she sighed, "Go ahead."

Mom shook her head and set down her cup, but instead of lashing out, her eyes liquefied. "You're just like your father. Always standing up for the underdog."

Underdog wasn't a label Willow would ever assign to Ashton Keller. Gothic hero perhaps. Or dark champion. But what did that make her in the story? The maiden? The nurturer? No, thank you. Maybe a crusader . . . like Dad.

Mom gasped as if realizing something. "He's our Pop-Tart-eating ghost." She glanced at the open doorway to the den where Rainn's cartoons were blasting, punctuated by his occasional laughter. "Does your brother know?"

"No! No one knows. Not even Lisa."

"What about Ashton's parents? I know they weren't the closest family, but why didn't he go to them?"

Willow shook her head. "They disowned him. He hasn't heard from them since his conviction."

"At all?" Mom's eyes flew wide. "He was fourteen years old!"

Which brought up another uncomfortable subject. "Mom, what happened to the letters I wrote to Ashton?"

Her mom's face froze, giving Willow the answer she'd expected. But she wanted to know why. "I don't understand. Why would you do something so horrible?"

"Willow, I'm sorry, but it wasn't your job to support him. That should've been his family's responsibility." She crossed her arms and stared up at the ceiling. "I thought cutting off your communication was the right thing to do . . . I was trying to protect you." She lowered her gaze, her eyes pleading for understanding.

Willow looked away, her fingernails digging deep into the flesh of her palms as she tried to maintain control. Picturing Ashton locked up and alone . . . year after year . . . thinking no one believed in him or cared what happened to him, made her heart ache. He'd always been a protector, but who was protecting him?

Pushing down her anger, Willow realized this was an opportunity to bargain. She leveled determined eyes on her mother. "Ashton has no one. And you kept us apart all these years. This is your chance to make that up to him. Do the right thing and let him stay here."

Mom turned and stared out the kitchen window, watching the workers as they gathered their things for the evening. When she spoke, her voice was barely audible. "I can't. I'm the only one watching out for you and your brother now. I can't allow someone I don't trust to stay under the same roof with you."

"I bet Pastor Justin would encourage Christian charity."

Mom glared and crossed her arms in front of her chest. "Leave him out of this."

Her double standard of secret keeping lit a fire in Willow. "Why don't you like Ashton, Mom? He served time for something he didn't even do!"

"How can you know that?"

"Because I *know* him." Willow shot to her feet. "Unlike you! You've never trusted him. Even when we were kids. Why? What did he ever do to you?"

Rainn appeared in the doorway, eyes darting between the two of them. "Why are you guys yelling?"

Mom crossed the kitchen. "Honey, everything's fine. Your sister and I are just having a difference of opinion." She ruffled his hair and smiled. "Why don't you head to your room and start your homework?"

"All right," he whined, his mouth twisting in a grimace before he stomped down the hall.

Mom came back and slid onto the stool across the bar. Willow took a gulp of tepid tea and waited for her mother to answer her question. "Why?"

"At first, it was more of an instinct. I didn't like the way you changed when you were with him." A small smile lifted her lips. "My little type A, structure-loving daughter became a wild thing. Do you remember when you came home with night crawlers slithering through your fingers, mud caked in your hair?"

Willow nodded. She and Ash had gone on a mission to dig up bait for fishing the next day, and she'd wanted to gross her mom out by bringing the worms into the house.

"Your dad said it was good for you. That Ashton helped you release your inhibitions and just be a kid. But it was more than that. Once Ashton came into your life, he was all you talked about, the only person you wanted to spend time with. It felt almost unnatural, the way you two bonded. Like . . ." She shrugged and looked away. "Like you imprinted on each other or something."

Willow could tell there was more. So she waited, her shoulders tensed as she braced for some horrid revelation—whatever Ashton had done that convinced her open-minded, peace-loving mother to distrust a little boy. But she wasn't prepared for what she heard.

"One night before a trip to the zoo, Ashton spent the night on our sofa. I had a nightmare about you . . . a dark force hovered near you. You were in danger."

"Momm," Willow groaned.

"Honey, you know I believe in spiritual dreams, and this one was unmistakable. When I got up to check on you, Ashton wasn't on the couch. I looked everywhere before I found him." One side of her mouth dipped down and she swallowed. "He was in your room, sitting on the edge of your bed, watching you sleep."

Ashton was watching me sleep? Willow's jaw had fallen open, so she snapped it shut. That didn't sound like him at all. She thought back to the zoo trip. Ashton would have been around twelve years old. "He was probably going to wake me up or something. He's always had insomnia. Too much energy."

"But the way he was looking at you, Willow. It was almost . . . possessive. I didn't like it." She took a slow sip of tea. "I felt like I was losing you to him."

"So you tried to separate us all of these years because a stupid dream made you question a twelve-year-old boy's intentions?" Willow's voice had risen again, but she didn't care.

"It was more than that, Willow. A thousand tiny things that set off my maternal instincts. When he was convicted, it confirmed my suspicions." Mom's lips pressed together and she lifted her chin. "I'm sorry. I did what I thought was right. Which is what I'm doing now too." She stood, her back rigid. "He can't stay here, Willow."

"But this is *his* house!" Willow shot to her feet. "He inherits it in less than three years!" When Ashton's grandfather left him the house, it had been a big deal. Ashton had seen it as the key to independence from his parents while still maintaining a connection with the grandparents he'd loved. But his father had not been pleased, and it had driven an even bigger wedge between them.

"Not right now, it isn't," Mom insisted. "My caretaker contract gives me full legal rights to use the home as my full-time residence."

"You don't think he could fight that if he really wanted to?"

Her brows drew together over her nose. "He wouldn't!"

A knock sounded on the front door. Willow offered to answer it, anything to escape their terrible conversation, but her mom was already halfway there.

Willow slumped over the bar and cradled her head in her palms. This discussion was not going as planned. Her mom truly believed Ashton was some sort of creeper. If studying history had taught her anything, it was that the best generals knew when to retreat. On her tiptoes, she crept across the kitchen and slunk into the hallway. Turning into a side corridor, she opened the first narrow door. A musty smell whooshed to greet her. The back staircase had been used by servants in the Victorian age. Crooked and eerie, Willow hadn't used it since they'd moved in. But desperate times called for—

A familiar deep voice immobilized Willow midstep. "I apologize, Mrs. Lamott. I'll have my things out tonight."

Spinning on her heel, she rushed down the corridor and into the foyer. "Ashton?" His hair stuck out on one side, his nose and cheeks ruddy, like he'd been riding his bike without a helmet. As usual.

He met Willow's gaze over the top of her mom's head. "Hi." He lifted a hand in an awkward wave before jamming it into his pants pocket. "I stopped by to check on you, but . . . um . . . how are you?"

Willow met his deep-blue gaze and had to push down the urge to close the space between them and throw herself into his arms. Instead, she walked around the tiny barricade that was her mother and offered him a warm smile. "Other than some bruises from my fall, I'm fine. Thanks to you."

The concrete set of his mouth relaxed a fraction, and he shifted his weight from one foot to the other. Plainly confused and unable to speak freely in front of her mother, he pinned Willow with a questioning gaze.

Her mother broke the tension. "Ashton, where will you stay?"

Was that concern Willow heard in her mom's tone?

Ashton ran a hand through his hair, taming the

wind-tossed waves. "Well, I'm not sure. I might try to rent a room at Hersey's B&B until I can find a more permanent place. Which reminds me—I'll need to get into the garage so I can sell one of my grandfather's bikes." His lips quirked in a self-deprecating grin. "I doubt many people would hire me around here."

"Sure, take whatever you need . . ."

"Thanks for everything you're doing, Mrs. Lamott." Ashton glanced around the foyer. "The house is starting to look familiar again."

"I'm just doing my job, but . . . thank you." Mom tugged on the tip of one dread, twisting it in a circle; a sure sign of turmoil brewing.

Willow stared hard at the familiar lines of her mom's face. Her mouth was slightly pursed, her eyes soft, head tilted to the side. Could she be having second thoughts? And if so, how could Willow nudge her to make the right decision and let Ashton stay? "Mom, do you think Ashton could eat dinner with us? You're making quesadillas, right?"

Her mom nodded. "Yes, with fresh guacamole and lime-chili rice."

"Yum! Ashton loves Mexican. Right, Ash?" He'd barely blinked when she added the clincher, "I heard Hersey's serves frozen, reheated dinners." Her mom let Rainn have the occasional Pop-Tart, but in general she believed processed food was of the devil.

"Oh! Well, I—"

A high-pitched scream cut off Mom's response.

"Help!"

Rainn's voice.

CHAPTER Twenty

Rainn's cries for help ricocheted in Willow's brain as she raced out the front door with Mom and Ashton on her heels. Once outside, she scanned the porch and the front yard for her brother's blond head, but there was no sign of him. This was all her fault. If someone had hurt him, she would never forgive herself. A choked scream escaped her throat as she ran down the front steps. "Rainn!"

"Help! I'm up here!"

All three of them raced out into the yard and spun to face the house.

"Oh my God!" Mom gasped.

Rainn dangled from a broken length of iron railing that edged the third-story roof. His little feet ran in midair, trying to gain purchase, but the gable was steep and too far out of his reach.

"Stay still!" Willow yelled, afraid his frantic movement would rip the rail from its mooring.

A few workers rushed around from the back of the house, where they'd been packing up, and one of them suggested, "I can reassemble a scaffolding below him."

The railing shifted a fraction and Rainn jerked, falling half a foot. He shrieked and Mom yelled, "There's no time!"

"What's the quickest way to the roof?" Willow asked Ashton, but he wasn't beside her anymore. He was climbing one of the porch columns like a tree. The muscles in his back bulged as he boosted himself up onto the overhang. Willow's heart catapulted into her throat.

gilt hollow

Her mom mumbled a prayer under her breath, and Willow joined her. *Please, God, let Ashton reach my brother in time.*

Ashton balanced on the porch roof, which was nothing more than a slanted sheet of metal, and made his way toward the second-story balcony. A gust of wind slammed into him and he sidestepped, slipping. Willow gasped, but he regained his balance and reached for the veranda above him.

"Mom! Help!" Rainn's voice tore a hole in Willow's chest. "I'm slipping!"

Tears streamed down her mother's face, but when she responded, her voice sounded strong. "Just a few more seconds! Someone's coming to get you!"

Ashton had scaled the narrower columns of the second-story veranda when a horrible wrenching sound ripped through the air. Rainn let out a bloodcurdling scream. Ashton pulled himself onto the tapered roof just as her brother dropped. Springing forward, Ashton threw out his arms. Rainn slammed into him, and Ashton pulled him tight to his chest. But as Willow sucked in a sharp breath of relief, the impact of her brother's body threw off Ashton's precarious balance and they both toppled backward.

Willow watched their freefall in horrified slow motion.

"Move!" A workman knocked her to the ground. Two painters stretched a blue tarp between them. "Pull it tight!" the foreman instructed. A split second later Ashton and Rainn slammed into the cloth with a whoosh. Their impact yanked the tarp out of one of the men's hands and pulled the other off his feet, causing the tarp to roll over Ashton and Rainn.

Stuck in a nightmare where she couldn't move or speak, Willow stared at the too-still cocoon of blue plastic. Why weren't they moving? Mom ran up and flung the tarp back. Rainn sat up and blinked. "Mom?"

Sobbing his name, she lifted him into her arms. Willow's eyes raked over her brother's body as he wrapped his arms and legs around their mom like a little monkey.

Willow turned back to the tarp, where one of the painters knelt over Ashton, blocking her view. "Hey, kid, are you okay?"

Willow scrambled up beside the workman, then sunk to her knees in the grass. Arms and legs sprawled, eyes closed, Ashton lay as still as a corpse.

"I think he hit his head on my knee," the man said.

Heart seizing, Willow leaned over and placed her hand on Ashton's chest. It rose and fell in a steady rhythm. Thank God, he was still breathing, but a fall like that could snap a spine or fracture a skull—paralyze someone for life. "Ash? Can you hear me?"

Years seemed to pass before he moaned and his head fell to one side. His eyelids cracked open to reveal a slit of midnight blue, and Willow's heart restarted with a shudder. Her throat burned, but she refused to let the tears come. He'd been strong. Now it was her turn.

"Don't move him," the foreman instructed. "I've called 911. The paramedics are on their way."

"Did you hear that, Ashton? You can't move, okay?"

His dark lashes fluttered several times before his gaze fastened on Willow's face. "Is . . . Rainn okay?"

Brushing his hair off his forehead, Willow smiled. "He's fine." She glanced behind her to where her mom sat on the front steps with Rainn in her lap.

Ashton lifted his head, but Willow held him down with a hand on each of his shoulders. "Whoa there. You can't move. Like, at all." When he relaxed, she asked, "Does anything hurt?"

"My head, a little."

Sirens wailed in the distance. The local fire department had an EMT squad, but the nearest hospital was twenty miles away.

Ashton's eyes flared wide. "I can't go to the hospital. I'm fine. See?" He rose up again, his head coming off the tarp before Willow could stop him. He groaned and fell back, his eyes squeezing shut.

"Hey." Willow cupped his face in one hand, brushing her thumb along his jaw. "It's okay. They can help you." The sirens grew louder, and she could see red lights flashing out of the corner of her eye.

"I can't afford their help, Wil." His eyes opened and focused on her face, his forehead creased in pain or worry or both. "Plus, I hate hospitals."

"Well, let's at least make sure you aren't broken."

Wheels screeched on the driveway as the ambulance barreled in at full speed, then slammed to a stop. The whirling lights and sirens cut off as a middle-aged woman dressed in a navy blue uniform opened the driver's side door and jumped out, snapping on a pair of disposable gloves as she walked. A man in the same uniform came around the front of the vehicle, carrying a red-and-white nylon bag. The foreman directed them to the tarp, where the male paramedic set down the bag and pulled out a stethoscope and blood pressure cuff before asking, "Where's the other victim?"

Willow pointed to her mom and brother on the steps. The paramedic walked over to Rainn as the female EMT knelt beside Ashton, directing her first question to Willow. "Hi, I'm Anita. What's your name?"

The moment Willow told her, the woman began to fire

off questions. "Are you hurt, miss?" Willow shook her head. "Can you tell me what happened?"

Anita listened as Willow described the fall, and then the EMT turned to Ashton. "What's your name, handsome?"

"Ashton Keller."

There was a flicker of surprise behind Anita's sharp brown eyes, but she covered it quickly. "Willow, I want you to hold Ashton's head with both hands. Keep the neck in line so I can assess him."

Willow moved behind Ashton and cradled his head on either side. She leaned over and gave him an upside-down smile, surprised by the fear she read in his gaze. Intent on distracting him, she said, "Hey, remember that time you jumped off the tree house roof?"

"Because I was Spiderman?" A smile tugged at his lips.

"Try not to talk, Ashton," Anita instructed as she pressed her fingers into his shoulders. "But tell me if anything hurts when I touch it." She moved down his right arm, squeezing every inch until she got to his hand, where she put two fingers into his palm. "Squeeze my fingers."

He did, and Willow blew out a slow breath as the EMT continued her examination on Ashton's other side. Willow looked back into his eyes. "You grabbed the branch, but your fingers slipped off. You had to get ten stiches."

He blinked rapidly.

"Eleven?" she corrected.

He blinked again.

She grinned. "Twelve?" When his lips quirked, she grinned. "Wow, twelve whole stitches. I insisted on going into the exam room with you, and when Dr. Beck put the numbing shot into the cut, tears welled in your eyes, and I started bawling so hard the nurse had to take me out of the room." His smile faded as the memory soaked into them both. When he hurt, she hurt, and vice versa. That's how it had always been.

Anita directed, "Ashton, push down with your feet like you're pressing on a gas pedal . . . Good. Now pull up, point your toes toward your head. Good, no paralysis."

When he'd completed her instructions with both feet, Willow turned away and blinked back tears.

"Great job." Anita crab-walked back up to where she'd left her kit. "Willow, you can release his head now."

Reluctantly, Willow let him go and moved back. The EMT pressed on Ashton's facial bones, his jaw, and then the sides of his neck. When she ran her fingers over the back of his head, he winced. "Does that hurt?"

"Yeah."

She threaded her fingers under his hair. "Did you hit your head on something?"

"I . . . I don't remember."

Willow chimed in, "One of the guys holding the tarp said he thought Ash's head hit his knee."

"Did he lose consciousness?"

"Yes."

"How long?" The woman removed her hands from Ashton's head.

"Just a few seconds, I think."

The male EMT walked over. "The kid checks out. Not a scratch on him." He squatted down beside Ashton. "Good job, man."

Anita turned a warm smile on Ashton. "You probably have a concussion. I have to take you in and let a doctor decide how long to keep you. Do you have a hospital preference?"

His gaze shifted to Willow and then back to the EMT. "I'm fine." He sat up but clutched his head with a groan.

Willow lurched forward and grabbed his shoulder as he swayed. "Ash, you need to go."

Ashton's lips pressed together, his brows lowering. "No."

She knew that look. Once he'd set his mind, there was no moving him.

"You can stay here tonight, Ashton." Mom and Rainn approached. "As long as you agree to see the doctor first."

Still seated on the ground, Ashton's gaze flicked to Willow and then back up. "Okay. Thank you."

Mom squeezed Rainn to her side, her eyes glistening. "It's the least we can do."

• • •

After Ashton was treated and released from the emergency room with instructions to have someone wake him every two hours, Pastor Justin picked them up and brought them all back to Keller House. Tucked into the massive four-poster bed that used to belong to his grandparents, with pillows propped behind his back and a tray full of Mexican food on his lap, Ashton's headache faded to the background. He could get used to the hero treatment.

He picked up a triangle of chicken and cheesy goodness and took a bite, savoring the soft crunch of the tortilla and the subtle spice. It had been too long since he'd tasted a home-cooked meal, and Dee Lamott's were the best.

As he shoved a forkful of rice into his mouth, a blond head peeked around the door frame and then disappeared. "You can come in, Rainn."

"Mom told me not to bug you," replied a disembodied voice.

"I don't mind." Ashton finished off the quesadilla in one bite, and when Rainn didn't appear, suggested, "It's kinda lonely in here."

The kid zoomed into the room like he had wheels on his feet and jumped up on the other side of the bed. "Are you really Ashton?"

Ashton choked back a laugh. The solemn look on the boy's face told him it was a serious question. "Yes . . . Do you remember me?"

Rainn cocked his head to one side and gave Ashton the once-over. "You're way bigger now, but your eyes are the same. I remember you coming over to hang out with my sister. And sometimes you'd play Super Mario Brothers with me."

Rainn had to have been around five years old when Ashton went away, but he'd followed Ashton around like a shaggy blond puppy since he could walk. After Mr. Lamott passed, Ashton had felt sorry for the kid and had spent more time with him. They'd bonded over Mario Kart, Teen Titans, and Twizzlers.

"You went to jail, right?"

Thankfully, Ashton's mouth was full, so he just nodded. "Why?"

Good question. "The police think I hurt someone."

"Daniel Turano?"

The kid was smart. Just like his sister. "That's right." Afraid of where this conversation was going, Ashton countered, "Why were you on the roof?"

Rainn leaned over and grabbed a quesadilla off his plate.

"Help yourself." Ashton chuckled.

After swallowing a bite, Rainn shrugged. "I saw one of the workers fixing the rail, and I wanted to know how he'd gotten up there." He took another bite and spoke with his mouth full. "I found the door on the third floor. You've been living up there, haven't you?"

The cat was out of the bag anyway, so Ashton nodded.

Rainn giggled. "I totally thought it was a ghost. Do you believe in ghosts?"

Ashton finished the rest of his rice and then said, "Not sure." He watched the kid squirm around for a few seconds. "Hey, don't go up there again, okay, Rainn?"

"Mom said she's putting a lock high on the door."

"Good. 'Cause I may not be around to break your fall next time. Plus"—he rubbed the goose egg on the back of his head—"ouch."

Rainn stopped moving, and his unwavering gaze tied a knot in Ashton's gut—he had the same piercing wintergreen eyes as his dad. Before he knew what was happening, the kid scrambled across the bed and threw his thin arms around Ashton's neck. "Thank you for catching me."

Ashton's throat contracted, making his voice rough, "Anytime, kid."

Rainn was off the bed and out the door before Ashton could blink.

He shook his head and popped three Advil into his mouth, washing them down with a swig of peach sweet tea. He stared at the glass and took another mouthful. The perfect mix of tang and sweet. *Delicious.* Dee had a gift.

"Ash, can I come in?" Willow stood in the doorway twisting the hem of her oversized T-shirt. Barefoot and wearing ragged, cut-off shorts revealing bruised knees, and her hair in a sloppy ponytail, she reminded him of the girl he'd left behind.

But when he told her to come in and she glided across the room, all long legs and swaying hips, he had to revise his assessment. Definitely not a little girl anymore. She came around his side of the bed, leaned over him, and peered into his eyes. A hint of her coconut and vanilla scent swirled around him, and he sucked it in greedily.

"Is your headache getting worse?" She placed the back of her hand on his forehead. "Do you feel hot? Any tingling or numbness in your extremities? Are you nauseous?"

Ashton chuckled. "Somebody's been on WebMD."

She drew back and crossed her arms under her chest, a dark brow arching into her bangs.

Ashton quirked a grin. "No, Nurse Lamott. I'm fine. Just a slight headache."

Seeming satisfied, she walked over to the rolltop desk, picked up the chair, and carried it over to the side of the bed. She sat, lowered a pair of dark-rimmed glasses onto her nose, and opened a book he hadn't noticed before.

He watched her for several seconds before asking, "What are you doing?"

Willow placed a finger on the page to hold her spot and looked up. "I'm watching you." Then her head tilted back down, hair falling across one eye, and she resumed reading.

Something heated in Ashton's chest, that undefinable thing she sparked inside of him that made him want to pick at her, to push her until he broke her perfect control. "No, you're not."

She glanced up and blew the bangs out of her face. "Yes, I am."

Ashton caught her gaze. "No. You're reading."

The delicate line of her jaw tightened. "Do I need to sit and stare at you?"

"I could have a seizure or lose consciousness and you

wouldn't even know. You're so caught up in . . ." He tilted his head but couldn't see the cover. "What are you reading?"

"None of your business," she snapped.

Gotcha. Ashton forced down a smile. "Why don't you read it out loud to me? I am an invalid, after all."

She lifted the glasses into her hair and glared.

Ashton patted the coverlet beside him. "Come sit beside me so I can see the pictures."

"There are no pictures, idiot." And then her lips stretched into a slow smile that kicked Ashton's pulse into overdrive. She was actually considering it.

He gave her his best disarming grin.

"You're a jerk."

"Come here."

"No."

"Please . . . I feel dizzy." He swayed side to side. "I might fall out of the bed and hit my head again."

"Stop!" She jumped up and grabbed his arm. "You're going to dump your food."

He stopped moving and seized her wrist in one hand while grabbing the book with the other.

"Hey!" She reached to take it back, but he held it at arms-length away from her.

"*Sense and Sensibility*," he read the title. "Sounds dead boring."

She raced around the other side of the bed, but he switched hands and opened to a random page. Hitching his voice up several octaves, he read in his best stuffy British lady accent. "Good God! Willoughby, what is the meaning of this? Have you not received my letters? Will you not shake hands with me?"

The words hit a little too close to home, and Ashton's voice trailed off as Willow plucked the book out of his hand.

She slumped back into her chair and muttered, "Not so boring, huh?"

To cover his sudden surge of emotion, Ashton took a long swig of tea, and then, no longer hungry, set the tray to the side. He cleared his throat, trying to push down the question fighting to slip out, but it was no use. "Did you really write to me?"

"Yes, she did." Mrs. Lamott stood in the doorway holding a fresh glass of tea.

Ashton's gaze darted between Willow and her mom. There seemed to be something going on with them that he didn't understand.

Dee walked into the room, gripping the glass with both hands. "Willow wrote to you for nine months, but I . . . I never mailed the letters."

CHAPTER Twenty-One

Willow watched the color drain from Ashton's face. Maybe it was selfish, but relief washed over her. He finally knew she hadn't abandoned him—at least not purposefully. But then pain, as sharp as broken glass, cut across his features, and her joy disintegrated. This wasn't over. Years of feeling betrayed wouldn't disappear because of one confession.

"Ashton, I'd like to explain." Mom set the iced tea on a table and stood on the other side of the bed, wringing her hands.

When Ashton nodded, his eyes looked dead, buffered against all emotion. "Fine."

Mom dropped her hands to her sides. "I'm only telling you this so you won't blame Willow. I don't expect your forgiveness."

Ashton's cheek tightened, and Willow could practically hear him grinding his teeth.

Willow hated conflict and she wanted to reach out to both of them—soothe Ashton's anguish and calm her mom's regret—but this was between them. She could only stand there and hope that they would find some common ground.

Mom took a step closer so her legs were pressed against the mattress. "Willow wrote to you every day for a while, then when she didn't get a response, she scaled back to a couple of letters a week. I pretended to mail them, but . . ." She broke off and turned pleading eyes on Willow. "Instead, I dropped them in the dumpster behind Bob's market."

The betrayal stung, and Willow bit her lip to keep quiet.

Ashton stared straight ahead, his eyes fixed on a faded painting of men perched in a leafless tree gazing at a cityscape in the distance. The dark, muted colors and desolate scene spoke of loneliness and loss, making it an odd choice for a bedroom.

Mom kept talking. "After Adam passed away, one of my greatest fears was not being able to raise Willow and Rainn on my own, provide for their needs, protect them from the world."

Raising her chin, Mom pressed on. "When the news reported that you pled guilty to killing Daniel, I knew keeping Willow from you was one way I could keep her safe . . . something I could control." Determination flared from her gaze. "Ashton, look at me."

He pushed himself up so he was sitting straighter and turned on her mom. When he spoke, it was with a quiet intensity that cut through Willow's gut. "You guys were like my second family. My first in many ways."

"We did care about you," Mom insisted. "We *still* do . . . I just assumed your own family would help you through." She shook her head and swiped at her leaking eyes. "I never imagined they would desert you. I'm so sorry."

The set of Ashton's jaw softened, and Willow had to fold her hands together to keep from reaching out to him.

Mom moved the food tray and perched on the other side of the bed. "Ashton, you saved both of my children today. Even risking your life . . ." Her face crumbled into a sob, but she pushed through it. "You risked . . . *your* life . . . to save Rainn. Why? Why . . . did you do that?"

There were several beats of silence before Ashton said, "The night before Mr. Lamott passed, I visited him at the hospital. He woke up for a few minutes and gripped my hand so hard, I thought for sure he'd had a miraculous recovery." A small smile ghosted across Ashton's lips. "He said you were a strong woman but would sometimes need help. And then he asked me to watch out for you all after he was gone." Ashton's throat contracted, and when he spoke again his voice was a low rumble. "I failed. But I'd like a second chance."

Mom reached out and took Ashton's hand, offering him a watery smile. "Thank you for telling me that." Her gaze moved from Ashton to Willow and then back to the boy beside her. "This place is enormous. If you'd like to stay, I think we have a bedroom to spare."

Ashton's eyes were damp when he squeezed her mom's hand. "I'd like that."

■ ■ ■

The next day, Willow did something she hadn't done in her thirteen years of schooling—she played hooky. She and her mom had taken turns waking Ashton up every couple of hours throughout the night, as the doctor instructed. After Willow's five a.m. shift, her mom had met her in the hallway and told her to turn off her alarm and sleep, which she'd done gladly.

It was almost noon when Willow rolled out of bed and into the shower. After she got dressed, dried her hair, and put on a little makeup, Willow rushed to Ashton's room and knocked on the frame. When there was no answer, she peeked around the open doorway, but his bed was empty. Surely he hadn't gone to school? The doctor had written him an excuse and instructed him to rest for the next day or so. With a shrug, she skipped down the stairs to the kitchen, hoping to find her mom. Brilliant sunlight flooded the room, but her mom wasn't there. She grabbed an apple and then stepped out the back door. The air felt warm with just a hint of autumn chill on the breeze.

"Hey, honey!"

Willow followed the sound of her mom's voice to where she knelt in the garden. Dreads held back in a multicolored bandanna, the woman yanked weeds like it was her job. Which, it kind of was. "Hey, Mom. Have you—"

"Ashton headed into the woods about a half hour ago." Mom sat back on her haunches and lifted a hand to shade her eyes. "Said he'd had enough rest and needed to stretch his legs."

"Did Rainn go with him?" Willow asked as she bent and tugged on a two-foot-tall stalk, the roots breaking free with a satisfying pop. She laid it in the basket atop the others, then gazed at all the other weeds waiting to be pulled and envisioned how neat the garden would look without them. Her fingers practically itched to dig in and clean the place up.

Mom chuckled. "Nope, I walked your brother to school when he insisted on going so he could tell everyone what happened."

"No one's going to believe him."

"That's what I told him."

Suddenly overcome with emotion, Willow fell to her knees and wrapped her arms around her mom. "Thank you! Thank you so much for letting Ashton stay."

Her mom squeezed her back. "I'm just sorry about the letters. I made a mistake. Ashton's a good kid." She pulled back and met Willow's gaze with dancing eyes. "Now, go on."

Willow grinned and hopped up. "Thanks, Mom."

Her feet knew the way, even though the fallen leaves had covered the path. She sunk her teeth into the green skin of the apple, juice bursting across her tongue as she crunched through the dried foliage. Once she reached the clearing, she chucked the apple core into the meandering stream below and stepped onto the old rope bridge, deftly hopping over the missing boards. As a kid, every time she crossed the bridge, she would pretend it was taking her into a different land, that when she set foot on the other side, she would be in Oz or Narnia or Brigadoon. But that day there was nowhere she'd rather be than walking up to her old tree house, her best friend grinning at her as she climbed the ladder.

"Hey." She popped her head through the open trapdoor.

Ashton sat with his back against the wall, an arm resting on one bent knee. "Hey."

Willow boosted herself up and stepped over his out-stretched leg, then sat on the deck. Folding her legs like a pretzel, she leaned back and stared up at the brilliant pumpkin-colored canopy above their heads. The sun shone through the variations of tangerine and amber, casting geometric patterns around them like confetti.

"It's beautiful, isn't it?" Ashton asked.

"Yeah. I haven't been out here in the fall in years. I guess I'd forgotten."

"I hadn't. I dreamed about this place. Sitting in this exact spot."

A soft wind rustled through the tree, swirling the leaves in a flashing kaleidoscope. Willow turned her head and watched Ashton soak in the sight. She'd taken so much for granted. Or maybe she'd been afraid—afraid of the memories, afraid of the future, afraid to live.

"I missed you." The words burst from Willow's mouth without any thought whatsoever.

A corner of Ashton's mouth curled up and he turned the full force of his deep blue gaze on her.

Willow's heart sputtered and then kicked into overdrive as their eyes locked.

"I missed you too. Even when I didn't want to." He reached out and tucked a strand of hair behind her ear, his smile tilting into something sad and regretful.

Regret for the time they'd lost or for what he'd done that had stolen that time from them, she couldn't be sure.

He brushed his fingers along her jaw, igniting a trail of tingles across her skin, and then he drew his hand back and fisted it in his lap.

As much as Willow longed to grab that hand and bring it back to her face, there were more important matters to resolve. "What happened that day, Ash? I know you didn't kill Daniel. But why did you take the blame?"

He didn't look away as she'd expected him to but instead searched her face. When he spoke, his voice was rusty, like the words were being torn from his soul. "We snuck away from our campsite when Mr. Martin and Cory went on a food run. We'd seen the falls earlier that day on a hike and had been talking about jumping off ever since. All of us except for Daniel." Ashton's mouth set in a straight line and he swiped a hand over his hair. "Once we'd climbed to the top, Daniel didn't want to do it. I taunted him. Called him every kind of coward. I was afraid if he backed out, so would everybody else. But Danny was really scared. He was even shaking. I backed off, and one of the guys suggested we check it out first. We all clustered together and looked over the edge. It was at least a two-story drop and there were rocks directly below, but beyond that a deep pool. I told Daniel all he needed to do was take a running jump. And suddenly he was falling."

Ashton's jaw clenched and his brows hunched over his eyes, but he still didn't look away. Almost like if he did, he wouldn't be able to say the rest. Willow reached over and put her hand on top of the one he had braced on the deck.

"As soon as he hit the rocks, I jumped. I honestly don't know how I cleared them myself, but I hit the water and sank to the bottom, then clawed my way back to the surface, my only thought"—he swallowed hard—"was Daniel. Everything after that is a blur. I remember screaming for someone to run back to camp. To get help. Isaiah, Brayden, and Colin took off and left me there with . . . the body."

Willow squeezed her fingers around his and scooted closer. He lowered his gaze to their linked hands.

"When they hauled me into the police station, I didn't understand what was happening at first. Until Chief Kagawa and two other officers took turns screaming in my face, trying to make me admit it was my fault." Ashton looked up, his eyes dark with anguish. "It *was* my fault, Wil. I didn't push him, but I might as well have. I bullied him. Told him if he didn't do it, he didn't deserve to hang with us. Plus, we were all standing so close. I couldn't be sure that I wasn't the one who bumped him."

Willow's eyes stung and she squeezed his fingers harder. "You were fourteen!"

"Old enough to know better." Ashton shook his head. "So I admitted it was my fault. The cops jumped all over it. When my lawyer finally arrived, he assured me it wasn't admissible. But after everything shook out and all three of my *friends* claimed they'd watched me push him and told the police how we'd argued, my attorney convinced my parents that it would be best to take the plea bargain . . . which required that I plead guilty to involuntary manslaughter. The DA had wanted to charge me with straight-up aggravated manslaughter, said she could prove I'd pushed him on purpose in the heat of anger.

"My parents told me to take the deal. My mom didn't want the scandal of a drawn-out public trial. And as I said, they washed their hands of me after that."

Ashton leaned back and stared up into the leaves.

"I've had a lot of time to think about what happened that day, frame by frame, backward and forward. I know I didn't touch Daniel before he fell, but when I came back here I was convinced one of the other boys accidentally pushed or tripped him and then pointed the finger at me. My intention was to uncover the truth and somehow clear my name. But someone's been working overtime to send me back to jail, which planted another idea in my mind."

He lowered his head and met Willow's gaze. "What if someone pushed Daniel on purpose and they don't want me to find out? What if that same person killed Cory Martin?"

A gust of wind sliced through the back of Willow's shirt and whipped her ponytail into her face. She removed her hand from his and hugged one of her legs to her chest. What Ashton said made perfect sense. The threats, the crimes Ash had been set up to take the fall for, even the flyers, all pointed to somebody or *somebodies* wanting him gone—badly.

"Say something, Wil," Ashton pleaded, his voice raw.

Realizing she hadn't spoken her thoughts aloud, Willow turned back to him. "I'm sorry. I totally believe you."

He let out a long breath and scrubbed a hand across his mouth, relief shining from his eyes.

A tingle buzzed along her leg, and she saw that her knee was resting on his thigh. Ignoring the giddy feeling, she said, "I was just thinking how it all fits together. Everything that's been happening seems a bit extreme. Why would someone work so hard, risk incriminating themselves to force you out of town?"

"Exactly." Ashton's hand moved to her knee.

Willow let out a gasp.

"Sorry." He jerked his hand back.

"No, it's not that." Willow guided his hand back to her leg and the heat of his skin reached her through her jeans. "Isaiah wanted to meet with me yesterday. Alone."

"What? Why?"

Willow told him about running into Isaiah in the hallway and her plan to have Lisa hide in the stacks to listen in. Ashton's eyes narrowed, but she cut him off before he could speak. "There's more. At the pep rally I got a SnapMail message that said, 'If you don't stop helping Keller, what happens to you will be worse than this,' and then they sent a picture of Cory in his casket."

Ashton's face turned as ominous as a thundercloud. "So that's what set off your attack?"

Willow nodded.

"Give me your phone."

Willow reached in her pocket and handed over her cell.

He handed it back. "The code?"

She swiped a finger across the grid, and her cheeks flamed as she realized her unlock pattern was the letter *A*. For Ashton. She'd used the same code since she'd bought the phone over a year ago and entered it without thought—until now.

Ashton didn't seem to notice as he took it back.

He clicked on something and smirked. "Brayden wants you to call him when you're feeling better. And Lisa . . ." He flicked his finger across the screen. "She texted you like a thousand times." Ashton shook his head, his grin widening. "Looks like she wants to know if you're playing hooky with Tall, Dark, and Dangerous."

"Give me that!" Willow grabbed the phone.

"Okay!" He laughed. "I'll stop reading about myself."

"How do you know Lisa's talking about you? Huh?" She punched his arm and pulled back stinging knuckles. "She could be talking about Brayden."

"Gingerboy, dark and dangerous?" He lifted a brow and took back the phone. "I don't think so."

Willow watched for a moment before peering over his shoulder. "What are you doing?"

"Shutting down your SnapMail account."

She snatched it away just before he hit the uninstall icon. "No."

"Do you like getting threatening messages?"

"No, but one of these times they're going to screw up and give something away." Willow shut the screen and tucked it into her hoodie pocket. "And next time I'm going to make them talk to me."

In that moment, Willow knew she had to help Ashton find out who really killed Daniel Turano. Whoever it was had taken Ashton from her once, and she wasn't about to let them do it again.

Willow set her jaw. "It's time to turn the tables."

CHAPTER Twenty-Two

I remembered her panic attacks from when we were kids. It's no big deal." Ashton shrugged, brushing off one of the most romantic moments of Willow's life with a wink and a smile.

"At least you kept her from passing out and ruining the pep rally," Yolanda commented.

"I know, right?" Penelope's high-pitched giggle abraded Willow's eardrums as she clutched her lunch bag to her chest and sped past.

Her stomach tightened as she searched the crowded cafeteria for a friendly face. Lisa's bright smile beckoned from a nearby table. Willow raced over and plopped down with a sigh—only to look back and see Penelope slide onto Ashton's lap and wrap her arms around his neck.

"This is going to be harder than I thought." Willow tugged her lunch toward her, knocking Lisa's water bottle over in the process. "Ugh. Sorry."

"No worries, chica." Lisa grabbed the bottle and sopped the water up with a napkin.

"Hey. Everything all right?" Brayden asked as he climbed over the bench and sat next to Willow.

"Fine," she muttered as she watched Ashton's hands encircle the hemp belt cinching Penelope's tiny waist. They'd agreed as part of their "offense plan" to keep dating Brayden and *Pen*—as Ashton called her—in order to see what they could learn from them and also as a cover to protect Willow and her family. But the logic behind it didn't make it any easier to watch.

Willow dug into her lunch, and Lisa shot her an encouraging smile. They'd had a long conversation the night before. Lisa had told Willow how she'd been camped out in the library during the pep rally, cell phone recorder at the ready, but Isaiah had never showed. And Willow had finally shared that she'd been hiding Ashton in the attic and that he was now living with them by invitation but still in secret.

Willow's account of how Ashton had risked his life to save Rainn—combined with the superhero-like reports of how he'd rescued Willow at the pep rally—were enough to make Lisa Gifford, jaded ex–New Yorker, irrevocably Team Ashton.

A chocolate chip cookie appeared under Willow's nose. She sniffed the sugary temptation and glanced over at Brayden. His warm brown eyes glimmered with that ever-present hint of humor that made her want to laugh and hug him at the same time.

"Take it. I know you want to." He wiggled auburn brows.

She snatched the cookie and took a big bite.

"Better?"

"Much," Willow mumbled as she chewed.

A tray plunked down on the other side of the table. "Why I pay for this slop, I have no clue." Colin Martin swiped the beanie off his golden hair and tucked it into his pocket as he sat next to Lisa.

Willow's friend froze with her sandwich halfway to her mouth. With as much subtlety as she could manage, Willow kicked Lisa under the table, which reactivated her arm but did nothing for the dreamy look on her face.

Colin tossed a tater tot into his mouth and launched a football conversation with Brayden that might have been in

Latin. Or at least that's how much of it Willow understood. Finally, Colin noticed the starry-eyed girl sitting beside him. He turned to her and extended his hand. "Hi. I'm Colin Martin. You're new, right?"

Proud that Lisa managed to introduce herself with minimal stuttering, Willow let her eyes wander over to Ashton's table where he and Penelope sat side by side talking to Yolanda and Ona. That's when she realized that they'd managed to split the popular table. For years Yolanda and her friends had exclusive rights to the Martin cousins, the two boys sitting beside her now.

"You're coming, right, Weepy?"

Willow turned to Colin and tried to hide her annoyance. He was the missing piece—the other boy with motive to want Ashton out of Gilt Hollow. She needed to get to know him better. "I'm sorry?"

"My end-of-the-season party this weekend."

"It's a blast," Brayden chimed in. "We do a bonfire, roast marshmallows, and play games." He grabbed her hand under the table. "I can pick you up and we can go together."

Willow returned Brayden's beguiling grin, and then, the smile dropping from her face, turned back to Colin. "I'll come on two conditions."

Colin quirked a brow in surprise. "What's that?"

"One, you invite Lisa." Willow lifted an index finger.

He turned and winked at her friend. "Done."

Lisa's cheeks flushed a brilliant pink.

"Two." Willow raised her fingers in a V and stared Colin down. "You never call me Weepy again."

Colin's eyes narrowed for a fraction of a second, and Willow thought he would refuse, but then his lips curled and he gave a single nod. "You got it . . . *Willow*."

■ ■ ■

"Isaiah!" Willow speed-walked through a maze of ambling students until she reached his side. "Hey, sorry I missed you the other day, but I guess you heard what happened."

"Yeah." He glanced over at her. "You okay?"

"Yes, but I was hoping we could reschedule our . . . meeting."

"Shh!" Isaiah scanned the people around them and walked faster. "I can't. I'm sorry. Just forget about it, okay?" He cut to the left and into his next class.

Willow stopped at the doorway and stared after him in stunned silence. Had it been her imagination or had he seemed . . . scared? She turned and headed toward the stairs. If Isaiah had been the one sending her threatening texts, then who was he afraid of? Or what was he afraid of her finding out?

She rounded the bottom of the staircase, and someone grabbed her arm, yanking her sideways through an open door. She screeched and tried to jerk away, but the person's hand clamped over her mouth as a powerful arm tightened around her waist from behind. "Wil, it's me," Ashton hissed just as he shut the door, thrusting them into complete darkness.

Slowly, he released her and pulled his hand away from her mouth. She drew in a sharp breath, and the scent of chemicals told her they were in a janitorial closet. Willow waited for the anger to kick in, but her adrenaline only fueled a hyper-awareness—of Ashton's solid strength pressing her back into the door, the heady taste of his breath, the fingers of his left hand a loose cuff around her upper arm.

The darkness giving her courage, Willow raised her palm and pressed it against the muscled wall of Ashton's chest.

Beneath a soft layer of cotton, his heart thumped hard and fast. She raised her chin, and it was like lifting her face to the sun. Heat buzzed across her lips as recklessness thrilled through her. If she rose onto her toes, threaded her fingers through his hair, and pressed their mouths together, would he kiss her back? Did he want that as much as she did?

Her pulse slammed in her ears as she flexed her toes and started to rise, but before she could, he released her and stepped away.

Fury and embarrassment flared through Willow in equal measure. "Was that really necessary? We shouldn't even be in here!"

"Don't worry about that. Do you have your phone on you?"

For a moment, she couldn't remember. Then she felt around her feet to where her bag had fallen and pulled her cell from the outside pocket. Blowing her bangs out of her eyes, she swiped in the code, the light of the screen almost blinding. Ashton took it and held it up to illuminate a piece of notebook paper. "I found this in my locker after lunch."

Willow met Ashton's gaze, his eyes glowing an ethereal blue in the radiant light. She tucked her hair behind her ears and stared at the note, reading the messy script out loud. "I know you didn't kill Daniel, but the person who did won't stop until you're gone for good."

Willow's eyes darted back to his. "Do they mean *gone*, gone?"

"I don't know, but check out the writing."

It looked as if the letters had been written by a child, scrawled in an odd combination of lower and upper case. "Why didn't they just type it?"

"I wondered the same thing. I think it indicates a spur of the moment decision."

Willow nodded. "That makes sense." She thought for a second. "We can show this to the police as evidence!"

Ashton shook his head. "It won't mean anything to them. I could've written it myself. Plus, I don't trust Chief Kagawa."

"That reminds me, I tried to talk to Isaiah—"

Ashton grabbed her upper arms in a fierce grip. "*Please* don't do that on your own. He could be dangerous."

The heat of his touch burned through the layers of Willow's sweater, scorching her skin. But it wasn't enough. She took a tiny step into him, and the very air between them went still. Ashton muttered a curse just before he pushed her back against the door, the cell phone falling from her hand. "Is this what you were hoping for?" His voice was low and rough, and Willow felt it vibrate through her spine.

"Maybe."

"Me too," he whispered as his lips pressed into hers.

Willow's world exploded, lights bursting behind her eyelids as Ashton's hands tangled in her hair. He captured her bottom lip and then he tilted her head, his mouth flush with hers as he deepened the kiss. Electricity flashed through her body and she gripped the front of his shirt.

Ashton groaned and wrapped his arm around her waist, pressing her full against him. He slanted his mouth the other way, and it was like they couldn't get enough of each other. The earth spun out from under her, and Willow clung to him, something wild causing her to pull at his hair and bite his lip. His fingers dug into her neck, and then he let her go.

Willow stumbled back, waves of heat washing over her as she sucked in ragged breaths. The air between them was so charged, she feared they might detonate the chemicals in the room. She pressed cool palms to her fiery cheeks and tried to clear her head.

Without warning, the door flew open. Automatically, Willow stepped into Ashton and he pulled her close. She raised a hand against the onslaught of fluorescent light, feeling a bit like a mole being unearthed.

"Go on. Get out of here, you two," a man holding a mop handle said in a tired voice, as if he encountered couples in his workspace every day. Maybe he did.

Willow shot Ashton an I-told-you-so-look as they grabbed their things and scrambled into the hallway. They were a total cliché.

"You might want to get a better lock, Charlie," Ashton quipped as he tossed something small and metallic at the janitor.

"I never thought of that before, Mr. Keller." The old man shot them a toothless grin and flicked the paper clip back at Ashton, who caught it against his chest with a laugh.

"How do you know him?" Willow asked as they walked away.

"Charlie? He's a good guy. Helped me scrub the paint off of Isaiah's locker. I would've been sanding away all night if he hadn't come to my rescue with an aerosol paint remover."

"They made you do that?" Willow gasped.

"Yeah, McNachtan said they couldn't prove it was me but asked me to do it as an act of good faith. It was either that or a week of detention." Ashton slanted a glance at her. "Which I didn't see as an act of good faith at all."

Willow rolled her eyes at his cavalier attitude. When were people going to stop blaming Ashton for every bad thing that happened?

They paused at an intersection, an awkward silence descending on them.

"I better go. We're already late." Willow pivoted toward Study Hall.

"Wait." Ashton reached out but just managed to pinch her sweater, pulling it off one shoulder. His eyes zeroed in on her exposed skin. "Talk tonight?" he asked as he stepped close, his exquisite blue gaze drifting to her mouth.

"Yeah," she breathed, hoping they would do more than talk.

His warm fingers brushed her cheek, and he leaned in, his breath tickling her ear as he murmured, "You taste like strawberries."

His words slid through her, weakening her knees.

He pulled away and shot her a wicked grin. "See you later."

All she could do was watch as he turned and strode away.

* * *

Ashton walked through the library. Tomb-quiet after school, it had always been Isaiah's favorite study spot. In middle school, he'd fallen asleep at one of the large slab tables and been locked in the building. That had been right after his mother left—when he couldn't stand the house he'd grown up in and all the happy memories.

That kid, the one who'd shared his heartache with Ashton, didn't seem capable of homicide, or of setting him up to take the fall. But psychopaths were notoriously good liars. Ashton had learned that the hard way in juvie.

He turned a corner and drew closer to the electronic glow of a computer monitor behind a partition. When he'd decided to chat with Isaiah, he'd known he would need to tread carefully—appeal to his old friend's sense of justice and rein in his own anger. But as he stared at the back of Isaiah's head, his pulse throbbed in his ears and he had to take a calming breath. Had this kid been threatening Willow? Rainn? Had he shot his best friend, Cory Martin?

Isaiah's head whipped around, his dark eyes wide. "Dude! You scared me!"

"Sorry, man." Ashton pulled a chair over, spun it around, and straddled it backward, hoping the barrier would keep him from throttling answers out of the kid. "How've you been? We haven't had much time to talk since I got back."

"I'm fine. How about you?"

"Not so good, actually. And I was hoping you could help me."

Isaiah closed his laptop and began to gather his things. "Um . . . well, sure."

"We used to be friends once, right?"

Isaiah gave a stiff nod.

"I could really use someone on my side right now." Ashton reached over and set the warning note on the table. "Would you happen to know anything about this?"

Isaiah blinked at it.

"Willow Lamott's also been receiving warning messages that have become increasingly threatening. Have you heard anything? Anyone talking about my friendship with Willow? Or anyone wishing I would leave town?"

Isaiah shoved his laptop into his bag, and he stiffened his shoulders, his whole demeanor changing. "Could be anyone. I've heard tons of people talking about how their parents don't think you should be allowed back at the school." He met Ashton's gaze unflinchingly. "Why put yourself through it? Why come back here when you could start fresh somewhere else?"

Isaiah sounded so much like his father, the self-righteous police chief, that Ashton had to clench his fists to keep from slamming his old friend against the wall. Instead, he took a deep breath and answered Isaiah with a question of his own. "Do you think Cory's death was an accident?"

The color leached from Isaiah's tawny complexion, and he looped his bag over his shoulder. "I've got to go. My dad's picking me up out front." He shot to his feet and darted toward the exit.

Ashton stood and grabbed Isaiah's arm. "Wait . . ."

Isaiah turned, his brows slanting over his nose. "Cory was my *best* friend." His eyes shifted past Ashton and then back. When he spoke again, his voice shook. "Just before Daniel's accident, Cory told me that Colin and Brayden had gotten into big trouble for something. Something illegal. You might want to start there." He jerked his arm out of Ashton's grasp and jogged out of the library.

Ashton watched him go; no way could he risk pursuing him with the police chief waiting outside. But clearly the kid was still lying. Either that or he'd just told a selective truth—or perhaps the perfect distraction to throw Ashton off his trail.

* * *

Willow decided to stop in town before going home. She needed time to think. Plus, Lisa's mom had picked her up after school for a mother-daughter shopping trip to a mall in the next town. Lisa had invited Willow, but she'd declined. Perusing clothes she couldn't afford was not her idea of fun. She'd drained the rest of her spending cash on the short leather boots she was wearing, an essential part of her current look. She'd taken extra care with her appearance that morning, agonizing over her hair and makeup. But did all of that really matter? When she and Ashton had kissed, he couldn't even see her.

Her lips buzzed at the memory, and she bit the inside of her cheek against a full-blown grin. Of course, walking down the street and smiling to herself was hardly the strangest thing going on in downtown Gilt Hollow.

As she turned onto Main, she passed a group of college kids knitting a sweater around a tree. It was called yarn bombing, and people had been doing it in Gilt Hollow for as long as Willow could remember. Some claimed it was a statement of rebellion against "the system" or a way to reclaim and personalize sterile or cold public places. Others saw it as art, a form of nondamaging graffiti.

The multicolored stitches appeared on everything from street signs to parking meters to an abandoned bicycle chained to a stand, but Willow's all-time favorite were the fuchsia leg warmers someone knitted onto the statue of the Annherst College founder, Deke Willis. She laughed every time she thought about the statue's dignified pose—chin lifted high, one hand on his hip, the other clutching a diploma like a sword—and fluffy leg warmers circling his boots. *That* was a statement she could get behind.

A guy wearing more makeup than Willow and with knitting needles stuck in his aqua Mohawk called out to her as she passed. "Come join us in vandalizing commercialism!"

Willow would hardly consider pastel rainbow yarn a tool for vandalism or a tree as commercial, even if it was in the business district. But whatever, it looked cool. "No, thanks. But keep up the good work!"

"Will do!" he shouted as she crossed the street and then opened the door of Gino's.

The scent of roasting coffee beans made her mouth water, but she was already hyped up enough. After ordering a hot cinnamon cider, she found a quiet table and pulled out her neglected homework, starting with biology—which used to be her best subject. She'd always gotten good grades, but they didn't come easy; she had to work for every A. Unlike some people who showed up for class, didn't crack a book, and still made the honor roll. Like Ashton.

And that was all it took for her to relive every delicious, mind-numbing detail of the kiss. She sighed and set down her notebook. Her neck and cheeks heated, which was the exact reason she'd forced it out of her mind all afternoon. Well, that and the guilt niggling at her gut. She'd kissed one boy and agreed to go out with another in the same day. And even though she'd decided to stay close to Brayden to see what he knew, she was beginning to have doubts.

She really liked Brayden. He was funny and thoughtful, and she enjoyed being with him. But her relationship with Ashton felt like something else entirely. As Lisa had so eloquently summarized it—there's always one who's good for you and one you can't resist. Brayden was like her favorite blanket, nice and cozy. But Ashton challenged her, lit a fire in her heart and soul. No matter what obstacles were thrown at them, they always found their way back to one another. Maybe that was fate or destiny. Or . . . what did Pastor Justin call it? *Providence.*

Willow cradled the warm mug in her palms and stared out the window at the blustery afternoon. On the surface, Brayden may seem good for her, but he'd been at the falls. And although she had a hard time believing he'd been the one to kill Daniel and point the finger at Ashton, he'd still lied and likely knew more than he was saying. She needed to find out what. But she would have to tread carefully.

"Hello, dear." An old lady slipped into the seat across the table. "You're looking much livelier than the last time we met."

Willow smiled, remembering the sweet, if slightly senile woman who'd helped her the day she was fired from CC's. "Oh! Hi, Mrs. McMenamin. How are you?"

A discreet glance beneath the table told Willow that Mrs. M wore her usual flannel nightgown and cowboy boots, but at least this time she wore a long wool coat on top.

"I hear you're dating my nephew." Mrs. M lifted a cup to her lips, steam wafting across her face.

"I am?" Willow tilted her head in confusion.

"Yes, dear, Brayden is my great-nephew." She blew on the hot liquid and then took a sip, making a satisfied noise after she swallowed. "And Colin too, of course."

"Oh, I didn't know." Willow took a drink of her own beverage, unsure what to say. "Um . . . Brayden and I, well, it's not serious . . . but we're going out. I guess."

"Well, he certainly thinks the world of you. Wouldn't stop talking about you at dinner the other night."

Willow had no idea what to say to that, so she took another sip of cider.

Mrs. M seemed to have no trouble filling the silence. "Are you doing okay with Ashton Keller being back?"

Willow blinked but realized everyone in town likely knew their history. "Yes . . ."

"Nice boy, that one. Did you know he used to mow my lawn for free?"

"No, I didn't." But it didn't surprise her one bit.

"It never sat well with me, what happened."

Willow set her cup down. "How do you mean?"

Mrs. M's gaze wandered out the window, and her eyes grew dreamy. Then she began to sway and hum as if she were listening to music that only she could hear.

"Mrs. M?" Willow reached across the table and took the woman's hand, the bones and skin fragile like papier-mâché. "What were you going to say?"

Her wistful gaze returned to Willow. "About what, dear?"

"About what happened to Ashton Keller."

"Oh yes. I just never trusted those Martin boys." She shook her head, her gaze focusing again. "When they'd come to my house as children, they were always getting into trouble and then lying to cover for each other. Mr. McMenamin and I called them the Trouble Twins, even though they were just cousins. As individuals they were fine, but put them together and havoc ensued."

Willow just stared.

Mrs. M chuckled. "Boys will be boys, I guess."

"I guess," Willow muttered, but her brain was spinning. What if Isaiah wasn't guilty at all? What if the Martins had convinced him to cover up their crime?

Bass pounded in Ashton's chest as he unloaded a box of new vinyl. He cut the packing tape and opened the flaps, breathing in the unique scents of cardboard, plastic, and history. A fresh shipment was like opening a treasure chest. Jeff never paid him for his help, unless you counted buying the occasional album at top dollar—like the 1969 Stones record Ashton had sold him that day. Jeff claimed he had a buyer lined up in the UK, but Ashton suspected that was bull. His old friend still felt guilty for the robbery fiasco—that he hadn't been able to convince the chief of Ashton's innocence.

Ashton slipped Metallica's *Master of Puppets* into a clear plastic sleeve, thumbed through the *M* section, and filed it between Metal Church and the Mighty Mighty Bosstones. Jeff couldn't keep Metallica in stock for long. But offering a minimal supply of each band made his clientele feel like they'd found something special and prompted them to buy.

Seeking a bit of peace, Ashton had opted to hang around after their transaction. Twisted Beauty had been his refuge since he could ride a bike to town by himself, but today every song seemed to claw at his heart. Even the act of filing reminded him of *her*.

He pulled another LP out of the box as the turntable in the corner dropped a new record with a soft plunk, followed by the anticipatory scratch of the needle. It was an old '80s tune, one of Jeff's favorites. Piano, haunting and sweet, wove through the shop before it melded into a throbbing rhythm that seeped into Ashton's blood and pulled him back into that closet with Willow—the curves of her face, the taste of her lips, the feel of her skin. Kissing her had blown his expectations out of the water. But with them it was more than physical. He knew her heart and she knew his. Willow was his rock, and he was her spark. She balanced him, reminded him of who he was. But more than that, she inspired him to become better—a person worthy of her.

Ashton would totally walk the world, as the song vowed, if it would make her fall for him. He had no clue if their make-out session had been an impulsive thing for her or something she'd been dreaming about . . . like him.

Suddenly he had to know. He picked up the box and carried it to the counter. "I gotta run, Jeff."

"That's cool, kid. Everything okay?"

Ashton felt a stupid grin spread across his face. "More than."

Outside he glanced down the street at a new tree sweater in progress and smiled. Only in Gilt Hollow. His phone vibrated. He pulled it out of his pocket and felt a rush of disappointment that the text was from Penelope.

Need to talk.

That situation was getting tricky. The girl had a one-track mind. He'd kissed her a few times, but it had become more like an obligation than a joy. Her connection to Colin made her a valuable resource, and not just to make Colin jealous—which he couldn't deny had its benefits.

Before he could reply, the phone buzzed again.

Meet me at the barn in 30.

Penelope's father owned an eighty-acre farm on the outskirts of town. They'd "hung out" a few times in an abandoned barn on the back forty. But Ashton had no desire to "hang out" with her at the moment.

He typed:

> Can't. Rain check?
>
> It's important. Overheard
> something that could help u.

Ashton had talked to Pen about the fact that someone was setting him up and trying to get him thrown back in jail. He'd kept his theories about who and why to himself. She didn't seem capable of connecting the dots, which was fine by him. But he'd asked her to keep her ears open to anything that sounded suspicious.

He hit the call icon. But the phone went directly to voice mail.

When he glanced back at the screen, she'd typed:

> Sorry, need to tell you in person.

With a sigh, he replied:

> Alright. C u soon.

■ ■ ■

The sun had begun to set, casting half of the barn in shadow. Ashton turned off his bike, lowered the kickstand, and dismounted. The place felt deserted. No sign of Penelope or the golf cart she usually drove around the property. Ashton ducked through the rotted-out door, and a flock of blackbirds exploded through a hole in the roof, setting his pulse racing.

A single ray of glistening sunlight bisected the dark interior. Ashton walked toward it and called out, "Penelope?"

A blur of movement to Ashton's right caused him to tense and raise his fists. Penelope jumped and threw herself into his arms, wrapping her legs around him with a giggle. "It's just me, silly. Were you going to punch me?"

"You startled me." Fighting annoyance, he walked forward, peeled her limbs from around him, and set her on the bed of an old hay wagon. Her feet were bare and filthy, making him wonder why she never wore shoes outside of school. "What did you want to tell me?"

Penelope grabbed his hand and tugged him closer. "Don't be in such a hurry." She blinked up at him, eyes wide, lips in a perfect pout.

"Sorry." Ashton swiped a hand over his hair. "It's just kind of important."

She dropped his hand and leaned back, sticking her chest out.

Ashton resisted the urge to roll his eyes. She had no idea how unattractive he found her pushiness. He crossed his arms and waited. Wind whipped outside, causing loose boards to clank together all over the barn. They might as well have been in a house made of Tinker Toys.

"Okay," she huffed as she slouched forward. "It's not even a big deal. I overheard Yolanda say Cory was at the falls when Daniel died. You knew that, right?"

"Cory Martin? Colin's brother?"

She nodded, and everything inside Ashton came to a grinding halt. He had to force air into his lungs before he could speak. "Cory wasn't there. He went on a food run with his dad."

Penelope shook her head. "Yo said something about him following you guys and hiding in the woods."

"Who was she talking to? What was the conversation about?"

Twisting a length of platinum hair around her finger, she sighed. "She was talking to Ona. And I don't know. I walked up halfway through the conversation."

"You didn't think to ask?" Ashton barked.

Her face crumbled, her chin quivering. "I . . . I didn't think it mattered . . . since Cory's gone anyway."

Ashton ran a hand over his face and took three deep breaths. The girl was either dumber than a box of pet rocks or she was pretending . . . feeding him information to set him up. Baiting him into doing something rash. When he'd asked her about the Martin cousins getting into trouble with the law just before Daniel died, she'd hedged and looked away, refusing to give him a straight answer. Could she be working for the other side? Playing him just like he was playing her? Either way, this information strengthened his suspicion that Cory's death wasn't an accident—established a possible motive. But he couldn't afford to let them know what he suspected, so he rummaged up a smile and took Penelope's hand. "I'm sorry. You're right, it doesn't really matter." She looked up, and he brushed the hair off her shoulder. "But I appreciate you telling me."

She leaned in for a kiss, but he pulled away. "We should go. This place is about to fall down around us." In confirmation, a gust pushed against the barn, whining through the rafters. The entire structure quivered.

Penelope hopped off the wagon and linked her fingers through his. "Come to the house? We can hang out in the basement." She leaned into him and lifted her chin, batting tawny lashes in flirtation. She was attractive, no doubt. And she was a nice girl. But now when he looked at her, he could only see Willow's dark, mysterious gaze, glittering with intelligence and fire. "Sorry, I have somewhere I need to be."

Her face fell, and guilt pinched Ashton's gut. How could he think she was working for the other side? There just wasn't enough going on in her pretty head to deceive him.

Ashton squeezed her fingers and quirked a half smile. "See you tomorrow?"

"Fine." She stomped over to where she'd hidden her golf cart at the side entrance of the barn.

Ashton strode outside, anxious to get home and tell Willow what he'd learned. It didn't bring them any closer to finding out who was behind the two tragic deaths, but it did point to a more sinister plot than he'd dared imagine.

As he mounted his bike, a light rain began to fall. He twisted and stared at the helmet strapped to the back. Something inside tugged at him to wear it. He grabbed it and pulled it over his head. Wil would be proud of him for taking the proper safety measures, for once. He fastened the strap under his chin, started the engine, and took off.

Two minutes later he was forced to throttle down. The velocity of the bike turned every raindrop into a tiny bullet pounding his chest and stinging the exposed skin of his hands and neck. It didn't help that he had to wipe the liquid off of his face shield every few minutes. So he didn't notice the vehicle on his butt until it was too late.

He rounded the first turn in a sharp S-curve as an engine revved behind him. Ashton whipped around just as the car accelerated and smacked into his back tire. The impact shot him forward and his heart slammed into his throat as the front wheel wobbled, weaving back and forth. He gripped the handles with all his strength, trying to compensate, but the frame began to shudder out of control.

As the car sped past, it clipped the left handlebar, jerking it out of his grip. Ashton sent up a quick prayer as the bike tilted into a sideways skid. Steel sparked across wet blacktop, and then the bike rocketed off the side of the road. He let go and flew clear of the screaming machine before smacking hard into a ditch.

He gasped, realizing two things at once—he was still alive and he couldn't breathe. His mouth opened and closed like a guppy as his lungs caught fire. He tore his helmet off and arched back. Nothing. Panicked, he sat up and pounded a fist against his diaphragm. His torso felt like ice. He gave his ribs another jab. With a sharp wheeze, his chest expanded, beautiful air inflating his lungs.

For several long minutes, Ashton lifted his face to the rain and relished the luxury of oxygen. But then a shiver wracked through him and he noticed he sat in water up to his waist, was soaked to the skin, and was likely going into shock. Hands trembling, he unzipped his jacket pocket, extracted his phone, and dialed 911.

So much for staying off Chief Kagawa's radar.

* * *

Willow walked faster and tried to stay under the trees. The rain had begun while she was still warmly ensconced inside Gino's. Now it was dark and the gentle showers had turned into a downpour. Since they didn't own a car, she couldn't call her mom to come get her, so she lifted her hood and marched on. But soon the protective material lay wet and soggy around her ears and she was chilled to the bone.

A gust of wind twisted through the branches overhead, dropping heavy leaves on her head and shoulders. She plucked at the slick foliage and resisted the urge to glance behind her. The hood muffled her hearing against the night—against the warning of someone approaching. A finger of panic traced down her spine and she picked up her pace. She never used to be afraid to walk the streets of Gilt Hollow alone. How quickly that had changed. After her conversation with Mrs. M, she didn't know who she could trust anymore.

The rev of an engine sounded behind her and she whipped around with a smile, anticipating a black Indian Scout motorcycle. But the dark-colored Toyota that pulled to a stop at the curb didn't look familiar. The window whirred down and a voice called her name. She stopped and bent down to find Isaiah Kagawa.

"Can I give you a ride?"

The back of her neck tingled in apprehension and she started to decline, but then realized this was an opportunity to talk to him alone. With a fortifying breath, she strode over to the car. Isaiah pushed the door open for her from the driver's seat, and she ducked inside.

"Thanks." She lowered her hood, a cascade of water falling around her shoulders. "Sorry, I'm soaking your car."

Isaiah pushed a button and raised the passenger window, muffling the rush of rain. "No worries. This thing is prehistoric." He shifted the car into gear, which automatically threw the locks.

When he didn't press the gas, Willow swallowed, trying to find her voice. "Um . . . you can take me to Keller House."

"That's right. I forgot you were living there now." Isaiah hooked his left arm on the steering wheel and turned toward her.

The car felt small and Willow resisted the urge to lean away. "Yeah, my mom's the new caretaker there."

"Does Ashton stay there now too?"

It was a legitimate question, so why had Willow's throat closed? Maybe because Isaiah felt too close. Or because rain reflected in streaky shadows across his face like tears . . . or blood.

Willow took a breath and reminded herself of what she'd learned from Mrs. M. Her assumptions about Isaiah could be totally off base. "No, well . . . Ash comes to pick stuff up once in a while." Wow, lying was really not her thing.

"Huh." Isaiah's gaze narrowed on her face, reminding her of his father. "Then where is he staying?"

"I couldn't really say." She shivered.

"Oh, sorry. You must be freezing." He turned to the dashboard and cranked up the heat.

"Thanks." She ran her fingers through the front of her hair and then wiped her hands on her leggings. "So why did you want to meet me the day of the pep rally?"

Without looking at her, Isaiah let off the break and accelerated into the street. "I just wanted to talk to you about something."

Obviously.

Forcing a light tone, she prompted, "I'm all ears. Even if they are a little wet."

He chuckled at her lame joke and turned onto Walnut Street. They were almost home.

"Seriously, Isaiah, I can tell something's been on your mind lately. If it's about Ashton, you don't have to worry; I'm not going to judge you. It makes everyone a little nervous that he's back. Including me."

Which was not a lie, even if he made her nervous for an entirely different reason.

"It's not that . . . Well, sort of."

Willow forced herself not to speak. Instead, she listened to the rattle of the heater and the whoosh of the windshield wipers. It was a trick she'd learned from her dad. Whenever he wanted her to confess to a rule she'd broken, he'd sit in the same room with her, patient and quiet. She would hold out as long as she could, which wasn't long. Not that she was scared of him. His punishments were never harsh; she just didn't like to see the disappointment on his face. But the silent treatment worked every time.

Isaiah let out a tiny sigh, like the air leaking out of a dying balloon, and Willow knew she had him. He turned into the driveway and put the car in park. "What I'm about to tell you cannot ever leave this car."

"I understand."

"I didn't see Ashton push Daniel off the falls that day."

Willow sucked in a breath and bit her lip. The wipers swished, and the rain beat against the roof.

"I hate that I lied. I can't even *look* at Ashton." Isaiah gripped the steering wheel until the bones stood out beneath his skin.

"Why are you telling me this?"

"Because I want you to convince him to leave Gilt Hollow."

"Why would I do that?"

"Because he's in danger."

Willow's mouth dropped open. "You're the one who put the note in his locker."

Isaiah turned to face her. "Willow, if you care about Ashton at all, you'll convince him to leave and never come back."

Headlights shone through the back window. Isaiah glanced in the rearview mirror, and all the color drained from his skin.

Willow pivoted to find a police cruiser parked behind them. The rain slowed to a drizzle, and Willow leaned farther into the backseat, peering through the foggy back window. "Oh no. Is that Ashton?"

Without another thought, she jumped out of the car and approached the cruiser. Ashton sat in the passenger seat with the door cracked, one foot against the cobbled drive. The set of his brows told her he was not happy, but at least he was in the front seat and not behind the Plexiglas divider. Willow drew closer and heard him say, "I told you, it happened too fast for me to see the driver's face, but it was a dark sedan and we were the only two vehicles on the road."

Willow tripped over her own feet but righted herself before she fell, and rushed up to the half-open door. "Ashton, what happened? Was there an accident? Where's your bike?" She swallowed the lump in her throat. "And why are you wearing pajama bottoms?"

He stood and towered over her with a scowl. "I'm fine." His eyes bore a hole into her skull, but it was as if he looked right through her. "I just came by to pick up one of my other bikes."

She blinked. He didn't want the police to know he was living there. "Sure," she said a bit too loudly. "Come on inside, and I'll get you the garage key."

Ashton leaned into the car, bracing his hand on the roof. "Thanks for the ride, Chief. Let me know what your *investigation* turns up."

What in the world was going on?

When the chief didn't respond, Ashton straightened and slammed the door so hard the window rattled. He winced.

"You're hurt," Willow accused and reached for him.

He stiffened and jerked away from her touch. "I said. I'm. Fine." Then he pivoted on his heel and stalked toward the house.

Willow shook her head in exasperation and noticed Chief Kagawa was on his phone, the sharp tone of his voice leaking outside the car. When she walked up to thank Isaiah for the ride, he was also on the phone; by his blanched face, she had to assume he was talking with his father. She thanked him for the ride, and he gave her a single nod before she shut his passenger door.

Worry for Ashton propelled her inside. The house was dark and quiet, and she remembered Mom and Rainn were serving dinner at St. Vincent's. Willow dropped her bag, toed off her shoes, and shrugged out of her jacket. "Ashton?" No answer.

After hanging her wet things in the laundry room, she headed up the stairs. Light leaked from under the door of the hall bathroom. She stood outside, debating whether to knock and ask if he was okay, when the door swung open.

Ashton stood there, framed by the soft yellow overhead light, wearing drawstring pants low on his hips and no shirt.

Sweet Baby James!

Willow stood completely motionless, her eyes drinking in the rippling plains of his stomach, his powerful chest, and his wide, solid shoulders. He was all smooth, tan skin over hard muscle.

"Like what you see?"

She raised her eyes, expecting to see a darkly amused grin. Instead, his face looked like stone—cold and unyielding. She blinked in confusion until she remembered that when he'd skinned his knee or fallen off his bike as a kid, he didn't want comfort. And if anyone tried to help him, he would lash out, covering his vulnerability with annoyance.

Steam curled into the hall, and she realized the shower was running. "I'll let you . . . um . . . finish what you were doing." When he got like this, the best strategy was retreat.

Willow spun away, but he grabbed her arm. "Why were you in Isaiah's car?"

She shot him a glare. Was he jealous or worried or just angry at the world? Either way, his demanding tone sparked something in her gut, and she yanked her arm from his grasp. "None of your business. Why are you wearing those"—she gestured to his thin, paper-like pants—"pajamas?"

Ashton stepped toward her, his face set in hard lines. "They gave them to me at the doctor's office because my jeans were half ripped off." He took another step, and Willow moved back. "When a car slammed into my bike and I slid across the pavement and rocketed into a ditch."

"Oh my gosh!" Her hand flew up to cover her mouth.

The ice in his eyes began to thaw, but he stood stiff as a board.

Willow lowered her hand and reached out to the bruise blooming across his ribs. She didn't touch it, afraid she would hurt him. "Are they broken?"

He gave a single shake of his head in response.

"What else?"

Their eyes locked, and she noticed his breaths were labored and shallow, his face flushed.

"What else?" she insisted.

With a grimace, he reached down and lifted his right pant leg and then pulled off a corner of the bandage covering his thigh. His skin looked like someone had taken a cheese-grater to it—red, raw, and seeping. "It's just road rash." Ashton reattached the bandage and lowered his pant leg, clenching his jaw as he straightened.

"You could've been killed!"

"I think that was the idea."

Willow blinked up at his rigid face for several seconds, her heart pounding a symphony in her chest, and then reached her arms around him as gently as she could and laid her head on his bare chest. After a brief pause, Ashton returned her hug but lost his balance and had to brace one hand against the wall. Awareness rippled up and down Willow's body as he pressed her tighter against him, the scent and texture of his skin setting her nerve endings ablaze.

She felt his breath in her hair just before he kissed the top of her head. "Sorry for being a jerk. I don't deserve you."

She glanced up, arched her brows, and quipped, "This is true." Then she shut off her emotions and went into organization mode. Helping him into the bathroom, she made him sit on the closed toilet seat while she turned off the shower spray and plugged the stopper. After she turned the water back on to fill the tub and checked the temperature, she grabbed two bottles from the ledge and grinned. "Batman or Ninja Turtle?"

She and her mom had their own bathrooms, but Ashton shared this one with Rainn. He glanced back and forth between the bottles. "Batman, all the way."

Willow poured a dollop of blue liquid under the faucet, releasing the overpowering scent of bubblegum.

"Seriously? Batman, the baddest superhero of all time, smells like chewing gum?" Ashton complained.

Willow turned the bottle in her hand. "It's Bubblegum Blast."

"Awesome. I can't wait to smell like an eight-year-old."

Willow took Ashton's body wash and shampoo from the shower caddy and set them on the ledge of the tub, got a fresh towel and washcloth out of the closet, and laid them within reach, and then turned to her six-feet-three, two-hundred-pound friend and bit the inside of her cheek. "Um . . ."

"I can get in the tub by myself, Wil." The devilish grin she'd been looking for earlier tilted his mouth and lit his eyes.

She swallowed hard, the fact that he could've been killed pressing down on her like invisible hands. A wave of fury tore through her, a storm brewing that threatened to take Gilt Hollow down in its wake.

Not wishing to upset him with her rush of emotion, Willow turned on her heel and headed out of the bathroom, throwing over her shoulder, "I'm taking a shower. Then we need to talk."

■ ■ ■

Sitting in front of a blazing fire—if one could call a gas-generated fire blazing—Willow combed out her freshly showered hair and watched Ashton drink his tea. He lounged in one of the overstuffed chairs in the sitting area of her bedroom, his legs stretched out and crossed at the ankles, his eyes at half-mast. He'd told her what he'd learned from Penelope, and she'd shared what Mrs. M had said about the Martins, as well as what Isaiah had told her in the car. Then Willow had forced Ash to take one of the pain pills Dr. Beck had given him. After he downed two PB&J sandwiches, a bag of chips, and two cups of chamomile, the medicine finally seemed to have kicked in.

Willow set down her comb and was about to suggest Ashton go to bed before he passed out, when his eyes flickered open. His voice barely audible, he asked, "Do you think there's someone out there watching over us?"

Willow stood from the hearth, then perched on the edge of the other chair and considered for a moment before answering. She'd gone to church her entire life. She'd had her ups and downs with God—like when her dad passed away and when Ashton was taken from her—but she never doubted his existence. The perfect order of the universe, the life-sustaining architecture of the earth, the miraculously complex information contained in DNA all spoke to the logic of a higher being.

She and Ashton had had this discussion before, but this time it didn't seem like he wanted to debate the issue. "You know I do. Why do you ask?"

He set his mug down and straightened with a wince. "Something told me to wear a helmet tonight . . . Granted, it was raining, but in some ways that makes wearing a helmet harder. They protect your face from the rain, but it can make it near impossible to see. The paramedic on the scene took one look at the banged-up helmet and said it probably saved my life."

Fighting back a wave of cold panic, Willow said, "I'm shocked they didn't send you to the hospital."

He cracked a grin. "When Dr. Beck checked me out, he said my new nickname should be Miracle Boy."

Willow didn't find it the least bit amusing. She pulled her chair closer to his so she could take his hand. "Do you think someone tried to kill you because they found out what Penelope told you about Cory?"

"Shh." Ashton pressed a finger against her lips. "I can't think . . . right now."

He threaded his fingers through her hair, cupping the back of her neck as he leaned forward. Willow closed her eyes, and their lips met in a single searing kiss that she felt all the way to her toes.

Ashton pulled away and murmured, "Just making sure."

"Of what?"

"That I didn't imagine how good you taste."

Willow grinned at the dreamy look on his face. "I like Morphine Ashton."

"If you like me so much, break up with Brayden." He met her gaze with wounded eyes, his mouth pulling down like an angry toddler as he swayed in his chair.

"Okay, that's it. Time for nighty-night, big guy."

After helping him down the hall and into his bed, Willow pulled the covers up to cover his chest and asked, "How's the leg?"

A goofy smile curled his lips. "Feels like baby dragons are tinkling on it."

Willow swallowed a giggle. "And your ribs?"

"Like marshmallow Peeps," he muttered.

"Perfect."

His eyelids lowered, and she reached over to shut off the light but stopped midreach.

"Forgive me?"

Willow lowered her arm slowly and met his unguarded blue gaze. Pretty sure he didn't know what he was saying but unable to resist this rare opportunity for a glimpse into his inner thoughts, she asked, "For what?"

He blinked long and slow but then worked hard to focus on her face. "For leaving you when you needed me most . . ."

Willow sucked in a breath. She couldn't move as their eyes locked. All the resentment she'd buried over the years— her anger that he'd gone off the deep end after her father died, that she had to pick up the pieces of the mess he'd made, that he'd screwed up so badly he'd destroyed a friendship she thought was unbreakable—all leached out of her in that moment. He'd suffered so much, and so had she, but they could turn it around. Make a fresh start. She took his hand, his strong fingers limp with the sedative, and wondered if he'd remember any of this in the morning. "Of course, I forgive you."

He grinned dreamily. "Good."

His eyes drifted closed again and his head fell to the side. Willow clicked off the lamp. Unable to tear herself away, she stood waiting for her eyes to adjust. Just enough moonlight filtered through the drapes to illuminate his beautiful face. She'd heard once that some wounds ran so deep they could never heal. When Ashton had first returned, she'd believed the betrayal and hurt between them was irreversible. But as her eyes traced the familiar freckles scattered across his nose, the stray curl that always hooked behind his left ear, and his thick, dark lashes at rest against his olive cheeks, she knew second chances were possible.

As his breathing deepened, Willow leaned down and dropped a quick kiss on his lips. "Love you."

She straightened with a start and blinked back hot tears. The words had popped out of her mouth without thought or premeditation, but it was true—had always been true. She loved Ashton Keller with all her heart.

Willow swiped away the moisture on her cheeks and walked to the door. She glanced back at his peacefully sleeping form, the steady rise and fall of his chest, and straightened her spine. She'd almost lost him, this time forever. No way was she going to let that happen. If the police wouldn't help them, then they would help themselves. She was tired of running blind through the woods, something dark and menacing biting at their heels. It was time to fight. Time to turn and look the monster in the face.

CHAPTER Twenty-Four

Though Willow tried to talk some sense into Ashton, he refused to accept a ride to school from Pastor Justin—who'd shown up on their back doorstep that morning as if by magic—and insisted on walking with her. Low gray clouds swept overhead, and a chilled wind whisked the breath from their mouths. Déjà vu hit Willow like a ton of bricks as they headed down Walnut Street. But the feeling shattered when she looked up and met Ashton's vivid gaze, and a fever rushed over her skin. Everything had changed.

To cover her reaction, Willow skipped ahead and walked backward. "Come on, old man. At this rate, we're going to miss first period."

He shuffled a little faster, and Willow could tell from the set of his jaw that he was in pain. So she strode back to his side and looped her arm through his. "Do you think what Mrs. M told me about Brayden and Colin is true? Or just crazy old lady ramblings?"

"We played war with those two. They always had each other's backs and they could be relentless. But so could Cory. I don't think we can make any assumptions."

A cold breeze whipped Willow's hair across her face, causing her to shiver. Ashton tugged her closer against his side, and she had to think for a second before she remembered her train of thought. "None of the pieces are fitting together. We need to find evidence. It's one of three people. Or maybe just two. Isaiah seems to want to help you."

"Either that or he's trying to throw us off his trail. What

better way to divert suspicion than make us think he's on our side?"

"I hadn't thought of it like that."

"Isaiah's car looked a heck of a lot like the one that mowed me down. When I described it, Chief Kagawa couldn't hide his surprise. After that, he acted like the whole thing was an accident."

Willow sucked in a quick breath. "What if Isaiah pushed Daniel and his dad knows it? What if they found out Cory knew and—"

Ashton's gaze drilled into hers. "Stop. Right now. This is over for you. Do you hear me?"

"What?" Willow dug in her heels, pulling him to a stop. "But that's what they want! For us to give up."

Ashton dropped her arm and faced her. "What if it's you next time? I couldn't live with myself if something happened to you." His finger snagged a strand of her hair and tucked it behind her ear. "Please, Wil. Promise me you'll let it go."

Willow searched his dark gaze. Together again, despite everything that had worked to tear them apart, she was starting to believe there was a reason they'd been reunited—and it wasn't so he could take the bad guy down on his own.

"I can't do that. We're a team." *And it's your turn to be my sidekick for once,* she thought before grabbing his arm and tugging him down the sidewalk. "Speaking of which . . . Are you going to Colin's party on Friday? We should *totally* coordinate our outfits."

"Ha, ha." He was quiet for a moment. "Are you going with Brayden?"

"Yes."

"Then I'm going."

■ ■ ■

Techno pop blasted from the patio speakers and reverberated across the pool and out to the lawn, where fifty or so of Willow's classmates milled around the raging bonfire like drunken moths to a flame. Willow sat in a lawn chair, balancing two metal skewers on her knees, while Brayden relived every play of the final football game with his buddies. Oh, and drank. She'd never been to a high school party, but it was way less romantic than portrayed on the CW.

Willow pulled one of the hot dogs out of the fire for inspection, decided it wasn't crispy enough, and stuck it back in the flames. Lisa had hitched a ride with her and Brayden but was currently flirting with a linebacker named Reggie. Searching for another familiar face, Willow met Ashton's stare across the fire. He'd managed to get another one of his granddad's old bikes running and had zoomed off to pick up Penelope, just moments before Brayden arrived. Their ruse was beginning to wear thin, in more ways than one.

Ashton's lips quirked up on one side and he winked. She shot him a playful grin but looked away before it melted. Even though she knew his relationship with Penelope was part of the master plan, it was hard to see their fingers laced together. And harder not to wish it was her by his side.

The wind shifted and the heat of the fire pushed hot against her skin. Deciding the dogs were crisp enough, she pulled them out and went to the condiment table for plates and buns. After assembling the hot dogs, she tentatively breached the mass of football players but didn't see Brayden among them. After asking, she learned he'd gone inside to "take a leak," so she handed the plates off to two eager boys and grabbed a Solo cup. She glanced over her shoulder and, when she found Ashton's back turned, knew it was time to put her plan into action.

As she approached the house, she took a sip of the dark yellow liquid, just to make it believable, but almost gagged. How did people drink that swill? Pasting a loopy smile on her face, she tripped over a deck chair and then laughed too loud as she stumbled into a nearby classmate and sloshed half her beer at his feet. "Whoops!"

"Take it easy there, Willow."

She giggled and wove her way around the sparkling pool and through a sliding door, which led her into a finished basement. Pulling the door closed behind her, she stepped into the warmth of the house. Soft music played from the huge flat screen, the perfect backdrop for the couples paired up all over the room. Keeping up her drunken act, she half shouted, "Where's the bathroom?"

Without raising his head from the girl in his arms, one of the guys pointed past the television. Willow strode across the room and into the darkened corridor. The first door had a light shining underneath, but when she tried the handle, it was locked. The next two doors revealed a weight room and a laundry area—which was occupied with more than dirty clothes. She quickly shut that door and headed toward the stairs. At the stop, she found a handwritten sign:

THE PARTY STOPS HERE!

Willow pressed her ear to the wood and listened. Nothing. After silencing her phone, she cracked the door and saw a dim kitchen but heard no footsteps or voices. She pushed on the door and stepped through, shutting it with a soft click. The kitchen opened to dining and family rooms and an office behind glass french doors. The space smelled of pine and the lingering scent of fresh-baked cookies. Hardly the lair of a killer.

There were two corridors branching from the main living area—one angled off the family room and the closer of the two just beyond the kitchen. If Colin had any secrets to hide, they would probably be in his bedroom. She glanced around cautiously and then rushed across the kitchen and into the closest hallway. Met with four closed doors, she hesitated. Should she start with the first door or the last? The closest was likely a bathroom.

A creak somewhere in the house propelled Willow down the hall. She heard footsteps and the murmur of voices in the kitchen before she slipped through the farthest door on the left and shut it behind her. Breathing hard, she leaned against it and waited for her eyes to adjust to the gloom.

She blinked a few times and saw a twin bed, neatly made with a navy blue comforter, a dresser topped with a TV and gaming console, and a floor-to-ceiling bookshelf. She took a few cautious steps inside. The room smelled stale, like a guest room rarely used. And somehow, she didn't picture Colin being so tidy. She crossed to the window, set her Solo cup on the dresser, and cracked open the miniblinds. As she turned, moonlight glinted on something in the corner. Willow gasped, her hand flying to her mouth. A saxophone. This had been Cory's room.

Willow was so focused on Colin that she'd nearly forgotten about his brother. The room was untouched, from the notebooks and pens on his desk to the stacks of books on his nightstand waiting to be read.

Feeling like an intruder on the Martin family's grief, she tugged the blinds closed and crossed the room, trying to control her shaking limbs. Her heart pounding in her ears, she rushed into the hallway and stopped. How could she even consider the possibility that Colin could have killed his own brother? She eyed the room across the hall. She had to be sure.

Willow slipped inside and knew immediately by the strong scent of Axe body spray and sweat that she'd found Colin's room. A low-wattage lamp on the bedside table illuminated the space, confirming her assumption—clothes strewn over every surface, the covers on the bed twisted in disarray, and a football uniform spilling out of a hamper in the open closet. She'd found it. Now what? It wasn't as if she expected him to have a confession typed out and waiting for her, but she had to start somewhere. So she crossed to his desk and tapped on the spacebar of his open laptop. A box appeared asking for a password.

Hacking not being one of her gifts, she typed in a few halfhearted guesses before moving on to search the desk drawers. When that produced nothing unusual, she went to the closet. On the top shelf tucked behind an assortment of beanies and folded clothes, she spied the edge of a box. Standing on her toes, she lifted a pile of sweaters and set them on the floor, then slid the wooden box off the shelf. The lid was engraved with Colin's name and held tight by a rusted lock with an old-fashioned keyhole. A perfect place to keep secrets.

She put the box on the desk and then turned in a slow circle. If she were hiding a key, where would it be? A door slammed somewhere in the house and she jumped, panic tingling down her arms. What if someone caught her in Colin's room rummaging through his private things? What if *he* found her? She took two strides toward the door and stopped. An image of Ashton's bruised ribs and torn flesh after his accident made her pause. She had to find out who was after him and why. Ashton couldn't do this himself. If he were caught snooping in the Martin's house, he'd get more than chastised or embarrassed; he'd be arrested and hauled into the police station—which is exactly what the real killer wanted.

Fisting her hands in determination, she turned back to search for the key. She rummaged through the nightstand drawer and then moved to the dresser. When that turned up nothing, she stared at the old chest of drawers again, something niggling at the back of her mind. It was dark cherry wood and built almost exactly like hers, with three small drawers across the top and two rows of larger drawers underneath. She snapped her fingers and pulled the small middle drawer all the way out.

Sure enough, in between the two drawers on the second row was a narrow, rectangular space. A hidey-hole just like the one she'd used for her diary. She reached in and felt around, her fingers touching cool metal. She pulled out an ancient-looking key and raced over to the box. Realizing Brayden or Ashton would start looking for her soon, her hands shook as she hurried to insert the key, but she had to try three times before she got it.

Glancing over her shoulder to ensure the door was still tightly closed, she turned back and lifted the lid, almost afraid of what she'd find—and Ashton's face stared back at her. The old newspaper clipping read: "Local Boy Confesses to Killing Classmate" and showed Ashton's eighth-grade class picture beneath.

The box was full of newspaper clippings. She riffled through, skimming headlines.

"Distinguished Keller Family Tainted By Scandal." Pictured were Ashton's parents rushing away, heads down. His mom covering her face with her purse.

"Three Young Heroes' Testimonies Key to Keller Conviction" showed Colin, Isaiah, and Brayden smiling into the camera.

Her stomach clenched. They were actually smiling like they'd done some great deed. Willow didn't remember seeing that one and realized it must have been published after she began to boycott the *Gilt Hollow Gazette*. She moved on to the next one.

"Winston Keller on Suicide Watch." Ashton's dad was shown in a business suit, his head low.

Willow's heart gave a squeeze and she paused to read.

> Sources close to the Keller family say the real estate mogul had seemed increasingly depressed since his only son, Ashton Keller's, incarceration for manslaughter in August. Appearing in public unshaven and haggard, and then disappearing for weeks at a time . . .

Willow skimmed to the end of the short article.

> It is unknown if Mr. Keller made an attempt on his own life, but it's believed he is now recovering in a treatment center in Arizona. His wife of nineteen years, Catherine Arnett-Keller, was unavailable for comment.

Willow shook her head and wondered if Ashton knew. Her time slipping away, she continued to shuffle through the box and, at the bottom, came across a single article about Cory's tragic death. But what did this mean? That Colin had a sentimental streak?

A loud scrape followed by voices made Willow start. She shoved the articles back in the box and turned the key, then realized the voices were coming from outside the house. She tiptoed over and lifted the edge of the blinds.

". . . can't do this anymore. I'm out!"

One shadow grabbed the other and yanked him forward. "You're out when I say you're out."

"Let. Me. Go."

That was Brayden's voice! Willow changed her angle to get a better view and could just make out Colin's face as he released Brayden's shirt. They stepped away, and Colin's next words were muffled, "You're . . . as guilty . . . the rest . . ."

A noise sounded from the hallway, and Willow spun around, dropping the blinds with a clang. Her pulse ratcheted out of control as she grabbed the box and raced to the closet. She shoved it back onto the shelf, just remembering to return the stack of sweaters. Deciding at the last second not to return the key, she slid the dresser drawer back into place and spun around as the handle began to turn. Why had she kept the stupid key? What if Colin found it missing?

Too late to change her mind, she dropped it into her bag and grabbed a tube of lip gloss. She'd just lifted it to her lips when Mrs. Martin walked in. "Oh, Willow! You startled me." Her hand pressed against her chest as her gaze focused on Willow's freshly glossed lips. A slow, knowing smile curled her mouth. "This isn't the way to win Colin's attention, dear." She shook her head, her eyes sympathetic, as if she were used to dealing with her gorgeous son's groupies.

Willow could feel her face flaming, which seemed to confirm Mrs. Martin's theory.

"Why don't you come with me to the kitchen? I just made cookies." She reached out a hand and gestured for Willow to precede her through the door.

A few awkward minutes later, Willow leaned against the

kitchen island and forced herself to shove the cookie into her mouth in two bites. "Mmm. So good. Thank you, but I better get back."

"Not yet."

Willow froze at the woman's tone, her pale blue gaze—so much like her son's—narrowed on Willow's face. Bracing for a lecture on promiscuity, Willow was shocked when a glass appeared before her on the counter.

"You'll need some milk to wash that down."

"Oh, thanks."

"Willow, I know things have been hard for you, but hiding in a boy's bedroom is not an appropriate way to get attention. Is it?"

And there it was. Willow swallowed hard. "No, ma'am."

The basement door swung open, and Willow whipped around ready to beg whoever it was to rescue her. Isaiah stuck his head in without coming up. "Oh, there you are, Willow. We're about to start Ghosts in the Graveyard, *in* the actual graveyard behind the house." He wiggled his fingers. "Spoookyyy."

"I'm coming!" Willow plunked down the glass, and turned on her heel as Isaiah backed down the stairs. "Thanks for the cookies, Mrs. Martin."

"I'm so very proud of that boy."

The random comment cut Willow off mid-flee. "Isaiah?"

Mrs. Martin wiped her hands on a dish towel. "Overcoming that nasty business with drugs."

"What?" Willow had no clue what the woman was talking about.

"Oh, I . . . it was a long time ago. Daniel thought he saw Isaiah dealing, but . . . nothing ever came of it."

"Daniel Turano saw Isaiah dealing drugs?" Willow asked in disbelief.

Mrs. Martin nodded, her cheeks reddening as if she'd been caught gossiping in church.

"But why haven't I heard about any of this? Why didn't Isaiah go to jail?"

Mrs. Martin busied herself cleaning up Willow's dishes. "I don't know. But I think it's best you get back to your friends."

Willow made her way out to the pool area and found it deserted. Belatedly, she remembered she'd left her Solo cup in Cory's room, but it was too late to go back. No one would know it was hers anyway.

"Where have you been?" Ashton's urgent whisper startled her, and she spun around to find him lurking in the shadows.

"Did you send Isaiah to find me?"

"No. Where were you?"

Willow glanced around to make sure they were alone before she replied, "Snooping."

Ashton pushed off the wall and stalked forward. "I thought we agreed we were done with that."

"No, you agreed. I—"

The back door swung open and an older gentleman, blond hair graying at his temples, walked out carrying a tray of marshmallows, chocolate bars, and graham crackers. "Willow, right?"

"Hi, yes." As he drew closer she realized it was Mr. Martin. She hadn't recognized him because he'd gained at least fifty pounds since she'd seen him last.

"Can you take this out to the bonfire for me?"

"Sure." Willow accepted the tray.

Mr. Martin turned and his face hardened. "Ashton."

Ashton gave the man a single nod. "Mr. Martin."

The door clicked shut behind Colin's dad, and Willow muttered, "Well, that was awkward."

"Don't change the subject." Ashton crossed his arms over his chest and stared down at Willow with lowered brows. "What did you find in the house? And don't bother lying. I'll get it out of you one way or another."

Wondering if he had any idea how menacing he could look, Willow set the food on a table behind her and crossed her own arms. She told him about finding Cory's untouched room, the box full of articles in Colin's closet, the overheard conversation, and then what Mrs. Martin had said about Isaiah. "Is the woman delusional or what? I've never heard that before."

Ashton let out a sigh and pushed a hand into the hair at the nape of his neck. "She's not crazy. I'd heard rumors, but Isaiah would never talk about it."

"I can't believe you didn't tell me. This changes everything, because if Daniel ratted him out, maybe Isaiah pushed him on pur—"

A bloodcurdling scream rent the air, joined by another, and then a cry for help. Willow and Ashton exchanged an alarmed glance before sprinting toward the field.

By the time they reached the edge of the graveyard, they had to push through a group of kids to see what had happened. In the center of the crowd, Yolanda and Ona knelt on the ground, crouched over a prone figure. Ona sat back, and Willow could see Penelope as still as death, her platinum hair spread around her, a dark stain spreading across the side of her white sweater. *Blood?*

"I called 911," Lisa announced in a calm, clear voice as she walked into the open. "Someone needs to meet them at the driveway so they know where to come."

"I'll go!" Several people, including Brayden, volunteered and took off at a run.

Willow gave Ashton's hand a quick squeeze just before he stepped forward and knelt next to Ona. "Is she . . . ?"

"She's . . . still breathing." Ona reached over and brushed Penelope's hair off her forehead. Yolanda was holding the unconscious girl's hand and whispering reassurances.

"What happened?" Ashton's voice sounded raw.

"She was . . ." Ona swiped at the tears streaking mascara down her face. "She was the ghost . . . and supposed to be hiding. I . . . I . . . found her like this."

Yolanda stopped her gentle murmurs and raised her eyes to Ashton. "She's been stabbed."

Just as Ashton started to rise, Colin flew through the air and tackled him to the ground. Insults pouring out of his mouth like fire, Colin slammed his fist into Ashton's gut. Ashton wheezed, gripping his damaged ribs with one hand. Willow stumbled forward, but someone held her back.

She whipped around to find Isaiah's stern face. "Don't."

Colin landed a blow to Ashton's face. "I'm gonna kill you for what you did to her, you lowlife—"

But he never finished. With lightning speed, Ashton wrapped a leg around Colin and flipped him onto his back. Colin flailed, trying to fight back, but Ashton pinned his arm and smashed a fist into Colin's nose. Without hesitating, Ashton followed with a left hook to Colin's jaw. Colin used his free hand to defend his face, and Ashton delivered a blow to the throat instead. Colin's eyes flew wide as he struggled for breath, but Ashton kept hitting him—his fist hammering into Colin's head over and over. The football team closed in and stood watching. Why weren't they stopping this?

Ashton's face was a cold mask of rage. Willow jerked

away from Isaiah and sprang forward. "Ashton, stop!" The pummeling continued. "Ashton Arnett Keller!" Something clicked behind his eyes, and his movements slowed. Colin moaned, his head falling to one side.

Willow approached slowly and touched Ashton's shoulder. "Ash?"

His jaw tight, he leaned into Colin's face. "I would *never* hurt Penelope, you scumbag. But I can't say the same for you." Giving his chest one last shove, Ashton rose to his feet as sirens sounded in the distance. He turned, his eyes burning into Willow's.

Reading his mind, she took his hand and led him away from the crowd. It was only a matter of minutes before he was arrested.

* * *

Blue and red lights swirled behind Ashton's closed eyelids, cutting apart his life with every rotation. He would never hurt Penelope—never stab *anyone*. But the police had found the knife, and the glimpse he'd caught of its curved, mother-of-pearl handle looked suspiciously like one of the blades from his grandfather's collection. Not that the police could know that, but Ashton knew. And the knowing carried piercing implications—whoever had done this had broken into Keller House, endangering Willow and her family, and stolen the knife with the express purpose of setting Ashton up for the crime.

His heart slammed inside his chest, the throb in his head intensifying with every beat. His return to Gilt Hollow hadn't been entirely altruistic. He could admit that revenge had fueled him. One vision had driven his every thought, his every action—the one who'd set him up losing his life, his future—just as Ashton had. Suffering—just as he had. Disappointing everyone they love—just as he had. The identity of the person didn't matter. In his mind, Brayden, Colin, and Isaiah had morphed into one hideous monster responsible for wrecking his life. And all he'd wanted to do was slay the beast.

But then Willow had given him a second chance, trusted him despite everything, and the terrible wrath swirling inside him had calmed. The need for vengeance had dissolved into dreams of clearing his name and starting fresh. He dug his fingers into his knees until his hands ached, the future he'd begun to hope for disintegrating with every whirl of the tires beneath him.

The cruiser pulled to a stop, and Ashton opened his eyes to see the brick facade of the police station. Deputy Simms exited the car and came around to open Ashton's door. When Ashton didn't move, Simms leaned in and gestured for him to get out. But Ashton's muscles had locked. What if the brief walk from the car to the station was the last free air he ever breathed?

"Let's go, Mr. Keller. The chief wants you booked and ready for questioning by the time he finishes his investigation at the Martin place."

Panic twisted his gut. He couldn't go back to being locked in a cage, and for a brief moment he considered running. He could knock Simms out, nab his keys, unlock the cuffs, and steal the cruiser in less than two minutes. He could run to Mexico, get a job on a farm, and never look back.

Simms grabbed his arm. Ashton sucked in a deep breath,

his muscles tensing. His instincts screamed for him to run as far and as fast as he could.

But then he exhaled and got out of the car. He couldn't do it. He couldn't leave the Lamotts with no explanation. Willow would worry herself sick, and besides, running would only make him appear guilty. He would have to stay and fight for his freedom.

Officer Simms steered Ashton from the cool night air through the double doors, a blast of stale heat blowing onto their heads. "I need to call my lawyer."

"Oh, you'll get your call." Simms tugged Ashton down a short hallway, stopped in front of a bank of cells, and unlocked the first door on the right. He gave Ashton a hard shove, and he tripped forward, his hands still cuffed in front of him. "When the chief is good and ready."

The metal door clanged shut, and as the lock clicked into place, déjà vu pressed down on Ashton's shoulders. He slumped onto the narrow cot. It was the same cage they'd put him in the day Daniel died.

CHAPTER Twenty-Five

W illow bit her lip hard to keep the frustration from pouring out of her mouth. Mr. Martin drove his Lexus at a snail's pace through the fog-shrouded streets. She tapped her foot against the floorboards and shoved her thumbnail between her teeth, knowing she could've run faster than this old man was driving.

The cops had questioned everyone at the Martin house as they'd huddled under blankets and sipped hot cocoa while Ashton had been handcuffed and shoved into a police car. It hadn't surprised Willow that Ashton was the primary suspect in Penelope's stabbing. She'd told anyone who would listen that they'd been together at the pool when Penelope had been attacked, but the cops just nodded and moved on.

What *had* been a surprise was Bill Martin turning up after the cops left and offering to drive Willow to the station. Brayden had protested at first, but when Mr. Martin insisted, he'd let her go. Heat blasted from the car vents, permeating the air with the sharp scent of burning dust, but Willow couldn't stop shivering. She *needed* to get to Ashton, to see him and make sure he was okay.

"Did you know my son Cory?"

Mr. Martin's voice cut through the thick silence, making Willow start. She turned and met his gaze. Purple shadows hung under his bloodshot eyes and deep lines bracketed his mouth. He and her mother had graduated from Gilt High the same year, but he appeared at least ten years older.

"Y-yes. I knew him." Cory's soft brown eyes and wide smile flashed across her memory.

"He was a good kid." Mr. Martin's voice trailed off as he applied the brake and steered the car into a sharp curve. "He loved to hunt." A smile lifted his profile. "He didn't really care for sports, like his brother. He didn't have that same competitive drive. Music and the outdoors, those were his passions."

Having no idea what to say or why Mr. Martin would talk to her about Cory at a time like this, Willow just nodded.

"Did you know we called him turtle-boy?" He chuckled under his breath, but the laughter held a bitter twist. "The turtle and the hare, those were my two sons to a T."

Willow stayed quiet.

"Colin rushes from one activity to another. Doesn't even stop moving when he's eating. But Cory couldn't be rushed through anything. He was thorough and precise in everything he did. Especially when it came to weapons."

The words hung in the artificially heated air between them, carrying an almost physical weight. Willow swallowed and turned back to face him, her question little more than a whisper. "You don't think what happened to Cory was an accident, do you?"

He pulled the car into the police station parking lot and guided it into a spot near the front door. When he turned to her, his fleshy face had set into hard lines. "No. No, I don't."

Willow sat stunned, implications swirling through her mind. Had Mr. Martin suspected someone murdered Cory but kept silent because his oldest son, his nephew, and the police chief's son where the most likely suspects? Why had he told her, of all people? And why was he getting out of the car? She'd assumed he was just dropping her off, but when she hadn't moved, he stopped and waited until she joined him, and they walked into the station together.

The first floor of the building was one large room divided by a reception area and then, behind it, two rows of desks. Hallways and several closed doors branched off the main room. Mr. Martin stopped at the front desk. "I need to speak with Chief Kagawa immediately."

The officer didn't even look up from what he was typing on the computer. "The chief is busy. Take a seat and I'll let him know you're here." He gestured toward a row of mis-matched chairs and a beat-up table marred with cigarette burns.

The bang as Mr. Martin's fist hit the countertop nearly stopped Willow's heart. "I need to talk to him now! Or, by God, I'll find him myself!"

The officer leaped out of his chair and rounded the desk, but Mr. Martin was already rushing into the station. "Kagawa!"

The cop ran after Mr. Martin and jerked him back by the shoulder. "Sir, you can't go back there!"

Mr. Martin whirled on the officer and stared him down. "He's got the wrong kid back there, and *this time* he's going to listen to me."

This time?

"What in all that's holy is going on?" Chief Kagawa barked as he strode into the room.

Mr. Martin didn't hesitate. "Ashton Keller didn't stab Penelope Lunarian. He was nowhere near the scene of the crime. I'd been watching him from the kitchen window as he paced outside by the pool for at least fifteen minutes before Ms. Lamott joined him." He gestured toward Willow, who nodded emphatically. "I came outside and spoke to both of them and then continued to watch from inside as they had a heated discussion. They were both in my sight when the call for help was raised."

Chief Kagawa's brows arched and he ran a hand over his buzzed head. "Are you willing to put that in writing?"

"Absolutely."

■ ■ ■

After Ashton was released, Deputy Simms drove Willow home. But Ashton had insisted on being taken back to the Martins' so he could pick up his bike and head to the hospital.

It had been one of the longest nights of Willow's life, and when sleep had refused to come, she'd camped out on a chair in the living room, dozing fitfully. She blinked late-morning sun from her eyes as the grandfather clock struck eleven and her phone pinged. She grabbed it, anxious for news. Ashton had texted her several times from the hospital with updates on Penelope's condition, which had been touch and go all night.

Even before swiping in her code, she saw the SnapMail notification on her home screen. She sat up and put both feet on the floor before clicking on the icon.

Back off or you're next.

She could guess what the threat meant, but why warn her? Why not just come after her like they'd done to Penelope? She typed:

Next for what?

The first messaged disappeared, and she demanded:

Who is this?

No response.

The front door clicked open. Willow jumped up and ran into the foyer just as Ashton shut the door behind him.

He looked terrible—red-rimmed eyes shadowed with dark circles, a cut on his cheekbone where Colin had hit him, his hair a chaotic mess.

Willow threw her arms around him, careful not to squeeze his bruised ribs. She leaned back and searched his face. "How is she?"

Ashton's voice was guarded, the way he sounded when he wished to hide his emotions. "Still in ICU, but they said she should make a full recovery."

"Oh, thank God!" Mom gushed as she joined them. "Come to the kitchen. Both of you. I'll heat up some chicken noodle soup."

Seated around the island, they all slurped the steaming broth until Willow finally asked what had been on all their minds. "Did Penelope have any idea who attacked her?"

Ashton stared down and twirled his spoon, the metal clinking against the edges of the ceramic bowl. A muscle in his jaw flexed before he glanced up. "No, all she remembers was someone grabbing her from behind and . . . the knife going into her side."

There was something he wasn't telling them. "Ash?"

He met her gaze, his eyes a turbulent sea.

"Ashton, what else?"

He stared up at the ceiling with a heavy sigh. "Just before she was . . . stabbed, a male voice said, 'You better keep your mouth shut.'"

Ashton closed his eyes and slumped back in his seat.

Willow asked, "You don't think they meant . . . ?"

"Someone tried to kill her"—he shook his head—"because she tried to help me."

"You don't know that." She took his hand, but his fingers remained limp.

"That's it." Mom grabbed their empty bowls and stood. "I'm canceling the party next week."

Mom had finally gained permission to host the Sleepy Hollow Ball after-party at the mansion and had been working her fingers to the bone cooking and decorating. Between the fake cobwebs, black candles, and skulls in every room, the first floor had begun to look like a movie set.

"That's a good idea." Ashton sounded defeated.

"No! Mom, you've worked so hard." Not to mention Willow had plans for that night.

Ashton slid off of his stool and slumped out of the room. "I need to sleep."

Willow followed him. "Ash, can I talk to you first?"

"Better make it fast."

They climbed the stairs, and when they reached Ashton's bedroom door, he leaned against the frame. "What's up?"

Willow gathered her courage and blurted, "Go to the ball with me?"

His half-closed eyes opened wide. "As a friend or a date?"

She smiled and lifted one shoulder in a shrug.

A corner of his mouth curled. "What about Brayden?"

"I don't want to go with Brayden." Willow stepped so close that her bare legs brushed the material of his pants. "I want to go with you."

He looked down into her eyes and rested his hand on her hip, his thumb brushing the sensitive skin below her ribs. "On one condition."

His touch weakening her knees, Willow braced a palm against his chest. "Anything."

"Wear your Pikachu costume." A full smile broke out across his face. In sixth grade they'd trick-or-treated as Ash and Pikachu. He'd worn normal clothes and carried a pokeball while she'd looked like an overstuffed chicken with a tail.

She smacked his arm. "No way!"

He winced.

"Oh, I'm sorry! Are you bruised there?"

He grabbed her shoulders, pulled her against him, and leaned down to whisper, "No, I just wanted to see your reaction." His breath ruffled the tiny hairs by her ear and she shivered. He was totally playing her.

"Idiot." She shoved out of his arms and propped her hands on her hips.

"Brat," he teased as he pushed off the wall.

Willow was poised to run, but Ashton sighed and stepped back into his room. "I'm too tired to fight with you . . . or kiss you, which is damn depressing." He turned and shot her a weary grin. "But yes, I'll take you to the ball, Willow-ella. Just plan your costume so you can straddle a motorcycle."

The door shut and Willow grinned. He was no Prince Charming, but he was hers.

* * *

After sleeping most of the day, Ashton awoke with a sad certainty pressing on his chest. Penelope's words had rocked him to his core. He'd been using her, and now she'd paid a horrible price. Next time it could be one of the Lamotts. And he could not allow that to happen.

His sudden release the night before had felt miraculous, but his hope had soon turned to fear as he realized his relentless need to clear his name and prove his worth to the people he cared about had only put them in danger. His return to Gilt Hollow had been a mistake from the start.

He rolled out of bed and grabbed the phone off his nightstand. Maybe if he took himself out of the picture, the violence would stop. He dialed the number he knew by heart and listened to it ring. Just when he was about to hang up, his father's brusque voice came across the line. "Winston Keller."

"Hey, Dad, it's me."

There was a pause and then, "Ashton?"

"Yeah." Ashton swallowed and pushed the words out without taking a breath. "I'm sorry for everything that's happened. I want to come to Cincinnati . . . maybe live with you guys for a while and finish my senior year there."

Silence.

"Dad, I came back to Gilt Hollow, but it isn't working out. There's nothing for me here." Except the only people he cared about. Which was exactly why he had to leave.

"We didn't think we'd hear from you."

Because they'd abandoned him and left him to rot in a jail cell? Ashton stared out the window and bit back his anger. There wouldn't be a plausible explanation for why he hadn't heard from his own family—not one Ashton would ever accept. But as a means to an end, he could swallow his pride.

"I know Dad, it's just . . . I have nowhere else to go."

"I don't know. I need to talk to your mother."

Not good. His dad was a teddy bear compared to Catherine Arnett-Keller. His mom definitely wore the pants, and the boots, in the family. But Ashton had inherited her single-minded focus. Tightening his fingers into a fist, he told the lie he knew would sway his father. "I've been thinking, and I really want to learn more about what you do. About real estate."

His parents had invested the family fortune wisely. His dad was a real estate broker and his mother an agent—the face of the business. They specialized in buying old commercial buildings, fixing them up, and selling them at top dollar.

"Well . . . I always said you had the mind for it. Wily as a fox, just like your old man." There was a smile in his voice. "I'll send a car for you tonight. Are you at Keller House?"

"Yes, but I need a bit more time to wrap things up here. How about next Sunday?" He had to make sure Willow would stop digging into things that could get her killed.

"Good thinking. It'll give me a chance to work on your mother."

"Okay, see you then." He lowered the phone.

"Ashton?"

Slowly, he lifted the speaker back to his ear. "Yes, Dad?"

"I'm glad you called . . . son."

The emotion in his dad's voice loosened something in Ashton's chest, but he wasn't about to let his father off that easily. He lowered the phone and disconnected the call.

Ashton sunk down on the edge of the bed. For four long years he'd dreamed of coming back home, and not just for revenge. He loved this house—where generations of Kellers had grown up and raised families of their own. He'd missed Gilt Hollow in all its eclectic glory. And a rough plan had begun to form in his mind; he'd graduate, work on a local farm, and defer college until his trust fund kicked in. Then he'd study business and eventually buy Twisted Beauty, expanding it to take over the whole building. Maybe make the first floor a pub with a stage where he could bring in indie bands.

He had zero interest in learning real estate and becoming a clone of his parents. His shoulders slumped. Maybe someday he could come back, but for now it was best for everyone if he disappeared.

He had one last hope. It was thin at best, but he had to try. After digging through his duffel bag, he unfolded a slip of paper and made another call. This time to an old friend.

CHAPTER Twenty-Six

I t's Isaiah. I'm sure of it. He came looking for me at the Martins' house. Probably to lure me outside." Willow jabbed her scalpel into the pumpkin's eye with a glee bordering on psychotic. It was two days until the big party, and Mom had sent her and Ashton to the backyard and put them on carving duty. Willow's life might be totally out of control, but jack-o'-lanterns she could handle.

"Heck of a lot of good that does us, since his dad's the chief of police." Ashton scooped out a spoonful of orange guts and splatted them onto a newspaper. "Besides, the knife they found at the scene had been wiped clean of fingerprints, and Penelope said the voice that threatened her was muffled. She hasn't been able to give the police any more information."

"Can't we go to the county prosecutor or something? Tell them that the police chief and his son are psychopaths? I'm pretty sure that sort of thing runs in families." An unseasonably warm breeze ruffled Willow's hair. The hint of dryness in the air made her want to soak up the sun before it disappeared for the long Ohio winter.

"Yes, but for that we'll need solid evidence. Which—"

Willow finished his sentence. "Which is what you're working on that I could ruin if I get too close. I know! But I'm starting to feel like you just made that up so I'll stop snooping. I'm telling you, Colin's family is hiding something. If I could just . . ."

A plop of wet goop struck Willow's face. She jerked back and crossed her eyes to see strings of pumpkin pulp hanging from her nose. Ashton bounced on his toes, eyes dancing, spoon loaded and ready.

"Ashton!" She swiped at the stinking mess and raised her knife. "I have a scalpel, don't make me use—" Another splat.

"That's it!" Willow lunged and grabbed a handful of guts, flinging them just as another mass smacked her chest. Ashton hooted his victory and ducked behind the table.

"Ugh!" She dodged another missile and then reached for more ammo, but the moment she did, pumpkin innards splattered her neck and face. Rethinking her strategy, Willow faked one direction, and then spun and sprinted around the end of the table. Ashton raised his hand to fling more gunk, but then froze, his eyes widening just before she threw herself at him. He let out a startled grunt as she tackled him to the ground and began to rub her arms and face against him like a cat.

Within a matter of seconds, she'd completely slimed him. His chest shook beneath her and she realized he was laughing so hard he couldn't breathe. Willow giggled as he sucked in a sharp breath.

He gripped her arms and rolled to the side so they lay in the damp grass facing each other. "You're surprisingly strong for such a little thing." Grinning, he pulled a clump of seeds out of her hair and flicked them away.

Willow brushed a glob of pulp from his throat, her fingers grazing warm skin. "I imagine that has something to do with my mass, times the velocity as I ran . . ."

Ashton wrapped his arms around her and pulled her flush against him. "I get it, science girl." He cupped her face and leaned in, his lips hovering a hair's breadth from hers as he murmured, "Velocity times mass equals momentum." He kissed her top lip and then lifted his head.

Sparks ignited all over Willow's body. He sure knew how to sweet-talk a girl.

He lowered his mouth again and kissed her with slow deliberation, as if she were a dessert and he wanted to savor every mouthful. Willow ran her hands over his strong shoulders and then laced her fingers in the hair curling against his neck. He gripped her waist and their mouths opened together. Urgency flooding her veins, Willow kissed him until she couldn't breathe—and didn't want to.

The sound of a throat clearing intruded into her bliss, but she ignored it, drowning in the feel of Ashton's skin, the taste of his lips. Until a deep voice said, "I didn't expect a heartfelt reunion, but a thank you might be nice."

Ashton pulled back and then leaned his forehead against hers. "Sorry. I've gotta take care of this." He planted a quick kiss on her chin, then released her and sprang to his feet. "This better be good, Rozelle."

Willow sat up and self-consciously straightened her shirt and plucked pumpkin bits from her hair. Ashton gripped the other boy's hand and raised it between them as they pounded each other on the back in a one-armed guy hug. Willow stood and examined the other boy. Tattoos swirled around the tan skin of his upper arms, and he wore some kind of pendant on a black cord around his throat. He was tall but not quite as muscular as Ashton. With his straight dark hair and the exotic tip to his eyes, he reminded Willow of a real-life Aladdin.

"Willow"—Ashton glanced back at her and then turned to the boy—"this is my old roommate from JJC, Toryn Rozelle."

When she shook his hand and his eyes danced with mischief, the image of the iconic Arabian thief was complete. She smiled at him, seemingly unable to help herself. He grinned back and then released her hand and pulled a roll of papers out of his back pocket. Turning to Ashton, he said, "I dug up what you asked for, man. But I'm not sure it's all that helpful."

Ashton took the papers, and Willow read over his shoulder. It was a police report from four years ago. She raised her eyes to Toryn. "Are you a hacker or something?"

His perpetual grin still in place, he replied, "Nope. I just know one who owed me a favor."

Ashton glanced up. "Doesn't just about everyone owe you a favor?"

Toryn shrugged. "It's a living."

"One that's going to get you thrown back in the clink. And I won't be around to back you up next time."

Toryn raised two palms in defense. "Whoa, okay, I'll lay off the criminal activity and go work at McDonald's."

"Yeah, right." Ashton went back to reading the report.

Willow skimmed the document and found Daniel Turano's name. She had to weed through the legal jargon but pieced together that Daniel claimed to have witnessed another boy selling drugs. The dealer was described as average build, average height, and wearing a beanie over his hair—which could be half the teen boys in Gilt Hollow.

"He covered it up," Ashton ground out. "I can't freaking believe it."

"But if Isaiah was dealing, Daniel still knew it. We could tell the DA that the chief buried the witness testimony." Willow was grasping at straws, and she knew it. Taking this to the county prosecutor would only make them look like fools.

"Sorry, man, I know you were hoping for something solid," Toryn said.

"Yeah." Ashton's shoulders slumped, his mouth dragging into a frown. This had been his last hope to reopen the investigation.

"I'm not giving up," Willow vowed. "We can still find the evidence we need."

"But at what cost?" Ashton spun on her. "No one else is getting hurt because of me!"

Toryn shifted from foot to foot. "Um . . . I gotta go, dude."

Ashton stared Willow down for several more seconds before breaking eye contact and digging in his pocket. He handed a wad of bills to Toryn, who folded them with a smile. "Nice doin' business with you. Let's hook up in Cincy next week. If you and your old man need an intern, I'm your guy. I'm not above making coffee or kissing a little corporate butt."

"Dude, shut up." Ashton strode forward, grasped Toryn's shoulder, and guided him around the side of the house.

"What? You told me to go legit, and real estate beats flippin' burgers . . ."

Toryn's words disappeared into the sudden vacuum swirling in Willow's head. What was he talking about? Ashton was going to Cincinnati? Had he talked to his parents? Was he going for a visit . . . or something more permanent?

When Ashton came back around the house, both of his hands jammed into his pockets, the look on his face confirmed Willow's worst fears.

"You're leaving?" Willow croaked.

He stopped a foot away from her. "Yeah."

"Just like that, you're giving up." It wasn't a question.

"This has to end before someone else is killed. The only way that's going to happen is if I'm gone." He reached for her, but Willow stepped away.

"When were you going to tell me?" She had to fight to keep the panic out of her voice.

He lifted a shoulder. "I don't know . . . I'd hoped Toryn would find something solid, but Kagawa covered his tracks too well."

"When are you coming back?"

"I'm . . . not sure."

She stepped into him, anger flashing across her skin. "Minutes ago you . . . you kissed me like you might die if you stopped, all the while knowing you were leaving! When were you going to tell me? After we did it?"

"No! Geez, Wil. I wouldn't do that to you." He raked a hand through his hair. "It sounds stupid, but I wanted to take you out. Just once. On a proper date."

"The ball? How ridiculously classic! You were going to show me the time of my life and then ride off into the sunset? Well, forget it!" She pushed against his chest with both hands. "Our date's off!"

Willow spun on her heel and stalked toward the house, her pulse raging in her ears.

"Can't you see I'm doing this for you?" Ashton called.

She spun around. "Really? Because to me it seems like you're running away."

Tears scalding her eyes, Willow turned and fled. She didn't want him to know he'd broken her heart. Again.

CHAPTER Twenty-Seven

The mayor's antebellum mansion appeared to float in a sea of fog as Willow and Lisa approached arm in arm, the gauzy material of their costumes brushing in a whisper. Eerie music filled the air, old-fashioned gas lanterns lined the winding driveway, and fairy lights twinkled in the trees. Beautiful and haunting, the atmosphere ignited memories from years past. All the times Willow and Ashton had attended with her dad, his eyes twinkling behind whatever creature he'd painted on his face.

Lisa squeezed Willow's hand. "I'm sorry I'm your date instead of . . . you know."

Willow had survived the last few days by stuffing her feelings down into the basement of her soul where no one would ever find them. She was good at it. She'd had a lot of practice after Ashton left the first time. But she didn't want to talk about him now. "Let's just focus on tonight. I've been coming to this ball since I was a kid. It's totally over the top. You're going to love it."

"I'm not so sure about that." Lisa's voice quivered as they reached the first bend in the driveway. Thick mist swirled up their legs and the sounds of moaning spirits echoed all around them.

"Don't be a ninny," Willow chided as a Victorian ghost drifted by covered in iridescent paint from her crow-topped hat to the sweeping hem of her bell-like skirt. "I'm the one who's supposed to have the anxiety disorder."

"Where I'm from, you follow your instincts, and if something doesn't feel right, you cut and run . . . or you die."

"That might be a tad bit dramatic." Willow's words were drowned out by the blast of organ keys as all the lights in the yard blinked off. Lisa shrieked, and every window in the house flashed like lightning with thunder booming close behind.

After a few beats of silence, the haunted tune wound back up and the lights flickered on one by one. There were a few nervous laughs, and a nearby Jack Skellington whooped and pumped a spindly arm.

"You were saying?" Lisa demanded. "That was just dang creepy."

"That's kind of the point."

Once inside, they checked their coats, and Willow stopped to look at her costume in the hall mirror. Lisa had painted Willow's face with swirls of black, purple, and silver so that it appeared that a mask was tattooed to her skin. The tiny crystals glued to her temples, fake violet-tipped eyelashes, and lavender-glitter lipstick transformed her into something magical—Willow the Wicked Fairy, to be precise. Lisa had thought it would be hilarious to make straitlaced Willow dark and herself light.

Willow had to admit, being someone else felt kind of freeing. She smoothed the gossamer layers of her skirt and straightened the laces of her bodice while trying not to imagine what Ashton would have thought. Not that it mattered, she reminded herself. He'd be gone tomorrow anyway.

Pushing down the rise of grief and anger, Willow lifted her chin and smiled as Lisa joined her in the mirror, all pink, gold, and fluffy—Lisa the Light Fairy. Willow scratched her scalp where the purple extensions clipped into her hair.

"Stop messing!" Lisa smacked Willow's hand away from her elaborate updo of braids and curls. "You'll ruin my masterpiece."

A woman with an enormous blue wig drifted behind them, and they both spun and shouted, "Effie!"

The woman turned her chalk-white face to them and lifted a gloved hand. "You look fabulous, darlings."

Willow and Lisa exchanged grins and followed the techno-beat of a Sam Smith-Disclosure remix into the packed ballroom glittered with candlelight and cobwebs. A life-sized mausoleum housed the DJ booth, where Jeff White, dressed as a zombified member of the Grateful Dead, mixed songs like a master. Colorful costumed couples mingled and danced across the floor, making it hard to know where to look first.

"Okay, maybe this is cool," Lisa admitted.

A hand touched Willow's shoulder, and she turned to find Brayden wearing a long black robe with his red hair combed over his forehead, a Gryffindor scarf wrapped around his neck, and wand in his hand. "Oh my gosh, Ron! It's perfect!" She'd always thought Brayden looked like a Weasley.

He smiled, but the expression didn't reach his eyes. "Can I talk to you for a minute?"

Brayden hadn't taken their breakup well. She'd stuck to the truth and explained that since Ashton had returned, she'd felt conflicted. But she hadn't talked to Brayden since Ashton told everyone he was leaving town. "Sure."

She turned to Lisa and found her heading off to dance with an alien who had fingers for teeth. With a shrug, Willow turned to Brayden and let him lead her to a corner by a black cauldron spilling mist onto the floor. Nearby, a green-faced witch ladled out cups of the bubbling brew.

"Willow, I tried to call you all day."

"I know. I wasn't answering."

Brayden ran his fingers through his hair, causing it to stick out on one side.

"Stop." Willow reached up and smoothed down his bangs. "You're ruining the Ron effect."

A corner of his mouth curled. "Thanks. You look awesome, by the way."

"Thank you." She glanced down at the sparkling layers of her skirt. She actually felt pretty.

"I'm glad you didn't come with *him*."

Willow didn't have to ask who he was talking about.

"Not that I'm jealous or anything, but now that he's leaving . . . I still kinda hoped we could—"

"I'm not ready, Brayden. I'm sorry." Willow glanced over her shoulder, hoping to find Lisa and lose herself in the frenetic mass of dancers.

"You're one of the smartest people I know," he said. "Have you ever thought that Ashton might be guilty? Even once?"

Willow clenched her teeth.

"No, really." He stepped closer. "Think about it. Everything that's happened since he returned . . . How do you know he didn't orchestrate it all? And then took advantage of your belief in him? Every bit of evidence I've seen points directly back to Ashton. Including the video we watched with our own eyes."

Willow shot Brayden a withering look. "I was with Ashton when Penelope was stabbed, remember?"

"But for how long? They don't know exactly when it happened. Could Ashton have attacked her before he came to find you?"

His brown eyes searched hers, and the blood seemed to

drain from Willow's chest. Thinking back, Willow had no solid proof that Ashton hadn't destroyed Colin's jersey or trashed Isaiah's locker or even robbed the record store. Only his word. He'd never been around when she'd received the threatening SnapMail messages. What if they were his way of warning her to stay out of it? What if he'd just wrecked his bike and no one ran him off the road?

A girl dressed as a ratty doll with long red hair and demented eyes smashed into Brayden's arm. "Dance with me, Ron!"

"Hold on, Yo." Brayden steadied the drunken girl. "Willow, just promise me you'll consider it."

Willow nodded as Yolanda tugged Brayden out onto the floor. When she and Brayden finally broke eye contact, Willow began to drift around the edge of the room in a daze. Was it possible her feelings for Ashton had clouded her judgment? Did she have any proof that one word Ashton had said to her was true? She believed he didn't push Daniel on purpose, but what if Penelope had learned about his other crimes and he'd tried to silence her? The insane rage on his face as he'd punched Colin had terrified her; it was as if he'd turned into a different person. Could he be leaving to escape before he was caught?

"Is that you, Willow?"

She turned to find Pastor Justin hanging out by the hors d'oeuvre table, wearing his usual costume of a floor-length brown robe and the heavy cross necklace of a monk. "Hi, Pastor."

"Can I offer a severed finger or gelatinous eyeball, perhaps?" He gestured toward the table of spooky treats.

"No, thanks."

Pastor Justin looked past her. "Is Dee here?"

"Nope, Mom's busy with last-minute preparations for our after-party. You should stop by."

"Of course." He grinned, and her suspicion that he had feelings for her mother solidified. But her mind churned with too many questions to analyze how she felt about her mom's dating life. She picked up a cake pop decorated like a miniature candied apple and twirled it in her fingers. "Pastor, do you think it's possible to be completely wrong about someone? To believe with all your heart that they're one way, only to find out you were wrong all along?" She felt stupid asking such a vague question, but she was desperate for guidance—for some idea how to deal with the doubts Brayden had planted in her mind.

The pastor seemed to consider for a moment. "Some people call it intuition, but I know that the Spirit of God lives within all believers. If you look for wisdom, you'll know the answer. Even if it isn't what you expect."

It was exactly the kind of mystical advice she'd anticipated from him, but for some reason it helped. "Thanks." She gave him a genuine smile before continuing on her way. An '80s punk song blared from a nearby speaker, the base pounding in her chest. She needed a minute alone to think.

Tossing the cake pop into a wastebasket, she headed across the enormous room to a set of french doors, but before she could walk outside, a clown snagged her arm. "Let's dance!" She didn't recognize the fake high-pitched voice, but she let the clown lead her into the mass of dancers just as a slow song began. Willow faced her partner and swallowed a gasp at the hollowed out eyes and enormous mouth full of jagged teeth. Multitoned hair stuck out of a bald cap at crazy angles, topped by a miniature hat. The clown tugged her close, and she felt a strong, muscled body beneath his colorful jumpsuit.

Willow pushed against his chest. "You're crushing my wings."

His hold only tightened, and as he leaned in, the scents of grease paint and Axe body spray made her want to gag. "You've been a naughty little fairy, haven't you?"

Willow arched back and stared into the cold blue eyes of Colin Martin.

Anger buzzed across her skin. She'd had enough bullying to last a lifetime. Gripping Colin's arms, she rose on her toes and hissed, "Let me go or I'll kick your balloons so hard you'll talk like Bozo for the rest of your life."

Colin reared his head back and laughed hysterically. Several faces turned at his display, but between the masks and makeup, Willow didn't recognize a single one of them. Colin twirled her in a circle and toward the doors leading out to the garden. Willow dug her heels in. No way was she letting him take her away from the party.

He bent down and whispered, "What's wrong? I thought you wanted to be alone with me. Isn't that why you were hiding in my room?"

A prickle crawled up Willow's spine. His mom must have told him. Colin released her just inside the doors and tipped her chin up so she was forced to look at his hideous face. "Bring me my key or I'll crush more than your wings."

He danced off into the crowd, and Willow stumbled out onto the veranda. After making sure she was alone, she leaned against the stone railing and opened the small glitter-covered purse hanging on a string across her chest. Tucked inside, next to her lipstick and phone, sat Colin's key. She didn't know why she'd taken the stupid thing in the first place, but fear of someone finding it had prompted her to carry it everywhere she went.

Worried Colin might see her, she snapped the bag shut. But that didn't stop the questions rattling through her brain. Why did Colin want it so desperately? What secrets did the ancient key unlock? Maybe she'd missed something vital hidden inside the box in his room. But did it really matter? Ashton had given up, so why shouldn't she?

Willow turned to lean on the banister. Flickering lanterns hung from the trees, illuminating disembodied ball gowns made of chicken wire that appeared to float across the lawn amid crooked tombstones. Laughter echoed up to her, and she saw a girl dart across the path, chased by a boy dressed as a werewolf.

Loneliness smacked into Willow like a wall of water, drenching her from head to toe in an icy chill. She'd believed herself invisible for years, but somehow this was worse. Knowing what it felt like to have Ashton back—how his presence jolted her into vibrant life—only to have that ripped away. It was as if all the color had been leached out of the world.

She wasn't sure about everything Pastor Justin had said, but when she felt confused, talking to her dad always seemed to help. She gazed up into the clear night sky sprinkled with stars. *Dad, could I really have been so wrong about Ashton?* Usually she could imagine her dad's voice in her head and exactly what he would say, but this time he was silent.

Awareness hummed along her shoulders, and she glanced to her right. Her heart skipped several beats. At the other end of the veranda, a figure dressed in head to toe black lounged against the railing, watching her.

CHAPTER Twenty-Eight

Willow studied the figure at the other end of the veranda, from his dark pants tucked into knee-high boots, to his billowing black shirt, to the silken mask that covered half his face and tied at the back of his head. His features were concealed, but Willow knew the line of his jaw, the tilt of his head. And yet she hesitated.

Was Ashton the villain everyone believed him to be or the boy she'd fallen in love with? She took a step forward, her breath misting the air, as images layered one over the other in her mind: Ashton climbing the house to save her brother, his sweet voice as he talked her down from her panic attack, his unguarded plea for forgiveness after his accident, and finally, his tortured gaze as he told her what had happened that day at the falls. Warmth flooded her soul, and before she knew it, she was halfway across the balcony.

Impatient as always, Ashton straightened and closed the distance between them in three strides. As he neared, Willow saw the sword swinging at his hip and her earlier chill melted into delicious tingles. The summer she'd turned twelve, they'd watched *The Princess Bride* so many times they could quote every line. Her eyes moved to his face. Stubble covered his jaw and upper lip, and his dark hair hooked behind both of his ears. The black of the mask contrasted with the blue of his eyes, making them appear to glow. Was he *trying* to make her swoon?

He stopped and crossed his arms in front of his chest, a smile hovering around his lips. The costume was perfect—the villain who's really a hero in disguise. But even better, she knew he'd worn it for her.

Willow arched a brow. "The Dread Pirate Roberts?"

"I saw no reason to change my costume just because Princess Buttercup canceled our date."

Her chest gave a squeeze. "Touché."

Ashton stepped closer and raised a finger to trace the crystals near her temples. "You're beautiful." His eyes held hers. "But you always are."

"Ash . . ." Willow's gaze flickered to his mouth, and she wished, despite everything, that he would kiss her—kiss her until she didn't care that he was leaving, until she forgot that her heart was breaking. She bit her lip to stop the plea from slipping out. "When are you leaving?"

"In the morning."

"Oh." She'd known it would be soon but had hoped for a little more time. "Why are you here?"

He stared at her, and for several long moments he didn't speak. His jaw hardened and she could tell he was clenching his teeth. A brisk wind tugged at her hair and the tails on Ashton's mask as the sounds of the party faded away.

"Willow, you not talking to me the last few days . . ." His voice broke off as he settled his hands on her shoulders, his thumbs brushing softly against her exposed collarbones. "You're wrecking me, you know that? I'm trying to do the right thing to keep you safe, but I can't think about anything but you."

Willow shivered hard and focused on his throat, watching the muscles contract as he swallowed.

"But that's exactly why I have to go. My judgment is totally clouded and I can't . . . I can't protect you when I don't even know *who* to protect you from."

"I don't need your protection," Willow snapped. But when she raised her eyes, his deep blue gaze seemed to drink her in, and her control shattered, her next words a plea. "Stay. Just tell me you'll stay."

He searched her face and after a long pause, whispered, "I will *never* make promises to you that I can't keep."

His words gouged at Willow's heart. How could she have thought for one second that he'd been lying to her? He was hot-tempered and sometimes impulsive, but he was good. So good and honorable that it made her feel like a selfish child. But she couldn't seem to help herself; she wanted him more than she'd wanted anything her entire life. Tears burned her eyes and clogged her throat.

"Please, don't cry." Ashton took her hand. "It's not like we'll never see each other again. We can Skype. You can come visit me in the city."

"That's not the point!" Willow jerked away from him and pivoted to face the lawn. "If you're willing to leave, then you don't feel the same way I feel about you."

He leaned close, and his next words brushed like a caress against her neck. "How do you feel?"

Willow didn't want to bare her soul, but maybe the truth would be the one thing that would change his mind. She turned into him and placed her palms against his chest. "Like I don't want to spend a day without you. Like together we can accomplish anything." Her throat tightened, but she pushed on. "Ashton, I'm in love with you. I think I've loved you half my life."

His chest expanded as he drew a shaky breath, his eyes softening just before he tore his gaze away. Willow searched his profile for some sign that he returned her feelings, but as he exhaled his mouth hardened, and when he looked back at her, his expression closed her out. "I love you too. But it doesn't change anything. I wish it did." Then he turned on his heel and strode away.

Stunned, Willow stared after him. Ever since the first time they'd kissed, she'd dreamed about Ashton confessing his love to her, but never like that—like it was a burden he had to bear, a mountain he had to climb. Hot tears spilled onto her cheeks. All the stories her father had read to her when she was a child had ended with the villain's defeat and true love's kiss. But they never told what followed the happily ever after. Or what would happen if you fell in love with a pirate and not a prince.

Willow dabbed under her eyes, purple and silver glitter coming off on her fingers. Clearly this was no fairy tale or her makeup would still look perfect—and the killer would be behind bars. Reining in her tears, she squared her shoulders and reentered the ballroom. A slow, romantic song played, and a disco ball spun overhead, flecks of light blanketing couples glued together at the hip. The sight made Willow want to scream. Maybe she should head home where she could lick her wounds in peace.

"Is that you, Willow Lamott?"

Willow looked down to find Mrs. M, wearing her ever-present cowboy boots, but this time with a black witch's frock and a pointy hat pinned to her gray hair. She patted the empty folding chair beside her. "Come sit with a lonely old woman for a moment."

Who could say no to that? Willow sat, and they watching the dancers. Lisa twirled in the arms of Reggie the line-backer, who'd removed his grotesque alien mask. The music transitioned into a slow, creepy tune, but that didn't seem to put a damper on the making out. An uncomfortable feeling in her hands caused Willow to loosen her grip on the edge of the metal chair.

Searching for a distraction, she turned to Mrs. M. "So, how have you been?"

"Right as rain." Her wrinkled cheeks stretched into a grin. "Every day not in the grave is a good one, I say." She chuckled and then looked around. "Would you happen to know the time?"

Willow grabbed her purse to check her phone, but the chain caught on her bodice, and half the contents spilled out before she unhooked the bag from her laces. She tucked her lip gloss back inside as Mrs. M bent down in slow motion and reached for an object on the floor.

"I'll get it." Willow swooped down and picked up the large metal key she'd taken from Colin's room.

Faster than Willow thought her capable of moving, Mrs. M snatched it out of Willow's hand. "Where did you find this?"

"Well . . . I . . . er . . ." Willow searched for some kind of lie, but so many possibilities entered her mind that she couldn't settle on one.

"It looks like part of a gift I brought back from England for Colin and Cory."

Willow reached for it, but Mrs. M deftly switched it to her other hand. "Handcrafted boxes with their names engraved on them."

Listening now, Willow lowered her hand. "You got a box for both brothers?"

Mrs. M stared at the key as if it could unlock the past. "Mr. McMenamin and I found the boxes at a quaint little shop in Somerset. They had all shapes and sizes, carved with hundreds of different names. We found Colin's, but we had to have Cory's specially made. So there was only one key." She turned tearful eyes to Willow.

"I'm sorry about your nephew, ma'am. It was a terrible tragedy. But this is just an old key I found at Keller House." She took it from Mrs. M's limp hand. "Tons of antiques in that place."

Willow slipped the key back into her bag. Perhaps there was a reason she'd held on to it after all. An insane idea began to form in her mind. "Mrs. M, have you seen the Martins here tonight?"

"Bill and Caroline? Why, yes." She pointed to a couple dressed like ketchup and mustard bottles out on the dance floor.

Perfect.

Willow stood. "I need to run. I just remembered I'm supposed to meet someone."

Mrs. M gave her a wave. "Have a good evening, dear."

Willow raced out the back doors and down the stairs into the garden. The Martins' house was just on the other side of the trees and through the graveyard. If she hurried, she could be back before the headless horseman's ride and sparkling cider toast.

If she found evidence that identified the real killer, then no one else would get hurt, and Ashton could stay. She flew down the lantern-lit path and patted the bag at her waist. Maybe the key *could* unlock the past.

CHAPTER Twenty-Nine

Ashton leaned against a Grecian pillar, sipping witch's brew and watching the ridiculousness on the dance floor. If his soul hadn't been a jumble of barbed wire and molten rock, he might find it hilarious that a man in a pink bunny suit was dancing with a woman dressed as a lamp—.fishnet stockings and all. Willow would have laughed and suggested they steal the idea for next year.

His spine stiffened. Willow actually *loved* him. It was beyond his wildest hopes, but it felt like she'd carved his heart out with a spoon. Love wasn't something he knew how to deal with. Hate, anger, indifference—all those he could process. Even so, he knew what he felt for her was real because it was transformative. It made him want to be the person she deserved. And that person was willing to give her up to save her life.

Not in the mood for a party, Ashton hung back and enjoyed the relative anonymity of wearing a mask. He would stay as long as Willow was here, just to make sure she was safe. He drained his cup and tossed it in a wastebasket, then searched the room for a glimpse of the purple and silver sparkles of his enchanting fairy girl. In the middle of the dance floor, he spied Lisa with Reggie and Yolanda, but he didn't see Willow. He scanned the nearby refreshment tables, and not two feet away stood a boy in a checkered suit with an enormous top hat perched on his dreads. Something inside Ashton snapped, and without another thought, he grabbed

Isaiah around the shoulders and forced him into a dark hallway. "We need to talk."

"Dude, let go!"

Isaiah and his crooked cop father had been at the root of every evil in Ashton's life. Red clouding his vision, Ashton shoved Isaiah through an open doorway and slammed him up against the wall. His voice a low growl, he demanded, "You pushed Daniel because he caught you dealing. Didn't you?" Isaiah struggled, and Ashton jabbed an elbow into his diaphragm. "Tell me now!"

Isaiah let out a grunt, his eyes watering as he fought to breathe. He shook his head, his hat toppling to the floor.

Ashton read the fear in his eyes. Good. "Did you lie to the police about it or did your daddy cover it up just like the drugs?"

When he didn't get an answer, Ashton pressed his forearm against Isaiah's windpipe. "Spill, or I swear I won't be responsible for what I do to you in the next two minutes."

"Okay." He croaked. "I lied. I lied!"

Ashton eased off Isaiah's throat but kept him pinned against the wall. "About what?"

"About . . . about you . . . pushing Daniel. I didn't see it."

"Yeah, you lied. Because *you* pushed him!" Ashton gave Isaiah another slam, his head snapping back.

"No, Ashton, I swear on my mother's life, I didn't do it. The Martins . . ." His throat convulsed. "The Martins gave their testimonies, and then my dad . . . my dad said it would go better for me if I just agreed with them." The tension left his body as if he'd been waiting to say those words for a lifetime.

"But Daniel saw you dealing drugs."

"Yes, but after Daniel talked to my dad, he agreed to keep

quiet if I promised to stop. And I did. I never touched the stuff again."

Ashton searched Isaiah's face. "But why would one of the Martins push him?"

Fear flickered across Isaiah's gaze, and this time it wasn't because of Ashton. That had to change. Ashton moved back, kicked the door shut, and then unsheathed the sword at his hip. Isaiah froze as Ashton pressed the tip to his throat. The sword had been his grandfather's, and although dull, it was very real. "I have nothing to lose by stabbing you. The chief already thinks I tried to kill Penelope. It's only a matter of time before he has me thrown in prison." Ashton twisted the sword, pressing the tip into Isaiah's skin.

"Stop! Please! I'll tell you everything!"

"You have sixty seconds."

Isaiah started talking in a rush. "I've been trying to help you guys. You and Willow. The threatening SnapMail messages were from me."

Ashton's heart skipped and he jerked forward, clenching a fist.

"No! I was trying to warn Willow. To protect her!"

"Go on."

"I've been . . . been following her since you got back to town. Afraid something might happen to her. But I knew she would never trust me, so I stayed hidden."

The tension in Ashton's spine released a fraction. "Why? Who did you think would hurt her?"

"I wasn't sure. But after I cleaned up my dad's flyers and my locker got—"

"*Chief Kagawa* put up the wanted posters of my face?" Ashton was floored.

Isaiah nodded. "He paid some kids to do it. He's terrified you'll learn that he covered up our lies."

Ashton shook his head in shock. All this time he'd thought the chief believed him a danger to the public, when really he was just covering his own butt. "So you took down the flyers?"

"Yes, I . . . I felt guilty. You'd already paid with four years of your life for something I was pretty sure you didn't do."

"Pretty sure?"

Isaiah met his gaze and then looked away. "I never actually saw who pushed Daniel. I just knew it wasn't me."

"Funny, I knew it wasn't me too, but that didn't stop me from going to jail for it."

Isaiah ignored his comment. "Anyway, after my locker was vandalized, I started receiving threats. Notes tucked into my locker or my binder. I even found one in my bedroom."

"What did they say?"

"That if I didn't stop helping you, they would rat on me and my dad."

"Who were they from?" Ashton realized he'd lowered his sword to the carpet.

Isaiah swallowed hard and stared into the dark shadows of the room. "I had my theories, but I couldn't be sure until the day of your accident." He gathered his dreads behind his head and then let them go and glanced at the door. He looked back at Ashton, his voice a whisper. "Brayden and Colin asked to borrow my car after school that day."

Ashton blinked, sprang forward, and raised his sword to Isaiah's chest. "You better not be lying to me!"

Isaiah raised his hands. "Dude, the Martins are crazy. I'm serious. I caught them sneaking out of the school wearing ski masks the night before my locker was trashed."

A vandalized locker didn't mean anything except they were punks trying to get Ashton kicked out of school. "But why would one of them push Daniel? What else do you know about their trouble with the law?"

"I don't know anything for sure." Isaiah was talking fast. "But both sets of parents met at Cory's house to talk to Colin and Brayden about it. Cory'd been sent to his room and couldn't hear it all."

"He had to have heard *something*. What was his theory?"

"Colin had all kinds of money suddenly. He bought a dirt bike and a huge flatscreen for his room. Cory thought he might have stolen something valuable and then sold it."

"And where does Daniel fit in to all of this?"

"Maybe he knew their secret, just like he knew mine."

Ashton thought for a minute. Daniel's parents were crazy rich. They were the ones who sponsored the Sleepy Hollow Ball every year. "Maybe Brayden and Colin stole from Daniel's family."

Ashton realized he'd lowered the sword again. He searched Isaiah's face for several long seconds. The guy appeared calm, almost relieved, his gaze clear. Over the last few years, Ashton had learned to trust his gut, and his gut was telling him that Isaiah was telling the truth—finally. But he had to be sure. "How do I know any of what you're saying is true?"

"I guess you don't. But I can tell you this. The day the Martins used my car to run you off the road, the moment I got it back, I went to find Willow."

Isaiah had brought Willow home that day in the rain. "Why? Why risk angering the Martins if you're so scared of them?"

A flush crept into Isaiah's cheeks, turning his tawny skin a reddish pink. He liked her. Not that Ashton could blame him. "One more question. What do you think happened to Cory Martin?"

Isaiah's jaw flexed and something dark flitted across his face. "I think he knew who pushed Daniel, and I think that person shut him up permanently."

Ashton sheathed his sword. If Isaiah wasn't the killer, then one of the Martins was, and Willow had no idea. He grabbed his phone and hit speed dial. After several rings, her phone went to voice mail. "Willow, call me immediately. Do not leave the party!"

● ● ●

Willow thanked the trusting culture of small towns as she slid open the unlocked back door of the Martin house. She'd determined that if she wanted her happily ever after, she'd have to slay the dragon herself. Adrenaline pumping through her veins, she sprinted across the basement and up the stairs, and then paused at the top to press her ear against the closed door. She'd seen all the Martins at the ball, but trespassing in their house still scared the fairy dust out of her.

When she didn't hear anything, she slipped into the dimly lit kitchen and jogged down the hallway to Cory's old room. For some reason, Colin didn't want her to have his key, and she was going to find out why.

She eased open the door and stepped inside, shutting it behind her. Even before her eyes could adjust, she knew something had changed. The shadows were off. Afraid to chance turning on a lamp, she took two steps toward the blinds and her knee slammed into something. She bent down and felt the outline of a box.

Navigating the gloom to the window, she cracked the blinds and turned around. The entire room was in boxes. The closet had been emptied out, all the books were off the shelves, and even the bed was stripped down. Surely they hadn't done this because of her . . . But what if they had? She had left her Solo cup on the dresser the night of the party.

Willow knelt by the first set of boxes and began to dig. She made quick work of the search because she knew exactly what she was looking for—a wooden box with Cory's name engraved on the top, one that opened with the key in her purse.

After going through several boxes full of clothes and books, she came across a plastic tub containing folders and desk items. She opened a blue folder labeled "English" and sat back on her heels. Cory had scrawled his name across the top of a paper on *To Kill a Mockingbird*. Willow's hands began to shake. She'd done the same assignment in seventh grade. These papers and books and old clothes were all that was left of a human life. And it took only one careless act to end that life forever.

Someone had killed this boy in cold blood, and it stood to reason they'd kill again to protect their secret. Willow returned the desk supplies to the box and sprang to her feet. Maybe Ashton was right—the truth wasn't worth their lives.

Turning in a quick circle, she made sure nothing looked out of place and fled into the hallway. But the half open door of Colin's room stopped her. What if Cory's box was right there? She slipped a hand into her bag and pulled out the key, gripping it in her fist like a weapon as she crept forward.

The door gave a loud creak as she pushed it open. Chaos greeted her, but this time makeup tins littered the desk and colorful costume remnants draped the bed and floor.

She stepped inside. A wooden box sat on the desk, and she rushed forward. But the name on top was Colin. She blew out her disappointment in a huff.

Quickly she unlocked the box and sifted through the articles but didn't find anything incriminating. She relocked the lid as a revelation hit her—if there had been a similar box in Cory's room, whoever packed up his stuff would have found it. And based on the disorganization of Colin's room, that hadn't been him. Willow rushed into the hallway. If Mrs. Martin had packed up Cory's stuff, she would have kept anything of importance.

A soft bang sounded somewhere deep in the house. Willow froze. Could it be the heat kicking on or someone returning home? She counted to ten in her head and when she didn't hear anything else, continued on. But with every step she took across the house, her conviction wavered. She'd been wrong so many times. Maybe she should just get out of there before someone caught her and called the police.

Willow paused outside the double doors to the master bedroom. A gut-level instinct that had nothing to do with logic or facts urged her to press on. She knew she would find what she was looking for on the other side of those doors. Pulse racing, she pushed them open and slipped inside.

She spotted it the moment she entered the room, sitting on top of a low dresser. Within seconds she'd fit the key in the lock and lifted the lid. What she found was beyond her wildest dreams. A journal. Her heart thudding in her ears, she leafed through to find the last entry.

Saturday, May 12

Leaving for Heartford Forest in the morning. I hope I'll gather the courage to talk to Dad about what I've learned.

It's a horrible choice . . . to do what's right or protect the ones you love.

Willow flipped back through the pages and skimmed several entries about band drama and a girl with red hair and freckles that he'd had a crush on. With trembling fingers, she turned to the next page and skimmed for names she might recognize. Then she found it, two weeks before he'd passed away.

Confronted Colin today. It didn't go well. Not that I expected it to. I told him I saw him that day at the falls, and he backed me against the wall. Something switched off in his eyes, like he'd turned into a soulless clone. When he demanded to know what I'd seen, I told him, "I saw you push Daniel and I know why you did it."

Colin was the killer! A noise made Willow raise her head. She couldn't place the sound. The prickles on the back of her neck urged her to go. But she just needed two more minutes to be sure. She kept reading.

He backed off then and slumped on the bed. I explained everything I knew about him and Brayden stealing Claire Turano's jewelry, selling it, and buying all that stuff. Then he admitted that Daniel knew what they'd done. And that Danny had threatened to tell. Colin said he hadn't planned to kill Daniel, just scare him.

I'm not so sure I believe him.

When Colin asked me what I planned to do about it, I told him I couldn't hold in the secret anymore. I begged him to turn himself in. Then I told him about the nightmares I'd been having about Ashton Keller chained in a damp cell, the flesh melting from his bones, and how it wasn't right for Ashton pay the price for something he didn't do.

Colin came at me again, this time wrapping his hands around my throat. He squeezed. His eyes popping out of his head. Just as I was about to black out, he released me and threatened to kill me too if I didn't keep my mouth shut.

I know it's crazy, but I'm scared of my own brother.

This was what she needed—the proof to clear Ashton's name and put Colin away for good. After stuffing the journal in her purse, she relocked the box and set the key on top, and then pulled out her phone to call . . . who? Ashton? Her mom? Chief Kagawa? What if he buried the evidence again? Before she could decide, she noticed a piece of paper tucked into the back pocket of her bag. She pulled it out and read:

Willow,

Meet me at Keller House by midnight. I need to tell you something important.

~A

She'd meet Ashton and show him the journal so they could decide what to do together. Clutching her overstuffed bag to her chest, Willow glanced at the clock sitting on the dresser. It was eleven forty. She would have to hurry.

CHAPTER Thirty

W illow jogged up the driveway to Keller House, feeling like she was trapped in a bad slasher film. Mom had replaced the outside lights with orange bulbs that flashed on and off at random intervals, and as Willow climbed the porch steps a dozen glowing jack-o'-lanterns leered back at her. She opened the front door to the dimly lit foyer and flinched so hard she almost peed her pants. A ghost with a skeletal face floated in the mirror. As she watched with her hand clutched to her thudding chest, the image flickered and she turned to see the hologram machine hidden behind a plant. Her mom had done too good a job turning the place into a haunted house. Not that it needed much help.

Shutting the door behind her, she called, "Mom? Ashton?"

No answer. She didn't even hear Rainn scampering around.

In the kitchen, Willow found trays of food covered in plastic, and the hot spiced cider simmering in the Crock-Pot made her mouth water. She set the journal on the counter, pulled out her phone, and saw that she had several missed calls from Ashton and a text from her mom saying she and Rainn had decided to go to the ball to catch the headless horseman's ride. Willow turned her ringer back on and checked the time. It was five minutes until midnight.

A bang from upstairs caused her to whirl around. "Ashton?" When she didn't hear a response, she began to worry. He tried to hide it, but he still hadn't fully recovered after his accident. She raced down the hall, then flew up the stairs and saw a light shining from his bedroom. "Ash?" She peeked her head in, but the room was empty.

A shuffling noise sounded down the hall, and her pulse leaped into her fingertips. If he was playing a trick on her, she would never forgive him. Her steps slowed. With the way they'd left things at the party, a prank didn't seem appropriate. The hairs rose on Willow's arms and she tiptoed back toward her room. Was someone in the house with her? Or had the famous Keller ghost finally come to call?

The curtains in her room were open so she could just see the outline of a figure sitting in one of the chairs by the fireplace. He was dressed all in black, a bandanna tied around his head, but his face was in shadow. "Ashton?" she whispered and took a step into the room.

"Do you believe we all have to answer for our sins?" The voice was gruff and unrecognizable.

Willow flipped the light switch, but the lamp didn't turn on. The dark figure tensed, his hands braced on the chair arms. What was it Lisa had said earlier? *"Follow your instincts, and if something doesn't feel right, you cut and run . . . or you die."*

With that in mind, Willow spun on her heel. But before she'd gotten two steps, something jerked her back. She twisted and struck out, but the guy in the mask held her wings in his gloved hands. She filled her lungs and screamed as he yanked her against him, wrapped an arm around her waist, and forced her backward into the room. He lifted her off her feet, and Willow kicked back, the heel of her boot connecting with his leg just before he hurled her onto the bed. He slammed the door shut and turned to face her.

"I told you if you didn't give me my key back, I'd crush more than your wings."

Willow gasped. Colin stalked toward her and she could

see he still wore his clown makeup under a ragged black cloth he'd cut eye holes into and tied around his head. Willow swallowed a rush of paralyzing fear. He'd dressed like Ashton for a reason. She sat up, but he rushed forward and pushed her back down on the mattress, grasping her calf as he pulled a wicked-looking knife out of his belt. It was curved at the end like the blade you would use to gut a deer.

"I'd stay still if I were you."

Willow stopped moving. Tingles rushed down her shoulders and numbed her all the way to her toes. He was going to kill her. She could see it in his eyes.

He pulled ropes from his back pocket and grabbed her wrists in one hand. She kicked out, but he shoved the knife in her face. "Ashton's grandfather was nice enough to supply me with this lovely blade. Did you know there's an entire collection of them in the garage?"

His eyes were wide and unfocused, the pale blue blending in with the white, his pupil a tiny speck of black. She'd never seen this side of him, but the insanity brewing in his gaze made her believe he was capable of taking human life without remorse. Fresh horror washed over her as the revelation sunk in—Colin had pushed Daniel to his death and murdered his own brother.

Desperate to pull him back from the edge as he tied her wrists, she asked, "You wrote the note and put it in my bag, didn't you?"

"Yes, and had Yolanda write one to Ashton and sign your name to it. Luckily neither one of you knows the other's handwriting well enough to spot a fake. Our friendly neighborhood killer should be here"—he glanced at his watch—"in about fifteen minutes, so we better get on with this." He set the knife down and moved to tie her ankles.

Willow bucked, her free foot connecting with something soft and fleshy. With a grunt, Colin released her and she rolled off the other side of the mattress. She jumped to her feet, but he recovered, grabbed the knife, and raced around the end of the bed, backing her into the corner.

Willow lifted her tied hands in front of her as he stalked forward. "Why are you doing this? I gave back your key!"

"I know." He cocked his head and blinked at her slowly. "I found it."

"What? You were there? Why didn't you stop me at your house?" She lowered her hands and began working the ropes, thanking the Lord for her tiny wrists.

"Brayden said you were smart." He shook his head and took another step toward her, the rope in one hand, the knife in the other. "Why would I attack you in my own house or even on the street when I could frame Ashton for your murder and kill two birds with one stone?"

The blood seemed to drain out of her head. Ashton would go to prison for life and no one would ever know Colin had killed Daniel or Cory—or her. Willow worked the ropes as her eyes darted around for something she could use as a weapon. "But how did you get here so fast?"

He grinned, his maniacal painted-on smile widening until it looked as if his face would split. "Quarterback, remember? I'm a fast runner." He stepped forward and, impossibly, his grin enlarged. "Passed your mom and brother. They both assumed I was Ashton."

Colin reached for her, but she sidestepped toward the bed. "Wait!"

He stopped and tilted his head, watching her like a bug in a jar, fully confident of his control.

A gust of wind slammed into the windows at the front

of the house, the glass rattling in time with the rioting trees. Her skin burned as she forced the rough fibers of the ropes down over her hands. She had to keep him talking. "What about Brayden? Does he . . . does he know about all of this?"

"Brayden is a gutless coward. After he helped rob Twisted Beauty, he refused to do what was necessary to close the deal." Colin rushed forward and pressed the cold steel of the knife against her throat. "Now, what did you find in Cory's box?"

"Nothing . . . nothing, I swear." She'd left the journal on the kitchen counter. If Colin didn't know about it, then Ashton could use it to clear his name. She forced herself to meet Colin's icy gaze and began to talk fast as she dropped the rope and inched her hand toward the nightstand. "Please don't do this. You asked me if people have to answer for their sins, and I believe that they do. I know you killed Daniel. But I believe in forgiveness and . . ."

His gaze narrowed, something dark and wild taking over his face. As his muscles flexed against her, she grabbed the lamp and swung. The stick reverberated against his skull with a resounding crash. He staggered back, shock flaring in his eyes. A sting of pain burned across her throat. Clutching the cut on her neck, Willow raced past him.

Caught in a living nightmare, she felt the hot blood seep through her fingers as her legs pumped in slow motion around the end of the bed. She reached out, the door just steps away. But before she could grasp the knob, footsteps thudded behind her, vibrating the floor. Remembering she still held the lamp, she whirled and swung it like a bat, hitting Colin's head with all her strength. The bulb shattered into a million pieces, and Willow held her breath as the knife clattered to the floor, along with the lamp. Colin swayed to the side, like a tree ready to fall.

"Willow!" Ashton yelled from somewhere in the house.

Willow screamed his name as she spun for the knob and flung open the door. But she'd only taken a step when Colin pushed her from behind. She stumbled down the hall, and when she looked back he was flying out of her room, blocking her path to the stairs.

Spinning on her heel, she sprinted down the corridor and took a sharp right, heading for the back staircase. The house was dark, and Colin didn't know its twists and turns like she did. Praying she could reach the door before he caught her, she pushed her legs faster. Colin crashed after her, his footfalls like gunfire.

Willow reached a fork in the hall, but before she could turn right toward the servant's stairs, Colin raced forward and cut her off. She spun and sprinted in the opposite direction, heading for the attic door at the end of the hall. She flung it open and hurtled through, but when she tried to pull it closed, Colin was already on the other side. She let go of the knob, ran up two steps, and then pressed into the shadows. Colin hurtled through the door, and she kicked his arm, knocking the knife from his grip.

His curses ringing in her ears, she raced up the rest of the stairs. At the end of the hallway was a door with a new bolt at the top. She threw the lock, slipped through the door, and shut it behind her. Unfortunately, there was no lock on the outside, but if Colin checked the other rooms first, it would buy her some time.

A gust tore at Willow's hair as she moved out of the sheltered archway and onto the roof. She took a few tentative steps and leaned over the edge of the widow's walk. The squeak of metal drew her attention up to the top of the turret where the weathervane twisted in the wind. When she lowered her gaze, vertigo took over and she staggered to the side. After catching her balance, she leaned over the edge at the spot where Rainn had fallen. If she dropped from three stories up, it could kill her. Colin screamed her name. She'd have to take her chances.

Ice pooling in her gut, she gripped the iron railing and stepped over onto the slanted roof. Easing herself down, her feet floated in midair. Her hope was that Colin would glance out the door to the roof, see she wasn't there, and then go back inside.

Afraid to move, she bit her lip and forced her gaze to the left. The turret was rimmed with a narrow gutter. She willed away a panic attack and reached between the spikes of the iron railing to her left. Once her left hand was secure, she lifted her right and grasped the rail in between the spikes. Just like climbing across the monkey bars . . . except three stories up.

She reached the turret and braced her foot on the gutter, taking some of the pressure from her hands. Just as she lowered herself so that her head wasn't visible above the roof line, the door burst open and Colin ran out. Willow prayed he wouldn't notice the white of her fingers wrapped around the dark rails.

His footsteps moved closer and a burst of wind pushed against her, ruffling the fabric of her skirt like a flag.

"Willow, I know you're hiding, but you can come out. I changed my mind. I won't hurt you."

Right. She squeezed her eyes closed. *And we'll hold hands and sing "Kumbaya" as we try to forget you stabbed your ex-girlfriend, killed your best buddy and framed Ashton for it, then murdered your own brother to cover it up. The perfect happily ever after.*

Willow's arms began to shake, and she didn't know how much longer she could hold on, or if she'd have the strength to pull herself back up. *Go back inside, Colin. Go back inside.*

A boot stepped so close to her hands, she ducked her head to hide her gasp.

"Funny, I thought fairies could fly."

Terrified to look, she gathered her courage and raised her eyes to find Colin peering down at her, the clown makeup melting in rivulets of sweat onto his neck, the butcher knife in his fist.

"And I thought clowns were supposed to be funny," a deep voice quipped.

Ashton! In her mad panic, she'd forgotten he was in the house.

Colin whirled. "Keller, so glad you're here. Now I can set this up good." He circled while he talked, and Ashton did the same. "The cops would totally buy a murder-suicide scenario from the two of you. Star-crossed lovers and all that." With their identical costumes and similar builds, it was hard to tell them apart. Then Willow noticed Ashton was holding a sword. His costume sword. How was he going to fight Colin with a prop? Her windpipe began to tighten, nausea rising in her throat.

Colin thrust and then Ashton parried, the sharp sound of metal on metal echoing into the night.

Willow's eyes flew to Ashton's weapon. It was real!

"I called the police; they'll be here any minute," Ashton said as he lunged. Colin caught the thin sword in the cross-guard of his knife and pulled Ashton forward. Chest to chest, with the blades locked between them, they grappled for control.

"Yeah, right. The ex-convict calls the cops. I don't think

so." Colin pushed Ashton back two steps. The flat surface of the roof was six feet by six feet, and the iron spikes of the railing only reached their knees. If one of them pushed too hard, it would be over. A heavy weight pressed down on Willow's chest.

As the boys struggled, Colin's knife ripped into Ashton's bicep, a brilliant red line seeping down his arm. Willow couldn't breathe and black began to close in on her vision. *No, No, no! Not now!* But her internal protests only fueled her panic. The familiar sensation of losing control rushed over her from head to toe, and her foot slipped. She cried out, her legs swinging in midair. She heard the unmistakable sound of flesh hitting flesh followed by the friction of blades untangling.

"Hold on, Wil!" Ashton called.

A steely clash sounded above her, but as Willow's vision became hazy, all she could focus on were her feet dangling three stories above the ground and the fire burning in her slipping fingers. If she passed out now, she would never wake up. Arms trembling, she wheezed in a breath and blocked out the sounds of fighting above her. She could talk herself through this. She had to.

With no hint of her focus color in site, she squeezed her eyes closed and pictured the sea-blue of Ashton's gaze. The image so clear in her mind, her pulse immediately slowed and she mouthed the first line of her panic script. "This is an opportunity for me to learn to cope with this problem."

Willow sucked in air through her nose and ground her teeth as she strained to pull up with her arms. "I have survived this before . . . and I can survive . . . this time too." She exhaled and opened her eyes. With her last reserves of strength, she swung her legs to the side, and her foot found the sloped edge of the turret but slipped on loose shingles. She glanced over her shoulder, found the narrow gutter, and then lowered her toes to rest on the edge. Relief flooded her as the weight eased from her hands. Pushing up, she poked her head above the roofline just as Colin kicked Ashton and he stumbled back toward the opposite edge of the roof.

Ashton's legs hit the rail, and she screamed. Arms circling, he tilted backward before he caught his balance and then charged. Sirens approached. Colin blocked the slash of Ashton's sword, but the power of the blow jerked Colin's arm sideways. Taking advantage of his opponent's distraction, Ashton slammed his fist into Colin's jaw, snapping his head back. Ashton stepped in, his sword pointed at Colin's throat. Willow could see the flashing lights of patrol cars out of the corner of her eye as they pulled up to the front of the house.

Ashton's gaze shifted down to meet Willow's, and Colin thrust his knife up, hooked it on Ashton's sword, and pulled it out of his hand. The weapon clattered to the roof's edge, and Ashton backed away, raising his hands in surrender.

"Police! Put down your weapon!" barked a voice that sounded like the police chief. "Simms, find a way onto that roof!"

Willow glanced down. Chief Kagawa and two other officers held guns pointed at the roof. Willow whipped back around. Colin lowered his knife to his side but didn't drop it.

"I can't tell who's who, Chief!" one of the officers called.

"Hold your fire, everyone!" the chief shouted

Colin's fingers clenched and unclenched on the knife handle. Ashton circled, his eyes darting to Willow. "Colin, give it up. If you hurt either one of us, the cops will see it."

"You think I care?" Colin yelled. "Why did you have to come back here? No one would've ever questioned my innocence. Now Willow knows what I've done. I'm going to prison. I might as well take you down with me!"

With a strangled cry, Colin raised the knife over his head and leaped at Ashton. Willow shrieked and pulled up with all her strength. Ashton stood frozen. Colin's arm slashed down, and at the last possible second, Ashton dove and grabbed Colin's ankles.

Colin stumbled forward, the knife flying out of his hand, the blade clattering down the shingles. Ashton leaped forward and tackled Colin to the ground. They struggled for control, and Deputy Simms rushed onto the roof. "Freeze!" Ashton rolled off of Colin just as the deputy dropped down and rammed his knee into Colin's back.

Colin fought, but Simms secured his arms behind him and looped handcuffs around his wrists. "Colin Martin, you're under arrest . . ."

Ashton crawled toward Willow and leaned over the ledge. "Wil, take my hand."

She latched onto his arms, and he pulled her up and over the rail. They sunk to their knees, and Ashton cupped both sides of her head, his eyes searching her face. "Are you okay?"

Willow nodded, and he brushed the tears from her cheeks with the pad of his thumb.

She touched his arm where he'd been cut. "You're bleeding."

"So are you." He reached toward the shallow wound on her throat, but she linked their fingers and tugged their joined hands to her chest.

"I don't care."

The wind tore at their clothes and hair, men yelled, and lights flashed as Ashton's gaze locked on hers, speaking a thousand things he didn't have to say. The same boy with the reckless grin and dancing eyes who'd stopped her from crashing her bike into a ditch the first time they'd met pulled her into his arms, and just as on that long-ago day, she knew she would never be the same.

A shton linked his fingers with Willow's and tucked her arm beneath his as they set off down the forest path.

"Are you going to tell me what we're doing?" she begged him for the eighth time since they'd left the house. "Just a tiny hint."

"Nope. Relax and soak up the nature." Birds chattered all around them, and a soft wind rustled the few leaves left in the trees. It was warm for November, likely the last nice day they'd have for months—the kind of day that when he'd been locked up made him feel like he'd bust out of his skin if he didn't get out in it.

Following Colin's deposition, where they'd both had to give statements, Willow had withdrawn inside herself. In super study mode, not even Lisa could coax her out for shopping and pumpkin spice lattes. Then, after Brayden had called Willow to apologize, explaining that Colin had forced him to start their relationship as a way to get information out of her but he had ended up really liking her, she'd disappeared for hours. Ashton had found her in the attic, cloaked head to toe in dust and cobwebs, organizing his grandma's massive record collection. Even after he'd sold the most valuable albums, there were hundreds of LPs for her to sort alphabetically by title.

That's when Ashton knew he had to do something.

"We're going to the tree house, right?" Willow guessed.

He pulled them to a stop and hooked his arm around her waist before checking the blindfold. "Are you peeking?"

"No! Just tell me something!"

"Okay. Productive pursuits are on hold for the rest of the day. No studying, organizing, or even thinking too hard." When she opened her mouth to protest, he put a finger against her lips. "This is about letting go. You know, spontaneity . . . Ever heard of it?"

"No, but I've heard of irresponsibility. I'm going to break an ankle walking out here!" A single dark brow arched above the fabric of the blindfold. "The least you could do is carry me."

He grinned as he scooped her up against his chest. "As you wish."

Willow looped her arms around his neck and leaned in, her soft breath tickling his ear as she whispered, "I love you too." Then her lips moved to his neck and fluttered a trail of kisses to his collarbone.

Ashton shivered hard. "Keep that up, Buttercup, and we may not make it to your surprise."

Her deep, throaty laugh vibrated against him, and he lengthened his stride. "Maybe we just need to get there faster."

When they reached the rope bridge, he lowered Willow to her feet and looped his arm around her waist.

As they made their way across, she said, "Did you see the news? Deputy Simms is the new police chief."

"Simms is okay. I'm just glad I never have to see Kagawa again."

"Do you think he'll go to jail?"

"Not sure I care." But with charges of perjury and obstruction, his days of law enforcement were over.

Ashton guided Willow over a missing board, and then she said, "Brayden told me that he and Isaiah recanted their statements that they saw you push Daniel. And they both received immunity in exchange for promising to testify against Colin. Every time I think about what they did to you and that they got away with it, I . . . I want to hit something!"

Ashton exhaled a low breath. He was still working through his own anger. They stepped off the bridge onto solid ground, and Ashton pulled Willow into his arms. He buried his face in her hair and whispered, "I feel the same, but I don't want to talk about them right now. This night is just for us. Okay?"

Willow nodded against his chest.

"Good." Ashton released her and instructed, "Wait here."

"Yes, sir!" Willow gave him a quick salute.

The sun sank behind the horizon, painting the sky in fiery streaks as Ashton started the generator hidden behind the base of the tree. He jogged back to Willow and took her shoulders, directing her gaze. "Ready?"

She gave an adorable jiggle of impatience. "Yes!"

He tugged off her blindfold.

"Oh!"

Ashton watched her face. The lights he'd strung up on the tree house sparkled in her eyes like fireflies, and her mouth dropped open in awe. "What's all this for?"

"I'm not very good at saying how I feel, so I thought I'd show you." She turned to him and searched his face. Feeling his neck warm, he grabbed her hand and tugged her forward. "There's more. Come on."

Inside, he'd arranged pillows in the corners, rolled out a plush rug, and set a dozen battery-powered candles of different heights in the center. A wicker basket stood open, displaying a narrow loaf of fresh bread and a glass carafe of chilled apple cider.

"It's a picnic!" Willow stood in the doorway and then

spun on him with an impish grin. "Did you make the food yourself?"

"Um, no. Your mom helped with that." His culinary skills extended to PB&J with the occasional boxed mac and cheese, if he felt ambitious.

Willow walked inside, kicked off her shoes, and sank her toes into the soft shag of the carpet. "Where'd you get all this stuff?"

"Keller House is like a treasure trove of unused finery." Ashton knelt in front of the basket and then glanced up at Willow, who paced around the carpet like a caged cat. She was *so* not good with surprises, but Ashton figured if she experienced enough good ones she'd learn to enjoy them. "Have a seat, Wil. This is supposed to be fun, remember?"

"Okay, fine." She dropped down and crossed her legs, then tugged a pillow onto her lap. Leaning over to peer into the basket, she squeaked, "Is that chocolate-pumpkin torte from Gales?"

Ashton just smiled.

Willow reached in and grabbed a plastic container, rich dark chocolate swirled with orange smashed against the sides. "How did you know this is my favorite?"

Ashton paused in unpacking the basket and leveled his gaze on hers. "Because I know you, Willow Elizabeth Lamott."

She ducked her head, the sheet of her dark hair falling across her face, but Ashton could tell she was smiling.

After pouring glasses of cider and distributing the sandwiches and fruit, Ashton leaned against the wall and stretched out his legs. Even sitting diagonally, his feet almost reached the opposite wall. The place had not been built for full-grown teenagers. A memory of Mr. Lamott laying each board and patiently instructing Ashton on the proper use of tools tugged at his heart. He would do everything he could to preserve this little retreat.

"I know you said you didn't want to talk about it tonight, but something's been bothering me. I never figured out how you knew that note Colin had Yolanda forge wasn't from me," Willow asked, breaking into his sappy thoughts. This was how it had been over the last weeks—so much had happened that night that as each of them processed through it, details would emerge, sparking questions at random moments. And although Ashton wanted to focus on each other, he knew Willow, and she wouldn't stop turning it over in her mind until she had all the answers. He bent one of his legs and hooked his arm around it. "At the ball, when Yolanda handed me the note, I knew it wasn't from you as soon as I read it."

Wil stared at him. "How?"

"You would never forget to dot your *i*'s, no matter how much you were rushing. That combined with what I'd learned from Isaiah set off my internal alarms."

Willow gazed down at her plate, running her finger along the fluted edge.

"What?"

She lifted one shoulder and raised her head. "I just feel stupid. I didn't recognize that Colin had faked the note from you."

He reached over and took her hand. "How about I hand-write sonnets to your beauty until you know every loop of my hideous cursive?"

Her lips quirked to one side. "Really? The boy who doesn't know how to express his feelings is going to write love poems? Doubtful."

"Song lyrics?" He lifted his brows.

She bit back a smile and shook her head.

"Limericks?"

"Now that, I'd believe."

Ashton let go of her hand and sat back. "There once was a girl named Willow . . ."

"Oh no, please don't." She shook her head emphatically.

"Her dark hair, how it did billow."

He popped a blackberry into his mouth, buying a second to think. "With the mighty strength of an oak, she is one you *do not* want to provoke." He drank in the sight of her eyes as they danced with amusement, and then finished his rhyme, "But if you can get close, her skin is as soft as a pillow, her kiss like . . ."

"Don't say it!"

Evidently she knew the limited words that rhymed with her name. ". . . an armadillo."

"Ugh!" Willow lobbed a pillow at his head.

He snatched it out of the air. "What? Armadillos are cute."

"That wasn't even a proper limerick! Please, no more love poetry, I beg you."

After their laughter died down, Willow resumed eating her sandwich and asked, "How did the visit with your family go?"

"Awkward." He tore off a chunk of bread and squeezed it between his fingers. "My mom can barely look me in the eye now that she knows I wasn't guilty, and my dad still acts like I'm the prodigal son returned to complete his life and join the family business."

"How do you feel about that?" Willow selected an olive from the antipasto tray. "About them?"

Ashton leaned back on his hands. "College first, and then we'll see about the business, but . . . I've forgiven my parents."

Willow's brows shot up.

"I didn't deserve your mercy or forgiveness after the way I treated you." He leaned forward, meeting her gaze. "But you showed me all the good that can come from second chances. Anger has torn me apart for too long . . . I'm ready to let it go."

Willow reached over and linked their fingers. "I guess . . . Colin deserves the same."

Heat flooded Ashton's chest as it did every time he thought about all the evil things Colin Martin had done— the years he'd stolen from Ashton and all the good people he'd hurt. He inhaled and turned his gaze to the stars twinkling outside the window. Forgiveness didn't excuse Colin from facing the consequences for his actions. Being tried as an adult meant he'd be living with those consequences for a very long time.

With a slow exhale, he turned back to Willow and offered a crooked smile. "I'm working on it."

Her dark eyes twinkled. "Good." She popped another olive into her mouth. "Now tell me about all the guilt gifts your parents bought you."

"Lots of clothes and electronics, and . . . a car."

"No way!"

"Yeah, a Nissan GT-R. It's being delivered next week. They let me pick out the color." The car wasn't going to fix anything, but Ashton knew it was their way of trying to make up for their mistakes.

Willow took a sip of cider and then watched him over the rim of the glass. "GT-Rs are crazy fast. I didn't think anything could be more dangerous than a motorcycle, but you're going to kill yourself in that thing."

Ashton ignored her. "I chose black with black leather interior."

"Of course you did." Willow grinned and shook her head.

"But this is still my favorite." He held up his wrist, where he wore the watch she'd given him. A gift to make up for all the birthdays she'd missed.

"It's just a watch." She shrugged, her cheeks flaming a gorgeous pink.

The watch itself was nice, but the inscription she'd had engraved on the back had rocked him.

I loved you at your darkest. Always, Wil

All those years when he'd felt alone, she'd loved him. The double meaning had not been lost on him, and every time he thought about it, he had to touch her. Ashton set down his half-eaten sandwich and crawled across the blanket. Willow lowered her glass to the hardwood and patted the carpet beside her with a slow smile.

Ashton gathered her into his arms and gazed into those exquisite dark eyes that still held countless mysteries he needed to discover. He tucked a wave of silken hair behind her ear as her hands ran up and down his back, igniting tiny sparks across his skin and filling him with the best kind of heat. His eyes drifted to her lips and then back to her eyes. "I've spent years burying my emotions, but when I touch you . . . it's like they all come rushing back at once."

She lifted a hand to his face, and even without words he knew she understood him. Ashton's heart was so full he thought it might explode. He felt superhuman, like he could scale a mountain with his bare hands or cure world hunger in a single day. Melodies swirled inside his head and wrapped around his soul. Songs had been written about this feeling since the beginning of human history, and he could see why.

He brushed his thumb across the gentle slope of her chin. "Wil, I told you once that I won't make promises to you that I can't keep, so for now all I want is to see you tomorrow."

He placed a kiss on the tip of her nose. "And the day after that." He kissed the rounded curve of her cheek. "And the day after that."

And *all* the days after that, but he kept that part to himself as he kissed her lips.

ACKNOWLEDGMENTS

Writing a mystery/suspense story is much more complicated than the Nancy Drew books made it seem. Combine that unique challenge with writing two novels simultaneously (*Forever Doon* and *Gilt Hollow*), and some pretty intense illness in my family, and you have the perfect recipe for insanity, but THANKFULLY I have many extraordinary people in my life who wouldn't let me slip over the edge!

It's a challenge to contain my gratitude within the boundaries of a few lines of print, but know that these words merely scratch the surface of my appreciation.

Gilt Hollow wouldn't have been possible without the remarkable publishing team at Blink. My heartfelt thanks to each one of you for your creativity, hard work, and vision!

To my ROCK STAR agent, Nicole Resciniti, for believing in this story even before I did . . . You were right, as usual. Thank you!

Thanks to my husband, Tom, for asking on our first date if he could see me the next day, and the day after, and the day after that . . . and inspiring the end of this novel. I LOVE *all* our amazing days together!!!

To my parents, who struggled at times to raise this idealistic dreamer. Thank you for giving me a solid foundation to stand on as I reached for the stars. I love you both!

Thanks to my second family, the Moeggenbergs, for accepting this odd, creative girl as one of your own. (This includes all the Fowlers and the Freemans) I'm GRATEFUL beyond words for each one of you!

To Carey Corp, my writing partner, co-conspirator, and friend. Our lives have become so intertwined that branching out on my own with this novel has been equal parts exciting and terrifying. But wherever this crazy life takes us, we will always be linked by our Calling.

A shout out to our Doonians all over the world! Words can't express my gratitude for your enthusiasm and support. THANK YOU for following me on this detour outside of our mythical kingdom!

To Melissa Landers, my critique partner, traveling companion, and sounding board; your friendship is a brilliant LIGHT in my life!

To Laurie Pezzot for falling in love with Ashton and Willow as I brainstormed this book between bites of chips and salsa. Thank you for continually reminding me that this story was worth telling.

Thanks to my brother-in-law, Jon Moeggenberg, for patiently answering my rambling, hypothetical law enforcement questions. If you read this book, hopefully they make sense now!

To the thriller queen, Natalie Richards, for beta reading and giving me a quote that still blows me away!

Thanks to my dear friends who see the same truth: Tricia Lacey, Angie Knopp, Brenda Hess, Jen Osborn, Sara (Ella) Larson, Mindee Arnett, and Kelly Innes Shults. Your faith and courage INSPIRES me to continue on the right path.

To all my other family and friends whom I haven't mentioned by name, I appreciate each and every one of you!

My writing career, and all that entails, is due to the MAGNIFICENT God who saw something in me that I did not, and called me to a bigger destiny that I could have imagined. I'm grateful every day that he drew me out of the boat and onto the turbulent waters of this amazing journey!

CPSIA information can be obtained
at www.ICGtesting.com
Printed in the USA
FFOW04n1701150516
24000FF